For Cindy Snow,

With warm regards!

Paul L Maier

2007

THE
FLAMES
OF ROME

Books by Paul L. Maier

A Man Spoke, A World Listened

Pontius Pilate

First Christmas

First Easter

First Christians

The Flames of Rome

The Best of Walter A. Maier (ed.)

Josephus: The Jewish War (ed. with G. Cornfeld)

In the Fullness of Time

A Skeleton in God's Closet

Josephus: The Essential Writings

Josephus: The Essential Works

Eusebius: The Church History

THE
FLAMES
OF ROME

A Novel by
PAUL L. MAIER
Author of *A Skeleton in God's Closet*

kregel
PUBLICATIONS

Grand Rapids, MI 49501

The Flames of Rome by Paul L. Maier

Copyright © 1981 by Paul L. Maier

Published by Kregel Publications, a division of Kregel, Inc.,
P. O. Box 2607, Grand Rapids, MI 49501.

Cover artwork: Ron Mazellan

Maier, Paul L.
    The Flames of Rome/Paul L. Maier.
       p.   cm.
    Includes bibliographical references.
    1. Sabinus, Flavius, ca. 8–69—Fiction. 2. Church history—
Primitive and early church, ca. 30–600—Fiction. 3. Rome—
History—Claudius, 41–54—Fiction. 4. Rome—History—
Nero, 54–68—Fiction. I. Title.
PS3563.A382F57   1991   813'.54—dc20   90-28622
                                                        CIP

ISBN 0-8254-3297-9 (paperback)
ISBN 0-8254-3262-6 (hardcover)

6 7 8 9 / 09 08 07 06

Printed in the United States of America

For
Laura and Julie

CONTENTS

CONTENTS

PREFACE

SOME of the most extraordinary, colorful, and tragic events in all of history shook Rome in the score of years following A.D. 47. Claudius and then Nero ruled over that volatile blend of idealism, sensuality, and cruelty which was the Roman Empire. Into such an unlikely setting Christianity made its own quiet—then shocking—entry, and a mortal struggle between the worlds of power and faith began. This is a serious attempt to reconstruct that conflict through portrayal of a Roman family caught up in the clash.

Since the true story of these times is so much more intriguing than the many fictionalized versions, I have not tampered with known facts in retelling it—unlike almost all historical novelists—nor invented characters that could never match the kind who actually lived in this era. The factual undergirding is documented in the Notes, some of which unveil new historical data.

But here as elsewhere in ancient history, yawning gaps in the original sources prevent any telling of the *full* story. I have tried to fill these in by devising a genre which I call the "documentary novel," resorting to fiction for such connective material as well as dramatization, dialogue, and subplot to flesh out the story and bring its characters to life.

To insure accuracy, I adopted these rules: 1) All persons named in the book are historical; no proper name has been invented—if it is not known, it is not given. 2) No portrayal of any personality, description of any event, episode, or even detail contradicts historical fact (unless by author's error). 3) Only where all evidence is lacking is "constructed history," based on probabilities, used to fill in the gaps. Such created segments are clearly identified in the Notes.

These rules in no way curb the drama of these incredible times, and readers should rather gain the added satisfaction of knowing that much of what they are reading actually *did* happen, while the rest could well have happened.

Though several episodes in these pages may seem lurid or jar our sensibilities, all are historical—none is contrived; as authentic fertilizer in the Roman seedbed of Christianity, it would have been dishonest to omit them.

P.L.M.

Western Michigan University
July 18, 1980—the 1916th Anniversary of The Great Fire

PREFACE TO THE SECOND EDITION

THE ENTHUSIASTIC reception accorded this book by both critics and the general public is most heartening. That scholars have also endorsed the research demonstrated in the 25 pages of Notes at the close of the text even more so. I hope that the genre of the documentary novel may serve to set higher standards for the "historical novel" so-called, which has been debased by too many authors relying on imagination rather than research.

PAUL L. MAIER

Western Michigan University
February 1, 1991

BOOK ONE

THE HEARTH

1

SPRING was daubing a drab and hibernating Italy with brush strokes of fertile green. High in the Apennines, the last patches of snow were surrendering to fragrant Mediterranean winds, and the boot-shaped peninsula seemed to quiver in rebirth, as if this year at last—A.D. 47—it would find the energy to give Sicily that great kick it had threatened for ages.

The city of Rome was already in full blossom, at least in mood, because in Roman reckoning this was the anniversary year 800 A.U.C. The Latin initials for *ab urbe condita*, "from the founding of the city," fairly shouted the fact that Rome had stood for eight proud centuries, during which she had spread across her seven hills and mastered all of Italy. Then, as if answering some trumpet call of destiny, she had gone on to conquer the entire Mediterranean world.

Claudius Caesar, Rome's bandy-legged but able emperor, was doing his imperial best to celebrate the anniversary with games, festivals, and religious observances. Once he even climbed up the endless staircase to the Capitoline Temple on his arthritic knees—Rome winced for him at every step—to inform Jupiter of the civic milestone.

Now in his seventh year as emperor—"and my fifty-sixth as a human being," he would quickly add, in a weak drollery that never quite succeeded—Claudius seemed shortchanged by life. A childhood paralysis had left him with a wobbly head, a speech defect, and a halting gait, though his own mother surely exaggerated his motor handicaps when she called him "a monster of a man, begun but never finished by Mother Nature." Some in the Senate would clutch their togas and ape his shambling pace, imploring the gods to loosen the stammering tongue of "Clau-Clau-Claudius." His critics were sure that the three new letters he had added to the alphabet —Ⅎ, Ↄ, and Ⱶ—would not endure (and they were right), and even his love life had become stock comedy on the streets of Rome.

But high above the Forum's laughter in his sprawling palace on the Palatine hill, Claudius Caesar was indulging in the final smile. He knew that a lucid mind lurked underneath his whitish shock of hair. Even his foes had to admit that he had stabilized the Empire after the mad Caligula, and had also added dramatically to its boundaries. Whenever he found himself listening too closely to criticism or gossip, Claudius would amble over to the colossal map of the Empire that covered an entire wall in his office suite and smile at the great island on the northwestern corner, now shaded in with Rome's colors: Britannia! He, Claudius the Clown, Lord of the Lurch, Wobblemaster of the World, had conquered Britannia!

It was because of this conquest that T. Flavius Sabinus had to have an audience with the emperor one morning early in May. A smartly dressed lieutenant commander, fresh from the Roman forces in Britain, Sabinus was waved inside the palace and now paced through its marbled corridors to the entrance chamber of Claudius' office suite. A Greek-looking man of slender build rose from his desk, extending a perfumed hand of greeting. "Ah . . . welcome, Flavius Sabinus!" said the second most powerful man in the Roman Empire.

"Greetings, worthy Narcissus!" Sabinus responded, while thinking, *Worthy* indeed—worth, say, 400 million sesterces as secretary of state . . . not bad for an ex-slave. But Sabinus ventured only the obvious query: "Is the emperor expecting me?"

"Indeed. Please follow me."

The aging, imperial huddle of flesh, well insulated in the folds of a plain white toga, sat at a sprawling desk of polished cyprus, squinting at reports from Britain. Looking up at Sabinus, Claudius stared for a moment, as if trying to recall who the tall, well-structured intruder might be. Then he brightened and came to life. "Well, well,

Ca-Commander, you don't seem to have aged any since we fought together in the north country four years ago. Not a trace of gray in that black thatch of hair. Why yu-you're handsome as ever."

"And you, Caesar, are looking admirably fit," Sabinus lied.

"So, y-you're just back from Britannia. Tell me, how's my friend Aulus Plautius? And w-when is he due back in Rome?"

The pleasant sparkle in Claudius' lead-blue eyes made Sabinus overlook the soft slurs and occasional stutters that pock-marked the emperor's speech. He also knew the stammer would fade once their conversation got under way. "The governor general sends you his warmest greetings, Caesar," Sabinus replied, in an officer's baritone. "I was sent ahead to report their arrival plans. At this moment they should be crossing the Alps, which would bring them to Rome about the Ides of June."

"Hmmm. A month from now." Claudius cupped his chin in thought, then turned to his freedman secretary. "Well, Narcissus, how shall we celebrate his return?"

"Ah yes." The secretary frowned slightly, for he had given no real thought to the matter. "Well, perhaps a . . . a state dinner would be appropriate."

Claudius' lips broke into a low smile. "And you, Sabinus? Do you think that would be sufficient?"

Sabinus reddened a bit and replied, "I'm sure the governor general would be honored by such a dinner, although—" He cut himself off.

"Although what?"

"Nothing, Princeps," said Sabinus, using the alternate name for emperor that meant "first citizen."

"Oh, but you had something else in mind," Claudius insisted.

"It's just that—now please understand that Aulus Plautius mentioned nothing of this—but doesn't Rome usually confer a *public* welcome on her conquering generals?"

"It was the *emperor* who conquered Britannia," Narcissus interposed coldly. "And he has already celebrated a triumph for it. Don't be impertinent, Commander."

An ex-slave talking to him of impertinence? Turning angrily to Narcissus, Sabinus spat the syllables out. "*Of course* Caesar conquered Britannia! But have you forgotten who designed the strategy? And who led most of the fighting? And who diplomatically held our forces to the banks of the Thames until Caesar could get up there and take command for the final victory? A victory Aulus Plautius had all but won?"

"Impudence!" Narcissus gasped, turning pale as his bleached tunic.

"*Impudence?*" Sabinus struggled to contain his rage. "Perhaps. But the truth nevertheless."

In an instant, Sabinus regretted his last statements. They were accurate, the gods knew, but they were hardly diplomatic. And talking that way before the person who could adjust one's destiny with the wave of a hand was at least foolhardy. He looked over to Claudius and saw his pinkish complexion turning turgid red. His lips had parted, and a string of drool started dangling from a corner of his mouth. His head was pitching slightly from side to side, the nervous tic that affected him whenever he was under stress.

"I . . . I'm sorry, Princeps," Sabinus apologized. "Our forces were . . . *much* heartened by your arrival in Britain. Forgive me."

Claudius made no reply. The room grew mortally silent. Had he really managed to offend the two most powerful men in the world *that* quickly, Sabinus wondered. Was truth that urgent? Cursed be that foolish tongue of his which had once again responded to mood rather than clear thought.

"Heh-heh-heh-heh."

Sabinus looked up to see Claudius grinning at him, and then chuckling some more in his inimitable cluck. Narcissus, too, appeared startled.

"Heh-heh-heh," Claudius affirmed. "Y-you're right, of course, Sabinus. I wasn't glaring at you at all just now, but at you, Narcissus."

"At *me*, Princeps?"

"Yes, of course. For daring to call Sabinus impudent. He's not impudent . . . no, not at all. *Honest* he is, not impudent."

"But Caesar . . ."

"Silence, Narcissus!" Then Claudius turned to Sabinus and smiled. "By the gods, Commander, that *is* the way it was: Aulus Plautius won Britannia for us. *He* did the work, but *I* got the glory. —Well, no matter. Now I'll share some of that glory, in the name of honesty alone." Pitching himself toward them, he chortled, "Yes, honesty . . . something we need more of around here, eh, Narcissus?"

"What do you propose, Caesar?" Narcissus asked coolly. "You know it dare not be a triumph."

"Oh, don't play the pedant with me, Narcissus!" Claudius huffed, sliding his bony fingers through whitish wisps of hair as he shuttled unsteadily between them. "Yes, I know: only the Caesars celebrate triumphs now. Very well, then. Let it be an ovation."

Sabinus broke into a beaming smile, while Claudius happily winked at him. The coveted *ovatio* was a lavish celebration nearly as impressive as the full-dress triumph.

"But, Caesar," Sabinus demurred, "will the Senate agree?"

Claudius turned to his secretary. "Isn't the Senate in session at the moment, Narcissus?"

"Yes, Princeps."

"Then go over and make the necessary arrangements. Immediately. Sabinus and I will look in there within the hour."

A minor guard of a dozen praetorians escorted Claudius and Sabinus as they walked down the heights of the Palatine and crossed the Forum to the Senate house. The emperor led Sabinus into an alcove that overlooked the Senate chamber, where they could watch the proceedings unobserved to avoid the fuss and formality of an official welcome. Below him, Sabinus saw a quorum of about 300 senators, all wrapped in the voluminous folds of their togas, listening to the presiding consul, who had already opened deliberations on an ovation for Aulus Plautius. In a sonorous Latin that rattled off the semicircular marble benches of the chamber, he called out the prescribed questions.

"*Iustum bellum?*" "Was Plautius waging a just war?"

"*Certe! Certe!*" responded the senators, "Certainly!" There was no opposition.

"*Quinque milia occisi?*" "Were at least 5,000 of the enemy slain in a single battle?"

"*Certe.*"

After further ritual queries, there were cries of "*Divid-e! Divid-e!*" —calls for the usual vote by separation.

The consul held up his hands for order. "All in favor of the ovation for Aulus Plautius move to the right side of the chamber," he directed. "Those opposed, to the left."

Several hundred toga-clad figures rose together, but instead of threading past each other, as on normal votes, they all walked to the right side of the hall.

"Done," Claudius whispered. "And unanimously. So you see, Sabinus, I didn't exactly keep Plautius' role in Britannia a secret."

"I'm delighted, Caesar. In the name of our legions, I thank you."

"A final matter. When did you say Aulus plans to return to Rome?"

"About the Ides of June."

Claudius' eyes had a playful sparkle. "I have a weakness, Sabinus —well, perhaps many weaknesses, but one in particular: surprises. I dote on them. Now, when you return to the governor general, you are to say *nothing* about the ovation. Only the banquet, do you understand? When you reach your last encampment north of Rome, you'll send a messenger to me, and this is how we'll work it out . . ."

As they broke camp at dawn on June 14, Aulus Plautius mustered his troops for a final review. He stood tall as a six-foot Roman javelin and almost as straight. Middle age had grayed his hair, and four northern winters had tautened his skin into a rough canvas which only accentuated his squarish forehead, the wide-set eyes, the determined mouth and chin. Now he mounted his great, bay-colored horse—a souvenir from Britain's Medway—and called over to his lieutenant commander. "Last leg of our journey, Sabinus, thank the blessed Fates! We should reach Rome just after midday, not?"

"Early afternoon. Which will leave us time to freshen up for Claudius' dinner."

"*Bah!* Couldn't you have talked him out of that?"

"Not one for fuss and ceremonial, are you, Governor?" Sabinus grinned. "Are you sure you wouldn't have preferred a parade? Perfect day for it."

"*Sweet Jupiter, no!*" He frowned. Then he gave the order to march.

They clattered onto the Via Flaminia and continued southward. A long column of legionaries followed them on horse and foot, each troop quickening its pace in anticipation of seeing Rome again. By noon they had approached the Tiber River bridge. Aulus Plautius halted his forces on the north bank and stared down at the sluggish yellow-green waters that sloshed around the northwestern edge of Rome. Then he peered at the maroon brick walls of the city itself in the distance and frowned. "Something's wrong, Sabinus. Haven't you noticed?"

"No, Governor. What?"

"The people. There aren't any *people* around!"

"Of course there are." Sabinus pointed to several old men staring at them quizzically from the upper story of a tenement, and a woman nursing her baby behind flapping curtains.

"Don't be foolish. Here we are, just outside the largest city in the world and no people! Something's wrong, Sabinus. Sickness? Plague?"

"I . . . I've no idea." Sabinus was trying his best to share Aulus' frown.

They marched across the bridge and finally reached the massive walls of the city, pierced only by two small arches of light that were the Flaminian Gate. Aulus took the lead in trotting through it, followed by his cavalcade.

An overpowering roar thundered down upon them. Tens of thousands were massed on both sides of the Via Flaminia inside the city, trying to burst through a double line of Praetorian Guards stationed along the roadway as far as they could see. Aulus Plautius' jaw sagged limply at the human forest of swaying arms and the shrill screams of the citizenry.

"It seems we've located a few of the people you were worried about," Sabinus chuckled, enormously relieved that the emperor's little game had succeeded.

"Your work?" Aulus demanded.

Sabinus shook his head and grinned. "Claudius'. It's a formal *ovation*, Governor, and eminently justified, I would add.—Ho there, Vespasian!" Sabinus called to his brother, a fellow commander who was mounted on the other side of Aulus. "Help me with this toga."

Ignoring Aulus' dazed protests and almost pulling him off his mount, the brother officers removed his traveling cape and draped him in the folds of a toga fringed with royal purple, standard dress for one receiving an ovation. Then they pressed a wreath of myrtle onto his graying locks and finally helped him back onto his horse. Raising an arm in stiff salute, Sabinus called out, "Hail, Aulus Plautius, conqueror of Britannia! *Io triumphe!*"

"IO TRIUMPHE!" the troops and multitude erupted in colossal unison, and the procession began. A large delegation of senators and magistrates joined the cavalcade, while a corps of flute players started piping. Straight as a spear, the Via Flaminia skewered their way through the shouting masses into the very heart of Rome. Three quarters of the city's million inhabitants were shrieking their appreciation to Aulus Plautius for delivering Britain to them. Incense smoked from every altar, flower garlands sprouted from the shrines, and everywhere the waving arms and endless cheering.

Flanking Aulus on each side a horse's length behind were Sabinus and Vespasian, exchanging grins of relief that their general had finally gotten into the spirit of the day, for at last he was smiling to acknowledge the cheers and waving his myrtle wreath from time to time.

Now they had reached the Roman Forum, a canyon of swarming humanity, reverberating with applause and shouting. The noise was overpowering, and Sabinus had some difficulty controlling his skittish mount, whose ears had flattened in a vain attempt to escape the sound. Suddenly a man dashed out of the crowd, yelling, "Remember, Plautius, you're *only a man!*" Then he shoved a scourge under Aulus' saddle. Vespasian leaned over and clamped the man's arm in a powerful grip.

"Let him go, brother! It's part of the ritual!" Sabinus laughed. "Whenever Romans treat somebody like a god, they also remind him that he's merely brother to a slave—"

"Hence the scourge," Vespasian nodded, sheepishly releasing his grip.

A brisk trumpet flourish plunged the Forum into incongruous silence. Sabinus squinted against the sun, but then his face bloomed with a great smile. Standing in the middle of the Sacred Way was the emperor himself. Claudius was not supposed to have joined them until the end of the procession, but here he was, honoring them even earlier. "*Hail, Caesar!*" cried Aulus, in formal salute.

"Hail, Aulus Plautius!" replied Claudius. "May I have the privilege of accompanying you to the Capitoline?"

"It would be a supreme honor, my comrade-in-arms!"

Just the right touch, Sabinus thought, for it underscored the emperor's role in Britain. Claudius beamed and then looked over to say, "Well done, Flavius Sabinus! A complete surprise, I take it?"

"My own brother here didn't know, Caesar!"

"Splendid. Just splendid!"

They all dismounted as the procession continued on foot. Aulus moved to the left of the emperor to accord him the place of honor. Claudius frowned and pulled him over to his right. "No, friend. Today we honor the conqueror of Britannia!"

Winding past the Senate house, the Sacred Way brought them to the foot of the great staircase up to the Temple of Jupiter Capitoline, the lofty citadel of Rome that was the goal of the cavalcade. Now a thunderous applause rattled down on them from every side.

"Turn around and smile, gentlemen," Claudius advised. "There are times when a person must not be modest. This is one of them."

After thirty ponderous steps up the staircase, Claudius lurched to one side and almost collapsed. "No, no!" he huffed. "Don't try to help me. I'll make it up this accursed mountain." He paused to catch his breath and then commented, "It seems Father Jupiter doesn't hear very well. We have to climb halfway to heaven before he catches our prayers."

Aulus chuckled and said, "You shouldn't have gone to this exertion, Caesar. Meeting us up at the temple would have been honor enough."

"Oh, I'm merely showing our Romans that they still have an ambulatory emperor. There are rumors that I'm a senile old carcass"—he grinned wryly—"and maybe I am. But, by Hades, I'm a walking one."

Finally, with Claudius wheezing and gasping, they reached the very summit of Rome, the ridge of the Capitoline hill on which towered the classic columns of the Temple of Jupiter. The afternoon sun splashed across its searing white marble, constricting Sabinus' eyes to narrow slits as he took in the breathtaking panorama of the city flowing down from them in all directions—the brick and marble, stadiums and temples, streets, parks, and baths that were Rome.

At last the whole procession had filed onto the esplanade in front of the temple. The emperor, now facing them on a lofty dais, nodded to the priest of Jupiter, who would serve as augur. The priest picked up a lamb and gently cradled its head in his left arm. Then he raised a mallet with his right and smashed it down on the animal's skull. The lamb twitched and died instantly. Several other priests slit open its belly, while the augur carefully probed inside to find the liver. For several moments he peered at the crimson viscera, then announced, "*Exta bona!*" "The entrails are favorable." The ceremony could now proceed.

"My fellow Romans," Claudius began, in a surprisingly firm voice. "Let us celebrate again the conquest of Britannia and honor the man who led our legions to victory." And the emperor's address all but conquered Britain again, tracing the invasion from the Channel to the Midlands.

Sabinus, standing at attention, was reliving the campaign when his gaze fell to the right of the dais and he saw a pair of smiling eyes fastened on him from among the official guests. Looking back to Claudius, he found his memory adding brush strokes to form the portrait of an uncommonly attractive girl. His mind was probably playing tricks. He stole a glance at her again, and found that he was wrong. The girl was not pretty at all—she was instead beautiful. Spectacularly so.

Again he stared at her, and felt a stab of chagrin: the girl's eyes were not locked on him after all but on Aulus Plautius, who was standing a half step in front of him. Aulus now stood forward as Claudius read from an official proclamation, engraved on a bronze tablet:

For extraordinary services rendered to
the Senate and the Roman People
in the conquest of Britannia

AULUS PLAUTIUS

was accorded an ovation
in the consulship of Lucius
Vitellius and Claudius Caesar, DCCC A.U.C.

Volleys of acclaim erupted, the sound cascading down the Capitoline, and it was fully five minutes before Aulus could acknowledge the ovation from the dais with a brief response.

Sabinus' eye was wandering again. The girl was still beaming at Aulus, and he noticed her profile for the first time. Too perfectly sculptured, he mused, even the nose. Then came the blunder he would never be allowed to forget. He failed to hear the emperor's final surprise. "Two Roman officers," Claudius was saying, "must also be commended for their wisdom during the Britannic campaign. It happens that they are brothers: T. Flavius Vespasian and T. Flavius Sabinus. Gentlemen, stand forward!"

Vespasian broke rank, presented himself, and saluted. But Sabinus just stood in place, apparently lost in thought.

Dumfounded, Claudius barked, "Flavius Sabinus, *stand forward!*"

Jolted back to reality, Sabinus complied at once, his face flushing a healthy shade of scarlet. Now the emperor solemnly approached them, hanging triumphal medallions around Vespasian's neck, and then his own, amid general applause.

A pair of white bulls, their horns painted gleaming gold, were now led before Aulus Plautius. Taking out his commander's dagger, he drove it deep into the throats of the pair and slit them. Bellowing in a frenzy, each bull collapsed, gushing dark crimson across the pavement. Then, while the priests completed the sacrifice, Aulus went inside the temple and laid his myrtle wreath at the base of the great statue of Jupiter. For several moments he gazed into the huge stone eyes of Zeus, trying to detect some glint of appreciation for his gift. Smiling at the useless effort, he then turned about and left the temple. With a final fanfare, the ovation was over.

"By all the gods, Sabinus, whatever happened to *you* just now?" Aulus asked, after the ceremonies. "Were my remarks really *that* boring?"

"Certainly not, sir. I was—"

"Great gods! There they are!" Aulus shouted. "My family!" He hurried over to a knot of people gathered to the right of the dais. Sabinus saw him rush into the outspread arms of a stola-draped woman in tears. "Pomponia, Pomponia," he whispered.

"At last you're ours again, my husband," she sighed. "It's been . . . so *many* months."

The surging joy of the moment nearly overcame Aulus. He pulled himself back to arm's length and caressed each gentle curve on Pomponia's face, as if to familiarize himself with old, and loved, territory.

"But where's little Plautia?" he suddenly remembered. "And who is *this* radiant young woman?"

"Yes, who *is* she?" Sabinus almost whispered. It was the face in the crowd that had immobilized him. No mirage that disappeared on approach, the girl, if anything, was even more striking at close range.

"Oh—you know it's me, Father." Plautia blushed. "Have I really changed *that* much?"

"A full metamorphosis!" He beamed, giving his daughter a resounding kiss. "When I left for the North, you were a pudgy little chub of a girl. Now look at you! Why you're almost as lovely as your mother."

An identification at last, Sabinus thought, and he had to agree with the family banter. Pomponia's features, crowned by chestnut tresses, were soft and balanced and not exaggerated in any part, something of a rarity among Roman women who so often just missed beauty by the bend of a nose or the warp of a mouth. Her serene face had blended with her husband's distinguished facial accents to produce the beauty in Plautia, Sabinus calculated, a bubbling, effusive girl of probably sixteen—younger than he had at first supposed and doubtless bravely reaching toward womanhood.

"Oho, there you are, Sabinus," said Aulus. "Poor bachelor—he has no family to welcome him. Well, we have more than enough family for you here." With that he began introducing Sabinus to the numerous Plautii and Pomponii, for all the relatives on both sides had gathered to help celebrate Aulus' great hour. Putting his arm around a broad-shouldered young senator, Aulus said, "Here's the pride of the clan, Sabinus, my nephew—"

"Quintus Plautius Lateranus!" Sabinus exclaimed. "How are you, friend?" He clasped both hands to his shoulders.

"Hello, Sabinus!" Quintus beamed. "You're looking marvelously fit."

"Oh, that's right," said Aulus. "You do know each other."

"*Know* each other?" Sabinus exclaimed. "Just before you dragged me off to Britain with you, I put every sesterce I could scrape together into Quintus' hands to invest. So how did we do, Senator?"

Lateranus' smile faded. "Not as well as I'd hoped, Sabinus." He paused, shuffled, and continued. "The orange groves in Apulia caught a blight. Then our pottery works in Arretium ran out of clay . . . and you know the grain ship we had half of?"

"Yes?"

"Our half sank. We're wiped out."

For exactly two seconds, Lateranus held his look of death. Then the corners of his mouth twitched out of control and he bent over laughing. "Just the opposite, Sabinus! It's all gone better than we schemed." He leaned over to whisper, "What would you say to . . . 150 percent on your funds in four years?"

Sabinus let out a whoop, lifting the stocky Lateranus off his feet. "Oh, put me down, do," Quintus said in an effeminate tone. "Else they may guess why neither of us got married."

Sabinus dropped him like a stone. "*Idiot!*" he laughed.

"Tell me, Quintus," Aulus interposed. "Was Sabinus here telling me the truth about the Senate's vote on my ovation? Wasn't there *any* opposition?"

"No, Uncle. The Fathers hurried over to the right like so many sheep at feeding time."

"You're sure you were actually *in* the Senate that day, and not off somewhere adding another hundred thousand sesterces to your fortune?"

"Uncle Aulus!" Quintus protested with mock surprise. "You know I consider wealth merely secondary to—"

"Women!" Aulus chuckled. "Tell me, young stallion, have you found the girl who will be your wife? Or are you still out wenching around?"

"The latter," Quintus admitted, grinning. "Though one of these days I'll have to submit to the 'happy tedium of marriage.'—But tell me, Uncle, what did you think of the sham out here today?"

"Sham? What do you mean?"

"I mean you should have had a *triumph*, not an ovation. Claudius spends all of sixteen days up in Britain, grabs credit for your victory, and celebrates a triumph, while you spend four years to get an ovation. He wears the laurel wreath, you get myrtle. He rides a chariot, you—"

"Still living in the Rome of a century ago, aren't you, Quintus? Still the diehard republican? You know the rules now. Triumphs go only to the emperor, not his commanders."

"Not back in the Republic."

"Ah, Quintus. If you'd been alive then, you'd also have stabbed Julius Caesar to save the Republic, right?"

"Probably."

"But Caesar *was* stabbed and the Republic still died. These are different times, Senator." He clapped him on the back. "But now get ready for the emperor's dinner, everyone.—Oh, Sabinus." He winked. "See that Quintus doesn't bring any daggers along."

A ruddy golden yolk of sun was just dropping over the hills west of the Tiber when Sabinus arrived at the palace with the other guests of honor. Perfumed fountains were bubbling in the polished marble corridors—a wild balsam fragrance—and a corps of servants glided up to them with great silver trays of exotic appetizers and snow-cooled wines. Sabinus found himself assaulted on all sides by friends he had not seen for months, former colleagues in the Senate, and well-wishers. At last he managed to reach the great dining hall for Claudius' feast, a gastronomic marathon that would feature a roast generously supplied by the two bulls sacrificed that afternoon.

He had nearly taken his place at the principal table when he noticed young Plautia reclining at the place assigned her across from Vespasian. In an instant, his hand was on Vespasian's shoulder. "Sorry, brother," he said, "your place is over there near Caesar."

"I don't think so," Vespasian remonstrated, until he felt pressure building on his clavicle. Then he rose and excused himself, while Sabinus reclined in his place.

Plautia wondered at all the shuffling and stared curiously into Sabinus' large brown eyes. He had a pleasant outdoor face, she thought, tanned from too much exposure to sun and wind, and it matched his lean and well-proportioned frame. Somehow, though, his ringlets of black hair seemed too neatly combed and deserved a good tousling.

"We met earlier this afternoon on the Capitoline," Sabinus began, flinching at his pedestrian comment.

Plautia merely nodded. Then she reached over to finger the gold medallion hanging from his neck. "Is this what Caesar gave you?" she asked. "What in the world are those animals doing?"

"The Roman wolf is biting through the throat of the British lion. Subtle, don't you think?"

"What's on the other side?" She flipped the medallion and said, "Oh, your name's engraved alongside Claudius'. How nice!" Suddenly she looked up at him to ask, "Incidentally, whatever was the matter with you today when Caesar asked you to stand forward?"

Her nearness only added to the impression she was making on him, and he barely restrained himself from saying, "*You* were the cause . . . you incredibly lovely stripling—too young for me even to think about." Instead he said, "I was merely lost in memories of Britannia."

"Your brother, Vespasian . . . he doesn't look at all like you. Why, he's stocky as a wrestler. Is he married?"

"Oh yes. Has two boys, in fact."

"And you're not married? Why?"

"A problem of the right woman appearing.—But tell me, pretty Plautia, what have you been doing these four long years while your father was in Britain?"

It almost seemed as if she had been waiting for him to ask, since she spent the next hour telling him in detail, well beyond the main course of sacred sacrificed bull. Sabinus hardly minded. It gave him a chance to watch the girl without risking the impression that he was staring at her. No girl had a right to be that . . . flawless, he thought, almost nettled at how Nature had likely robbed from others to create this masterpiece. Lustrous, light brown hair, free as a waterfall, flowed around sea-blue eyes, a—thank the Fates—non-aquiline nose, and lips that—

"Could I see you for a moment, Sabinus? If my beauteous cousin will permit?"

Sabinus looked up at Quintus Lateranus. "Of course, Senator. By the way, where have you been keeping yourself all evening?"

"I . . ." He faltered and frowned. "I'll explain in a moment."

Sabinus pushed himself up from that delightfully languid position in which Romans dined and followed Quintus out of the dining hall to a balustrade that overlooked much of central Rome. Lamps had been lit in the city below, and flickering daggers of orange flame were stabbing the evening sky. But Quintus seemed too disturbed to enjoy the view. "Has Claudius been asking for me?" he inquired, with a worried glance.

"No, but I think he's been looking for Messalina."

The very name seemed to raise globules of perspiration on Quintus' brow, and he uttered a soft oath.

"Yes, Senator?" Sabinus laughed.

"Sorry, friend. But you can't believe the . . . the terror I'm in because of"--he quickly looked about—"because of Messalina . . . 'wife of Claudius Caesar' . . . 'empress of Rome' . . . 'Beauty Incarnate'—but Sensuous Slut!"

"Now really, Quintus, surely you don't believe those wild stories."

"Shhh! Believe? You can't imagine what's happened since you left for Britain, Sabinus. The empress Messalina is . . . simply the most improbable woman in all our history." His brow knitted even more deeply. "And now she's all but demanded that I—how shall I put it gracefully?—well, that I spend the night with her."

Sabinus' jaw dropped. Then he broke out laughing. "The empress? With you? Ridiculous!"

"No, it's not. And I'm far from the first," he sighed. "Lately, Messalina's been, ah, 'entertaining,'—let's see, her doctor, Valens . . . that Rufus who runs the gladiators' school . . . Mnester, the actor . . . and several of our colleagues in the Senate. Probably half a dozen others, too."

"But that's not possible, Quintus! Claudius . . . doesn't he know? Wouldn't he put them to death if he found out?"

"Of course he would. But no, he doesn't know."

"Beyond belief! Why not?"

"No one dares tell him. Messalina would deny it—Claudius dotes on her and would believe her—and they'd both lash out at the informer. One or two *did* threaten to tell Claudius, but . . . they're no longer with us."

"What happened?"

"Messalina had them condemned to death for treason. Using false testimony, of course."

Sabinus' features grew taut. Finally he asked, "How did you answer Messalina when she . . . issued her invitation?"

"I told her no, because a senator shouldn't aspire to the imperial level, but I'm afraid *that* excuse won't work again. Just now, though, I could tell her it was too dangerous with all the people here for Aulus' celebration."

"Just now?"

"I just came from her," Quintus moaned. "What, in the name of all the Olympian gods, am I supposed to do, Sabinus?"

Indulging a bit of whimsy, Sabinus said, "Well, she *is* very beautiful . . ."

Lateranus merely looked at him with widening eyes.

"Sorry, friend! I shouldn't be joking when you're under such . . . pressure. But here's some quick advice. Get back inside immediately, or Claudius may connect your empty place at his board with Messalina's. We'll talk it over later when we total up all those sesterces you owe me, all right?"

"Right. And thanks, friend."

At last the celebration for Aulus Plautius drew to a close. Twice Claudius had dozed off during the lengthy banquet, and that was the proper sign for guests to depart. Leaving after the emperor's first nap would have been an affront; staying on after the second, equally bad taste. While Aulus was gathering his clan, Claudius roused himself and conducted the guests of honor to the vestibule of the palace. A great cheer arose from crowds still gathered outside, who were waiting to escort Aulus to his mansion on the Esquiline hill. Torches were lit, and the corps of flute players struck up a tune.

"Aha, my Aulus," Claudius crackled, "you won't lose your way home with these guides. But please don't make Duilius' mistake, dear friend." He was looking expectantly at Aulus, for he had just dropped a typical Claudianism: some obscure reference from Rome's lengthy past that would have delighted only another antiquarian like himself.

Aulus surrendered. "You have me, Caesar. What *was* Duilius' mistake?"

Claudius beamed, for he prided himself on knowing every nook and cranny of Roman history. "Doesn't *anyone* know about Duilius?" he asked.

"Back in the First Punic War, wasn't it, Caesar?" Sabinus volunteered. "Duilius was so proud of his victory that for the rest of his life whenever he returned home at night—"

"He had torches and flutes marching in front of him to celebrate," Claudius interrupted, nodding enthusiastically. "Well done, Sabinus!"

"Ah, *vanitas!*" Aulus smiled. "But thank you for today, my friend. You too, Sabinus. Quite a day you planned for me!"

"Good night, Governor." Then, seeing Plautia under the arm of her father, Sabinus looked a last time into the eyes that had bedeviled him but were frustratingly removed from him by time and circumstance. "Good night, Plautia," he said softly.

She smiled. *"Vale,* Commander."

2

VALERIA MESSALINA twisted about on the broad expanse of her bed with half-opened eyes. Ever so slowly, she came to terms with the new day. "Claudius?" she called, in a languid tone. There was no response from the adjoining room. Evidently her husband was up and about his emperor's business. She thought back to the previous night and the brief appearance she had put in at the banquet for Aulus Plautius. By the gods, how such functions bored her!

For that matter, Claudius himself bored her. True, he had seemed a desirable enough prize when she married him eight years ago. But she was only fifteen then and Claudius was a member of the imperial house—the family idiot, to be sure, but an idiot of the Caesars. He had gone on to make her empress, the envy of the world. And for several years she had tried to be a decent wife—the gods knew she had tried—and didn't their little children, Octavia and Britannicus, help prove that?

There was no doubt that Claudius loved her. And why shouldn't he, after two marital failures? His first wife was a real prize, Messalina mused. Urgulanilla! That murderous Amazon was every bit as ugly as her name. Ha! Poor Claudius had to divorce her for reasons of personal safety! And the second was a transparent little fawn—Paetina—whom Claudius never really loved. No, he never knew what love was until *she* stepped into his life and made him supremely happy.

Yet she herself was anything but happy. "Love is the center of a woman's world," she explained to her intimates, "and a husband thirty-three years older than I can't possibly satisfy me." Messalina stood up to dress, smiling at the solution to her plight. She had surely owed it to herself to take lovers, she reasoned, for love was very much like food: its taste and enjoyment depended on its freshness and, above all, on its variety. Let the moralists rage. Let jealous women gossip and bewildered elders shake their heads. She was empress and not to be shackled with the customs binding ordinary women. She would live—and love—to the very summit of her inclinations.

Shrugging off her nightdress, which fell into a circlet of purple around her feet, Messalina glanced down at her generous breasts and exquisitely matured figure of twenty-three years. Was it fair to limit such a view to the dimming eyesight of a doddering wreck of a man older than his fifty-six years? Claudius, that spent satyr, could amuse himself with various palace girls at trysts he supposed were secret, so why shouldn't she have similar privileges? She had incriminating documents on all possible informers in the palace, as they well knew, so her own liaisons were shrouded in a conspiracy of silence.

She rang a chime. Several attendants fluttered in to help her dress. One combed the tresses of her raven-black hair, another took jeweled clasps to fasten a crisp white tunic around her body, and then draped the saffron stola she had selected for the day. Messalina gave her girls only wooden responses, for her thoughts had focused on the events of the night before—and on the person called Quintus Plautius Lateranus, that devilishly attractive rogue who was spurning her love with threadbare excuses. But why did he make them? She knew he found her appealing, and he had no wife to answer to. Obviously, the poor dear was afraid of Claudius. Yes. Yes, that had to be the reason. Well, no great problem.

Messalina emerged from her suite to share a light breakfast with her husband. It was not until he had finished munching his wine-soaked bread and cheese that Claudius finally responded to her careful pouting and asked what was wrong. Messalina's sulk darkened into a scowl. "I don't want to talk about it," she snapped.

"All right, don't then." Claudius shrugged.

"Tell me, Claudius," she suddenly demanded, "is it wrong for an empress to interest herself in financial matters? Investments? That sort of thing?"

Claudius looked puzzled, but before he could reply, Messalina resumed. "Does the name Quintus Lateranus mean anything to you?"

"You mean the young senator? Aulus' nephew?"

"The same. Well, I saw Lateranus at the banquet last night, and since he's making a fortune for himself, I asked him for investment suggestions. And do you know what he replied?"

"What?"

" 'Caesar's wife couldn't possibly be interested in how I collected my few crumbs.' Then he turned and walked off."

"Why, the impudent churl! I'll send and have him flogged."

"No you won't. You can't flog a Roman citizen, not to say a senator. But you should punish him somehow."

Claudius was about to summon a guard when Messalina demurred. "Wait, dear. Let's be more subtle. Why not make the man swallow that fierce pride of his? That's the best humiliation." She brushed a delicately manicured hand across her mouth in thought, then smiled. "I have it. Summon Lateranus to the palace and tell him that an empress should be able to expect common courtesy from a senator. That in the future he must cooperate with *all* my requests, or face some dire consequences."

"All right." Claudius smiled. "I won't mind lecturing that fellow. Why must these young dandies always find success and conceit at the same time?"

"Thanks, dearest." She turned to leave but then stopped. "Oh . . . one more thing, Claudius. Don't deliver a lecture to Lateranus and don't say anything about investments. Be very curt with the man. Say simply, 'Cooperate with her. Do *whatever* she says.' And let it go at that. Above all, don't tolerate *any* back talk from him. A one-minute interview would be too long. The shorter the audience, the more effective the humiliation."

"Fine thinking, carissima.—Guards! Send in a messenger."

The summons from the Palatine renewed the torque of anxiety deep inside Quintus. Certainly he hadn't made a cuckold of Claudius, but what if he'd learned of Messalina's interest in him? Or, more probably, what if she had used that ancient stratagem of the

spurned woman and accused him before Claudius of making indecent advances to her? The emperor would never believe him.

Fear, but anger too, tingled inside him as Narcissus opened the
door to Claudius' office for his audience. Ominously, the state secretary was staying with them. As witness?

"Oh yes, Lateranus," Claudius gurgled. Then he cleared his
throat and resumed. "The empress has informed me about last
night. I . . . I wouldn't have thought that the nephew of my com-
rade Aulus would have been so . . . indiscreet."

Quintus' eyes appeared to bulge. "But what indiscretion, noble
Caesar?"

"You were rude in not complying with the empress. Now, Senator, may I advise you that from now on you are to answer any
request my Messalina may make of you, and I shall not discuss the
c-consequences if you refuse."

Quintus was dumfounded. Quickly shifting his stance to keep his
knees from buckling, he asked, "*Any* request?"

Claudius nodded.

"You mean," Quintus swallowed, "even—"

"Yes, yes, yes, man!" Claudius grumbled, without trying to understand Quintus.

"But, Princeps, you—"

"Enough, Senator!" Narcissus interrupted with a glowering
glance. "Caesar has spoken. The matter is settled." Impatiently he
waved Quintus out of the room.

For one last moment Quintus peered directly into Claudius' eyes,
trying to fathom his intentions, but he found nothing which would
suggest that his directive had been only a bizarre joke. Then he
whipped about and left.

Returning eastward to his mansion on the Caelian, Quintus was
baffled and thoroughly alarmed. And he found only one solution to
the ridiculous puzzle: Claudius was actually to be taken at face
value. He only too clearly meant what he said—the debauched
pander! Jaded in his twilight years, Claudius was evidently giving
his wife free rein, probably as part of an agreement by which his
own privileges were also unlimited. Messalina *had* dropped broad
hints that this, in fact, was their arrangement.

He glanced skittishly about the city, now blanketed by the shadows of late afternoon and finally shook his head. After burying the
Republic, had Rome really come to this? It certainly explained Mes-

salina's conduct. Why addle one's brain trying to figure out how Claudius could be so dense about his wife? He knew all the time!

Quintus stepped inside his town house. No sooner had he shaken the dust off his toga than two bejeweled arms tenderly wrapped themselves about his waist. Messalina's eyes gleamed and her lips glistened as she pulled him into the shadows of the vestibule and whispered, "Quintus . . . my Quintus."

The change from military to civilian life was exhilarating for Flavius Sabinus. He had not really wanted to leave the Senate for duty in Britain—he was not a soldier at heart, like his brother Vespasian—but military service was obligatory for anyone with political ambitions. He had put in his time. But now everything was falling handsomely into place for him back in Rome. The beast that hounds all men—financial insecurity—had been easily tamed by Quintus' uncanny ability to make sesterces spawn sesterces. As a leisured Roman, then, he had two options: indolence or politics. No contest. The choice had been as inexorable for him as it proved to be for Aulus Plautius.

Both, in fact, were formally welcomed back into the Roman Senate on the same day. The consul designate, Gaius Silius, was presiding over the chamber with another of his bravura performances at the dais. It was said that the golden-tongued Silius could have fended off any of Rome's enemies by syllables alone, not swords.

"You, Aulus Plautius," he exclaimed in peroration, "and you, Flavius Sabinus, we shall no longer style as 'Commanders' but as 'Conscript Fathers,' fellow members of this august body. We forgive you your absence over the past months: something detained you in the north country, we understand." He paused for the laughter he had anticipated, and then concluded, "Resplendent as you appeared in armor on the day of your ovation, the public togas you are now wearing strike us as even more glorious uniforms. You will, of course, be courted fiercely by every political faction in the state— what else would one expect of returned military heroes?—but we wager in advance that you will pursue your own independent strategies. Welcome back, gentlemen! Help us govern Rome!"

Aulus and Sabinus, who were seated front and center on the marble benches, now stood to receive prolonged plaudits from the chamber, and even some rather unsenatorial cheering. When the session was adjourned and senators were filing out into the Forum, Sabinus felt an arm across his shoulders and heard the same voice, now subdued. "And how is dear Polla? Still up in the hill country north of Rome?"

"My mother is fine, Gaius. I visited her in Reate last week. And thank you for the . . . brilliant reception inside just now."

Gaius Silius merely raised his palm by way of acknowledgment. Then he inquired, "How long has it been since your father died?"

Sabinus winced inwardly while responding, "Six years." His father had been a customs collector in Asia Minor, so exceptionally honest that the citizens there had actually erected a statue to him with the inscription, "TO AN HONEST TAX COLLECTOR." (It was said to be the only such statue in the Empire, because this was the only occasion for one!) Sabinus' father had, in consequence, returned penniless to Rome, but Gaius Silius' father had befriended him, lending him the capital necessary to establish a bank in Switzerland. So when the younger Silius made reference to his father, Sabinus guessed that he was setting up a mood of obligation for him, even though the financial debt had been repaid.

He was not mistaken. As they strolled through the Forum toward the late morning sun, Silius carefully probed into Sabinus' political views. Sabinus gave guarded responses, trying to fathom the intentions inside that boyishly handsome head next to him. "Gaius Silius is the only man in Rome who can truly be called beautiful," the women of Rome agreed.

At a secluded corner of the Forum, Silius stopped, looked about to make sure no one was near, and then confronted Sabinus directly. "You may or may not agree with what I shall now tell you, Senator, but I must ask your word, no, your *oath* of secrecy—absolute secrecy —in this matter. Your father once told mine, 'If someday we can repay this favor, command us.' Well, Sabinus, the time has come. This is the only favor we'll ever seek."

Sabinus nodded. "You have my oath for secrecy, Gaius."

Again Silius looked about and then whispered, "A growing number in the Senate—and elsewhere—are *tired* of the Empire, Sabinus, disgusted with Claudius' performance, and we aim to restore the Republic.—Now, before you say anything, hear me out. Yes, Augustus was necessary as a strong man—he ended the Civil Wars— but that randy old hypocrite Tiberius fled any statecraft in Rome for the tangled sexual games he loved to play on Capri. And he was a saint compared to Caligula—"

"A madman, Gaius," Sabinus interrupted. "No commentary necessary."

"And now this dawdling cripple of a Claudius who runs at the mouth both literally and figuratively, this stuttering simpleton who is making Rome the laughingstock of the world—oh, what a *magnificent* succession of Caesars: a hypocrite, followed by a madman, and then a fool!"

Sabinus was hardly shocked by Silius' language—it was standard fare in republican circles—but he did ask why Silius was singling him out.

"Because of your prestige, Sabinus. Because—*if* you sympathize with us—we want you to approach Vespasian and possibly Aulus Plautius too—but only when the time comes. We already have the night watch on our side, and some of the praetorians. It *can be done*, Sabinus! We can restore the Republic and return real power to the Senate." Silius' eyes were glowing, piercing those of Sabinus for some response.

Sabinus carefully looked across the Forum to the palace on the Palatine. Then he replied evenly, "Claudius is no paragon, Gaius. I'll grant you that. But he's no fool either. I won't be part of his assassination."

"He wouldn't have to be assassinated, Sabinus. Exile would do. He could spend the rest of his life with his beloved scrolls in Spain. Or Egypt. Anywhere."

Slowly, Sabinus nodded. "The matter requires much thought, Gaius. I'll give it that thought. Meanwhile, I *quite* understand your need for secrecy."

It was so studied an understatement that both broke into laughter.

"I will say this," Sabinus added. "It's not the emperor who has made Rome a laughingstock so much as the empress."

"Messalina?" Silius' eyes suddenly flared toward, then avoided, his. "Ah yes, the empress. She . . . ah . . . *is* a problem." Color was suffusing Silius' youngish cheeks, and he asked a final time, "Absolute secrecy? Even if you decide not to join us?"

"You have my word, Gaius."

"I ask you on the bones of our dead fathers, Sabinus."

"I *gave* you my word, Gaius."

They parted, Sabinus returning to the Quirinal hill, where he was staying with Vespasian and his family. Soon he would move into his own newly purchased town house on the Quirinal, now being redecorated. He gave a moment's thought to discussing Silius' conspiracy with his brother—he was *supposed* to contact him eventually—but then he dismissed the idea. Vespasian held secrets like cracked crockery held water. Besides, he knew what his brother's response would be without asking him. Tough, loyal soldier that he was, Vespasian would have headed directly to the Palatine to warn Claudius. Lucky for Silius that Vespasian wasn't wealthy enough to sit in the Senate, because if he had been party to their conversation, Silius' conspiracy would have been pried wide open.

But what of his own attitude? Would nudging Claudius aside be a crime—treason—or patriotism? A healthy Republic, governed by a truly independent Senate in place of the present chamber, always deliberating with one ear cocked toward the Palatine, had to be preferable. But he had many more questions to ask, many more assurances to be pledged before committing himself.

Sabinus was also struck by Silius' strange reaction, his almost telltale response to one word: Messalina. And speaking of Messalina, why hadn't Quintus said anything more about his predicament?

3

OVER THE NEXT MONTHS, Senator T. Flavius Sabinus was indeed wooed by various factions that tugged away at the Roman body politic—and by one in particular. The eyes of the consul designate, Gaius Silius, turned to him embarrassingly often during deliberations, hungry, imploring eyes. At the close of each session, Silius would seek him out to comment cryptically: "The number grows." "Soon now." "Have you decided?" Freighting about conspiracy and treason in his head, yet sworn to secrecy, Sabinus wondered whatever happened to his peace of mind.

Aulus Plautius caught him after adjournment one day and said, "You'll be seeing less of me in the Senate from now on, Sabinus, because I've . . . given in."

"Your memoirs of the campaign in Britain?"

Aulus smiled and nodded.

"*Excellent,* Governor! I've been urging you to get started ever since we returned."

"Which is almost as long as we've been inviting you to dinner at our place, Sabinus. You've declined twice now. 'Courtesy' has been served. But now, barring revolution, catastrophe, or death itself, we'll expect you this coming Saturday evening. Can you make it?"

"Delighted," Sabinus concurred, with a sheepish grin.

The Plautii lived on another of Rome's seven hills, the Esquiline, which loomed up northeast of the Forum. Near the crest of its pine-encrusted slopes stood the Plautius mansion, target of some controversial gossip in Roman society. One of Aulus' rivals in the military wandered through its Doric columns and commented, dourly, "A palace? For a Roman officer?" Yet Caligula once took the same household tour and grumbled, "Oh, it's shelter, Aulus, but why don't you climb out of this hovel and build yourself a *real* home?" But Caligula, of course, was mad.

Sabinus found Aulus' twenty-two rooms at least adequate for a family of three. All of them opened onto one of two large adjoining courtyards: the atrium, nearest the street, and the more richly ornamented inner peristyle. The servants lived upstairs in rooms that also faced the interior courts.

Pomponia's dinner was savory in taste and conversation. Whatever reserve Aulus' wife showed in public seemed to disappear in the privacy of her own home. And daughter Plautia showed no reserve at all. Sabinus felt curiously unnerved, reclining across the table again from this radiant slip of a creature. How old was she, anyway? Whatever age, she was too young for him, and he privately cursed the Fates that had placed them almost a half generation apart.

To make matters worse, Plautia was chattering away about a young girl's favorite topic—herself—and the boys in her life. "Roman girls are terribly sheltered, Senator," she complained. "Why, I can't even go down to the Forum—or anywhere else for that matter—unless Mother or Father comes along."

"Nonsense," Aulus countered. "Any one of the servants would do."

"And marriage will change all that, Plautia," Sabinus laughed. "You'll be spared your chaperones someday when the proper man comes along."

"Someday? I'm old enough for that right now."

"No you aren't, daughter." Pomponia smiled.

"Oh yes I am. I'm sixteen, and three of my friends are sixteen and engaged. One is even married."

"Well, then," said Aulus, in a patronizing tone. "When do we announce your betrothal, Plautia? And what Roman male has Fortune favored?"

"Don't think I haven't had the chance." She pouted. Then she brushed her tawny locks aside, turned toward Sabinus, and said,

"You can't believe how it goes, Senator. The boys my parents want me to like—proper family and all—well, they're a collection of curiosities." She paused as the others laughed. "But the men I like all seem to have a 'hopelessly wrong background,' as Mother puts it. So I suppose I should have become a Vestal Virgin," she sighed. "I could have, you know. When I was ten years old, the high priest invited me to become a novice.—Just think, I could have spent my whole life in sacred spinsterhood!—But Father said no."

"Oh, thank the Fates," Sabinus said to himself.

"I really should have joined the Vestals, I think," she persisted, pouting, and then jabbered on about her sheltered existence and the lot of Roman women in general.

Her comments and bearing tended to cool Sabinus' interest, for they showed the girl to be a flighty adolescent after all, and much too young to take seriously. He almost felt a perverse consolation in learning that, for all her beauty, she was also shallow and immature. Nature had dealt normally with her after all.

Pomponia had been staring curiously at her guest. "You know, Sabinus," she said, "I find that you resemble our nephew Quintus rather *closely*—except for your build. He's heavier than you."

"*Aha!*" Sabinus chuckled. "Now you'll understand why we chose the name we did for our joint business ventures."

"What's that?"

"*Gemini.* The Twin Brothers."

"Who's Castor and who's Pollux?" Aulus laughed.

"We haven't decided yet."

Plautia, who had said nothing for some minutes, now seemed to change tack. "Suppose for a moment, Senator," she said, in a more serious tone, "that you possessed the same mind and talents that you now have . . . but that you had a woman's body. Do you realize how drastically different your life would be? You could never have become consul or commander. Or senator. You could not even vote for one of these offices. You could never serve as juror or judge. The law would treat you almost as a minor. Now, is that fair, I ask you?"

Sabinus was taken by surprise. "Perhaps not," he replied. "But the women of Rome are marvelously free when compared to those of Greece and elsewhere."

"True. But that's like a rich man telling a peasant to be glad he's not a slave," she countered. "Could it be that you men are afraid of us? Wasn't it Cato who said, 'On the day that women are our equals, they will be our masters?' "

Sabinus swore to himself. He had misjudged the girl. She had a mind after all. And a fine one.

A servant entered the dining room, excused himself, and then whispered something into Aulus' ear. The face of the paterfamilias suddenly took on a serious cast, and he rose from the table.

"It's all very confidential," he said, "but Narcissus is here. Alone."

"No aides?" Sabinus asked, for Claudius' state secretary was always accompanied by a train of assistants.

"No one else. He has to see me privately. A *very* urgent matter, he says."

"Time for my exit," said Sabinus, rising from the table to thank his hosts. "Your family suits you well, Governor. Now I know the sacrifice you made to leave them for Britain."

Aulus walked toward his library with a knit brow. He numbered the emperor's secretary among his friends, but he had purposely kept a respectful distance from him. Narcissus was indeed the second most powerful person in the world, and any closer involvement with him meant swimming in waters close to the treacherous vortex of Roman politics.

Narcissus' greeting and apologies for his sudden visit seemed sincere enough. Then the pleasant-looking Greek started frowning as he nervously brushed aside the scented strands of his black hair and tugged at one of his earlobes, pierced from the days of his slavery. "Rome's in desperate danger, Aulus," he said, with a deadly serious cast to his eyes. "Claudius is threatened. We have a situation that's nearly out of control. But I hope your commander's mind can help devise a strategy to save us."

"Sounds like a Parthian puzzle, Narcissus. What do you mean?"

"You've heard the stories about the empress Messalina?"

"Yes, but what does that gossip have to do with your problem?"

"Everything. But first of all, you should know that the 'gossip,' as you call it, is not only accurate, it's really very kind to Messalina. No one's yet compiled a full inventory of her lovers, but I'm trying. We're up to nineteen."

"The wife of a Roman princeps? That's beyond belief!"

"But true, Aulus."

"How do you know, Narcissus? Were you around, taking notes behind a curtain, I suppose?" he chortled.

"I have more than enough proof." Reaching into his tunic, Narcissus extracted a folded piece of papyrus. "Look. Here are only a few of the prominent Romans who . . . have violated the emperor's bed. In alphabetical order. I have written proof on each of them." He handed a list to Aulus:

> Suillius Caesoninus
> Decrius Calpurnianus
> Mnester, the actor
> → Traulus Montanus
> Polybius
> Titius Proculus
> Sulpicius Rufus
> Gaius Silius
> Saufeius Trogus
> Pompeius Urbicus
> Vettius Valens
> Juncus Vergilianus

Aulus studied the names. "Thundering Jove!" he growled. "Senators . . . magistrates . . . prefects. Messalina certainly has aristocratic tastes."

"Not necessarily. Remember, these are only the prominent names. There are many more."

"What's the arrow doing there?"

"I'll explain in a moment. Now, which would you say is the most dangerous name on the list?"

Aulus studied the names again. "Probably that 'rising star' in the Senate, Gaius Silius."

"Exactly. And there lies the danger. Messalina is after more than passion now. She wants power too. We've learned that she has an overwhelming infatuation for Silius. She even wants to marry him and make him emperor in place of Claudius. And Silius *is* consul designate, you know."

"*Emperor?*" Color was draining from Aulus' face. "But I thought Silius had republican sympathies."

"Oh, he does, he does—*when* he's trying to enlist support. And he may have been an honest republican at one point, but now he has loftier goals in mind. Messalina may have corrupted him. Or his own ambitions did. No matter. He now promises to restore the Republic only to build a following."

Aulus' brow wrinkled into a deep frown. What were only the mad flagrancies of an empress-strumpet now seemed to shake the very foundations of Rome. Not that Claudius himself was so indispensable, he knew, but an Empire ruled by a palace whore and that vain and limited Gaius Silius, a pretty youth who spoke too often and too grandiloquently in the Senate, would surely court disaster. He stepped over to his wine cabinet, extracted a bottle of strong, aged Falernian, and poured cups for both of them.

"She can't stop showering gifts on the man," Narcissus continued. "She paid for Silius' new mansion and then hounded his wife out of it. And she's all but moved in herself. She's there day and night. She's moved much of the palace furniture over there too. Ah, but dear Claudius! He never seems to notice anything missing."

"You mean he *still* doesn't suspect? Why haven't you told him?"

"Because I'm very selfish about my life, Aulus. I want to keep it, you see. Was it Homer who said, 'Pity him who brings bad tidings to the powerful'? Everyone in the palace agrees that Claudius must be told, but no one wants to tell him."

"Why not Pallas?" Pallas, also a freedman, was Claudius' other most intimate secretary and in charge of the state treasury, while a third ex-slave, Callistus, supervised all petitions addressed to the emperor.

"I know what you're asking," Narcissus replied. "Claudius . . . is a charioteer drawn by three horses: Pallas, Callistus, and Narcissus. Why doesn't one of them turn about and neigh loudly enough to warn his master? And you're right, of course. But the other two are even more afraid than I, if that's possible. Messalina has threatened that if we inform on her, she'll 'prove us liars,' and have us executed for treason."

"Could she?"

Narcissus thought for several moments. Then he said, "Yes, she probably could. Claudius is still helplessly in love with her, and he'd *much prefer* to believe her innocent than guilty. He loves the children she gave him. Against these odds, an accuser would be courting suicide. And even if Claudius *did* believe us, he'd be furious that he wasn't told earlier, since Messalina's been . . . deceiving him for the last five years." He threw up his hands. "We're all caught . . . caught in a horrible trap."

"So. You'll say nothing, and let Rome pass over to that conceited fool, Silius?"

Narcissus looked down, grabbed his goblet, and drained it. Then he clipped his words. "No, we can't let it go on any longer. That's why I'm here. I need ideas. I need advice. I need support. Let's talk about support first. When the crisis breaks, I'm asking you to use your influence with the officers of the Praetorian Guard to keep them loyal to Claudius. That way Claudius must eventually win—*if* he isn't assassinated first."

"You have my word on that, Narcissus."

"That's a relief." He smiled. "Now for the advice: if you were in my position, Aulus, how would you go about breaking the news to Claudius?"

Aulus slowly twirled the cup in his hands, staring at the crimson inside. Then he tightened his lips and said, "Draw up detailed documentation on Messalina's . . . conduct. Have Pallas and Callistus at your side with corroborative *proofs* of her infidelity. Have witnesses in waiting. Claudius will *have* to believe such evidence."

Narcissus pondered briefly and then nodded. "Yes, that's really the only way."

"But you'll have to hide your plans from Messalina at any cost, or she'll strike first.—But you were going to tell me about the arrow on your list there."

Narcissus winced. "No detail escapes you, does it, Aulus?" He drew in a deep breath and said, "The name of your nephew Quintus Plautius Lateranus belongs in the list at that point. I . . . I'm sorry, friend."

Aulus' features froze in disbelief, only his eyes reflecting the pain. "Are you certain?"

"As it happens, I witnessed the very start of your nephew's involvement. But you'll be glad to know he was duped into it. Didn't he ever tell you what happened?"

"No. Never."

Narcissus then reported the strange interview on the Palatine. When he had finished, Aulus snapped, "Why didn't you warn Quintus then?"

"At the time I had no idea what was involved. Later, when I learned, it was too late. But now I must ask you: does this change your opinion that Messalina should be exposed?"

Aulus' knuckles whitened around the stem of his goblet. "No," he muttered, then more distinctly, "no, of *course* not."

"Honorably spoken. I can only promise that we'll . . . try to keep Lateranus' name out of the affair. But if this fails, he'll certainly have a solid defense: Claudius innocently ordered him to do the very thing for which he will have been accused! I'll testify to that."

"Mmmm. Kind of you, Narcissus."

"Oh, one last thing, Aulus. The moment I leave, you will probably send a warning to your nephew, and I can't blame you for that. But Lateranus does have republican connections, as you know, so I would say *nothing* about Silius and his conspiracy . . ."

"I'd already thought of that, Narcissus."

4

FOURTEEN MILES southwest of Rome, the Tiber River spilled into the Mediterranean at Ostia. This was supposed to be the port of Rome, but the yellow sludge disgorged by the river had silted up the harbor for years. And so the grain ships from Africa and Egypt that kept Rome fed had to stand offshore and unload their vital cargo onto heaving flat-bottom barges that ferried the grain up the Tiber. When Mediterranean storms made chaos of such transfers, the people of Rome went hungry. Several such famines and they would start looking for another emperor, Claudius knew, so he conceived his grand plan of carving out a deep new harbor at Ostia to the north of the old one.

Claudius' engineers told him the scheme was impossible. He quite agreed, but ordered them to go ahead anyway. Their kind had been arguing over the project for some ninety years now—ever since Julius Caesar first dreamed about it—and it was time to move. An army of laborers converged on the area, and a huge basin was slowly dredged out, while breakwaters, built over a base of sunken ships, gradually took shape.

Claudius decided to spend several weeks of Rome's glorious autumn at Ostia, surveying progress on his beloved harbor, and he asked Messalina if she would care to accompany him. She'd love to go along, she said, were it not for indigestion. Kissing her tenderly, the emperor left for the coast with a minor entourage, leaving Narcissus in charge on the Palatine.

Messalina watched her husband's retinue wind its way out of the palace courtyard and then called for a writing tablet. She inscribed only two words on it: "Now, Darling." Sealing the tablet, she summoned her most trusted aide and told him, "Deliver this to Senator Gaius Silius on the Esquiline. Immediately."

Roman financial circles were starting to watch the activities of "The Twin Brothers" with increasing interest. Sabinus and Quintus Lateranus not only bore a curious resemblance to each other, their personalities also matched. They were both outgoing, adventurous sorts, a little bored with the status quo; both were bachelors, both senators, and both, lately, were making a fortune with their joint business ventures. The money men of Rome tried to ape their style, always a step behind them in timing—and profits. Until now, the shrewdest businessman in Rome was supposed to have been Narcissus, the "Sage of the Sesterce," but when the mighty Narcissus conceived his bright idea of buying property near Claudius' harbor works at Ostia, he found that most land titles on both sides of the new basin were already vested in the name of the Twin Brothers.

Lately, though, Quintus seemed more interested in politics than business, and Sabinus almost regretted it, because Quintus, with his republican sympathies, had been trying to draw him into Silius' conspiracy. Shrewd as they were in financial matters, neither of them had any idea that Silius might have higher ambitions for himself.

Because it was midautumn, Gaius Silius' great party would have a harvest motif. Quintus carefully hand-delivered Sabinus' invitation and added, "It's going to be *the* social event of the season, Sabinus, and I'd like to emphasize that it is to be social indeed—not political. So you can bury your qualms about what we're doing and come and have a good time." Sabinus was predictably disinclined, but Quintus could be extremely persuasive.

The Twin Brothers arrived together early on a bright and warm October afternoon. Decorated in a vintage motif, the atrium of Silius' mansion was now a country vineyard, framed by actual vines laden with luscious grapes. Huge wooden vats stood in the peristyle, in which guests were merrily trampling grapes with their bare feet

while gulping down wines of every variety. Threading their way between the vines and vats, a corps of stewards bore great silver flagons
emblazoned with signs advertising their contents: Setinian or Falernian, hot or cold, sweet or dry, watered or straight.

Several smiling slaves surrounded Sabinus and Quintus, whisked
them out of their togas, and presented them with rustic costumes
made from animal skins, for this was to be a festival of Bacchus, god
of wine and revelry, whose harvest and fertility rites dated back to
the dawn of Mediterranean civilization.

"Darling Quintus!" Messalina cooed, as she implanted a lingering
kiss on one of the two bucolic figures just entering the atrium-
vineyard. "You have forgiven me for my . . . for my friendship with
Gaius, haven't you?"

Shaking his head but smiling, Quintus replied, "Don't ask the impossible, my goddess."

"Oh, you did bring him along, didn't you? Welcome, Flavius
Sabinus!" She extended her hand, which Sabinus kissed mechani-
cally, too stunned to do anything else.

"Before this is over, you should be able to do better than that,
Senator." She smiled coyly.

Sabinus flushed, the color rising as he noticed Messalina's outrageous costume—or lack of it: a narrow band of bleached leather
barely covering her breasts, tied to another that wound between her
legs and around her waist to form a belt.

"I designed it myself, Sabinus," she beamed. "Excuse me for now,
gentlemen. Enjoy yourselves . . . as much as I *know* you will!"

As she turned away, Quintus planted a goblet of cold Setinian
into Sabinus' hand and said, "Drink this, friend. And *don't* try to
understand the woman."

Mingling with the merry mélange of guests, they chuckled at how
the women were adapting to their scanty costumes, also designed by
Messalina, which were little more than loose-fitting loincloths and
halters of skins bleached to match flesh tones.

The shrill blast of a cornet blanketed the hall with silence. Gaius
Silius stood up to greet his guests. "A cordial welcome, my friends!
Today we celebrate Italy's bountiful harvest!" He held his cup high.

"But more!" Messalina cried, reclining at his side.

"We also celebrate our Cause, which has nearly triumphed!"
Silius exclaimed.

Sabinus leaned over to whisper to Quintus. "So public? Has he gone mad?"

"*Shhhh!*"

"But more! But more!" Messalina was squealing with delight.

Silius stopped, leaned down to place a passionate kiss on Messalina's lips, and then continued, "Ah yes, more indeed! Today, my beloved friends, we also celebrate . . . my marriage . . . to the empress Messalina!"

A sepulchral silence followed. Sabinus inhaled a breath which hung in his lungs and did nothing else. Quintus raised himself from a reclining position to stare at Silius.

"Some here were witnesses to our wedding several days ago," Silius continued, "but we swore them to secrecy so we could surprise you all. This feast, my friends, will go down in Roman annals because it marks a bold and public change in Roman government, not a clandestine assassination. I took only Claudius' wife, not his life! So raise a cheer for the bridal couple!"

Everyone about them jumped up in a frenzy of applause and wild cheering, as Sabinus and Quintus stayed reclining opposite each other at the table. "Madness," Sabinus whispered. "*Madness!*" he now fairly shouted.

"By all the gods," Quintus murmured, still staring at Silius.

"No, no, no, *no!*" a piping voice behind them broke in. "It isn't madness at all." A middle-aged rail of a man reclined next to them.

"Sabinus, this is Vettius Valens," Quintus said softly, still in obvious shock. "He's a physician."

"Not necessary, I know the senator," said Valens. "No, the empress' problem isn't madness at all but *kindunophilia.*"

"Which means?"

"Love of danger. It's the last resort for a jaded soul that has tried all the pleasures life can offer and wearied of them. It was Messalina who arranged—who demanded—this marriage, not Silius. She was tired of deceiving Claudius so easily—night after night, month after month. She's just a . . . a child of excess."

When he got no response, Valens added, "You doubt me? Look, I'm Messalina's doctor, and I've also examined her thoroughly. Many times." He gave a wicked chuckle. "No, her only refuge now is danger itself. She needs it to prod and revive her senses. Messalina needs danger like a party needs wine."

"And Silius?" Quintus wondered.

"Had to go along with her plans. *Had* to. Probably wants to, though, now. The husband of an empress is an emperor, isn't he? Heh-heh."

"But . . . *bigamy?*" Sabinus demanded.

"What else?" Valens shrugged his shoulders. "After adultery, theft, conspiracy, treason, and maybe murder . . . why not bigamy too?"

Sabinus felt ill. Silius' vaunted "return to the Republic" had been only the thinnest tissue of lies, then, a screen of deception to mask his own ambitions. "Let's go, Quintus," he said.

"Wait. Just a little longer. I can't . . . really believe this . . ."

"*Let's go,* I said."

"Just a few minutes longer. I . . . have to think."

Their wine-soaked wits were responsible for their staying on, they later argued. And it was true that, in a more sober state, they would easily have abandoned such a theater of treason. Perhaps, though, the madness of the moment also held them in thrall, infecting them with a curious rage also to taste danger at first hand. In fact, no one was leaving the hall.

From one corner of the room, a company of drummers started tapping a languid beat, answered from the opposite side by other drums. An orchestra of flutists and lyrists, all dressed as satyrs, struck up a sensuous tune. The throbbing rhythms grew in volume. "The Dance of Bacchus!" a herald cried.

One by one, the women got to their feet and started a slow series of bends and whirls, which soon picked up tempo and intensity. The music cast a spell over the guests, luring more of the women into a wilder dance across the artificial hills and dales erected in the great court.

Messalina and Silius lay on a nuptial couch in the center of it all, luxuriating in the success of their party. Breathless from the dance, her hair as disheveled as a genuine bacchante, Messalina screamed with delight and shook the ivy-twined staff of Bacchus. She was cheerfully aware that one of her breasts, its tip carefully painted gold, was now exposed in her torn halter. Silius, with his crown of ivy, was impersonating Bacchus himself. His legs, laced with the buskins of the god of drink, were twitching about in time with the music, and he grasped his bride from time to time in an ecstatic embrace.

The music grew even louder, coaxing echoes throughout the marbled mansion and overcoming everyone's reserve. All the women now joined in near-manic choruses of delirious, frenzied dancing, vaulting about like crazed fawns.

The men could stand it no longer. Stumbling off the couches where they had been reclining, they started chasing the women. A planned delirium broke out, a laughing, shrieking, howling chase throughout the premises. The skin costumes, poorly stitched at the seams, started coming apart as they were meant to. Couples found each other between the hedgerows of the vineyards, in shady glens contrived in the rear garden, in any convenient nook. Several actually embraced while thrashing about in the slimy purple mash inside the wine presses.

Sabinus watched it all with an exotic mixture of disbelief and his own unavoidably rising lust. Quintus had left him for adventures in the vineyards, but some nagging shred of conscience told Sabinus that he should remain an observer at the bacchanal, not a participant. And then a woman dropped down next to him. She was staring at him through the coolest orbs of green he had ever seen, eyes that seemed to pierce and study and smile at him all in the same instant. Her smallish mouth parted into a delightful smirk, as she sat up to comb curly strands of brown hair that had become disheveled from the dance.

"Are you enjoying all this, Flavius Sabinus?" she finally asked, her voice caressing his ears, assaulted as they were by the shrieks about him.

"How d'you know me?" Sabinus slurred even as he tried to speak distinctly.

She reached over to finger the triumphal pendant hanging from his neck. "Only two men in all Rome can wear this," she said. "I was at the ovation."

"You were? Well, forgive me, then, but who're you?"

"You really don't know?" Her green eyes suddenly narrowed a bit.

Sabinus studied her uncommonly pretty face, but then shrugged. "No. No, I don't. Should I?"

"That's not important now," she smiled, leaning over to brush his cheek with her lips and kiss his ear. "This is."

The unexpected tactile shock unleashed the passion that had been building inside him, and he clasped the woman to his chest as she crossed his cheek and mouth with insistent kisses. "Come, Sabinus," she finally whispered. "An olive grove in back. No one's there."

Later he tried to recall exactly what followed—so bizarre was the scene—but it all seemed a wine-hazy, frustrating dream. The woman with the green eyes—*if* he remembered correctly—led him by the hand outside into the grove, where she caressed the pendant off his neck, untied the thongs of his exhausted skin tunic, and began running her hands across his bare chest. What happened next? Was it the fresh outside air cooling him down, or some moral impulse warning him that he must *not* do this with a stranger? Whatever it was, he grabbed her exploring hands and halted them.

Puzzled, she demanded an explanation. Sabinus, searching his wits for some excuse, came up with the worst one any woman can hear: "You . . . you don't appeal to me . . . that way."

He had not meant it, but evidently he'd said it, for his one sure memory from the delirium that afternoon was the woman hissing like a furious feline, lashing out with both her hands and scratching ten painful trails of red down his bare chest. Then she hurried back inside, but not before unleashing a withering curse: "May the Gorgons turn *all* of you into stone, you simpering eunuch!"

Earlier that day, Pallas, the emperor's financial secretary, stormed into Narcissus' quarters in the palace. Pallas had let his dark, scented locks grow long enough to hide his earlobes, pierced when he was a slave boy. Now they trembled with fury as he bellowed at Narcissus, "She's done it! Our palace prostitute has gone and done it. She *got married* to Gaius Silius!"

Narcissus cringed. "She *what?* How do you know?"

"You know my source. He was invited to the ceremony—witnessed the whole thing."

"When did it happen?"

"Last Tuesday. He tried to tell me immediately, but I've been away."

"An official *wedding?* Is she *insane?* Bigamy?"

"Yes. Or automatic divorce from Claudius, depending on which law you follow."

Slumping into a chair, Pallas continued. "To all appearances it was a normal wedding—the witnesses, the vows, the sacrifices. They ate cake on bay leaves. They were constantly kissing and slobbering over each other. Oh, it was a regular marriage, all right, including the wedding night."

"How would you know?" Narcissus asked woodenly, scarcely comprehending the news.

"Well, at the end of the feast, Messalina shooed the guests out of the house because—how did she put it?—oh yes, 'We must pass the night in that freedom which marriage permits.'"

"Unbelievable."

"So now the happy couple are man and wife," Pallas sneered, his grim humor only barely disguising the anxiety they both felt. "Well, what do we do now?"

"There's no option. We have to tell Claudius. At once."

Pallas shook his head. "No. Not now. It's too late. He'd have our heads for not telling him sooner. Gods, he might even accuse us of conspiring in the affair."

Narcissus shot Pallas a chilling stare. "Well, do you want to do that? Make Silius emperor?"

Pallas bristled. "Are you suggesting . . . are you trying to get me to commit treason? Is that it?"

"Calm yourself. I'm just showing you the consequences of not telling Claudius."

Pallas thought for several moments. Then he said, "All right, Narcissus. He has to be told, then . . . But you're his chief of staff— you wear the dagger, not I—so you'll have to tell him. And, by flaming Hercules, leave me out of it." With that he stalked out of the room.

"Coward," Narcissus muttered. "Simple, spineless dastard!"

Not that Pallas' attitude was any real surprise. A leaden certainty had hung over Narcissus that eventually he would have to convey the terrible truth. He rehearsed his strategy and then recalled Aulus' advice some weeks earlier. Yes, he thought, that's it.

Before hurrying off to Ostia, Narcissus sent this message:

Narcissus to Aulus Plautius, greeting! Messalina has just committed public bigamy with Gaius Silius. We are informing Caesar. Urgent that you control the praetorians as planned. Farewell.

It was not Narcissus' visit that surprised the emperor so much as the fact that Calpurnia and Cleopatra, Claudius' own concubines, had made the trip too. "Proceed now, as planned," Narcissus quietly told them. "We will confirm everything."

An anxious, dour look on her face, Calpurnia asked, "Master, may I see you privately? A matter of gravest importance?"

"Certainly, my dear."

While the others waited outside, Calpurnia threw herself on Claudius' knees and began weeping.

"But what is it, child?"

"I . . . I know this will hurt you terribly, Master, but"—she burst into fresh tears—"*someone* has to tell you. You should have been told long ago, but we all wanted to spare you, I suppose. But now you must know the terrible truth."

"What happened, Calpurnia?"

"Your wife, Messalina . . . she's married."

"Aha! Of course she is. Heh-heh. Else how could I be her husband?"

"No, no. Several days ago, she . . . got married to . . . Gaius Silius."

Claudius gave Calpurnia an empty stare. She waited for him to digest the poisonous tidings, but he did not seem to comprehend.

"What do you mean, Calpurnia?" he croaked, then cleared his throat.

"Senator Gaius Silius, the consul-elect, married my lady Valeria Messalina. At his home . . . while you were here in Ostia. There were public vows. And witnesses. They . . . they," she faltered, "they also consummated the marriage." Then she broke into sobbing.

Absentmindedly, Claudius began stroking her head, but the deepening furrows on his brow showed that the news was finally taking some effect.

"*My* Messalina?" he wondered. "The empress?"

"Yes. Oh, my lord, how we tried to—"

"I don't believe it."

"It's public knowledge in Rome, Master . . ."

"She loves me too much to do something like that."

"But, Caesar, there's no question—"

"And I love her too much," he grumbled. "It's not possible."

"Cleopatra!" she cried. "Cleopatra, come in here! Maybe he'll believe you."

The door opened and the other concubine hurried inside, her eyes filling rapidly with tears. Cleopatra nodded and said, "It's all true,

Caesar. The empress and the senator are man and wife. She now has two husbands."

For some moments there was total silence. Finally Cleopatra shouted, "Narcissus! Come in and help us!"

The state secretary entered the room, hunched over with anxiety but prepared to deliver the most carefully rehearsed speech of his life.

"Narcissus," Claudius crackled, coughed, and then continued, "explain these . . . lies about the empress."

"Would that they *were* lies, Caesar. Unfortunately, they're quite true. An official wedding *did* take place: a dowry . . . omens . . . banquet . . . everything."

Claudius glared at the three and then finally exploded, "Thundering Olympian Jupiter! Are you telling me that my own wife married somebody *else*? Without telling me first? Without divorcing me? Bigamy was outlawed seven centuries ago among the Romans!"

"But it happened, Princeps," said Narcissus. "You can confirm it with the praetorian prefect and the chief magistrates. The tragedy is that so much more is involved."

"What else? What possibly else?"

"Silius . . . isn't the first. Actually, he's the last in a series. The empress has been deceiving you for several years, Caesar. We can document perhaps twenty men. There may be more."

Claudius' face became a glowering mask of anger and incredulity. The women, terrified by the hideous transformation, started weeping again.

"Who?" Claudius gargled. "W-who else was involved?" A string of saliva started dangling from his lower lip, and the twitching of his left cheek caused him to wink.

"Here are the names, Caesar," said Narcissus, handing him the list he had shown Aulus, with some additions.

Claudius' hands were trembling, and he had to squint to make out the names. Each one induced a new ripple in the muscles around his eyes. When he laid the list down, he asked, "What does that arrow mean?"

Narcissus winced. He had forgotten to erase the arrow! He groped for some explanation other than the truth in order to spare Aulus, but then gave up the attempt. "The name of Quintus Plautius Lateranus belongs there," Narcissus admitted. "And I make a special point of his case to show that several on the list were involved against their will. Do you recall the interview with Lateranus in which you said, 'Do whatever the empress says'?"

"Yes, but I thought she wanted some . . . business advice."

"She was lying, we found out later. Poor Lateranus thought you were ordering him to commit adultery."

Claudius' face reddened, and his blue-gray eyes sparkled the awful sheen of a wounded animal. He sprang to his feet, grabbed Narcissus by the arms, and bellowed, "If all this is true, why didn't you tell me long before now?"

"For several reasons, Caesar," Narcissus replied, trying to stay composed. "At first, we also knew nothing of the empress' crimes. And when we did learn, we had to be *sure* of her affairs before exposing them. It would have been worse to accuse her if she were innocent." He paused to let Claudius digest the logic, then resumed. "But I will admit, Caesar, we also tried to overlook her infidelities, hoping she would mend her ways. We knew how much you loved her and how this would wound you. Then there were the children, too."

The prime reason for the delay—fear of Messalina—could not be mentioned, since imperial secretaries were expected to risk their very lives for the emperor.

"But her affair with Senator Silius is *far* more dangerous than the others," Narcissus continued. "Her bigamy suggests that she and Silius are planning to depose you and take over the Empire. Our informers tell us of overtures they've made to the legions, members of the Senate, and even the praetorians."

"*What?*" Claudius darkened. He clapped his hands. "*Guards!*" he shouted. "Get me Geta and my whole staff. Bring them here immediately!"

Lucius Geta, the praetorian prefect who always attended the emperor, made a hasty entry, as did other powerful friends of Claudius who had accompanied him to Ostia. Heads lowered and eyes askance, they all confirmed Narcissus' noxious report.

"W-well, wo—, w-what do we do now?"

Narcissus looked over to Geta and asked the questions on which the future of the Roman Empire depended: "Well, Prefect, will the praetorians stay loyal? Or will they support Silius?" The guard commander was somewhat unreliable, Narcissus knew, and he *might*

abandon Claudius if he thought Silius could win. Or if he were
bribed enough.

Geta flashed a scornful glance at Narcissus, then turned to Claudius and replied, "The Guard will stay loyal, Caesar. But only if
you return immediately to the Castra Praetoria and *show* them that
you are still in charge of the Empire."

For a moment Claudius did nothing. Then he slowly nodded and
said, "Pack up! We return to Rome at once."

The journey back to Rome was fourteen miles of exquisite agony
for Narcissus. Besides the emperor and himself, two others were
seated in the jogging imperial litter, Claudius' friends Vitellius and
Caecina. Both were spineless opportunists, he knew, and could only
complicate the crisis. Vitellius had even made a fetish of Messalina's
slipper, carrying it inside his tunic and kissing it from time to time!
What if they should induce Claudius to spare her? In that case, he
himself would surely die, Narcissus knew. Everything now depended on Aulus Plautius keeping the praetorians loyal, since Geta
could be leading them into a trap at the Castra Praetoria with his advice.

Claudius suddenly broke down and wept convulsively. The odi-
ous revelations about the woman he truly loved had burned through
the logical part of his mind and were now searing his emotions.
When he partially recovered, his comments were random and distraught. There were long, lugubrious silences. Then he would roll
his eyes and babble, almost incoherently, "You *couldn't* have done
this to me, my beloved . . . my pet." The next moment he would
snarl, "Oh, but a harlot must be paid for her services!" After that he
muttered darkly about those who withheld information from the emperor, for whatever reason.

Vitellius became unnerved. He thought the only safety lay in
aping the moods of Claudius, and so he wept or threatened in tune
with the emperor, wringing his hands extravagantly. Caecina
chimed in with slavish echoes.

Later, Claudius did become lucid enough to ask, "Well then,
gentlemen, what shall I do about . . . Messalina?" Significantly, he
looked first to Narcissus for an answer.

"If it were only a matter of her adulteries, Princeps, you might
banish her to an island. But since the empress also conspired to
depose you, there is only one punishment for such treason." Even in

exile, he knew, Messalina would have her agents try to assassinate him for his disclosure. And what if she were pardoned?

The litter was silent. Several tears slid down the ruddy, wrinkled cheeks of Claudius. "And what would you do, Vitellius?" he groaned. "What if you had the misfortune to preside over such a garden of adultery as Rome?"

Vitellius' hands grappled with one another for an answer. He could have joined Narcissus in recommending death, but what if Claudius should finally forgive Messalina? "Ah, Princeps," he whined. "The gods have put you, rather than us, to such a test, for they know that your superior wisdom will unfailingly choose the proper course."

Narcissus shot Vitellius a loathing glance. "Come, come, worthy Vitellius," he challenged. "Let's hear you more plainly. Clear up those ambiguities, like a good emperor's adviser should."

"I merely hate the taking of any human life. I'm only trying—"

"To be as vague as possible," Narcissus cut him off. "You're a weathervane, Vitellius. A jellyfish! You used to have some backbone —like the time you dismissed Pontius Pilate as governor of Judea— but now—"

"Insolence!" Vitellius cried.

"'And from an ex-slave!' · you'll say next," Narcissus mimicked. "But we really have no time for this, gentlemen. I fear, Caesar, that you're underestimating the danger to Rome and to your own life. If this treason isn't punished immediately, you'll lose the Empire."

The distraught Claudius actually began weeping again and cried, "Am I . . . am I still emperor of Rome, Narcissus? Is Silius still my subject?"

Before he could reply, they heard the clatter of horses' hoofs outside the litter. Narcissus looked out and saw that it was several of his aides, fresh from Rome. They whispered something in Narcissus' ear. A gleam of triumph lighting his eyes, Narcissus said, "Tell Caesar. Tell him everything."

The men reported the bacchanal in progress at Silius' residence. As the lurid details unfolded, Claudius' self-pity melted into smoldering rage.

"May I issue the orders in your name, Caesar?" Narcissus inquired.

Claudius nodded emphatically.

"Take a cohort of men, Tribune, and arrest Senator Gaius Silius, the empress Messalina, and all who are at his residence on the Esquiline."

"The empress too?" he asked, with widening eyes.

"The empress too. Take them to the Castra Praetoria and hold them there."

5

SABINUS tied his skin tunic together and returned to Silius' party, but only to find Quintus and then leave the premises as quickly as possible. The nameless woman's fingernails and her seething curse must have overcome the effects of the wine, since he remembered the rest of the day more clearly. Inside, the bacchanal had moderated somewhat, and couples were returning to the tables. Everyone was watching the irrepressible Dr. Vettius Valens scampering atop a large cask. Holding up a crystal goblet, he called out a series of treasonable toasts.

"May our magnificent Messalina mother a new dynasty of emperors!" he cried.

"*Io! Io!*" the guests shouted.

"And may her children be *normal* Romans, not slobbering old satyrs from Hades like Ci-ci-claw-claw-claudy-claudy-Claudius!"

"*Io! Io!*" This time there was laughter and wild cheering too.

"And may our new emperor Gaius rule for many, many years!"

"*Io! Ave Imperator!*" Many of them stood up and took long sips from whatever cup was nearest.

"Silius, you hypocrite traitor, I'll see you in —— first!" Sabinus swore. He looked everywhere for Quintus but could not find him.

Someone shouted a lewd remark about Valens' professional services for the empress, and several young revelers scrambled up the cask, trying to grab the doctor. Valens playfully sprang down from his perch and the girls chased after him. They ran out into the garden, where he escaped by climbing up a tall pine tree—a remarkable achievement for one in his condition. "Oho, what a view!" he shouted.

"What do you see?" the girls called up to him.

"A terrible storm coming from Ostia!"

Everyone knew Claudius was in Ostia at the time, and they roared with laughter at the clever remark. Sabinus, meanwhile, finally located Lateranus sleeping under one of the tables. He pulled him out, slapped some cold water on his face, and said, "Let's go, friend!" Quintus grunted his consent as Sabinus lifted him to his feet, and the two began a swaying exit.

Suddenly they heard a loud banging at the doors of the mansion. Silius was called out to the vestibule. Not a minute later he reappeared with an ashen face and trembling lips, holding up his arms for silence. "Your weather forecast is correct, Valens," he shouted in the awkward stillness. "A storm is coming from Ostia! Claudius is on his way to Rome. He knows everything!"

For a moment, nothing happened, and some drunken guests never did get the message. Then a low moan arose, a babbling, hysterical chaos of confusion. People rushing for the door knocked Sabinus off balance, pitching Quintus onto the terrazzo floor of the vestibule, where his head struck the hard marble. Sabinus made a lunge to prevent his friend being trampled, and managed to drag him behind a column. Husbands were snatching their wives, if they could find them, and scrambling off in their party costumes. Tables were overturned in the panic to escape, one of them crashing against the spiggot of a great cask, which now jetted spurts of wine across the marble floor—little help for those fleeing, who slipped and slid across the slick.

When all who were able had left, Sabinus turned to the host for help with Quintus. But Silius ignored him. He was holding Messalina by the shoulders and saying, "Get hold of yourself, carissima. We'll use the other plan. I'm going down to the Forum as though nothing happened, and, remember, you have to get to him *before* he reaches Rome."

"Help me with Quintus, Silius!" Sabinus called again.

"Go to Hades!" Silius barked, hurrying off.

"*You* will for certain, you adulterous reptile!" Sabinus shouted after him. A rage that pulsed down to his fingertips gave Sabinus the strength to hoist Quintus' sturdy frame onto his shoulders and hurry away.

Moments later, a large company of praetorians converged on Silius' place just as the last guests were scattering in every direction. But they had little trouble chasing down and arresting some of them because of their bizarre dress. "Just look for skin-covered savages, reeking with wine!" the tribune ordered his men. When they burst into the house, they found only a besotted few, snoring in drunken slumber. The host and hostess were missing. "Seal up the place as is," the tribune commanded. "No one gets in or out till Caesar arrives."

Messalina and three of her women companions were hastening southward on foot to the Ostian Gate. There they searched desperately for transportation down the Via Ostiensis, but found none. Finally Messalina noticed a tethered mule standing in a park. A cart was harnessed to it, but no one seemed to be attending it at the moment. Rushing over, they untied the beast and scrambled onto the wagon. It was muddy and stank from garden refuse. No matter. Messalina gave the reins a jerk, and the cart clattered out onto the Ostian Way.

They did not have far to ride. About three miles down the road, they saw Claudius' entourage approaching them. Messalina pulled in the reins, but the trotting mule, happy to be free of hauling manure and blissfully unaware that it was approaching the lord of the world, refused to obey. The imperial litter-bearers, in fear of collision, dropped the gilded litter in a swirl of dust and took to the ditches. With all four women tugging at the reins, the mule finally came to a halt, inches from the imperial party.

Narcissus stuck his head outside and flinched. There, incredibly, was Messalina, stained with what appeared to be compost, climbing off the cart and running up to the litter. Eyes tearful but flashing, she cried, "My husband! Listen to me!"

Claudius stared at her, then sullenly turned the other way.

"Everything can be explained, dearest! Listen to the mother of Octavia and Britannicus! You've been listening instead to false rumors."

"False?" Narcissus turned to her with a sneer. "Your public bigamy with Senator Gaius Silius . . . is *that* a false rumor?"

"The marriage was only a sham!" Messalina insisted. "Claudius, you remember the portents threatening 'the husband of Messalina'? I *feigned* marriage with Silius to avert the danger from *you*. I did it to save you."

Claudius turned and looked at her blankly. Then his eyes shifted to Narcissus.

"Here, look at this," she said, thrusting a document into Claudius' hands. "That's your signature, isn't it? This is the contract for the dowry. You signed it with your own hand so that the marriage would *look* legal."

Claudius studied the signature. Then he said, "I . . . I don't remember this. But I must have signed it, I think. It *looks* like my signature."

"Which proves *nothing*, Princeps," Narcissus objected. "You sign dozens of documents each day. She merely slipped this in with the others. It's all a lie, Caesar, an incredibly audacious lie designed to cover her crimes."

"No," Messalina cried. "My husband, you do remember those threatening omens, don't you?"

"Yes . . . I remember your saying something about them."

Narcissus' eyes widened. "If there *were* portents, Caesar, she must have bribed the priests to find them. But did you ever give her permission to marry Senator Silius? Even in a sham wedding?"

Claudius' hands teased his silver locks and his forehead wrinkled. Slowly, he shook his head. "I . . . don't think so. Wouldn't I have remembered . . . something like that?"

"Of course you would, Caesar," he rushed on. "And even if you had agreed to a mock wedding, you didn't intend that it be *consummated*, did you? If it's documents you need, begin with this stack." He thrust a pile of papers into Claudius' hands.

Painfully, Claudius began reading the testimony. Even that was part of Narcissus' strategy: the emperor's eyes must be drawn away from Messalina. Her unkempt, though still lush, beauty must not continue working its spell on him. The old feeling dared not be rekindled.

Messalina fired a glance of mortal hatred at Narcissus and her lower lip quivered. She flashed about to order guards to arrest the upstart state secretary, until she realized that only her three attendants would follow her orders now.

Narcissus ordered the litter-bearers to continue toward Rome. They bent to their task. Claudius did not interrupt his reading. Messalina protested and cried, but Narcissus called back that she should not disgrace herself further. The four women and their mule stood astride the Ostian Way, watching the litter jog on toward Rome.

Silius' mansion was surrounded by smirking guards who had occupied their time by telling the latest Messalina stories. But when the imperial litter lumbered up they quickly wore faces of sympathetic concern. Narcissus helped Claudius out of the litter and told the two who were still inside, "You'd better join us, gentlemen. We'll need witnesses"—you equivocating dastards, he added, to himself.

At that moment, Aulus Plautius galloped up to the imperial party, dismounted, and saluted.

"Oh . . . Aulus," Claudius moaned. "I'm glad you're here, my friend. Have you heard the terrible news, too?"

"Yes, Princeps. But—"

"What about the Guard, Aulus?" Narcissus interrupted. "What's Geta doing?"

"Good news. Silius *had* sent agents to bribe the praetorians, but when I got there I lectured the men on the subject of treason and its consequences. Geta arrived toward the close of it. Now, I'm sure I didn't influence the prefect"—Aulus smiled—"but he promised us his loyalty and full cooperation. They're all waiting for you over at the Castra Praetoria now."

Narcissus was beaming, while Claudius put his arm around Aulus and hugged him. "You've saved Rome for us, Aulus," he exulted. "You've saved Rome for us. But first there's this . . . matter of evidence here. Join us, friend."

The imperial party inspected the site of the bacchanal, a shambles of wine-smeared floors, scattered food, toppled decorations, and broken furniture. The resinous, fermented odor of drying wine saturated the place, which had all the atmosphere of the inside of a dank barrel. Narcissus, whose agents had briefed him on what to look for, appointed himself as tour guide, identifying which furnishings had come from the palace, and which had been confiscated from the estates of those whose death Messalina had caused. Claudius had to hear a painful running commentary:

"Those murrhine vases used to stand in your atrium, Caesar . . .

"You were wondering about that missing Cupid? Over there . . .

"Oh, here's one of your slave boys. Hello, lad!"

Claudius' emotions churned away from grief and self-pity toward fury and revenge. But it was in the master bedroom that he lost control of himself. There, at the end of the bed, stood a magnificent inlaid table that he had presented Messalina as a wedding gift. Standing on it was a carved, obscene wooden caricature of himself. His face flushed purple and his left cheek quivered as he thundered, "Sh-she will *die* for this! By the Olympian home of the gods, sh-she will die!"

"But first, Princeps, save the Empire," Aulus cautioned.

"Ye-yes indeed! To the camp, everyone!"

By an agile zigzag in and out of the roadways, malls, and alleys of eastern Rome, Sabinus managed to avoid Claudius' troops. Fortunately for his aching shoulder, Quintus' concussion was only minor, and when Sabinus heard him yell, "Put me down. I'm not a blathering baby," he knew all was well. At last they reached the safety of Lateranus' town house on the Caelian, where a cold bath did much to restore their wits.

News arrived that Claudius was on his way to the Castra Praetoria to place Silius and Messalina on trial for treason. Quintus brightened and said, "Into your clothes, Sabinus. We can't miss this: Claudius the Cuckold, quaking up to the rostrum and bawling out to his praetorians, 'Strange, I never noticed that my wife was playing the prostitute these last years—'"

"Much too dangerous, Quintus. What if—"

"None of Claudius' men saw us at Silius' place. And we don't exactly have to stand in the front row over at the Castra . . ."

"No! We should stay out of sight for a while!" Sabinus kept remonstrating all the way over to the Castra Praetoria, for naturally he could not leave his foolish friend in the lurch—nor stifle his own gnawing curiosity.

When they reached the praetorian barracks, the Guard cohorts were all standing at attention before a raised tribunal. Their helmets, each sprouting a curved red plume, flashed gilded silver in the late afternoon sun. Claudius, evidently, had just finished his pathetic confessional, since Narcissus was calling out to the guards: "Do you, then, maintain your allegiance to the emperor?"

"Hail, Caesar! Ave Imperator! Hail, Caesar!" they all shouted.

Brushing a tear from his eye, Claudius addressed the guards, "It was seven years ago that you men first declared me emperor as I stood on this very platform. I'll not forget your loyalty!"

"Let those arrested now be brought before this tribunal," Narcissus announced. "Caesar's assessors—his advisory justices—have taken their places. Let the trials begin."

Sabinus, who was standing next to Quintus in the midst of a large crowd of spectators, whispered, "There's your Uncle Aulus sitting to the right of Claudius."

Lateranus whistled softly. "I guess he's one of the assessors too."

"You still think we should have come?"

Quintus merely chuckled. It was, perhaps, the last time he smiled that day, since they both found the trials unnerving. The very guests they had been partying with just hours earlier were now being sentenced to death. Gaius Silius himself, white as the senatorial toga he was wearing to bely the revels, looked defiantly at Claudius and said, "I am *guilty*, Caesar, guilty of wanting a better emperor for Rome than your silly self. I ask only a quick death."

"And you shall have it," replied Claudius evenly. He turned to his assessors and briefly tallied their response, which was unanimous. He then pronounced sentence of death. Silius was led off to a block set up at the opposite end of the camp courtyard, where he bent over and bared his neck for one great slash of the sword.

Silius' late-blooming courage became contagious, and the other accused also requested a quick execution. Decrius, prefect of the night watch, was very soldierly and professional about it. The tree-climbing Dr. Valens even had a twinkle in his eye as he asked Claudius, "I trust the palace no longer has need for my . . . services?" There was a ripple of laughter from the praetorians.

"Silence!" Narcissus shouted, and the trials and executions ground on. Each time Sabinus and Quintus heard the muffled thud of sword on flesh, they cringed. "Let's get out of here, Quintus," Sabinus whispered.

"No, wait. They're about to try Mnester, the actor."

Mnester surprised everyone by making a spirited defense for himself, pointing his finger at Claudius and telling the imperial face, "You yourself ordered me to do Messalina's bidding, Caesar! Remember your own words: 'Serve the empress in *any* manner'! And she threatened me with death itself if I didn't cooperate."

Quintus shook his head in disbelief. Evidently Messalina hadn't even used a fresh stratagem in seducing him! Claudius, meanwhile, seemed touched by Mnester's appeal, and Aulus flashed him the thumb-up signal for mercy. But then Pallas walked over and advised, "When you are felling so many illustrious Romans, Caesar, will you then pardon an *actor?* And did this mime really sin from compulsion? Or choice?" Like the others, Mnester was sentenced to death. Quintus looked at Sabinus in horror.

Claudius now leaned over and asked Narcissus, "By the way, where's that arrow fellow, anyway?"

Narcissus tried to ignore the question, primed as it was by Mnester's parallel experience.

"The name you didn't have down," Claudius persisted. "Quintus Lateranus, wasn't it?"

"But Caesar, I don't think—"

"Arrest him! Bring him here! He's an adulterer like the rest of them and must also be punished. By very Hades, he must."

Narcissus tried valiantly to dissuade Claudius, but the emperor was clearly losing control of himself. The relentless succession of shocks seemed finally to be macerating his mind, for he now got shakily to his feet and bawled out to the crowd, "One of the culprits is still at large! Do any of you know where the Senator Quintus Plautius Lateranus might be?"

Up on the tribunal, Aulus' mouth sagged open. Down in the crowd, Sabinus, paralyzed by disbelief, barely seemed to notice a figure to the right of him leave his side and make his way up to the tribunal. Quintus stopped in front of the emperor and said simply, "I am here, Caesar."

An excited babble welled up from all sides. What could Quintus possibly do, Sabinus agonized. His defense was not only shopworn by now, but obviously impotent. And yet, as eloquently as he could, Lateranus simply reported his interview with the emperor in detail, calling Narcissus to witness that every word of it was true. Narcissus nodded emphatically. Then Aulus, who had disqualified himself from the bench, stepped forward to testify in his nephew's behalf. He had only begun when Claudius cut him off.

"Enough, dear friend. Rome remains indebted to the conqueror of Britain, and we need no further testimony than your word. It is our decision that Quintus Lateranus will *not* suffer the death penalty."

A commotion broke out among the guards.

"Aha! You're suggesting that Caesar is not fair?" Claudius turned to the praetorians. "That I am pardoning one for the defense ignored in the case of another? You should know, then, that the adultery of the actor took place over many months, in which time he should have learned the truth! That of the senator was brief and almost innocent. Still, he will not go entirely unpunished. Oh no, especially since—I am informed—he was foolish enough to attend the disgusting debauch at Silius' residence."

A low rumble of surprise swept the crowd. Sabinus felt blood rushing to his head.

Turning to the defendant, Claudius said, "Senator Lateranus, you are herewith expelled from the Roman Senate, with loss of all attendant privileges. You may no longer wear the broad purple stripe of the senatorial class. Guards, remove the *ex-*senator from my sight!"

As Quintus was forcibly escorted out of the camp, Claudius called out: "Did anyone else here attend the . . . treasonable 'festivities' at Gaius Silius' residence?"

The noise of the crowd stilled to a hush, although Flavius Sabinus heard a ringing in his ears. Claudius was looking back and forth across the crowd, when he stopped and looked expectantly in his own direction, Sabinus saw, with a sense of despair. Did he have any choice in the matter, or was it all over for him in Roman statecraft? There was the matter of honor, too: should he not step forward and share his friend's fate? Of course he should.

He started to shoulder bystanders out of the way and move forward, but then he stopped. He might also be playing the fool, he realized. Oh, how Lateranus would curse him for stupidity afterward!

But no. Claudius was staring directly at him. There he was, only waiting for him to confess like an honest Roman. The emperor knew, somehow. He would have to make a clean breast of it.

Sabinus threaded his way to the front of the crowd and cried, "Hear me, Caesar—" This was all he managed to say before a brawny arm crossed his face and he tasted the salt of arm flesh pressing into his open mouth. Jerked backward, he saw the horizon dropping below his eyes and then only the deepening purple of twilight overhead. Pinned to the ground by two ponderous figures he had never seen before in his life, Sabinus seemed to hear a voice saying,

"It's the falling sickness, Princeps. Poor fellow . . . excitement always brings it on."

Sabinus tried to get up, but his head was slammed down on the brick courtyard with such force that he saw only pinpoints of gleaming gold in his blackening vision. And then nothing more at all.

Up on the Palatine, Claudius was reclining at dinner—drained of energy, but almost master of himself again. His secretaries were dining with him to celebrate their success in the Silius affair. But for Narcissus, the agony of suspense was far from over: Messalina continued to live, and while she did, the sword was only inches from his own neck. They had just discovered her whereabouts. She had withdrawn to her favorite grove in the Gardens of Lucullus, composing letters of love and appeal to Claudius.

The emperor had dined sparingly and was allowing himself more wine than usual. A messenger arrived with another of Messalina's notes. Claudius read it, folded it up, and tucked it inside his tunic. Now he smiled and ordered more wine. Warmed with its effects, he began reminiscing about happier times he'd had with the empress. Narcissus grew tense, for he knew Claudius better than any of the palace staff, and easily recognized the sensual smile that was mellowing the emperor's face. The evening had descended; the night was bringing its memories. And Claudius was obviously recalling happier nights with Messalina.

"Will someone do something for me?" asked Claudius, the half smile broadening.

"Yes, Princeps?" Narcissus volunteered, casting a worried glance at Pallas.

"Why doesn't someone go and inform that poor creature that she must come back home tomorrow and plead her cause?"

"You . . . you mean Messalina, Caesar?" asked Pallas, losing all color.

"Yes. The empress."

Narcissus' hands grew clammy and he flexed them to regain control. "I . . . Princeps," he said. "I'll do it." With that he left the dining room and hurried to the vestibule of the palace. There he told the officer in charge, "Instructions from the emperor, Tribune: take the centurions who are on duty and their troops and go at once to the Gardens of Lucullus. There you will find the empress Valeria Messalina. Execute her."

The tribune showed no surprise. "We've been expecting *that*." He smirked but then grew serious. "Still, since it *is* the empress, shouldn't we have a signed order from Caesar?"

Narcissus glared. "Almighty Jove, Tribune, hasn't Caesar been plagued enough by that harlot? He wouldn't deign to draw up something so formal as an order. Messalina has simply ceased to exist for him, and if you delay any longer in carrying out these orders, you'll be under arrest for treason."

"All right, all right! Done!—Guards!" He clapped his hands.

"Oh, Tribune," Narcissus added, in afterthought, "if she wants to . . . take her own life rather than having her neck severed, give her the time."

"Certainly." He gave a stiff salute and led his men out of the palace.

"Evodus, go along and see that it's done properly," Narcissus told the youthful staff assistant at his side. "Better yet, get there first and see she doesn't escape. Kill her yourself if she tries."

Evodus nodded, grabbed a dagger from the palace arsenal, and was off into the night.

After the fiasco on the Ostian Way, Messalina finally realized that she had been living in a fool's paradise. When her child's mind finally awoke to the impending disaster, she did what any child would do: she ran to mother. Or rather, she asked her mother to join her at the Gardens of Lucullus, a favorite haunt, where she had been writing her succession of notes to Claudius. Mother Lepida had long since tried to warn Messalina of the catastrophe awaiting her conduct, but the advice was spurned and the two had become estranged. Now it was too late for Lepida to do anything, she thought, but help prepare her daughter for death.

Yet Messalina knew Claudius' weakness, and she was composing messages in the erotic imagery she knew he could not resist. But still there was no reply. An hour passed, then several more, yet no hint of a response from the Palatine.

Then Lepida heard it first—a rustling of men and weapons. "It's all over, dearest," she said. "You couldn't have hoped for mercy—no, not after all that." She burst into tears. "But Messalina"—she suddenly straightened—"let your last act be noble, and people will al-

ways remember it: take your own life. Don't wait for the executioner. It's better that way." Weeping, she drew out a stiletto and
handed it to her daughter.

Messalina moaned and threw herself to the ground, crying and
kicking like a child. At that moment Evodus arrived and saw, to his
relief, that Messalina was still inside the grove. He heard the pathetic dialogue: a mother urging an honorable death, a daughter
complaining that the ground was cold and damp, then crying,
"*Don't* show me that awful dagger!"

And now the tribune arrived with the troops. They cordoned off
the area and then burst through the gateway into the gardens.
Evodus held a flickering lamp over the two women and said, "It's
the one on the ground. Spare the other."

The tribune hovered over Messalina. She looked up, terrified,
then started sobbing hysterically. The tribune drew out his sword
with a shrill rasp.

"No!" Messalina shrieked. "I'll do it." She grabbed the dagger
and pressed its point against her throat, making only a minor cut.
Then she tried pushing it into her breast, with no effect.

Evodus sneered, "You've sent a dozen others to their deaths, little
bawd. Can't you take the journey yourself?"

"Shut up, Evodus!" the tribune barked. Then, laying his sword on
the ground, he bent down to Messalina and said, gently, "Don't
worry, Empress. Here, let me see the pretty little handle on that
dagger."

While Messalina opened her palm to show him the hilt, the point
still aimed at her breast, the tribune struck a sudden blow at the end
of the handle, driving the blade deep inside her. She gasped, wild-
eyed, tried to clutch at the dagger, and then huddled over in death.

Lepida burst into convulsive sobbing and cradled the body of her
daughter in her arms, heedless of the crimson saturating both their
garments.

"You all saw it," the tribune commented. "Her hand was on the
dagger. The empress died a noble death." He and the guards
marched out of the grove.

For some minutes, Lepida rocked Messalina in her arms, shedding
bitter tears for the daughter who had just died, and for the Messalina who, in many respects, had died years before. Only the stars
now shared the vigil over the body of Rome's beautiful third empress, dead at twenty-four.

Claudius was finishing his dessert when Narcissus returned to the dining room and said, "I was too late, Princeps. The empress Messalina is dead. By her own hand."

Claudius, who by now was well fortified with drink, frowned momentarily. Then he shrugged his shoulders, banged his cup down on the table, and shouted, "More wine!"

The freedman secretaries looked at each other in surprise—and profound relief. Had Claudius meant to condemn her anyway, they wondered. Even after a hearing?

About midnight, a figure stealthily evaded the ring of guards around Silius' mansion and climbed over the garden wall in bright moonlight. Near some olive trees, he dropped down to the grass on all fours and began a frantic search for a missing medallion pendant.

Earlier that evening, Sabinus had awakened in a park just outside the Castra Praetoria, rubbing a painful bump on the back of his head. Someone, obviously, had not wanted him to admit attending the bacchanal. But who? The someone had been dead right, of course, for here he was, a free Roman, albeit a Roman with a substantial headache. Massaging his scalp, Sabinus almost welcomed the pain, for now no one need ever know about his presence at Messalina's bacchanal.

It was only then that he suddenly clutched at his throat to feel for his triumphal pendant. It was missing! The green-eyed girl in the grove . . . he'd forgotten to put it back on! It took several moments for the full implications to splash icy apprehension over him. Claudius was planning to sift out every crumb of evidence at Silius' place, and the large, golden medallion, engraved with his name, which all but shouted his participation in the collective treason, now lay waiting to be found—unless someone had discovered it already.

Combing the grass desperately, Sabinus squinted for something that would reflect the moonlight. Suddenly a guard emerged from the residence and began a leisurely patrol around the perimeter of the grove. Sabinus planted himself against a gnarled old olive tree, and had to make a slow, agonizing full circuit of its trunk to stay out of view. The guard loitered, apparently enjoying the moonlight. But eventually he returned inside. While hiding, Sabinus realized that this, in fact, was the very tree under which he had almost been seduced by the nameless woman. Dropping down again, he probed the entire area, but found nothing.

Someone else must have found the pendant, then. Someone in Rome could now easily prove that he had been part of the tainted, disastrous festivities. Was it the woman who cursed him? Who was she, anyway? And who had assaulted him at the Castra? And what was happening to Rome, that such grotesque actors as Messalina and Silius had commanded center stage? And almost triumphed? *Madness!*

6

AULUS PLAUTIUS was also trying to make sense of it all but could not. Like Rome itself, he was in a patchwork of moods. He could cheer with the common people as they pulled down statues of Messalina and chiseled her name off the monuments. He was relieved that Claudius had triumphed and could abandon the ugly role of cuckold which had threatened to make Rome a laughingstock among the nations of the world. He was naturally elated to hear Narcissus and himself styled as "saviors of Rome."

But he also worried for Rome, that such an imbecilic conspiracy might nearly have succeeded. He was embarrassed by his nephew's role in it, however innocent. He sympathized with the domestic tragedy on the Palatine that had now left little Britannicus and Octavia half orphaned. And above all, he was concerned for Claudius. Unquestionably, the emperor was deeply scarred by the affair. Stories told of him wandering around the palace in bewilderment, asking where Messalina was. He had settled down to a wooden existence, Narcissus reported. He merely sat at his gaming boards with a vacant expression, shooting roll after roll of dice, his tired eyes hardly bothering to count the throw.

One day, Aulus paid a quick visit to the Palatine, hoping to cheer Claudius a bit. And it seemed to be a proper tonic, for the emperor was glad to see his old friend, though he did apologize for having had to expel Lateranus from the Senate. "But you saw the mood of the guards," he added.

"Forget that, Princeps." Aulus smiled. "I thank you for his very life."

But what worried Aulus was the pallor and weariness he found in Claudius, who seemed to have aged five years in as many weeks. It was only when he was invited to go along that afternoon for a visit to the Castra Praetoria that Aulus again caught a glimpse of the old Claudius. For, after reviewing the guards, the emperor seemed to come alive again. A twinkle in his eye, he announced, "I understand there's a new bit of gossip making the rounds in this rumor factory with seven hills. It deals with the silly question, 'Will Claudius take another wife?'"

The praetorians rippled with laughter.

"Oh yes," he continued, "and the answer, supposedly, is: 'Yes, Caesar *will* marry again.' And you should see the candidates being suggested . . . you should hear the names."

The men laughed louder.

"There isn't a hopeful patrician mother in Rome who isn't planning 'a little party for the princeps' so that he can meet her 'lovely' daughter." Claudius said it in an affected way, and the men howled.

"But hear me, my praetorians! Marriage and I just don't get along. I should know—I've tried three times, and that's enough. From now on, it's the bachelor's life for me!"

"*Io Caesar!*" the Guard broke out cheering.

"And if I change my mind—by the sword of Mars, you men can happily kill me!"

Claudius was applauded and cheered all the way to the gate. Aulus thought it a remarkable performance, played by the Claudius of old, who had little trouble establishing rapport with his troops. The emperor would survive.

Aulus was more concerned that the great family name of the Plautii was tarnished by his nephew's disgrace. He also knew that time would erase the smudge, but the aftermath of the affair now led him to spend less time in the Senate and more on his memoirs. Julius Caesar had made his literary reputation with the *Commentaries on the Gallic Wars*. Could he do less for Britain?

Composing had been difficult at first. He would sit for hours in his scroll-lined library, a weather-beaten battle diary at his elbow on the broad worktable strewn with maps and blank rolls of papyrus. Yet only a quarter of a scroll bore any writing. He would stare at the inkwell and tell himself it was merely a matter of scratching black fluid onto papyrus—certainly simpler than slashing a heavy sword to victory in Britain. But each chapter was a special problem child that seemed to require its own nine months to produce. He found his library stuffy and constricting, and he crossed out phrase after phrase that failed to pass muster.

It was a magnificent day in golden autumn, bright, warm, and beautiful, that suggested a solution. Aulus set up a table and chair in the rear garden and carried his writing materials outside. Peering at his cedars and cypresses, he filled his lungs with fresh air and sat down to reach for his quill. Soon the British campaign itself descended on him, and he wrote with ease and relish.

Before the afternoon was over, he had finished a whole chapter. Pomponia read the material at supper and thought it moved nicely. He tried the outdoor scheme again the next day, and the lines continued to flow. "I know this sounds ridiculous," he told Pomponia, "but I conquered Britain in the outside air, so I suppose I'd best write about it there too."

There were some distractions in his garden study. An occasional insect would scuttle out of the way of his pen, and the sun sent shifting spears of blinding light across his pages. A passing bird once splattered his scroll with a preliminary critique. But when a sudden squall drove him back inside one morning, the oppressiveness seemed to return, household noises interfered, and the work ground to a halt.

"Just as well. I have to quit anyway." He threw down his quill. "Claudius wants me to go to Ostia with him."

"How long will you be gone?" Pomponia inquired.

"About a week. He wants me to see the new harbor works."

Just long enough, she thought.

No sooner had he left for Ostia than she called in a Syrian carpenter who had installed some handsomely worked cabinets in their kitchen. She asked him to build a roofed porch facing the garden, where her husband could escape the sun and rain, and still write in the fresh air.

The wizened little Syrian, whose name was Hermes, probed about at the rear of the house. Finally he said, "Happily done, my lady. But may I offer a suggestion?"

"Yes?"

"I'm afraid a porch of any size would mar the appearance of your home. But if you merely want some shelter for your husband, why not a canvas awning? I'd build a floor of crushed stone and gypsum —say here"—he pointed—"arrange supporting ropes over there, and when your husband isn't working, the awning could be rolled back to preserve the beauty of the garden."

Pomponia brightened. "A good plan, Hermes. Excellent in fact. What would it cost?"

The canny Syrian cupped his chin. "Oh . . . I'd estimate no more than, say, seven or eight thousand sesterces."

Pomponia said nothing, and for some moments there was an embarrassing silence. It was simply her method of bargaining. No counter offer. No hint that the sum was too high. Just a patrician silence until the vendor grew worried about losing a sale and offered a lower figure.

"Yes, my lady. It'll come to eight thousand sesterces—*if* we get the canvas from the usual sources who supply the Palatine. But I know a dealer on the Aventine who imports his fabric from Cilicia and sells it for less. If we used his canvas, I could do the job for, say, six thousand."

"Is the quality as good?"

"Frankly, it's better—thicker, more weather resistant—better."

"Done, then. And use the Cilician fabric."

Three days later, when the concrete base had hardened sufficiently, Hermes appeared with a red-haired, bearded fellow who stood a head taller than himself.

"This is Aquila, noble Pomponia, the man who deals in Cilician canvas."

"Peace be with you," Aquila nodded.

"Yes, this Aquila is quite a bird," Hermes punned.* "He's a Jew, and you know we Syrians aren't too friendly with the Jews. But I'd trust this one with my own daughter."

Aquila flashed a brief, indulgent smile, and then went out to pull four large rolls of canvas off a pair of donkeys that were braying im-

* Aquila is "eagle" in Latin.

patiently in front of the house. He stretched the fabric on the ground and began taking measurements. It was largely mohair, which Pomponia had ordered in a rich, Tyrian purple.

"Well, my work's finished, noble mistress," said Hermes. "I'll be back tomorrow and see if this Jew has spoiled what I've done." He clapped Aquila on the shoulders and was off.

For the rest of the morning, Pomponia found excuses to visit the garden and watch her project take on final shape. Aquila was a nimble craftsman, sewing the material into seams that had no bulge or crease. He cheerfully showed her several stitches she had never seen before, and she was pleased enough to invite the tentmaker in to lunch.

He was a slender man, perhaps in his early forties, with a well-clipped russet beard edging the lines of his jaw. A ruddy complexion enhanced the slight Semitic cast to his face. With typical Roman prejudice, Pomponia had at first recoiled a bit when Aquila was introduced as a Jew. Jews were supposed to be canny, clannish traders who had some absurd belief in an invisible god who disdained statues and pork flesh and was never satisfied with the world he was supposed to have created.

Pomponia inquired about Aquila's background—he came from Pontus in Asia Minor—and about his family—he was married to a woman named Priscilla, and they had no children. Finally, she also ventured to ask him about his "Jewishness," as she expressed it, with less tact than candor. But Aquila seemed pleased with the query and gave a spirited explanation of Judaism, setting the lofty, single God of the Jews in stark contrast to the "many immoral deities who clutter up your Greco-Roman myths," as he candidly phrased it. Pomponia might have been offended, but she had abandoned her own belief in the Olympians ever since girlhood.

Then Aquila said something that mystified her, for it seemed to go beyond Judaism—mention of a recent special revelation of the Jewish deity in the form of some victim crucified in Jerusalem. But she could make little sense of it.

Aquila returned to his work on the canvas, and by late afternoon the awning was finished. With pride of craftsmanship, he showed Pomponia how to raise and lower the tarpaulin. Then he bowed respectfully and took his leave.

When Aulus returned, still dusty from his trip, Pomponia happily shoved him into the garden and lowered the awning over his new outdoor study. For a moment he scratched his head at Pomponia's surprise, but then he beamed. Reaching out to the stola flowing off the head and shoulders of the lovely woman standing next to him, he pulled her into his arms and kissed her.

The ominous summons from the Palatine arrived just about the time Flavius Sabinus expected it would: when Narcissus had finally finished investigating the Silius conspiracy. The curt note suggested that Claudius himself would be seeing him. Painfully, he anticipated the emperor's opening statement: "I once hung this medallion personally around your neck, Senator. Why was it found at the house of bigamist traitors?"

Sabinus tried not to look anxious while entering the palace, grateful that no one could see his pounding heart. Not in his wildest fancies did he imagine that his interview with Claudius would have nothing to do with the missing pendant, or that an hour later he would be leaving the palace in an aura of exhilaration as he hurried to share the glad news with Aulus Plautius.

He found his former commander writing in his outdoor study, and before Aulus could even greet him, Sabinus declared, "Claudius has just appointed me Provincial Governor! In Moesia!"

"*Well done*, Sabinus!" Aulus beamed. "Congratulations! Oh, I'll admit, this doesn't come as a complete surprise: there have been inquiries about you from the Palatine. And what could I say but that your experience in Britain easily qualified you for service along the Danube."

"I'm afraid Moesia won't be anything like the challenge we had in Britain."

"Nonsense. One day those Dacians are going to cross the Danube and give Rome a terrible fight, so watch out for them.—By the way, what's been happening to your brother Vespasian lately?"

"He's trying civilian life for a while. Narcissus is grooming him for a public career."

A touch of color now crept into Sabinus' face. "Just wondering . . . I'll . . . be leaving for Moesia very soon. So may I say good-bye also to . . . ah . . . Plautia? And Pomponia too, of course," he hastily added.

The slightest smile played at the corners of Aulus' mouth as he tried to guess the reason for Sabinus' halting performance. "Certainly, Governor!" He grinned. "Pomponia isn't home, but Plautia's here, I think. I'll send her into the peristyle."

Sabinus sauntered toward the bright inner court, trying to reflect a casual air. Several times he nervously flexed his hands, rehearsing what to say to a girl he barely knew. He was sorry he seemed to have made so slight an impression on Plautia during their few contacts, and even sorrier about their age difference.

"Oh, there you are, Senator." Plautia's voice had a lilt that Sabinus found delightful.

"Plautia!" he greeted her, smiling. "I wanted to bid you good-bye before I leave for Moesia."

"Moesia?"

"Yes . . . our province north of Greece."

"Flavius Sabinus, I certainly know where Moesia is," she said, somewhat irritated. "But why are you going so far away?"

"The emperor has just appointed me governor of Moesia."

"He has? Congratulations, Governor!" She beamed. "How long will you be there?"

"That's indefinite. If I'm a poor administrator, Claudius will see I return to Rome soon enough."

"Which means you'll be there for years and years."

He smiled, groping for an appropriate rejoinder, but found nothing. What tied the man's tongue, what converted a hero of the British campaign into an almost simpering adolescent was the exquisite girl standing before him. Here and now he wanted to declare his feelings for her, but that would have been stupid, he realized. His demeanor probably shouted that. He also had a fierce pride and dreaded the thought that Plautia might, after all, have no interest whatever in him. Why should she indeed?

"I didn't think I'd be leaving Rome this soon, little Plautia," he finally said. "And I'm sorry . . . because I will miss you."

She looked at him with a widening stare and said nothing.

His eyes, which had been flitting about in a vain attempt to escape hers, now stopped their dance and focused on her with a new intensity. "I should be coming back to Rome on rare occasions," he said. "May I . . . see you on one of the return trips?"

"Well . . . certainly, Governor."

"Could you call me Sabinus, instead?"

"If you like . . . Sabinus." Color suffused her cheeks.

He studied her features to etch them firmly in memory. Yes, he thought, several more years for nature to add her finishing touches to this creature and she would be something spectacular. Then he leaned over and kissed her on the forehead. "Good-bye, pretty Plautia," he said. "Next time I see you . . . I may not be so brotherly."

Plautia blushed and looked at him with a curious glint in her blue eyes. "*Vale*, Sabinus," she said, smiling. "The gods protect you."

Just as he was leaving, Aulus called him back into the library and closed the door. "I've been meaning to give you this for weeks, Sabinus, but it slipped my mind. Here, hold out your hand." Aulus took the lid off a little box and turned it over onto Sabinus' palm.

"Your medallion, Governor," said Aulus, with a wry grin.

"How did—"

"I found it the day I inspected Silius' place with Claudius. No one else saw it, the Fates be thanked!"

Sabinus turned scarlet and tried to stammer out an explanation, but Aulus stopped him. "Don't bother. Quintus told me about that, ah, party. Not *everything*, I'm sure!" he chuckled. "By the way, you haven't had any headaches from that blow you got over at the Castra, have you?"

"No, but I was going to ask if that was *your* voice telling Claudius that I had the 'falling sickness.'"

Aulus unleashed a broad grin. "Yes—*epilepsia*—I'll confess it. You see, once Quintus was on trial there was no way I could protect him. But when I saw you standing there too, I knew you'd try to play the noble fool, so I sent a couple of my men to . . . dissuade you. They were sorry they overdid it, and they stayed with you till you started coming around. But I saw no reason for you to ruin your career also. Claudius didn't even know it was you: he's nearsighted."

"Thank you, Aulus!—I saw Quintus a short time ago, and he's not at all resentful. In fact, that rascal claims he can use his time better now, supervising sesterces. Quintus *will* pull out of all this, won't he?"

"Someday. I'm sure of it. But do you think you two lads will ever grow up?"

"Possibly." Sabinus smiled sheepishly. "Let's hope the East will be a . . . maturing experience."

7

WOULD Claudius take another wife *anyway?*

Narcissus shuddered viscerally at the prospect. The emperor was almost sixty years old, so why should he be grumbling about "the curse of celibacy" like some young stallion? And yet here he was, padding about alone in the palace, starved for the companionship of a wife, seized by an almost perverse desire to be bothered, even dominated, by one.

"Give me a good marital quarrel instead of this monotony, Narcissus," he wailed. "I'd take even the shouts and threats and tears of Messalina about now. I . . . I actually miss her sharp tongue. I really do! And at night, I miss the *rest* of her, the gods know!"

"But, Princeps, aren't Calpurnia and Cleopatra . . . serving you well?"

"They're docile. They're no challenge. They *have* to perform. But I crave an equal in status. A friend. A companion. An *alter ego.* In a word, a wife."

"But, Sire, your vow to the men of the Praetorian Guard?"

Claudius' smile faded only momentarily. "Surely those lads are lusty enough to understand me. And to forgive me."

"But, Caesar—"

"So open up the palace to some festivities, Narcissus. You, Pallas, and Callistus should think up a list of candida— I mean guests, of course! Heh-heh-heh."

Narcissus dared enter no further objections, even while cringing at Claudius' resolve. Women had been the very bane of his life, and three failures should have been enough for him. The machinery of Roman government was finally stabilized again, thanks to his own efforts, but another empress could upset everything. Cursed be Claudius' incontinence!

Well, he would try to make the best of it. He would get together with the other secretaries and they would all agree on some harmless beauty, shove her at Claudius, go through the ceremonies, and then let the aging bull content himself with a docile heifer which they would keep well tethered. Yes, he resolved, that had to be the solution.

Narcissus spent the next days thinking of candidates to suggest to his colleagues. The loveliest girl in Rome, to his mind, was Aulus Plautius' daughter, who, at seventeen, was more than nubile. She also came from a perfect pro-Claudian family. But when he tried to picture the wrinkled, aging form of Claudius embracing Plautia's fresh beauty, he dropped the idea, shuddering at the sort of Latin Aulus would have used in rejecting the abhorrent prospect!

He thought further. Again and again he lingered at Paetina's name. Claudius' second wife *was* something of a "docile heifer," not very interested in politics. Paetina, yes. He must get his colleagues to accept her as their joint candidate, and then let Claudius rekindle the embers of a past love. He hurried to discuss the scheme with Pallas and Callistus.

A plague on their greedy ambitions! They had candidates of their own, Narcissus was shocked to learn, for whoever sponsored the woman Claudius chose would have enormous leverage with the future empress—and therefore the emperor. Claudius, meanwhile, was roguishly encouraging the competition, enjoying his little game as some compensation for the domestic disaster he had suffered. With all the resolve of warm putty, Claudius inclined first to one girl, then another, depending on his moods. Finally he called his three secretaries into conference and, much as a judge deciding a lawsuit, he actually had them plead their candidates' cases before him.

"Narcissus, you first," Claudius grinned. "As usual."

"As you know, Princeps," he began, a little defensively, "I've been urging you to marry the lovely Aelia Paetina, your second wife, whom you divorced for—"

"Used merchandise," Pallas commented, a contemptuous warp to his mouth.

"Silence, Pallas! To continue: you once loved her, Caesar. Above all, you're used to her. There won't be any unhappy surprises."

Callistus, a fat and squinting Asiatic, interrupted, "Then why did Caesar divorce her if she's such a gem?"

"You recall why, Caesar. It was only 'for trivial offenses.'"

"Ha!" Claudius cackled. "The real reason was because I was infatuated with Messalina at the time."

"So," Narcissus resumed, "it's merely a matter of welcoming back the woman who was your wife. What could be easier?"

"No!" Callistus objected, in his buzzing, abrasive voice. "On that point you're wrong, Narcissus. Your Paetina would be an arrogant hussy. I can hear her now: 'I'm the only woman ever to marry an emperor twice.'—Now, Lollia Paulina, the woman I've been suggesting, would make a magnificent empress, Caesar. She's fairly young and has the desirable patrician background. And, of course"—he smiled—"she's also very wealthy."

"Since when does Caesar need money?" asked Pallas, with lofty eyebrows.

"I mean, she'd not drain the imperial treasury like Messalina. Why, I've seen Lollia at an ordinary dinner party wearing 40 million sesterces' worth of jewels."

"She needed that many to cover all her wrinkles," Pallas sniffed. "Really, Caesar, Lollia is older than our worthy colleague suggests. Isn't it time we talked about a real possibility?"

"Do you really think I should marry the younger Agrippina, Pallas?" asked Claudius, with noticeable interest.

"Who else, Princeps? The blood of the Caesars already flows in her veins. Both the Julian and Claudian houses unite in her."

Narcissus raised his voice. "But she's Caesar's—"

"She's still young and very beautiful," Pallas continued.

"But she's your *own niece*, Caesar!" Narcissus broke in. "Her father Germanicus was *your own brother!*"

"*Must* you tell Caesar who the members of his own family are?" Pallas huffed. "Of course Agrippina is related . . ."

"Related? Why she's—"

"Do spare us information we already know, Narcissus," Pallas yawned.

"But you're all overlooking the obvious impediment to such a marriage! Civilized Romans have a name for unions between uncles and nieces—or brothers and sisters, for that matter. We call it *incest!* An ugly term. And it happens to be grossly illegal."

"A mere detail," said Pallas, with a wave of his hand.

"But it's against our customs."

"Customs can be changed," he snapped. "But to continue, Caesar: Agrippina has royal blood. She was sister to an emperor—your predecessor Caligula—and she has proven fertility: a son who would make a good companion for Britannicus. And since her husband died, she's free to marry again. My point is this: her bloodline alone makes her a very powerful woman. It wouldn't do well to have her marry someone else and transfer the glory of the Caesars to another family."

Claudius was visibly moved by that argument. Though the other two continued extolling their candidates, Claudius kept peering at Pallas, reflecting on his unsettling comments. Finally he stood up and said, "Thank you, gentlemen. I wish I could marry all three girls to keep you happy," he chuckled. "But I suppose bigamy *is* worse than incest. At this moment, I don't know when I'll choose the girl. I may even let my heart decide the matter."

Aulus Plautius had every reason to be satisfied with his own marriage. Pomponia Graecina was the full name of that serene and gracious woman he had married more than a score of years ago, and she was a good wife. Their life patterns had easily coincided, and they had few quarrels. Besides, anyone who had borne the Plautia on whom he doted could do no wrong. At a time when some illustrious ladies were reckoning the year not by the names of the consuls but by those of their changing husbands, Aulus thought his marriage a happy enough exception.

Pomponia did, however, have one curious quirk. A close friend of hers had been forced into suicide by Messalina, who was jealous of her beauty. The fact that Pomponia had not been able to help her friend, along with Aulus' absence in Britain, made her almost despair at the time. Doctors had not been able to dispel the melancholy entirely, and they told Aulus that she had suffered a mental wound or *trauma,* as the Greek physicians called it.

Recently, however, Pomponia seemed to be winning her battle with depression, although she still wore mourning garments on anniversaries and religious holidays. Aulus thought such devotion to her friend's memory excessive and unnatural—it had been six years now —but he was careful not to say anything that might reopen the wound.

His wife, he knew, was a highly sensitive woman. Back in the days of their courtship, one coarse or careless word from him and she would "blush all the hues of Vulcan's forge," as he told his friends. But nowhere did Pomponia's sensitivity show itself so clearly as in her concern for things mystical and mysterious and religious. "When it comes to spirits, my wife has a woman's curiosity and a child's credulity," Aulus claimed.

"Not so," she would object. "I merely want to answer this question for myself: if Jupiter, Apollo, and the other Olympians don't exist, is there anyone else who does? *Are* there gods after all, or are there not? Are there many? Or is there only one?"

Well and good to ask such questions, Aulus thought, but to try and answer them by dabbling in Jewish beliefs was shocking. And yet his Pomponia had actually invited that red-bearded Jew, Aquila, back to their home not to check on the canvas awning but, of all incredible things, to discuss religion! He appreciated the man's talents with needle, thread, and mohair, and certainly his memoirs were going much better in his garden study now that spring had returned. But if only that fellow would control his tongue as well as his fingers. If he succeeded in making a Jewish proselyte out of Pomponia, the Plautii would be scandalized. Pomponia had told him not to worry—she would not convert—but the thought nagged at him all the same.

One day Aulus returned to the Esquiline, barely concealing a smile of satisfaction. "Well, carissima," he told his wife, "you won't be seeing your friend Aquila anymore . . ."

"Oh? Why not?"

"You know those riots the night before last over in the Jewish quarter across the Tiber?"

"Yes . . ."

"Well, they were a religious squabble between two different Jewish groups. It seems your friends can't even agree on their own beliefs." He smiled.

Pomponia looked pensive. "How was Aquila involved?"

"He was a leader of one of the parties. Claudius investigated the affair to see how it began, and it seems the chief culprit was a Jew named Chrestus."

Pomponia seemed startled at the name, but she said nothing.

"Well," Aulus resumed, "Aquila spoke out for this Chrestus and that must have touched off the rioting. Most of Region XIV got involved in that fanatic turmoil. Anyhow, Claudius is now preparing an edict banishing Aquila and the other Jewish leaders from Italy. And don't frown, Pomponia. It could have been much worse for them. At first Claudius was so furious he wanted to banish all Jews from Rome."

"What changed his mind?"

"Well, that would have been impossible because of their numbers. So only the Jewish leaders will be exiled. The rest can stay here, so long as they don't gather in groups larger than twenty."

"But what about their synagogues? Their worship?"

"No more of that. At least, not for the time being."

"So?" Pomponia tried to look unconcerned and said nothing more.

But the moment Aulus returned to his memoirs, she sent her personal messenger over to the Aventine to try to contact Aquila. An hour later he returned with the message undelivered. "He and his wife Priscilla have left Rome," the servant reported. "They're sailing for Greece. Neighbors said they'd probably settle in Corinth so long as Claudius' ban is in effect. They have friends there."

The next day, Aulus was summoned to the Palatine. Claudius had convened a special conference to discuss foreign cults in Rome and what should be done about them. He was furious that they were prospering at a time when the Roman state religion was languishing and the city's many temples stood almost empty.

Aulus feared that Claudius had somehow learned of his wife's interest in Judaism, but he had not. Aulus was there because the emperor had decided to include Druids in his decree banishing the Jewish leaders, and Aulus, with his experience in Britain, was the ranking available authority on Druids.

The conference labored much of the morning and finally submitted to Claudius a document headed by three lists:

ABSOLUTE PROHIBITION
The Druids
Astrologers
Magi
Sorcerers
Noxious cults

RESTRICTIONS
Judaism
The Neo-Pythagoreans
Cybele
Mithraism

SUBSIDY/REHABILITATION
Roman state religion
Public morality

The rest of the document detailed how this program might be implemented.

Claudius studied the recommendations and nodded. Then he turned to Narcissus and asked, "Did you get any more information on that Chrestus fellow who raised the riot in the Trans-Tiber? Have you captured him yet?"

The scented cheeks of Narcissus flushed rosy pink as he slowly cleared his throat and said, "It seems our first information on that was . . . a little faulty, Princeps. Although the riot took place because of Chrestus, he himself did not lead it. In fact, he could not possibly have led it."

"Oh?" Claudius scowled. "Why not?"

"Because he died about sixteen years ago."

For some moments there was silence. Finally Claudius broke it with a touch of ire. "Clarify your own stupid riddle, then, Narcissus. We know that this Chrestus was involved somehow."

"One of the Jews we arrested explained it to us. Chrestus was some prophet in Judea who roused the people. But our governor there, Pontius Pilate, crucified him at Jerusalem—oh, about three years before you recalled Pilate, Vitellius."

Vitellius, Claudius' indecisive litter companion on the awful trip back from Ostia, was sitting adjacent to Narcissus at the conclave. He nodded in recollection, for in his younger days he had served as governor of Syria in the reign of Tiberius.

"Anyway," Narcissus continued, "several days after his crucifixion, the prophet supposedly reappeared from the dead. They searched his grave—it was empty—so someone must have stolen his body. And now a sect of Jews believes he's a god or something. But the other Jews deny it. That's what the riot was all about."

Vitellius stood up and asked, "Princeps, may I go to our imperial archives for a moment? I want to check something." Claudius nodded, for the archives were just across the Forum from the Palatine.

Just as Vitellius was leaving, a young woman with light brown hair combed into a vortex of curls whirled into Claudius' office and planted herself on his lap. Ignoring the men in conference, she nuzzled her pretty face against his cheek and then kissed it. "Hello, Uncle Claudius," she cooed coquettishly. "Are you coming to lunch?"

Now she deigned to notice the others present. "Who are these people?" she asked, her limpid eyes of aquamarine flashing in Aulus' direction.

"They're my advisers, Agrippina." Claudius beamed. "Now you'd best go and leave us, little darling. I'll be ready for lunch in half an hour."

"All right, Uncle," she said, stroking him, while pressing a lingering kiss on his lips.

Aulus looked with shock at Narcissus, who returned a glance of tired resignation and a sad shrug.

Claudius had reddened perceptibly and coughed. Agrippina giggled and left the room. "Such a sweet niece," said Claudius, as he returned to the matter at hand.

The emperor now prodded Narcissus for further information about the bizarre Chrestus story. He told what he knew, which was admittedly very little, though he did add one significant detail: the grave had been officially sealed under Pilate's orders, but the seal was later broken.

Soon Vitellius returned, carrying several sheets of parchment. "Here it is," he smiled. "An excerpt from Pilate's *acta* for 786 A.U.C."* He handed the copy to Claudius, who read it aloud:

IESVS NAZARENVS, age 36
Galilean teacher, "prophet," and pseudo-Messiah or "Christus."
Case was remanded to the jurisdiction of the tetrarch Herod

---

* A.D. 33. The *acta* or "acts" were official yearly reports sent to Rome by provincial governors.

Antipas, who waived his authority and returned the defendant for Roman trial. Convicted of capital blasphemy by the Great Sanhedrin, with verdict endorsed by the prefect. Also convicted of constructive treason for claiming to be "King of the Jews." The prosecution: Joseph Caiaphas, high priest, and the Great Sanhedrin. Tried, sentenced, crucified, and died on April 3, A.U.C. 786, in Jerusalem.

When the emperor had finished reading, Vitellius made the obvious comment: "So you see, gentlemen, the prophet's name was Christus, not Chrestus."

"Hmmm," Claudius pondered. "I wonder why Pilate made no mention of that hubbub following the crucifixion. And don't say he was incompetent, Vitellius. I disagree with you on that."

"Shall we summon Pilate and ask him, Princeps?" Pallas ventured. "He's living over in Antium, isn't he?"

"Gentlemen!" Aulus broke in. "What are you suggesting? That a responsible Roman governor should have cluttered his official records with details on every religious fanatic to appear in Palestine? They have a new pseudoprophet crawling out of the desert every other year out there. I could have sent you sheaves of records on the Druids in Britain, but I had more important things to report."

Claudius and the others chuckled. "That's why we always like to have a military man in on these sessions, Aulus. You keep us in line." The emperor grinned. "No, we won't disturb Pilate's retirement. But there is something in this Chrestus—or Christus—story that bothers me: the grave robbery . . . the fact that the culprit's body was stolen. Out of his very grave. That's bad. Impious."

"What . . . do you propose we do about it, Caesar?" Vitellius wondered.

"Perhaps we ought to draw up an edict for Palestine, warning against any form of grave robbery."

"And the penalty?"

"Why death, of course."

Aulus thought the idea unnecessary, if not a little ridiculous, but since the others were nodding their agreement, he did not feel the issue important enough to bother opposing. Soon the conference had drawn up the following edict, with all the circumlocutions so dear to government administrators:

ORDINANCE OF CAESAR: It is my pleasure that graves

and tombs remain undisturbed in perpetuity for those who have made them for the cult of their ancestors, or children, or members of their house. If, however, anyone has information that another has either demolished them, or has in any way extracted the buried, or has maliciously transferred them to other places in order to wrong them, or has broken the sealing or other stones—against such a one I order that a trial be instituted. . . . Let it be absolutely forbidden for any one to disturb them. In case of contravention, I desire that the offender be sentenced to capital punishment on charge of violation of sepulture.†

"Yes," Claudius said as he reread it. "This will do. Narcissus, see that this is inscribed in stone and set up at several places in Palestine. In Jerusalem, of course, and, ah—what was that prophet's name?"

"Chres—Christus?"

"No. The full name. The legal name . . ."

"Oh. Iesus Nazarenus—Jesus of Nazareth."

"Yes. Have another copy set up at Nazareth. Wherever that is."

"In Galilee, Princeps," Vitellius advised.

"All right, all right. In Galilee, then."

When the conference ended, Aulus managed to draw Narcissus off to a corner and ask, "So what does the performance by that brazen little minx inside just now signify?"

Narcissus replied, looking about to make sure they were not overheard, "Only that she's the one. And Pallas—that serpent!—has won the game. Claudius intends to marry the girl."

Aulus was thunderstruck. "But . . . but his vow of celibacy to the Guard?"

"Means nothing.—Oh, this all began innocently enough. Little Agrippina claimed a niece's right to kiss her 'Uncle Claudius' anytime she pleased. And kiss him she certainly did, and we couldn't raise an eyebrow at such tender displays of affection among relatives, after all. When we weren't looking, of course, she did more than kiss. They've been sharing the same . . . quarters for several weeks now."

"But . . . but that's incest! Agrippina is his *own niece*."

† This ordinance is authentic, and was found at Nazareth in Galilee. For further discussion, see the Notes.

"Obviously," Narcissus agreed. "But worse than all that is the darling little *son* she'll bring to this wedding from a previous marriage. Her Domitius is three, maybe four, years older than Britannicus. So can you imagine the rivalries? Can you see how the palace here is about to turn into another battleground?"

Aulus nodded darkly. "We have to stop this, Narcissus."

"How?"

"Doesn't the Senate have to approve such a marriage?"

"Yes, but Vitellius is introducing a bill of approval in the Senate. Tomorrow morning, in fact."

"Vitellius? That craven toady?"

"Oh, Vitellius is equivocating only when the gusts of politics blow in crosscurrents. Once a prevailing wind is established, that human weathervane snaps quickly into place."

"I haven't attended the Senate since I started my memoirs. But I'll be there tomorrow."

Vitellius had prepared himself well. Yesterday's sycophant was today's orator, Aulus had to admit. With gilded tongue, Vitellius easily convinced the senators that, with all the cares of empire, Claudius truly needed another wife, and that, ideally, such a wife should also be related to the imperial bloodline. His colleagues, in fact, were now rising to heap praises on Agrippina by name, while Aulus himself squirmed uncomfortably on the marble bench. Incredibly, not one voice had raised the obvious impediment to such a marriage. Well, his would.

Standing up in the quieted chamber, Aulus let just a touch of spleen spill into his tone. "Forgive me, Conscript Fathers, for venturing onto a tender issue, but someone must. If Claudius Caesar marries his own niece, why should this not be construed for what it actually is? Incest! And if incest, the Senate and the Roman People must *not* condone something impious in itself, unprecedented in all of our annals, and which would make the emperor, indeed, the Empire itself an object of derision in other lands!"

Aulus glared several moments more at his colleagues, then sat down. A pall of silence descended on the chamber, then a sudden flutter of whispering. Aulus glanced about him and saw more heads nodding than shaking.

"You are correct, Senator," Vitellius stood up to reply. "Such a marriage *would* be something of a novelty among Romans. But it is permitted in other countries. Even here, marriages between cousins were unknown centuries ago, but now they are common. Custom adapts itself to change. Marriage between uncle and niece will cease to be incestuous the moment the Senate so decides."

Pallas, meanwhile, had orchestrated a huge demonstration in front of the palace that was shouting: "CAESAR MUST MARRY!" "CLAUDIUS AND AGRIPPINA!" "IO CONNUBIUM!" And soon the figure of the emperor himself could be seen leaning over the balustrade of the palace, waving to the people below. In a short time, Claudius was threading his way through congratulating masses in the Forum to the Senate chamber, where he submissively bowed "to the will of the people." The Fathers had just legalized uncle-niece marriage, against the votes of Aulus Plautius and painfully few others.

Claudius' marriage to Agrippina was feted at a great celebration on the Palatine, to which all of Roman aristocracy was invited. The emperor had never seemed happier. In giving the groom's toast, he bubbled, "The very gods, including the Divine Augustus, owe me a happy marriage." Then he smiled adoringly at his pretty bride, who looked younger than her thirty-four years, and said, "After three . . . false starts, let this one succeed!"

He said it almost as a prayer. The hundreds of guests, wearied by Claudius' marital misadventures, rose from their recumbent positions at the banquet in an honest cheer. But Aulus and Pomponia, who could not disregard the imperial invitation, remained reclining at their table. The bride carefully noticed this. She whispered to Claudius, "Isn't that the man who called us incestuous in the Senate?"

8

PLAUTIA, now a ripening eighteen, had been attracting more and more attention from the patrician young men of Rome. Several eligible but persistent suitors she eluded only with the cunning native to her sex. Her father's younger colleagues in the government made constant visits, and it was obvious that they had more than politics in mind.

Aulus, however, cheerfully endured the callers—Pomponia had to play hostess on such occasions, and this drew her out. Yet for Plautia it often led to friendships that started innocently enough, but then grew serious much too quickly for her liking, and she would break them off. She had outgrown her girlish weakness of falling in love instantly and ardently with every handsome Roman she met. But was she now becoming too discriminating for her own good?

Or did Flavius Sabinus have something to do with it, she wondered. By now he was little more than a pleasant phantom of memory, although every four months a letter from him arrived, usually filled with news of his province. One letter began with a playful parody on the way emperors started their official correspondence:

> Titus Flavius Sabinus, never *pontifex maximus*, consul but once, acclaimed *imperator* at no time, governor of Moesia (that he will confess!) to the pulchritudinous Plautia, greeting.

I often wonder when I shall have finished my term of office here so that I can return to the only really civilized city on earth—or so I would have written before news of the emperor's incest. Is it true that on his wedding day, the statue of Virtue fell over on its face in the Forum? Or did its white marble blush into pink granite? We've heard both stories here in the East, but rumors from Rome come to us very much like waters of the Danube: sometimes in a flood, but always heavily freighted with dirt.

I worry about Rome. It controls the world, but does it deserve to? I'm anything but a moralist, little one, so matters must be bad indeed to alarm even me. Yet I keep reminding myself that Roman woman is not Agrippina but Plautia, and that Roman life is truly lived not on the Palatine but the Esquiline . . .

The letter moved on to events in Moesia. It was clear to Plautia that Sabinus enjoyed being governor of the province, but he was not overly impressed with his own importance. "Poor Ovid," he wrote, "because of his delightful (though pornographic) poetry, he was exiled to the very province I now govern—which speaks volumes for the importance of this place!"

Plautia enjoyed his lines and smiled at all the places Sabinus hoped she would, but she looked in vain for any revelations of a personal or intimate tenor. And so she usually replied in kind—except once when she allowed herself to ask when he planned to return to Rome. All she got by way of reply was:

When shall I return? I looked into the terms of several of my predecessors, and I found that one governor of Moesia stayed in office here for *twenty-four* years! Since it's always my policy to excel and exceed, you may expect me to hobble back to Rome a quarter century from now as a three-legged antique: two aging limbs and one cane.

So much for attempts at romance by correspondence. She had better forget Flavius Sabinus, she told herself. But then another letter would arrive from Moesia and she would hurry to share it with her friends.

She had been seeing much of them lately—too much, Pomponia thought—but it was all normal enough. Plautia and several daughters of the senatorial nobility had reached the age when they were finally allowed out into the city for longer periods—accompanied, of course, by a member of the household staff. The girls celebrated their new freedoms by manufacturing opportunities to leave home whenever possible.

Today it was the baths. Plautia and her companions were enjoying themselves at a swimming party in the great pool of the Baths of Agrippa. Since neither sex wore any clothing in the public baths, men and women bathed at different times: women in the morning hours, men in the afternoon and evening. The girls were playing water tag, jumping in and out of the pool like so many merry dolphins.

It was while she was being chased that Plautia darted behind some statuary set in a broad alcove near the center of the pool. To her horror she found several young boys hidden behind the statues, leering at her and the other girls. Shrieking, the girls all scrambled into the arms of attendants, who covered them with towels and shouted at the boys. Nothing daunted, the youths scampered after the girls with screams of laughter, and a pimply lad who seemed to be their leader shouted something lewd to Plautia.

"I know who that one is," one of her friends whispered. "It's Domitius Ahenobarbus."

Enveloped in towels, Plautia was so furious at his remark that she picked up a strigil and threw it at him. The skin-scraper struck Domitius, gashing him in the cheek.

Wiping away the blood, he spluttered, "I know you—you who threw that. You're Senator Plautius' daughter, aren't you?"

Plautia was startled. But because of the circumstances, she was even angrier that he knew who she was. "And what if I am, you vulgar wretch?"

"Well," Domitius smirked, "you've marked me now, little Venus. And I think I'd enjoy returning the compliment one day."

Plautia, now burning with embarrassment and rage, shouted back, "They tell me your name is Domitius 'Bronzebeard,' you beardless, disgusting whelp! Now get out of here and play your children's games elsewhere!"

When Domitius saw several of the bath guards approaching, he and his friends ran off.

"Don't you really know who that is, Plautia?" a friend asked.

"No. And I don't care. I hope I never see his pimply face again."

However unpleasant at the time, it was a small incident, really, and Plautia told her parents about it only after a long lull in the family dinner-table conversation. Aulus looked at Plautia and his mouth tightened. "You say the fellow's name was Domitius? You don't mean Domitius Ahenobarbus, do you?"

"Yes, that's what the girls said his name was. 'Bronzebeard.' That's what Ahenobarbus means, doesn't it?"

Aulus nodded and asked, "What did he look like?"

"Oh, he was about twelve or thirteen, with a thick neck. Light, curly hair. And"—she flinched—"his face was covered with pustules."

Aulus nodded several times. Then he said, "Think now, Plautia. Do you know whose face you really cut?"

"A disgusting weed of a boy with a foul mouth."

Aulus sighed. "Well, my dear, I must compliment you on your aim with that strigil, but I do wish you'd have chosen a different target. Perhaps next time you won't aim at a . . . prince of Rome . . . the son of the new empress?"

Plautia caught her breath, while her father continued. "Yes, Domitius is Agrippina's son by her first marriage. You didn't attend the reception honoring his betrothal. That's why you didn't recognize him."

"*That* blighted little boy is *engaged*?"

"Yes. To Octavia, Claudius' daughter."

Plautia frowned at the implications. "And anyone who marries the emperor's daughter may have hopes for the throne? Even Domitius the Pimple?"

"Exactly. And it's becoming clearer that young Domitius is *the* reason why Agrippina wanted to marry Claudius."

"Didn't she marry him simply to become empress?"

"More than that, evidently. She was sister to one emperor— Caligula—and wanted to be not only the wife of another, but the *mother* of one as well! She's already starting to groom her Domitius for the succession."

"But he's only a child," protested Pomponia, who had been quietly listening.

"Still, everything points to it. You've heard of the philosopher Seneca?"

"Yes." Pomponia nodded. "One of the finest minds in the Empire."

"Well, Agrippina has appointed him personal tutor to Domitius."

"But Claudius' *own son* is Britannicus," Plautia objected. "Surely he'll be next in line for the throne."

"Ordinarily, yes. A son would be preferred to a stepson—son-in-law-to-be like Domitius. But don't forget the age difference. Domitius is *older* than Britannicus—only about three or four years older—but still, older. If anything happened to Claudius, who would be more likely to succeed?"

Slowly Plautia wrinkled her brow and nodded.

"Poor Britannicus," said Pomponia. "I understand the empress is forever humiliating him at the palace."

Aulus shrugged. "Let's hope Claudius is alive ten years from now. Britannicus will be almost twenty—old enough for succession." Then, putting his arm around Plautia, he said with a twinkle, "And let's hope you haven't marked Domitius for life with that strigil."

Some version of this conversation was being repeated in almost every Roman home, for the question of who would succeed Claudius was being gossiped and debated everywhere. Once again Aulus felt a clutch of apprehension. Rumors were cracking off the Palatine and tumbling across the city, forming sinister mosaics on a common theme: Agrippina smashing all hurdles between her son and the succession. Her former rivals fell: the wealthy Lollia was accused of consulting astrologers and forced into suicide. If Claudius' wandering eye chanced to find some patrician lady attractive, Agrippina quickly secured her ruin. If some wealthy Roman had gardens that she coveted, they were confiscated. Or if any doubted her power outside the city of Rome, she merely flaunted it—even to the point of renaming the Rhenish town where she was born "Colonia Agrippinensis."*

Still, Aulus was heartened by Claudius' refusal to formally adopt her Domitius as son, even though Agrippina hinted about it every time she had her husband's ear. One day, however, Aulus returned from the Senate with a wounded look and said, "He's given in, Pomponia. Claudius finally asked the Senate for permission to adopt Domitius."

"And did the Fathers grant it?"

"Of course!" Aulus threw up his hands. "But without my vote, in any case."

---

* Today, Cologne, Germany. Mercifully, the second name did not survive.

Pomponia pursed her lips and looked down. "So," she sighed, "Caesar now has a stepson, a son-in-law-to-be, and a son—all in one youngster named Domitius."

"Correct, my dear, except for the name. The Senate found 'Domitius' too common for the young prince, so they awarded him an old name from the Claudian *gens:* Nero."

"*Nero?*"

"Yes. It's supposed to denote strength or courage. And, of course, young Domitius has neither." He turned to her with a frown and said, "I fear for young Britannicus now. If only we knew what was happening inside the palace."

Pomponia offered a suggestion. "What about Titus, Sabinus' nephew?"

"Vespasian's son! Yes, he's attending the palace school with Britannicus, isn't he?"

"Yes, and I understand they're great friends. They even eat together. Narcissus managed it all as a favor to Vespasian."

Aulus invited Vespasian's family to dinner, and there was much reminiscent chatter about the British campaign. After the repast, however, Aulus spirited Vespasian and young Titus into the library, where the ten-year-old was treated to a barrage of questions. A bright lad with tousled brown hair and a robust build for his age, Titus supplied answers that confirmed Aulus' darkest suspicions.

This picture emerged. Agrippina was behaving toward Britannicus like the worst sort of stepmother, kindling a loathing in the lad which prompted his ugly comments—all of which were then carefully reported to Claudius. Britannicus was particularly furious that he had to appear on public occasions wearing only a boy's tunic, while Nero stood next to him clad in a toga of manhood although he was only thirteen years old.

"Tell me, Titus," said Aulus, "how does the *emperor* feel toward Britannicus?"

"Well, he *seems* to like him. Though he spends a lot of his time shaking dice, you know."

Aulus flashed a wry grin at Vespasian. "Claudius has just published a *treatise* on gambling!—Now tell me, lad, how does Pallas behave toward Britannicus?"

Titus shook his head. "Pallas hates him, I think. Of course, he and the empress . . . well, maybe I shouldn't say." He blushed.

"Please do, lad," Aulus urged.

Now flushed with color and wishing he had not moved into an area that was new and embarrassing to him, Titus hung his head and said, "Britannicus tells me the empress has been—no, forget it."

"Speak, son," Vespasian insisted.

"Well," Titus drawled, "that the empress has been . . . doing naughty things with Pallas."

Aulus' wide-stretching eyes flashed at those of Vespasian for several moments. Then he said, "I wonder if Narcissus knows all this."

Titus had reported it all accurately enough, and soon he would have a new story to tell. One morning, he and Britannicus were strolling in the central garden on the Palatine when they chanced upon Nero. "Hello, Britannicus," said Nero, with a certain contrived affability, while ignoring Titus.

"Hello, Domitius," Britannicus replied, carefully using his old name.

Seized by anger, Nero spun around and spat out the words, "There no longer exists any Domitius Ahenobarbus, you little cur! Not since my adoption!"

"Oh, excuse me, Tiberius Claudius Germanicus *Nero Caesar,*" Britannicus responded, with sham pomposity. "Do I have it right?"

His eyes burning, Nero stalked inside the palace to tell his mother.

" 'Bye, Domitius!" Britannicus called after him, an impish grin rippling across his lips.

Agrippina was up to Claudius' office in a trice. "An urgent matter, dearest," she said breathlessly. "The first dreadful sign of discord in our happy family. Out in the gardens just now—your Britannicus refused to call our Nero by his proper name."

"What did he call him?"

"Domitius."

Claudius dropped a wan smile and said nothing.

"Well, aren't you going to do anything about it? Must decrees of the Senate be undone by a . . . a ten-year-old changeling?"

"Britannicus is *not* a changeling, Agrippina!" He was glaring at her. "And his comment was only a childish remark."

"Oh no. It's more serious than that. Britannicus' tutors *told* him to say that to Nero. And if you don't punish this kind of insubordination in the palace, woe to the Empire!"

Agrippina had lied about the tutors, but it had the desired effect.

Shifting moods in an instant, Claudius stalked angrily into the palace school and dismissed the entire lot of Britannicus' instructors. Later he would replace them with inferior teachers who, to no one's surprise, were partisans of Agrippina. Meanwhile, the philosopher Seneca was giving Nero the best education available in Rome, while Agrippina launched rumors that Britannicus was an epileptic and slowly going insane.

9

AULUS PLAUTIUS threw down his pen in disgust. He had gotten as far as the Thames River in his memoirs of the Britannic War, but seemed unable to cross it. The present was intruding hopelessly into the past. The new plotting on the Palatine was slowly shattering his peace of mind.

Was Claudius sleeping—again? Why didn't Narcissus act? Why didn't he warn the emperor? To be sure, Narcissus had been grateful for the information supplied by Titus, but he had added, ominously, "What can I really do, Aulus? You know I've . . . drained away all my credits."

He had indeed, Aulus reflected, staking his future to that huge, smelly swamp fifty miles east of Rome called the Fucine Lake. Narcissus had had 30,000 men working there for eleven years, tunneling through the limestone of a surrounding mountain so that the stagnant marsh could be drained and thousands of acres of new farmland be cultivated. A grand celebration was planned for the Day-of-the-Draining, Aulus recalled with a grimace, a mock naval battle before half the population of Rome camped on the banks. But he could still hear the ghastly gurgle of an emptying tunnel when less than half the lake had drained away. Narcissus' engineers had not tunneled deeply enough. More excavations were needed, more millions of government funds expended.

Then dawned the glorious Day-of-the-Second-Draining, when Claudius invited them all to a great banquet next to the sluice gates at the outflow. But when the gates were raised, Narcissus' impressive waterfall broke through the substructure and became a hideous tidal wave that nearly drowned Claudius, Agrippina, and the rest of the imperial party, who had to run for their very lives. Aulus himself had barely managed to carry Pomponia to safety.

If there had been any doubt, there was none now: Narcissus had indeed drained away his credits, Aulus mused. Pallas and Agrippina would win, then. And Domitius the Pimple—her darling Nero— would be the next emperor. Aulus shoved his writing desk away from him and stood up. "No, by all the Furies of hell, he will *not* be the next emperor!" he bellowed, stalking inside the house. Hearing the commotion, Pomponia rushed over to ask what the trouble was.

"I'm going to see Claudius. I'm going to stare into his blue eyes and shout: 'Wake up, Caesar! Put away those cursed dice of yours and learn what's been happening under your ruddy nose! Your wives are the very bane of the Empire, and each is worse than the last. Your Agrippina is a ruthlessly ambitious vulture: she'll stop at nothing until her Nero sits on the throne, and you are safely across the Styx!' "

"No, Aulus," Pomponia pleaded. "If you intervene at the palace, you endanger your life! Stay away from the Palatine, I beg you."

"Someone *must*. This is no time to abandon Rome!"

Narcissus arranged the audience for a night when Agrippina, Nero, and Pallas were presiding over a festivity in the city and the emperor would be alone. "Thank you, friend," Narcissus greeted Aulus as he arrived at the palace, knowing that his was the one voice in Rome to which Claudius might still pay some heed. They found Claudius in his suite, sitting upright in bed, reviewing some reports from the provinces.

"Greetings, Aulus," said Claudius, laying his material aside. "Sorry you find me like this, but my bowels refuse to do what's expected of them. Oh, the cramps I get!" He struggled toward the edge of his bed to get up.

"No, please stay as you were, Caesar. And don't go, Narcissus. This is something that concerns us all." Aulus took a deep breath, hoped he had searched out the proper language to pry the blinders off Claudius, and then launched into a lengthy, well-documented warning on the activities of Agrippina and Pallas. The phrases were more diplomatic than those he had unleashed at home, but they conveyed the same message.

Claudius listened to it all without betraying any emotion. He merely pushed himself to sit up straighter in bed. When Aulus finished, the emperor stared at him vacantly, lips slightly parted but saying nothing.

Narcissus finally broke the silence. "What Aulus says is true, Caesar. For months the empress has been—"

"Marvelous consistency, Narcissus!" Claudius cut him off. "You called the empress a ruthless plotter before I married her. And now after, as well. I should have your head for that."

"And you *shall have it*, Caesar, if you wish," Narcissus replied. "My only purpose is your well-being and security—"

"Or is it to ruin as many of my marriages as possible? First Messalina. Now Agrippina."

"This is not our intention, Caesar," Aulus interrupted. "We're concerned only for your safety—perhaps even your survival—as well as that of young Britannicus."

"Britannicus?" Claudius scowled.

"Yes. If I may be candid, Princeps, you seem to be denying the young prince his birthright and handing it instead to Nero."

Claudius frowned for several moments. Then he asked, "Why do you think that?"

Patiently and cautiously, Aulus enumerated all the political advantages conferred on Nero over the past months, culminating with the latest: his marriage to Claudius' daughter, Octavia. "Everything points to Nero's succession, Caesar," he concluded. "The empress has arranged all the details, even to making her supporter Afranius Burrus the new praetorian prefect. The Senate seems to think Nero will be the next Caesar. The people assume it. Don't you?"

Claudius pushed his covers aside and got out of bed. Padding across the chamber, he poured himself a cup of wine. Swishing the crimson liquid through his teeth as if to cleanse them, he suddenly looked up at the other two and thundered, *"No!* I don't think Nero will be the next emperor! The next emperor *will be my own flesh and blood, Britannicus!"*

A hush of silence ended when Aulus whispered, "The Father of the gods be thanked."

"I gave Nero those favors to keep peace in the palace," Claudius huffed, "and because Britannicus isn't old enough to receive them yet. In three or four years he will be. I've only been playing for *time,* gentlemen, as well as feigning a little ignorance just now so you'd bare your souls. You two don't know what it's like to live with that domineering woman. She hounds me from one end of the palace to the other. By the very gods, I should have taken your advice and never married the prostitute."

"The . . . prostitute?" ventured Aulus.

"Yes, prostitute. With Pallas, I found out.—Heh-heh-heh. Don't look so surprised, my friends: the old cuckold has his own sources of information."

"Do you . . . intend any action, then, Caesar?" Aulus inquired.

"What do you suggest?"

"Well, clearly you must guard Britannicus very carefully over the next months, and pray that the lad grows up quickly."

"I've already encouraged him to do so," Narcissus said, with a wan smile. Then, pacing the chamber, he unveiled his plan. "With your permission, Caesar, I'll have my men set up a secret surveillance over Britannicus' bedroom at night, as well as your own."

Claudius nodded. "And by day?"

"By day, all who have an audience with you will first be searched for daggers. We used to do this some years ago, so the empress will not suspect."

"Exactly," Aulus interposed. "She and Pallas must not suspect, or they'll take countermeasures. Play the mime. Play for time. But if you discover any plot against Caesar, Narcissus, we'll have to act immediately—with or without the praetorians."

Again Claudius nodded. "Splendid, Aulus. I've always thanked the Fates for your loyalty and friendship."

"And may those blessed Fates measure out a good long thread for the span of your life, Caesar!"

"Oh, they will, they will," Claudius tittered. "After all, I'm only sixty-two. And I really don't plan on leaving the stage for a long time yet. Just to spite the empress, of course!"

One evening at dinner, Claudius and Agrippina were having a disagreement over a minor household matter, and Claudius drank

more wine than usual to blot out the nagging voice and presence reclining next to him at the table. Cup followed cup. Finally, half intoxicated, he propped himself up on one elbow, opened his mouth,
and emitted a resounding, imperial belch.

"Claudius!" Agrippina reprimanded. "The servants might hear."

"Oh s-silence, woman!" he slurred his words. "I thought of introducing a law permitting people to break wind at the table too. . . ."

"Enough, you drunken sot!"

Claudius lay back and gazed at the ornate ceiling of the palace
dining room. "Ah me," he sighed. "It's become my destiny to have
wives—all of them unchaste. But not *unchastened!*" Then he turned
and gave her a long and chilling stare.

Agrippina excused herself and left the room. The look in Claudius' eyes thoroughly alarmed her. They had a fearful, deadly earnest. Under other circumstances, his pun might have been no more
than a cranky comment, but with that look they were a mortal
threat. "Unchaste," he had said. Could he possibly know?

The next day she was sure of it. Pallas told her of a scene he had
witnessed that morning before breakfast. Claudius had greeted Britannicus and then, as if on impulse, he had walked over to the lad
and hugged him. "Then, dear Agrippina, mark well what he said
next: 'Soon you'll be a man, my son, and then I'll explain everything that's happened. I may have wounded you, Britannicus, but
I'll heal that wound. And do you know what, lad? I'm going to give
you the toga of manhood a year early: I want the Roman people to
have a *genuine* Caesar after me.'"

Agrippina winced and then reported Claudius' comments the
night before. "So, this is how matters stand. Young Britannicus is
growing older and older. By the month. By the hour."

"And soon, of course, he'll be legally entitled to all the privileges
Nero now enjoys," said Pallas.

"If *only* Claudius would . . . *pay nature's debt* and join his ancestors."

Pallas nodded, but his next thought dared not be put into words.
Agrippina, however, felt no such restraint. She looked at her lover
and said, slowly, "So, dear Pallas. We no longer have any alternative. Do you understand me?"

Pallas frowned, teased his left earring several times, and finally
nodded slowly.

"But what's to be done about Narcissus?" She knew better than to attempt anything with Claudius' loyal secretary fluttering around the palace like a solicitous mother hen, keeping the bodyguard in trim.

"Can't we eliminate him?" Pallas wondered. "No, that would only alert Claudius to our plans." Then he brightened. "I have it! My dear colleague has been complaining about swelling in his joints —obviously gout. Now surely he should go away for a rest cure, don't you think?"

Agrippina smiled. "Where, dear Pallas, do they heal such a dreadful malady?"

"The standard spot is the bubbling sulfur bath at Sinuessa."

"Yes, and Sinuessa happens to be almost as far south as Naples."

"Far enough for our purposes."

"Yes. Yes, indeed. I'll have one of the palace doctors advise Narcissus that he's been working too hard and should go to Sinuessa for his health."

"That's it. Only he must *not* say that the suggestion came from you."

Narcissus' health had indeed been failing, as much a result of his political anxieties as his gout, but affairs seemed stable enough on the Palatine for him to follow the palace doctor's orders. Early in October, he set out for Sinuessa, accompanied by his chief aides, glad for a brief vacation at the salubrious waters of the resort. He sent word to Aulus telling him where he could be reached and when he would return but, inexplicably, the message was never received.

Trying to shorten the life of a Roman emperor was a particularly dangerous venture, Agrippina knew. If he were universally detested, main force could do the job—a committee of assassins clutching daggers and swords. Her dear, crazed brother Caligula had gone that route.

But Claudius presented a special problem. He was far more popular than his predecessor, and Rome would never tolerate his assassination. He would therefore have to die "naturally," an apparent illness, followed by a very real death. Only poison, she and Pallas decided, filled these qualifications.

A woman named Locusta had the greatest reputation in Roman toxicology. To most people, Locusta was merely a legend—a witch and sorceress who never really existed except to frighten disobedient children. Agrippina knew better. Locusta had recently been condemned to death for poisoning—her arts were in considerable demand in the city—but Agrippina had secretly intervened to save her life. At the moment, Locusta was under house arrest in her dwelling near the Palatine, guarded by a tribune who was directly responsible to the empress.

The evening after Narcissus left Rome, Agrippina disguised herself and made her way to Locusta's house. At her knock, a young praetorian opened the door just enough to peer out quizzically.

"It's I, Pollio," she said, lifting her veil.

"Come in, Empress."

"Wait here and see that no one else enters."

Agrippina descended a steep flight of stairs to what looked like the kitchen of a large villa, poorly illuminated by several flickering clay lamps. She almost retched at the strange, acrid odors of the place, so unlike the essences of rose and balsam that were continually sprayed about the palace. As her eyes adjusted to the darkness, she noticed shelves with dozens of ceramic pots, many marked with strange, occult symbols. Glass bottles stood on an adjacent table, filled with liquids and powders of various colors.

At a central work table sat Locusta, a swarthy, corpulent woman clad in a stola that looked yellow, whether from age or the flaming lamplight Agrippina could not tell. Locusta now looked up suspiciously with jaundiced eyes. "Well, what do you want?" she demanded in a rasping voice.

"Do you know who I am?" Agrippina lifted her veil.

Locusta's eyes squinted, then widened in recognition. "You . . . you're the empress?"

"Yes, the one who saved your life. Now it's time to return this favor . . . without asking any questions. Agreed?"

"Agreed. Certainly. Agreed."

"I must have a special poison."

"For what purpose?"

"I thought we agreed you wouldn't ask any questions."

"But Empress, the potion must *fit* the victim," the hag wheezed. "Those jeweled sandals of yours: they were made to fit you, not your husband. So if it's to have proper effect, the poison must be specially prepared for its victim and administered in the proper dosage."

Agrippina was silent, pondering.

"Empress, I owe my life to you, so I swear that nothing of this conversation will ever pass my lips. What is it? Do you want the horses slowed down at the circus so your colors will win? Eh? I've got a beautiful mixture for that. And there's no way to detect it." She grinned proudly. Agrippina noticed that several of her teeth were missing. "And the horses recover again in a day or so.—No? Not horses? So . . . it's more serious. You want somebody's death? Describe her. Or him."

"A human being, about sixty years old."

"Male or female?" Locusta continued, now very businesslike.

Agrippina hesitated, then replied, "Male."

"How tall? How heavy?"

"Five feet and three-quarters. About 180 pounds."

Locusta gave her a startled look, but did not disrupt the inquiry. "Must he die quickly, or of a lingering illness?"

"Yes, that's important. He must *not* die immediately, for then poison would be suspected. But he should lose consciousness and die within several hours."

"I see." Locusta thought for a moment, stained hands tugging at her wrinkled chin. Then she reached over and uncovered a large pot with bright green crystals. "Here . . . four, no, five pinches of this in his wine at supper. The green won't discolor the wine, even though you might think so. Even if he drinks only half the cup, he'll collapse and die by morning."

Agrippina shook her head. "No, it won't do. This man has all his wine tasted first."

"Ah, well, a different carrier, then," Locusta shrugged. "Is his food tasted too?"

"Yes."

"No matter. Food can be separated. What are his favorite dishes?"

Agrippina pressed her lips in thought. "Well, roast boar, mullet, oysters—"

"Does he like mushrooms?"

"Oh . . . yes, of course. He loves mushrooms. But he knows them so well he'd recognize the poisonous kind."

"I don't mean poison mushrooms . . . *edible* mushrooms as hosts for the poison. We merely have to find a toxin that won't interfere with the delicate taste of a mushroom." Locusta glanced into an aged scroll, then took a dusty amphora off a shelf. "Yes," she said, pulling out the cork and smelling it, "this will do. It's a very rare compound: the juice of the Palestinian wild gourd, and it has almost no taste. Take one or two large mushrooms—that should be enough—

cook them, and then let them steep in this essence overnight. But see that he eats at least one of them completely."

"What will happen then?"

"In a minute or two he'll start gasping for air and then faint. Death will follow in three or four hours."

"How do I know it will work?"

Locusta scowled for a moment but then grinned. She dribbled a single drop of the poison onto some wheat in a feed tray. Next she went to a wall stacked with cages, pulled a pigeon out, and stuffed several grains down its squawking throat. "Now watch that bird," she said.

The pigeon pranced around for several minutes. Then its wings flapped out of control, and it flipped over dead.

"It will be slower with Clau—ah—the man involved," said Locusta, her yellow skin turning orange with embarrassment. "Don't worry, Empress," she added hastily, "we *both* have reason enough to keep our lips sealed."

"Thank you, Locusta. I'll see that you're . . . properly rewarded."

Agrippina climbed the stairs, clutching a flask under the folds of her stola. At the doorway she whispered to the guard, "Locusta is not to leave here for the next two days. She's not to receive any visitors. If she tries to escape, kill her."

"As you wish, Empress."

October 12, A.D. 54 had been a good day for Claudius. His engineers at Ostia had given him a glowing report on the harbor works, and already he was thinking of what extraordinary spectacles to schedule for the opening of the port.

Even Agrippina seemed friendlier than usual. She inquired about his health as if genuinely concerned about him. At lunch she chatted about plans for the coming spring and wondered if they might take a trip to Greece. Could they yet make a success of their marriage, Claudius wondered.

That evening the imperial family dined together, including Nero and his Octavia, and Britannicus. Nero was badgering Britannicus in some argument, but Britannicus took it well: someday he, not Nero, would be emperor. The thirteen-year-old seemed less excited over the prospects of ruling a world empire than in having the chance to pull Domitius off his high horse. He still refused to call him Nero.

The first course of Circeian oysters and crab was followed by green beans and a silver platter of steaming mushrooms. The emperor was always served first, and when the lid was raised and he spied his favorite delicacy, he sighed with contentment.

On this particular evening, the eunuch Halotus was on duty as Claudius' butler and taster, for Agrippina had made him party to the plot. Halotus' fingers deftly poked about for several small pieces of mushroom and he put them into his mouth. He nodded and served Claudius.

Claudius was about to pluck several of the large tainted mushrooms when he looked about the table and stopped. "Aha ha!" he chortled. "You all know about Caesar's weakness for mushrooms, don't you? And you expect to see a hungry old man slobber all over them? Eh?" He looked about with a twinkle in his eye. "Well, I can control myself. Here, Halotus, serve the others first."

Halotus stepped back and looked blankly at Agrippina. She had been watching the mushrooms from the corner of her eye and now had to take her hands off the table to disguise their trembling. Nero knew nothing of the plot. What if he—or anyone else—took the wrong mushrooms?

"Just put some on his plate, Halotus," she said. "We know how much he loves them."

Claudius spread his hands over the plate. "The others first. I have spoken."

Agrippina coughed several times and said, "All right. But remember all of you, save the large, choice pieces for Caesar. Here, Halotus, give me just a few." She extended her plate, hoping the others would follow her in letting the butler serve them rather than making the selection themselves. With a silver fork, Halotus skewered several small mushrooms near the edge and put them on her plate.

In agony she watched the platter go round the table. Only four of the largest mushrooms in the center of the dish had been steeped in Locusta's brew, and Agrippina's eyes never left them. They were safe until the platter came around to Nero. A playful gleam in his eyes, Nero slowly opened his fingers and plucked the largest mushroom off the platter. "Haha, Papa!"

The mushroom was saturated with poison. Agrippina felt dizzy.

Then, as playfully, Nero put it back on the platter for Claudius. But what if he should lick his fingers? Agrippina signaled a slave boy who came running over with a bowl of water and carefully washed Nero's hand. Since Romans ate mainly with their fingers, they were regularly washed between courses. No one noticed anything amiss.

When the platter finally returned to Claudius, he dropped a pleasantry about his self-control, and then plucked two of the four large mushrooms for his plate. Agrippina now added to her helping, taking the two remaining poisoned mushrooms so no one else would eat them.

For endless minutes Claudius seemed to eat everything on his plate but the mushrooms. Agrippina was appalled. The same thumb and index finger Claudius had used to take the tainted mushrooms were poking the other delicacies into his mouth. If enough poison had contaminated his fingers, he might sicken before he got to the mushrooms, but that small a dose would hardly kill him.

"Mmmmm," mused Claudius, and then, still munching, "these mushrooms aren't nearly as good as they look."

Agrippina's eyes swooped over to his plate. He was chewing one of the mushrooms! At last he swallowed it and reached for the second, carefully probing it apart with his fingers.

"Hmmmm. Looks all right, but these really have an odd taste. I wonder if they're spoiled."

Agrippina felt a painful throbbing at her temples as her pulse raced madly. Claudius was showing no ill effects whatever. Had he taken some antidote? Had Locusta or the tribune betrayed her?

"Halotus!" Claudius bellowed. "How about the rest of you? Did everything taste all right to you?"

The others looked surprised and nodded. Then they saw Claudius' right arm fall limply from the table and his eyes roll up in their sockets. His face contorted. He coughed once and then slumped back onto the couch, unconscious.

The dinner circle sat up, stupefied. "Poor dear," Agrippina said, "he's probably had too much to drink. But let's be sure. Halotus, summon Xenophon."

Xenophon was the Greek palace physician who had recommended Narcissus' vacation and, of course, was also in on the conspiracy. He came rushing in to examine Claudius. But in a short time he turned around and smiled. "Nothing to be alarmed about. Caesar has simply had an attack of indigestion, along with the effects of the wine, of course. Let's carry him up to bed, Halotus."

"Poor dear," said Agrippina, stroking the silver hair of her stricken husband. "Finish your dinner, all of you."

The emperor of Rome, his face now hideously flushed, groaned as he lay in his bed. Agrippina allowed no one but Pallas, Xenophon, and herself inside the bedroom. The rest of the palace had accepted the doctor's story and saw no reason for concern.

Suddenly, Claudius regained consciousness, looked around with wild eyes, and staggered out of bed to go to the bathroom and surrender his dinner. Then, without saying a word, he crawled back into bed, breathing very deeply but regularly.

A half hour passed. Then another. And another. Now Claudius, belching, propped himself up in bed and said, "The mushrooms . . . spoiled. But I feel better now. Bring me some cold water, Agrippina."

"Certainly, dearest." Outside the bedroom she asked Xenophon, "He *can't* be recovering, can he?"

"I'm afraid he is. He may have thrown up much of the poison. Or purged it."

"By all the infernal gods," she cried, "what shall we do now?" She looked at Pallas, who stood mute and ashen-faced.

"Cursed be the day I agreed to all this," Xenophon muttered. "But we'd better finish what we started. I have another drug here." He inserted a feather into a jar of slimy blue substance and swirled it around. Then he carried it into the bedroom.

"You're doing much better, Princeps," he said. "But we must be certain that all the spoiled food is out of your body. So we'll use this feather to induce nausea, as usual."

Claudius nodded. It was a standard remedy.

While Agrippina held out a bowl, he quickly swabbed Claudius' throat with the undiluted poison. The emperor retched, gagged, and fell unconscious.

"Now it's done," Agrippina whispered.

Xenophon nodded. "It's a very rapid-acting poison."

But by midnight Claudius was still alive. His pulse, after almost stopping, was now beating regularly again, and his breathing seemed almost normal. He stirred and nearly regained consciousness.

"How does he do it?" the doctor whispered, grinding a fist into his palm.

"I'll kill the witch who gave me that poison," Agrippina seethed.

"No. I know that essence of gourd. It's very powerful. It would have killed him if he'd kept it down. Then, too, his body is used to all kinds of excesses. He can probably absorb anything . . . even poisons."

"Well, what can we do? Smother him with pillows? We've got to end this all *now*. Britannicus won't go to sleep. He keeps asking about his father."

"We can't smother him. There's a chance he might waken and cry out. What did you do with Locusta's poison after you steeped the mushrooms in it?"

"I . . . I put it back into the flask."

"Good. Get it. Quickly."

When she returned with the flask, the doctor ordered, "Roll him over." Then he opened his case and took out a strange-looking vessel, which he filled with the fluids remaining in Locusta's flask. Then he applied it to his patient.

Claudius Caesar, fourth emperor of Rome, died fifteen minutes later of a poison enema.

BOOK TWO

THE TINDER

10

"IT'S DONE, Pallas!" Agrippina whispered to her paramour. "Go. At once. Everything must work exactly as planned, or we'll still lose everything."

Pallas embraced her warmly and hurried out of the room. "Understand, everyone," he told his aides, "the emperor is *not* dead. He's seriously ill—a sudden stroke—and Rome must now pray the gods for his swift recovery. All right, then, everyone to his assignment."

News of Claudius' death had to be withheld until transfer of power was safely accomplished. While aides hurried off into the night, Pallas went to the Castra Praetoria to alert the prefect Burrus.

By dawn, the Senate convened in extraordinary session as the consuls led the chamber in supplications to Jupiter. Citizens were gathering in the Forum, shouting vows for the emperor's health. And all the while, the lifeless body of Claudius was being wrapped in blankets as if to warm him. People clustered outside the palace saw a troupe of comic actors rush inside. Claudius had revived, guards said, and was calling for entertainment.

Agrippina went up to the chamber of her private astrologer, who was carefully studying the charts of Claudius and Nero and consulting scrolls.

"Well, Balbillus? When shall it be?"

The astrologer looked up from his figures. "Is Caesar dead?"

Agrippina looked at him suspiciously. "Don't your stars tell you that he is? Yes. Six hours ago."

Balbillus coughed with slight embarrassment and busily adjusted his calculations, drawing new lines and scribbling down occult signs and configurations. Then he frowned and said, "Your son must *not* be declared emperor this morning. Something dire would result."

Agrippina blanched. "What would happen?"

"The stars are not that specific. But it would be calamitous."

"Well, what about this afternoon?"

The astrologer returned to his charts, staring at them with hypnotic detachment. At last he nodded and said, "Yes. Noon or after will be favorable. Very favorable."

Agrippina hurried off to prepare Nero. She had awakened him at early dawn with the news that he was now emperor of Rome. Sleepy and bewildered, he yawned and replied, "Whatever you say, Mother."

Now Pallas had returned with Burrus, and all the heads of Agrippina's party held a final strategy session. The philosopher Seneca, Nero's tutor, started writing down what his ward was to say in his first public address. But Afranius Burrus, the praetorian commander, was the crucial key to empire, and they now asked him the momentous question: "Will your men declare for Nero?"

Burrus brushed a hand through his auburn hair, which had been cropped short in the military manner. Then he massaged his maimed left arm—an old war wound—and nodded.

Just after high noon, October 13, the gates of the palace suddenly burst open and Nero, resplendent in imperial purple, marched out with Burrus at his side. A light rain was falling, and Nero tried to brush the droplets off his cloak, overconscious of his first appearance as Caesar. The elite First Cohort of the Praetorian Guard was standing at attention in front of the palace steps.

Nero and Burrus stopped at the center of the staircase. Slowly, the prefect made his announcement: "Tiberius Claudius Caesar Augustus Germanicus is dead!" The red plume across his helmet seemed to quiver with each syllable of the imperial name. "The end came this morning. A stroke."

A commotion of surprise and sorrow broke out among the praetorians.

"Attention!" Burrus barked. "I have the supreme honor to present to you the new emperor and princeps of the Senate and the Roman People: Tiberius Claudius *Nero Caesar!*"

Some of the praetorians looked startled. Burrus backed off and saluted, "Hail, Caesar!"

"*Hail, Caesar!*" many of the men joined in, but others continued to look perplexed.

"What about Britannicus?" someone shouted.

"Yes, where is Britannicus?" cried another. "Whom did Claudius appoint in his will?"

"Order!" Burrus fumed. "Stop this incredible display! For shame! Now, whoever fails to hail the new emperor will be arrested on the spot for treason!" He scowled several moments more, then turned, slowly extended his right arm, and cried, "Hail, Caesar!"

"*Ave imperator! Long live Nero Caesar!*" came the now unanimous refrain. Burrus' eyes combed through the ranks and saw every arm saluting.

Nero entered a litter and was carried over to the Castra Praetoria. He cursed the rain. He would have preferred riding triumphantly to the camp on horseback, but he could hardly show himself to the praetorians spattered with mud and soaked to the skin. He made a brief speech to the assembled troops, who paid most attention to what he said at the close: "As a reward for your allegiance, I pledge each of you a gift of 15,000 sesterces."

The jubilant roar from the Castra could be heard as far away as the Forum. Nero and his party left for the Senate with the men still shouting, "*Ave imperator!*"

Earlier that morning, Aulus Plautius had thought the sudden summons to the Senate ominous enough. But when Claudius' possibly mortal illness was announced, he had jumped up from his bench and left the chamber. Outside he met one of Pallas' junior aides and asked him where Narcissus was. "Why he's down in Sinuessa," he replied, smirking. "He's taking the baths."

A dozen thoughts raced through Aulus' mind. Why hadn't Narcissus stayed in touch? Was there still time to reach him and make a move for Britannicus? No, hardly enough—unless Claudius were not that seriously ill. Painfully, he returned to the Senate.

Just after noon, the official prayers were interrupted with the bulletin that the emperor was dead. Aulus sank back on his bench and covered his face with his hands. His friend, his comrade-in-arms was no more, and he immediately had very dark thoughts about the circumstances of his illness. At the moment, there were no further details of any kind, but the senators were already gossiping about his successor.

And now young Nero himself was presented to the Senate. The Fathers rose to bestow honor after honor on the prince, and soon it was official: the Senate solemnly declared the blondish-haired youth emperor of Rome. One of the senators even stood up and said fawningly, "I propose that our beloved new princeps also be awarded the title *pater patriae!"*

Immediately Nero was on his feet. "Father of the Fatherland?" he protested. "No, my elders in government. My seventeen years do not justify so esteemed a title. I must refuse."

The chamber broke into deafening applause, and Seneca, off to one side, beamed his approval. Squinting and blinking a bit because he was nearsighted, Nero now delivered a eulogy for Claudius, and the Senate formally decreed divine honors to the dead emperor.

During Nero's address, Pallas had been sitting in a gallery behind him, watching the faces of the senators and jotting down names on a slip of papyrus. He recorded those who seemed less than pleased with the succession, and he underlined the names of the only two Fathers who had given no external sign whatever that they approved of Nero. They were the Stoic senator Thrasea Paetus and Aulus Plautius. Not once that afternoon had either man applauded or even smiled.

Nero returned to the palace after the most dizzying day of his life. At dawn the sleepy teenager had learned of Claudius' death. By dusk all Rome had acclaimed him emperor. Agrippina was waiting for him at the portal, radiant and triumphant. Nero saw her at the head of the stairs and he paused to smile adoringly at the woman who had made it all possible.

Just then, a tribune of the palace guard came up to ask him what the watchword for that night would be.

"*Mater optima!"* he said. "The best of mothers!"

Meanwhile, alone in his bedroom, an inconsolable Britannicus was weeping bitter tears at the loss of a father—and an empire.

The next morning, the palace awoke to the smell of smoke. It seemed to be coming from Claudius' office. Rushing in with several guards, Agrippina found Narcissus burning all of Claudius' secret documents in a brazier. Haggard from a furious ride back to Rome, Narcissus had a tired smile as he watched the last papers turn to ash. "There," he sighed. "I've kept faith with you, Claudius. Until the end."

"It's the end, all right," Agrippina seethed. "Guards! Throw this . . . filthy wretch into the dungeon. The deepest and rankest cell you can find!"

Less than an hour after Narcissus was dragged off, Pallas visited him in the subterranean prison on the Palatine. "You knew it was suicide coming back here, Narcissus," he said. "Why did you do it?"

"Loyalty, Pallas. You wouldn't understand the concept."

Pallas unleashed a scowl at his rival and said, "Well, your situation's hopeless, you arrogant fool. So you might as well use this." He threw him a dagger and left.

"I'll just borrow it, Pallas," he called. "You'll need it again some-day . . . because of the usurper you created!"

Not since that of the great Augustus had Rome witnessed such a funeral. Aulus led the senatorial pallbearers carrying the body of Claudius in solemn procession down to a Forum crowded with Romans. Young Nero ascended the rostrum and delivered what even Aulus had to admit was a brilliant address, promising wisdom, moderation, and clemency as the hallmarks of his future administration. Seneca must have written every word of it, Aulus assumed.

The funeral procession continued northward to the Campus Martius, halting before a tall pyramid of stacked logs which had been saturated with spices and sprinkled with incense. Aulus and the pall-bearers carefully hoisted the bier onto the apex of the pyre. Nero was then handed a torch. Averting his face, he touched the kindling of cypress boughs which had been threaded between the logs, and the pyre quickly ignited in a great blaze.

Aulus and his colleagues waited in respectful silence until the pyramid collapsed in a shower of sparks but left before the embers were quenched with wine and Claudius' ashes collected for his urn inside the Augustan Mausoleum. While returning to the city, Aulus was astonished to find Nero's tutor-adviser Seneca falling in line at his side. The philosopher was a man of short stature and spare build, but his deep-set, penetrating eyes and well-chiseled nose lent dignity to what otherwise would have been an unattractive face. Turning to

Aulus, he asked in an amiable tone, "May I presume to accompany the conqueror of Britain?"

"You are welcome, Annaeus Seneca."

"Tell me, Senator. How did the princeps' remarks in the Forum strike you?"

Aulus frowned. "Moderation? Clemency?" he challenged. "Then why did Narcissus have to die?"

Seneca flushed. "Believe me when I tell you that Nero was furious when he heard the news. He would have pardoned him. It was Agrippina and Pallas who drove him to suicide."

Aulus said nothing. His mood was as smoldering as the embers he had just left. For a moment he thought of demanding from Seneca the full details of Claudius' death, but then he decided that this was neither the time nor place for such a discussion.

"But again, Senator, what did you think of the new Caesar's address?" Seneca persisted.

"A fine performance, certainly. I only hope he'll be able to do exactly as he promises."

"I too. But why are you smiling, if I may ask?"

"Nothing, really. I just happened to think that the new emperor must be precocious indeed to have written such a speech at his age."

"Oh, he is, he is . . . though I think he *may* have had a little assistance." He smiled. "Sometime, Aulus—if I may call you that—let us meet to exchange views on Rome's future. May we?"

"Of course."

So, Aulus thought, as he watched Seneca rejoin the imperial party, the new government was losing no time in trying to conciliate possible opposition. But Seneca's singling him out also proved what he had already suspected: in the new administration, Aulus Plautius was a marked man.

One afternoon, late that fall, a strange figure appeared at the door of the Plautius residence, demanding to see the master of the house. When Aulus appeared, he saw a scalp full of dark hair bent low toward him in the posture of a suppliant and a hand thrust out with a note in its open palm:

I cannot speak. My tongue was cut out by Rome's enemies in
the East. I have no employment, but would like to add myself

as client to this noble household, and receive the patronage I deserve from so famous a family as the Plautii.

Aulus was startled and asked, "Who are you?" before he recalled that the man could not talk. The figure only grunted in a miserable baritone.

"Enough *obsequium!*" Aulus snapped. "Hold your head up, man!" The stranger lifted his head and unleashed a broad smile, exposing the perfect teeth of which the Flavii were so proud. "Hello, Governor!" he said, in perfect Latin.

"Flavius Sabinus, you *scoundrel!*" Aulus bellowed. Then he shouted for Pomponia and Plautia. Sabinus had just returned to Rome after resigning his governorship in Moesia, for when an emperor died, all magistrates tendered their resignations. He was now sweeping back into their lives with the exuberance of a Mediterranean gale, breaking up the gloom that had overshadowed the Plautii.

Inevitably, he and Aulus took a long excursion into the new political climate of Rome—until Plautia could stand it no longer and all but snatched Sabinus away from her delighted parents and pulled him out into the peristyle. Now that they were alone at last, he flashed a great smile and asked, "Have I aged much, pretty Plautia?"

"Yes, you have. You look about a week older than when you left for Moesia."

"Five years ago?" Sabinus laughed. "It's not fair, then. I'm the same, but you—you're astonishingly different."

"How I've grown? That sort of thing?"

Sabinus shook his head and grinned. "It's not a question of growth. The term is transformation. Alas, the lovely little slip of a girl I left is no more." He said it with mock grief.

"Disappointed, Sabinus?"

He looked at Plautia carefully. Her now-mature beauty made him almost uncomfortable, for nature had added several soft finishing touches to the girl that both surprised and delighted him. Her perfect nose had not been spoiled by time, her once-thin lips had fleshed out into a handsome, patrician mouth, and her blue eyes had more sparkle than he ever remembered.

"Disappointed?" he finally replied. "With a woman of . . . incredible charm?"

"You shouldn't say that to me." Her cheeks were flushing. "At least, not so directly. And besides, I've a score to settle with you, and how can I do that when you're saying such nice things?"

"What's wrong?"

"Well," she bit her lip. "Let's put it this way: why didn't you bring your wife along on this visit?"

"My wife?"

"Yes, and your children too, for that matter?"

Sabinus looked at her uncomprehendingly. "But I'm not married."

"Pity!" Plautia smiled. "Because I am."

"*You? Married?*"

"Yes, didn't Father tell you? I'm just visiting here today."

He looked at her blankly. "Who? When?"

"Last fall. After all, Sabinus, I was becoming an old woman. I was twenty-one at the time—twenty-two now."

"Who? Why didn't you mention it in a letter?"

"I . . . think you know him. What's the matter, Sabinus? You wouldn't be disappointed now, would you?"

He put his hands to her shoulders and pressed them. "Enough of this! Whom did you marry?"

"Marcus Otho."

Sabinus stepped back. "Marcus Salvius Otho?"

She nodded, avoiding his eyes.

"But that wild dandy is still a bachelor! I know it for a fact!"

"*Hades!*" She stamped her foot. "He's my age, but I picked the wrong name!"

Sabinus shook with a hearty laugh and hugged her. "*Vixen!*" he cried.

"But that's the point, Sabinus." She pouted. "I could easily *have* fallen in love and gotten married during the five years you were away—for all you cared."

"But I *did* care, Plautia . . ."

"Then why didn't you visit me on your trips back to Rome?"

"I did."

"Once. Hurriedly."

"But I got back to Rome only once. I thought I'd return more often, but Moesia was *quite* a chore. And my letters certainly showed I was . . . well, concerned about you."

"Did they? Oh, I appreciated hearing from you, Sabinus. But there was never anything really personal in your lines. And you were away for so *long*."

"I'm afraid that's the political side of me, Plautia. I hate to express feelings in words. But you're right, you know. I really was presuming to find you here—still unmarried. And it has been a long time."

"A *very* long time." She frowned, but then brightened. "I suppose I do understand, though. Men in government have very full lives. Time passes rapidly. But we gir—ah—women think about other things."

"Maybe I'm still presuming too much, Plautia, but I forgot to ask you. You've never said anything about it in your letters—but *is* there someone in your life? Or have your parents arranged anything?"

"I'd love to tease you some more and parade a whole list of names—"

"Aha! Then, at least, there would be safety in numbers."

"And don't for a moment think there haven't been suitors around."

"More than were buzzing around Penelope as she waited for Ulysses, I'll wager!"

"Oh stop it, Sabinus, I'm serious, and—what are you looking for?"

"Where do you keep it?"

"What?"

"Your loom, of course. Remember, Penelope promised to marry when she'd woven a shroud, but each night she unraveled the day's work?"

"*Monster!*" Plautia shouted, playfully pommeling his broad chest with her smallish fists. Then she broke into childish laughter. He *had* changed after all, she thought. He was ever so much surer of himself than when he had left for Moesia. Five years of issuing commands as governor of a province had finally made a man of that shy semisuitor who had first shown up on the Esquiline, eyes askance and foot in mouth.

"Tell me about Moesia, Sabinus," she said.

"You must see it with me some time, Plautia, its lush, rolling hills, heavily wooded at places. A greenish river called the Danube rims it to the north . . ." The description lasted until the dinner hour, after which Aulus and Pomponia retired early, leaving Sabinus and Plautia alone.

In bed, Pomponia heard the chatter and laughter as well as the intriguing silences, and she smiled, remembering the days when Aulus had wooed her—and had won so easily. Would that distinguished-looking Sabinus try to steal their only daughter from them? For Plautia's sake, she hoped so. For herself, she dreaded the day.

It was the small hours of the morning when Plautia finally saw Sabinus to the door. Hours earlier, they had easily fallen into each other's arms, kissing and embracing with an intensity that astonished them. He leaned over to brush her cheek with his lips one more time. Her skin—soft, resilient, tingling—inflamed him as much now as their first rapturous kiss earlier in the evening. And when his lips met hers a final time, their very souls seemed to flow together.

Tradition ruled that it was the wrong time to fall in love. Romances, like nature, usually blossomed in spring. But the wind and rain of that Roman winter found Sabinus and Plautia glowing with a deepening attachment that easily took command of their lives. They seemed to see everything with a new intensity because joy had added a fresh dimension to life. The marble columns of Rome's public buildings never seemed so majestic, the art in the Forum never so impressive. Nature herself, though she lay in mourning for spring, seemed bursting with color for the lovers. Patches of lead blue in the cloud-flecked skies overhead became living azure, and even the pines shed their drab for a brilliant wintergreen. The very air they breathed seemed to acquire, for the first time, a special aura of its own, so that something so common as breathing itself had meaning for them.

So magnificent was love, Plautia told her parents. But it was also demanding. Love possessed one. The image of Sabinus was always there, whether or not the man himself was. Everything in her day— every plan, hope, detail—seemed related to him. Her life now had a new set of values: things were no longer good or bad in themselves; they had meaning only to the extent that they brought him to her or took him away.

Sabinus had resumed his seat in the Senate, and this filled much of his day, wrenching his thoughts away from the Esquiline and Plautia. But he could never really put her out of mind, and he found every excuse to visit her as often as possible. He was intrigued —no, astounded—by life's happy surprise called love, and he now regretted the years he had spent apart from Plautia.

As they watched the relationship ripen, Aulus and Pomponia found it difficult to conceal their enthusiasm, though they had the good sense not to flaunt their approval. Pomponia's parents had favored Aulus' courtship too eagerly—and almost ruined it in the process.

Sabinus was listening carefully to what Annaeus Seneca had to tell him in the privacy of his suite at the palace. For some minutes the philosopher confided—in muted tones—the tragic circumstances of Claudius' death, but swore that he had no part in it. His mood brightened, however, as he paraded out for Sabinus the great hopes he had for Nero's regime. Then he gave abrupt focus to their conversation.

"The emperor and I have studied your record in Moesia, Sabinus. Frankly, we're impressed." Touching the tips of his fingers together, he asked, "Do you suppose you could tear yourself away from the Senate long enough to do a job for us?"

"What is it, Seneca?"

"We'd like to appoint you *curator census Gallici*, supervisor of the census in Gaul. For once we need an accurate count there, Sabinus. Everything depends on it—taxation, the military, representation in the Senate. You can take a staff along with you, of course."

Sabinus was disappointed. After a governorship, this hardly seemed a promotion, and the thought of leaving Plautia at this point was painful. "How long would I be gone?" he finally responded.

"Shouldn't take more than a year. Probably less. But let me add this, Sabinus: Caesar and I feel you're capable of *much* more in Roman government, of course. Do a good job for us up in Gaul, and we'll take you into the administration here in Rome—if you're willing."

Sabinus was too diplomatic to press Seneca for details on the last interesting point, so he exhaled a long breath and asked, "May I think about it for a day or two?"

"Certainly.—By the way, I have no idea how the empress mother knew you were coming here, but she's asked that you see her before leaving the palace."

"Agrippina? But I've never even met her—thank the gods! What could she possibly want of me?"

Seneca shrugged. "Here's her note: 'I should like to see Flavius Sabinus immediately after your interview today, Annaeus Seneca.' So I'd best show you the way."

Seneca escorted Sabinus up a staircase and across a hall. Then he pointed to a doorway and excused himself.

A servant girl admitted Sabinus into a lavish waiting room, and then withdrew. Several minutes later, Agrippina appeared, wearing a robe of spun silver, a light smile on her lips. Sabinus looked at the cascades of dark curls and burning green eyes. Glints of recognition started piecing themselves together in his memory. Then he gasped. It was . . . yes, it unmistakably was the woman he had spurned at Messalina's bacchanal!

Several moments more she let him suffer, and then said, "So, Sabinus, you *do* recognize me, don't you? That's the first compliment you've ever paid me, since it *has* been some years . . ."

"I . . . *you* are the empress Agrippina?"

"That's rather lame, Senator. But, then, I always did have the advantage of knowing who you were, rather than vice versa." Then she flashed an almost malicious smile. "Well, Sabinus, it seems the Gorgons didn't turn you into stone after all." She broke into a low, mischievous chuckle.

Sabinus was struggling for composure. He thought he had banished from memory the hissing voice that had once called him a simpering eunuch, but here it was again, belonging to the most powerful woman on earth, who had become empress-mother over the bodies of her victims and the poisoned flesh of her husband.

"Nothing to say, Sabinus?"

He was struggling for something as simple as a coherent sentence. "I . . . I was drunk then, Empress," he finally managed. "So was everyone else."

"I wasn't," she said, giving no quarter. "How did you put it that day? 'You don't appeal to me . . . not that way.'" Now her voice shifted to a lower register. "No one has *ever* told me that, Sabinus. Ever. Before or since."

"I dare say not." Desperately, he tried to shift their excruciating conversation. "You are surely to be congratulated for achieving the very—"

"No need for that, Sabinus. No garlands. No politics. No obvious comments." She stepped over toward him, eyes fixed on his as they flaunted her superiority and his helplessness, flashing green versus constricting brown. "Did I leave any scars?" she finally asked, stroking the front of his tunic.

"No, Empress."

"Too bad. I wanted to mark you for life, I think." Now she reached out to pull his head down to hers, giving him a long kiss

with penetrating tongue. Then she did something that had never before happened to him. No woman had ever taken off her robe in his
sight. Roman women didn't do such things. But Agrippina was
never detained by such minor restraints as custom, Sabinus realized,
while trying to tear his eyes away from Agrippina's remarkably sup-
ple figure as she plunged into a milk bath at the corner of her bedroom.

"I'd best be leaving, Emp—"

"Come over here, Sabinus," she commanded. "Don't worry: I'll
stay submerged if you're prudish." She ran her fingers along the skin
of his forearm and said, "You're very rough, Sabinus. A bath would
do you good, too. Join me?"

Sabinus jerked his arm away and moved out of range. "I'll be
going now, Empress," he said in a strained tone, turning to leave.

She wore a dark smile. "I'll be seeing more of you, Sabinus.
Much more."

On the way out of the palace he stopped again at Seneca's office
and told the philosopher, "I've just made my decision, noble Seneca.
I accept the post of *curator census Gallici,* but under one condition."

"Which is . . . ?"

"That I leave for Gaul as soon as humanly possible."

The wise Seneca pondered only a moment or two before replying,
"Of course, Senator, of course. So much the better!" Then he smiled
and shook his hand.

Sabinus went directly to the Plautii. He decided not to mention a
word about Agrippina for fear it would frighten the family. Aulus
supported his decision on Gaul, intrigued by Seneca's closing comments.

Telling Plautia, however, proved an ordeal. She had grown too ac-
customed to having him near her to even consider his leaving Rome
once again. She immediately conjured up for herself another five-
year absence and ran off to her room crying. Vainly he stood outside
her door, protesting that it would merely be a matter of months. Finally he tried the door. She had barred it.

"Be reasonable and let me explain, Plautia," he pleaded.

"Go away," she cried, between sobs.

"But Plautia. It won't be that long—"

"Good. *Leave then!* Go off to Gaul! Go off to Hades, for all I
care!"

"Please, darling . . ."

"And don't come back. *Ever!*"

It had been quite a childish performance, Plautia decided the next day, something that could have been expected from a thirteen-year-old, not a woman of her maturity. She should not have carried on so. Flaunting custom, she decided to go over to his town house on the Quirinal and apologize personally.

At the same time, though, she would announce the end of their romance. His decision showed all too clearly that he was much less serious about their relationship than she had imagined. She was always presuming too much. He could so easily have declined the post in Gaul and continued in the Senate. Even if Seneca had exerted pressure, he might have pleaded his five long years away from Rome, or even told Seneca about herself. No, Sabinus was plainly a bachelor sort who really wanted to stay single—probably for the rest of his life. She was a temporary infatuation—nothing more. But she would redeem herself.

When a servant answered at Sabinus' place, she carefully avoided going inside, asking only that he summon his master. Sabinus appeared, but she cut off his greeting with a brisk apology for her tears the night before.

"You darling girl," he soothed. "There's no reason for you to—"

"I'm not finished yet, Sabinus." Then she proceeded to unload all the thoughts that had been tormenting her on the way over to the Quirinal, embellishing them as her ire—and voice—rose.

Finally she reached under her palla, pulled out a jeweled bracelet and necklace Sabinus had recently given her, slapped them into his hand, and said, "It's best for us not to see each other again, Sabinus."

For a moment he looked thunderstruck. Then, slowly, he nodded in sad resignation. "I suppose you're right, little Plautia. Our wonderful romance is . . . is over, it seems"—he stopped just long enough to be effective—"but our *marriage* should be just as wonderful, shouldn't it?" Instantly he was smiling. "Now, I leave for Gaul in two weeks and return in about ten months. We can either be married before I leave and you come along with me to Gaul, or we get engaged now and married the moment I return. Which do you prefer, *carissima mea?*"

She merely stood there, dumfounded.

Sabinus had a radiant flame in his eye.

"You . . ." she faltered, "you're just saying that because . . . you'll think I forced—"

"Darling, darling Plautia." He threw his arms around her and pressed her to himself. Then he lavished kisses on her forehead and cheeks and lips. "Don't you *know* how much I love you? Didn't you realize I would have come to carry you off had you said no?"

Hot tears flowed down her cheeks and she smothered her face in the folds of his tunic.

Neighbors, who had been watching the argument from windows on both sides of the street, now burst into applause and cheering. Sabinus and Plautia broke off their embrace and laughed ecstatically.

They hurried over to the Plautii with their joyous announcement. Mother Pomponia wept for happiness, and Aulus could at last tell Sabinus how very much he had hoped exactly that would happen. However everyone—even Plautia—agreed that a proper patrician wedding would take months to prepare, though if they worked quickly, they could at least manage the formal betrothal before Sabinus left for Gaul.

In a matter of hours they had drawn up a lengthy guest list and dispatched messengers to deliver the sealed invitations. Two weeks' notice was a little brief, though quite acceptable. There was some debate on whether the new emperor should be invited, but Aulus would not have it, and Plautia worried lest Nero remember her aim with a strigil. Sabinus roared with laughter at the story. As a courtesy to the palace, however, Seneca was invited.

On the day of the betrothal, a parade of litters invaded the secluded lane on the Esquiline, depositing a throng of guests at Aulus' mansion. At the appointed hour, Flavius Sabinus walked out to the center of the atrium, his stocky brother Vespasian standing at his side.

The chattering crowd stilled to a hush when Aulus entered the hall, his daughter on his arm, followed by a serene and stately Pomponia. Solemnly they walked to the center of the atrium and saluted the Flavian brothers.

With a broad, confident smile, Sabinus then asked Aulus, in the legal formula, "*Spondesne Plautiam, tuam filiam mihi uxorem dari?* Do you solemnly promise to give me Plautia, your daughter, as wife?"

After a slight pause, for due dramatic effect, Aulus replied, *"Di bene vortant! Spondeo.* The gods bring luck! I betroth her."

"Di bene vortant!" Sabinus replied.

Even though Plautia had said absolutely nothing, they were now legally engaged, and the atrium broke into cheering and applause. Sabinus tenderly kissed Plautia, his *sponsa* or betrothed, and presented her with several traditional gifts: a jeweled comb and other toilet articles, and a gold ring which he carefully placed on the third finger of her left hand. A nerve or sinew ran directly from this finger to her heart, so they all believed. Plautia, in turn, gave Sabinus a golden stationery kit, whose purpose was at least obvious.

The formalities were over, and festivities followed, lasting well into the night. Everyone had to agree: it had been a very proper betrothal in the best traditions.

When all their friends had left, Aulus congratulated Pomponia on how well she had managed the affair, embracing her happily. It was just the kind of tonic she had needed, he thought, for her moodiness had disappeared in the excitement of preparation. At the celebration, in fact, Pomponia had been so rarely effusive in a circle of confidantes that she had expressed herself quite candidly about the empress mother. "These delicacies are more 'reliable' than Agrippina's," she said, in urging food on her guests.

How was she to know that one of the senators' wives, whom she thought a friend, was a very aspiring sort who was on intimate terms with Agrippina? The next morning, the empress mother learned everything that was said at the reception to which neither she nor her son had been invited. She was more than interested.

At the same moment, Sabinus was saying a very tender farewell on the Esquiline, cradling the cheeks of his beloved between his large, strong hands.

Plautia looked up at him and murmured some poetry:

> Whenever I see you—
> sound is silenced and
> my tongue falters;
> thin fire steals through my limbs;
> an inner roar shrouds my ears
> and darkness my eyes.

"Catullus." He smiled.

"But he was translating Sappho. It's how a *woman* feels . . ."

"It's how *I* feel," he objected. "A short time now, darling. A very short time. Meanwhile, you prepare the best wedding ever." He caught the lithe, willowy figure in his arms and trembled at the touch of her body and the delicious tickle of her warm, pliant lips.

"Please take care of yourself, *mea vita*. If anything happened to you, I . . . I couldn't go on living."

11

ANNAEUS SENECA had a villa just south of Rome, where he retreated each evening after a busy day at the palace. He had invited Aulus here for dinner and the long-promised chat. After a wholesome repast, the host invited his guest into the library, which was stacked from floor to ceiling with a diamond-shaped latticework of wooden pigeonholes, projecting thousands of scrolls. They were grouped into the main sectors of Mediterranean culture, with "Greece" by far the largest category. Three lemonwood tables were covered with open scrolls, while the fourth, with inkstand, contained pages of papyrus on which Seneca had been working.

"It's a treatise on clemency I'm writing for Nero," he explained to Aulus. Then he showed him some of his rare scrolls, including an Aristotle autograph of his *Metaphysics*. "Do feel free to use this collection at any time, Aulus, even when I'm not here."

"That is most kind of you, Seneca."

"But let us move to the present, my friend. Now, shall we start with the assumption that, having been close to the Divine Claudius, you're—shall we say—not too enthusiastic about the new regime?"

Credit the man for candor, Aulus thought, and then replied, carefully, "It's really too early to judge, isn't it?"

"Well, then, let me ask, how did you regard the circumstances of Claudius' death?"

"As a profound disgrace to the state. As the disgusting, premeditated murder that it was." Despite precautions, details of the poisoning had seeped down from the Palatine.

"Good, I agree. And don't raise your eyebrows, Aulus. You may not believe this, but I had nothing to do with Claudius' death. True, Pallas and Agrippina tried to entangle me, but I absolutely avoided any involvement."

"I see." Aulus darkened. "Then why didn't you warn Claudius? Like a good citizen?"

Seneca frowned. "Put yourself in my place, Aulus. Claudius banishes you from Rome for eight years—ninety-six months on that dreadful island of Corsica."

"But was your exile justified, Seneca? *Did* you . . . commit adultery with Caligula's sister Julia?" The question had passed his lips before, on second thought, he would not have uttered it.

His face coloring, Seneca replied, "You know it was Messalina who made the charge, Aulus. Need I say more?"

In fact, yes, thought Aulus, but he let it pass while Seneca continued. "Some people like to play the hermit, but not I. For a person who *must* have intellectual exchange, Corsica was a living death. None of my letters to Claudius did any good. Gods, he didn't pardon me even after Messalina's death! It was Agrippina who secured my recall. Can you really think I'd then betray her to favor him?"

"Probably not," Aulus had to agree. "But did you and your brother really have to cackle that loudly when Claudius died?"

Seneca looked surprised. "Which brother do you mean?"

"Gallio."

"Oh." Seneca smiled. "You mean his remark about Claudius being dragged up to heaven by a hook?"

"Yes, a hook—just like they use to drag criminals' bodies down to the Tiber."

"Oh, just a bit of satire.—In any case, we have more important things to discuss. Now, I know you've every reason to be suspicious of the new government. All we're asking is that you give us a chance."

Aulus nodded, now a little amazed at his candor with Seneca, who was one of the most powerful men in Rome. But he would have retracted nothing. Aulus Plautius hated hypocrisy, worshiped honesty, and feared no man.

"Now, Aulus, do you remember what Plato once said about the ideal government? 'Until philosophers are kings, or kings and princes have the spirit of philosophy . . . only then will the state behold the light of day.' Well, we *may* have a chance to test his theory here in Rome. Perhaps Nero is that prince."

"And you the philosopher?" Aulus smiled.

"Well," Seneca chuckled, "don't we have a unique opportunity to create an enlightened government for Rome? Nero's a fine pupil so far. He's young and quite pliable. He can easily be molded for the good—if *only* we can win out over Agrippina and Pallas."

"What . . . do you mean?" Aulus was obviously surprised.

"This shows the confidence I'm placing in you, despite your . . . critical comments, Aulus. But reveal this to no one: a *fierce* household struggle is raging in the palace over who will control Nero. It's Burrus and I against Agrippina and her minion Pallas."

"But Agrippina recalled you from exile . . ."

"I know. And I suppose I should be obligated to her for a whole lifetime. But I place the welfare of Rome higher than this personal debt. You see, Agrippina has no intention of letting Nero rule Rome —at least not without her. Ever since his password that first day— 'the best of mothers'—she's acted as if she were empress in fact as well as title. A month ago we had a scene that could have made us the laughingstock of the world. Some envoys from Armenia were paying a state visit to the palace. Nero was sitting on his throne when his mother suddenly appeared and tried to climb up the dais to sit on a throne beside him."

"As *co-regent?*"

"So what could we do? I told Nero to stand up and 'greet' his mother. He caught on immediately and did so—he's quite bright, you know—and then he led her out of the hall, returning alone. The Armenians saw only a son's courtesy."

"Well, I hope you succeed in your campaign against her, Seneca. And you *must* guard poor Britannicus from any evil plots. His position is quite precarious, you realize."

"I know. We will."

During a lull, Aulus, somewhat puzzled, asked, "Why are you . . . kind enough to tell me all this, Seneca?"

"In other words, why this visit?"

"Yes. Surely Aulus Plautius can't be that important to you."

"Oh, but he is. You have enormous influence in the Senate, Aulus, and the public has not forgotten about Britain. You'll also be father-in-law to a man we'll soon need in our administration. Now, if I hadn't told you where we're aiming the new regime, you might have assumed that Burrus and I were merely Agrippina's creatures and have influenced your colleagues to work against us. Now you know the truth. Mind you, Burrus and I aren't asking you to *campaign* for our policies in the Senate. Not at all. We're only asking for a little time to try to bend Nero for the better. It *is* worth a try, isn't it?"

Aulus softened, smiled, and nodded. "All right, Seneca. Much luck in your noble experiment. And do tell Burrus I knew he'd make the right decision, ultimately."

"Oh . . . I almost forgot to give you this, Aulus." Seneca walked to his writing desk and pulled a document out of the drawer. "And I want you to know you'd have received this even if you'd sworn to fight us to the death."

"What is it?"

"Another token of Nero's clemency. Go ahead. Open it."

Aulus took a knife and slit the imperial seals on the document Seneca handed him and read the following:

Nero Caesar, son of the deified Claudius, great-grandson of Tiberius, great-great-grandson of the deified Augustus, *pontifex maximus*, consul, holding the tribunician power for the first year, acclaimed *imperator*, to the Senate and the Roman People, greeting.

By agreement with the censor and to further our expressed policy of clemency, we herewith restore

QUINTUS PLAUTIUS LATERANUS

to his full rights and prerogatives as Conscript Father in the Roman Senate. Given the Calends of February, A.U.C. 808.

"Will you see that your nephew receives this?"

"Happily done!" Aulus beamed. "And the timing is superb: Quintus is finally getting married. Three weeks from today. Thank you, Seneca. Thank you *very* much indeed!"

"Oho! Don't thank me," he said with a twinkle. "Thank Nero's clemency, remember?"

"True. And may the gods guide your efforts to . . . Platonize Rome."

Later Aulus thought about their frank exchange and shook his head in amazement at that extraordinary phenomenon who was Annaeus Seneca. Born in Spain, he had come to Rome and quickly won fame as a Stoic philosopher, until disaster struck and he was forced into exile. But now, as Nero's tutor and adviser, Seneca virtually ruled the Empire, for his pupil was too busy growing up to be bothered with government and merely signed the documents Seneca prepared for him. Burrus, as prefect of the Praetorian Guard, was equally powerful, Aulus knew, but he represented the brawn more than the brain of the new government, and he was quite content to let Seneca chart Rome's course. When not tending the government, the versatile philosopher penned a stream of satires, tragedies, and treatises that were being read from the Nile to the Rhine.

However much Aulus had wanted to despise young Nero, he had to admit that the lad was making all the proper decisions, due, undoubtedly, to Seneca's promptings. Rich sycophants begged Nero to let them cast statues of him in gold and silver, but he refused. Toadies in the Senate suggested that the new year begin with December, when Nero was born, not January. He vetoed the proposal. And when Burrus once asked him to sign orders for the execution of a condemned criminal, the seventeen-year-old Caesar looked up and said, "How I wish I had never learned to write!"

Perfect freedom of speech and pen were again permitted—Seneca saw to that—and Rome's provinces prospered as never before as a result of Nero's strategy of peace. "The Empire is large enough for now," he said. "Let's consolidate what we have. That should be enough of a task."

Aulus saw Nero in the Senate rather frequently, a deferent, respectful youth who was even trying to learn all the Fathers by name. When he heard that several worthy senators were resigning because of financial reverses, he supplied them a subsidy so Rome would not lose the benefit of their advice. Aulus thought it all too good to be true. He caught Seneca after one of the sessions of the Senate and told him, "The Palatine *is* becoming Plato's Academy indeed. Bravo!"

Northward, in Gaul, where he hurried to complete the census, Sabinus received a scroll with two different handwritings: one, an effusive love letter from the girl he missed more than he thought possible; the other, from a future father-in-law who seemed to be changing his politics. "Despite its violent beginning," Aulus wrote, "Nero's principate may yet be the best since that of Augustus himself. It's Seneca's work. I've misjudged the man, I think. I only hope he continues to shape the emperor . . ."

Just when Pomponia seemed to be improving, she suffered a relapse. Aulus fretted over what to do. Not that his wife was getting moody again—preparations for Plautia's wedding kept her much too busy for that. It was religion, once again. Not only had that fanatic Jewish tentmaker Aquila returned to Rome, he had even dared to show his ruddy face on the Esquiline, ostensibly to see if the garden canopy was in good repair.

Such a pretext! The real purpose of his visit was apparent when Pomponia spoke excitedly about what had happened to Aquila and his Priscilla in the meantime. During their temporary exile in Corinth, they had met another Jewish tentmaker named Paulus. And this fellow, evidently, was a leader of sorts in that Jewish sect called the Christiani.

Aulus was appalled to hear Pomponia tell their daughter wild tales about that Chrestus or Christus who had started it all, and of the tentmaker who was spreading the stories. It seems Paulus had so impressed Aquila and his wife that they had invited him to live with them while they were in Corinth.

Aulus thought of a solution. He would pry his wife free of this foreign cult by proving some discrepancy or falsehood in Aquila's bizarre stories. It was easy in the case of the founder himself: rising from the dead was so obviously a fairy tale it required no further thought.

"I don't know why you're so hostile about the Christians," Pomponia complained. "They teach morality. They help people. They believe in one supreme God who created everything. And that he sent a . . . an extension of himself into the world—Jesus, the Christ —who lived and died and rose again to save all mankind. They believe he forgives their errors and helps them also find life after death. They tell others about this 'good news,' as they call it, and they've organized congregations to do this. They offer hope and love—"

"*Bah!*" Aulus snorted. "If they get started here like the other foreign cults, they'll soon be a menace to Rome."

"Oh no." Pomponia laughed. "In fact, there's already been a . . . a 'test case,' I think you call it. Paulus was tried before one of our governors, and he was declared *not* guilty."

"When did this happen? Where? What governor?"

"In Corinth . . . oh . . . about two or three years ago."

"Who was the governor, I asked."

"Don't get so excited, dear," she soothed. "You can ask Aquila all about the trial. He was there."

"I don't want to talk to him. Or see him. You tell me. Who was the governor?"

"I'm not sure. I think his name was Gallus . . ."

"Gallus?"

"Or Gallio . . ."

"Not Junius Gallio—Seneca's older brother? The 'wit' who said Claudius was 'hooked up to heaven'?"

"That *could* be the one . . ."

"Gallio *was* governor of Greece about that time." A shallow smile lit Aulus' face. "The next time I see Gallio in the Senate, I think I'll have a word with him."

There it was, that providential flaw that would expose Aquila's story for the hoax it was. Roman governors were far too busy to bother with zealot preachers. Then Aulus frowned. It was ominous how religious fanatics like Aquila so often fastened themselves, leechlike, to wives of the wealthy. He might have to introduce protective legislation.

Aulus knew L. Junius Gallio only casually. Originally he had shared his brother Seneca's family name "Annaeus," but changed it when he was adopted by the wealthy Gallio family. Since his brother now virtually ruled Rome, Gallio had never been more popular, and he was not at all surprised when Aulus detained him one day as they were leaving the Senate chamber, probably to seek a favor.

"I've an odd question for you, Senator," Aulus led off. "Several years ago, when you were governor in Corinth, did the case of a Jewish tentmaker named Paulus ever cross your tribunal?"

"A Jewish *tentmaker,* you say?" Gallio smiled. Then he shook his head. "No, I don't think so. The proconsul of Greece has more important things to do than keep the canvas merchants honest."

"Just as I thought," Aulus frowned. "I was merely trying to trace down a story I'd heard. But it's not important."

"What story?"

"Oh . . . this Paulus was supposed to be leader of a Jewish sect called the Christiani."

"Yes, now I remember," Gallio nodded. "Sorry, Aulus, but the climate in Greece didn't agree with me. I got malaria over there and I've been trying to forget the year I put in at Corinth. It was a rabbi or teacher named Paul. I didn't know he was a tentmaker too. Smallish build? Big nose?"

"I don't know, Gallio. I've never seen him."

"Well, it was nothing much. Some of the Jews in town brought him to my court and accused him of—what was it?—teachings about their god contrary to Jewish law. Something like that."

"How did Paul defend himself?"

"He didn't. I threw the case out of court. I told the accusers I wasn't about to decide the fine points of their religious law. Besides, this Paul was a Roman citizen."

"He was?"

"Yes. And how *could* I decide it, Aulus? The Jews themselves were divided about Paul's teaching. Yes, I recall it now. Some in their synagogue believed the same way Paul did. Others didn't. Anyhow, I washed my hands of the case."

"Hmmmm. Just like Pontius Pilate. Does that name mean anything to you?"

"Pilate? Of course. Although I must confess I've lost track of what he's doing now."

"It's not important, and thanks for the details, Gallio."

"I hardly think I was any help. *Vale,* Aulus."

It had been a blind effort. It did not disprove Aquila's story, as he had hoped, but it was far from the "test case" that Pomponia was claiming. Evidently Paul had never even opened his mouth to defend himself. It was probably little more than the Chrestus riot in Rome transferred to Corinth.

Why did his wife get involved in these matters?

12

AGRIPPINA looked out across Rome from the veranda of her bedroom suite in a mood of limitless superiority. Romans had fallen into a ridiculous habit, she mused, assuming that their rulers must be males. Hatshepsut and Cleopatra certainly proved that the Egyptians were wiser than that. Some of the greatest rulers in far-off Mesopotamia were queens. But now at last, she swore, future ages would speak with awe about Agrippina of Rome: the sister, the wife, and the mother of emperors, to be sure, but also empress in her own right with supreme power as her son's co-regent. She had seen to it that *two* thrones stood in the palace reception hall, and her image was engraved on imperial coinage next to Nero's.

Who could challenge her? That vile Narcissus was dead, Callistus was dismissed, and her dear Pallas controlled the treasury, as always. Seneca and Burrus were her creatures, and Nero would live the rest of his life in debt to her—docile, faithful, obedient—the doting son who owed her absolutely everything. Agrippina of Rome—the first woman to rule the greatest empire in history.

Tears welled up in her eyes. A sweep of her arm sent the breakfast crystal flying across the veranda and smashing onto the courtyard below. Then she parted her teeth and screamed, "*Why*, by the very fiends of Hades, is it all coming apart?" Her authority was being undermined insidiously, she knew, her power eroded. There was that disgraceful day with the Armenian ambassadors. She saw Seneca whisper to Nero and prevent her assuming her rightful place next to him. Burrus was slighting her. And recently, even Nero was showing her a certain coolness and independence. By the gods, even a colorless sparrow like that Plautius woman could ridicule her in public!

Pallas, who had heard her scream, came running in to see what was the matter. With smoldering epithets, Agrippina quite candidly told him.

"It's all the work of Seneca and Burrus," Pallas confided. "From morning to night, they're telling Nero: 'Be your own man' . . . 'You're old enough to make decisions for yourself' . . . 'Caesar isn't a mother's boy, is he?'—that sort of thing."

"The treacherous ingrates!" she fumed. "I made both those men. Seneca was rotting on Corsica and Burrus was a maimed nobody. And this is the thanks I get for it."

"They're swine, certainly." Pallas brushed his lengthy strands of hair aside to scratch one of his pierced earlobes.

"Only you've stayed loyal, darling Pallas." She kissed his cheek. "Well, how shall we stop them?" Her green eyes flashed in appeal.

"I've been thinking about that. You'll have to do one of two extremely different things to restore your control over Nero, and I can't for the life of me tell you which is the better course," he fretted. "Either you reassert yourself as a strict mother—cow the wayward son into submission—or, quite the opposite, you become his partner and confidante rather than mother. In either case, you have to win him back. Then Seneca and Burrus will be powerless."

"So. The flavoring must be sour or sweet."

"Anything, I think, would be better than ignoring the situation . . . letting it all crumble away."

"Yes, it can't go on like this. All right, I'll wait for the proper moment and then show him he still has a mother to deal with. Don't worry, dear Pallas, we won before"—she caressed his cheek—"and we'll win again. And when we do, there are a few other scores I have to settle." Her thoughts drifted over to the Esquiline.

Nero was not very happy with his wife, Octavia. Even though the sixteen-year-old girl was starting to show some of the beauty of her mother, Messalina, Nero had never fallen in love with her and complained about her complexion. Their marriage had been arranged. It was totally political. Worse than that, their politics didn't agree. Torn between loyalties to her brother, Britannicus, and her husband, Octavia tried desperately to avoid taking sides in the murky rivalries swirling about her. But soon she and Nero were sleeping in separate bedrooms and spending as little time together as possible.

One day Nero stalked into her quarters and found a dark-haired girl in charge of the domestics there. Her profile had a classic cut to it, and when she turned to Nero and smiled a greeting, he was momentarily stunned. Olive-skinned and with hair cascading freely down her back, she was so very striking that Nero lost his composure.

"Who . . ." His voice had an unnatural, squeaky sound. He swallowed and tried again. "Who are you?"

"My name is Acte, Caesar. Claudia Acte."

"By the very gods! Some relative I haven't heard about?"

"Oh no," she laughed, revealing her small, perfect teeth. "Quite the opposite. I was a slave until the Divine Claudius freed me. I adopted his name in gratitude."

"A freedwoman, eh? I find a trace of Greek in your Latin. Where are you from?"

"You have a good ear, Caesar. I was born in Ionia."

"Doesn't Acte mean 'the place where waves break'?" Seneca's Greek lessons were serving him well.

"The beach, the seashore. That's right."

"Perfect name for you. What's more beautiful than the coastlands?"

Acte blushed and replied, "Don't forget, *acte* also means 'bruised grain.'"

"Aha! A bit of wit behind that Aphrodite's face of yours. But why haven't I seen you before?"

"There are hundreds of us in the palace, Master. I worked in the kitchen until my mistress Octavia placed me in charge of her personal staff."

"*Hades!* The kitchen? Did we hide an Olympian goddess in the *kitchen?*"

She laughed and continued with her chores as Nero followed her about, asking details of her Greek heritage. Seneca's tutelage had instilled in him a vast appreciation of Rome's debt to Greece, and

Nero was smitten not only by Acte's beauty but her Hellenism as well. The combination was overpowering.

Heedless of whether Octavia or anyone else knew, much less approved, Nero mooned about the palace, setting up trysts with his beloved. At first perplexed but then flattered by the emperor's attention, Acte soon returned his affection but was clever enough to withhold the ultimate gift. Nero was frustrated, then maddened, and finally so captivated that he decided to divorce Octavia and marry Acte. He was utterly serious. Brimming with surprise and joy, she agreed.

Nero was heady with elation. He hurried over to Seneca's office suite and shared the glad news with his tutor and Burrus, who was conferring with Seneca at the time. Burrus darkened and said, brusquely, "You're planning to *what?!*"

Seneca quickly covered for him. "I think news like this can't wait, Caesar. Hurry and tell your dear mother immediately!"

Nero whipped about and ran upstairs. It took Burrus exactly five seconds to comprehend. Now he knew why they called Seneca a genius.

Agrippina had at first dismissed Nero's infatuation with Acte as a temporary madness. But the illness lingered, and with Nero's announcement, it had become full-blown insanity. Yes, now was the time, she decided. "You say you want to *marry* Acte, my son?" she asked, trembling to control herself.

"Yes, Mother. I love her deeply. So very deeply."

"More than you love me, Nero?"

"Well," he mumbled, "not more, dear Mother. It's a . . . a different sort of love, isn't it?"

"Well," she huffed, reddening with fury, "I will not have a *freed-woman* as a *rival!*" she shouted, just inches from his ears. "The empress mother of Rome will *not* have a *slave girl* as a daughter-in-law!"

"Sweet Jupiter, will you lower your voice, Mother! I'm almost deaf!"

"And you must be *blind* as well to want such a marriage! I've overlooked your colossal ingratitude so far, Nero, listening to the Spanish Tongue and the Praetorian Cripple instead of your mother."

"Who?"

"Seneca and Burrus, young fool, who else? Now Pallas and I for-give your many discourtesies . . . above all, your failure to realize that you wouldn't be Caesar today *if it weren't for me!*" She fairly spat the words, as Nero cringed.

"But, Mother, I—"

"Hear me out! Do you know what you'd be today if it weren't for me? A worthless wreck . . . like your ridiculous father, the first Domitius Bronzebeard. He took one look at your horoscope the day you were born and laughed like a hyena. It was a horrible forecast! And why shouldn't it have been? The only thing he ever did for Rome was to aim at a child on the Appian Way and run him over."

"When did that—"

"Oh yes, he also gouged out someone's eye in the Forum. And he slept with his own sister, your Aunt Lepida."

"You never told me *that*, Mother."

"I wanted to spare you, my son."

"What . . . what did the horoscope predict?"

Agrippina blanched. "I . . . can't tell you that, Nero. Not now. Someday, perhaps. But this is the point: despite what the stars said, I planned night and day to change all that. Your father died when you were only three, and then came years of persecution by the Im-perial Harlot."

"Messalina?" Nero always had to be sure of her terms. Agrippina had her own names for everyone.

"Yes, yes, yes. And when she died, why, dear son, do you suppose I wanted to marry Claudius?"

"Why? Well, I know you didn't really love him, Mother. You just wanted to become empress."

"No!" she cried, with mock shock. "I did it all for *you*, my son. So that *you* would succeed Claudius. So that *you* would become em-peror one day."

It was time for her to pause and let several tears trickle down her cheeks. Even Seneca would have approved that dramatic touch. But Nero was not entirely taken in by his mother's performance.

"Yes, dear Mother, I appreciate all you've done for me. I've ex-pressed my gratitude a dozen times to the Senate, to Rome, and to you. But what does all this have to do with my forthcoming mar-riage to . . . my darling Acte?"

"*Dolt!*" she shrieked, again losing control of herself. "*Don't you see?*"

He was cowering, trying to protect his ears. "Gods! Softer, Mother!"

"If you divorce Octavia and marry Acte, you'll ruin everything! The only reason you were accepted as emperor was not that artificial business of Claudius adopting you as son, but the fact that you married Julio-Claudian blood in his daughter Octavia. The imperial line really continues through *her*, not you. Divorce her and you'll have to give back her dowry: the Empire. Marry Acte and Rome will be so scandalized by a Caesar being seduced by a slave girl that—"

"Freedwoman."

"—that you'd have a revolt on your hands. Think about it, my son. And isn't it time you started listening to your mother again?"

Nero sulked for some moments. Then he threw up his arms and said, "I think I'll give it all up: I'll marry Acte, and we'll sail off to Rhodes for the rest of our lives."

For a moment Agrippina glared again. Then she stroked his cheek and said, "No you won't, dear son."

Nero was deeply troubled. He found his mother's performance abusive, but there was some logic to her comments about a marriage with Acte. Yet in moments when it seemed their wedding could not take place after all, Acte became an even loftier object of his love by her very unattainability. In hopeless confusion he sought out his mentor Seneca.

In contrast to the scene with Agrippina, his conversation with Seneca was conciliatory, subdued, friendly. The philosopher had to admit that marriage with Acte would indeed be a false step "at this time." But then he continued, "Tell me in candor, Caesar. If Acte hadn't appeared in your life, couldn't you perhaps have returned to your love for Octavia?"

"I never loved her. Never at all. I rather loathe her, in fact. They forced us to marry, you know."

"Yes, yes. But a divorce just wouldn't do right now—for reasons of state."

"So everyone tells me."

"Yet you truly love Acte?"

"By the Goddess of Love herself, I adore her."

"Well, then. Why not take Acte as your mistress?"

Nero looked startled. "Will . . . will she?"

"Yes." Seneca smiled. "Burrus and I had a long talk with her,

explaining why marriage just was not possible for the present. But
that you loved her more than any wife and that she should . . . ah
. . . cooperate. And I know she will."

Nero's eyes gleamed with gratitude and he threw his arms about
his teacher.

"You two must be very discreet, of course," Seneca warned. "And
we've worked that out too. Annaeus Serenus, my relative, will quite
publicly pretend to be in love with Acte. Any notes you want to
send her, any gifts you want to give her will all come 'from Serenus,'
you understand. You may also use his home for your trysts." For this
help, Seneca knew his enemies would call him a pander, but, given
a lusty young emperor whose passion would not be bridled, it was
better to let him indulge in an affair with a harmless freedwoman
than risk worse scandals with some of the powerful and ambitious
women of Rome.

Nero was beaming with joy. "In all the Empire, only two men
have my interests at heart, beloved teacher: you and Burrus. I shall
not forget that."

Seneca smiled, then had a sudden thought and replied, "No,
Princeps. There are *three*, at the very least!"

"Who's the third?"

"Flavius Sabinus, who is taking the Gallic census."

"Sabinus? Oh yes. Tall man. Good build?"

Seneca nodded and said, "Well, he's achieving a masterstroke for
you up in Gaul."

"How?"

"By lowering the Roman tribute."

"Lowering?" Nero was frowning.

"And yet our tax income from Gaul will almost double!"

"But how is that possible?"

"Well, Sabinus replaced our fiscal 'experts' up there with a Gaul
who studied in Rome—Julius Vindex. And Vindex convinced his
countrymen that Sabinus was right with his slogan: '*If everyone registers, everyone pays less tribute!*'" Seneca started chuckling, and
then continued, "Ah, Princeps, it certainly worked. There are far
more Gauls up there than Rome ever knew!"

Nero was smiling. "Good for Sabinus! A masterstroke indeed!"
Then he returned to his favorite theme. "And thank you for helping
me . . . with my beloved Acte."

Pallas had to break the news to Agrippina that they had been completely thwarted by Seneca, who was now higher than ever in Nero's favor. "I think it's time you tried the opposite approach," he said. "I only wish I would have had the foresight to suggest it the first time."

"If the Spanish snake hadn't come slithering in as procurer, I would have succeeded. But you could be right, Pallas. Maybe it *is* time for honey."

One evening, after the rest of the imperial party had left the dinner table, Agrippina sat pensively looking at her son until Nero asked what was wrong.

"*Mea maxima culpa*," she sighed. "My greatest error was to regard you as my son and apply what I thought was a mother's proper discipline. But . . . you're so much more than that, my darling Nero. You're young, but you are no longer anyone's son. You are father to the whole Empire. I'm no longer your mother, just a humble subject, and I shouldn't have been so strict with you."

"You'll always be my mother, Mother." He winced, knowing Seneca would have disapproved his syntax.

"No. Nero is emperor. Nero must decide his life from now on. And please forget my ill-timed remarks and harsh words. I've wept over them. Repeatedly. But what caused our quarrel, beloved? Was it Acte? Well, if you love her, then I love her too."

"You . . . do?"

"Oh yes. She *is* a magnificent, charming girl, and there's really no need for you to have to go sneaking off for your trys—ah—appointments with the lovely Acte. You might be seen. No, indeed. Why don't you simply meet in my suite instead?"

"W-where?"

"In my rooms. And anytime, dear one. Just drop a hint, and I'll be gone. Don't look so surprised, my son. Why shouldn't you be permitted these indulgences? You're burning with the flames of life and you need Acte. And besides, Caesar can do anything he pleases."

"That's very generous of you, Mother."

"Now come with me. I'll show you how to lock the door."

Astounded at the change which had come over his mother, Nero found himself being led up to her lavish quarters, where she showed him a concealed latch. Then she turned to him and said, "I know you, my son. You're thinking that your mother isn't capable of so complete a change of heart. But she is. Let this prove it."

Agrippina walked over to her desk and took out a piece of parchment. "Here, dearest," she said. "This document lists my personal funds in the palace treasury . . . and grants you access to all of them."

Nero looked at the totals and his eyes bulged. "By Hercules, Mother. This is almost as much as we have in the imperial treasury!"

"I know. I inherited much. And Claudius was quite lavish with his gifts to me."

"Well, this is amazingly generous of you, dear Mother. But I won't touch your funds. I have quite enough."

"No, dear one. What's mine is yours."

As they left the suite, Agrippina clasped Nero in an almost passionate embrace.

Over the next days, Nero was puzzled. The change in his mother seemed too good to be true. He decided to test the promised arrangement regarding her room and found his mother happily compliant. Though Acte was almost quivering with fright, he led her triumphantly into Agrippina's suite. Everyone had vanished. Inside there was merely candlelight and a gift of perfume for Acte.

Nero reported the change to Seneca. The philosopher was careful not to dash his hopes, but he did urge him to be wary. "Aesop said it first," he added. " 'Appearances are deceptive.' " Seneca, of course, had a reason for saying that, Nero realized, for he saw clearly enough the battle lines being drawn in the palace. But what if his tutor were wrong? Agrippina was, after all, his own mother, and seemed to have recognized her proper role at last. Yes, he decided, he must do his own part to repair their relationship.

One day he inspected the imperial wardrobe, selected a jeweled turquoise robe from India, and sent it to his mother as a gift. He also told one of his aides to go near her quarters and report her reaction, but to stay out of sight. He wanted to know every joyous comment she made. Surprises were such fun.

The aide returned fifteen minutes later, a lugubrious warp on his face. "Pallas was there at the time," he reported, "and perhaps the Lady Agrippina was only . . . trying to impress him."

"Let me draw the conclusions. What did she say?"

"I'm . . . sorry to report this, Caesar, but . . . I can only tell you what I heard. She said, 'Oho, will you look at *this*, Pallas? Nero thinks he's furnishing my wardrobe—with a single, ridiculous dress!

What about the others in his collection? They're probably for that silly little strumpet, Acte! Such a son! He's only sharing with me one scrap of what I gave him in the first place.'"

Nero was livid. He began trembling, and his lips moved to form several words without succeeding. Finally he stammered, "Fa-Father Zeus knows it was done in good faith! And then this! What did Pallas say?"

"Something like: 'Behold what Nero gives in return for an Empire: one robe.'"

"That does it. Fetch Seneca."

Several hours later, Pallas was summoned to appear before Nero. With his heart throbbing, but determined not to betray a trace of emotion, Nero looked up at his finance minister and said, "Antonius Pallas, I thank you for your services to the Divine Claudius, and to me. However, that service is at an end as of this moment. You have two days in which to remove yourself, and all your effects, from the palace."

Pallas seemed less surprised than Nero thought he would be. "Very well, Caesar"—he bowed—"as you request, so shall it be."

"You didn't ask the reason for this decision, but I shall tell you anyway: you betrayed your loyalty to me by sharing my mother's terrible arrogance this morning. Do you understand?"

Pallas nodded.

"And don't alter any of the state accounts in the next two days, Pallas. At the moment, my agents are sealing all your records."

"Perfectly understandable, Caesar. But you'll find all my accounts with the state in balance." He bowed and left the room.

Nero sat and waited for the approaching storm. He knew it would break within a half hour, and he was not disappointed. Agrippina came roaring in with the fury of a Mediterranean tempest. "*Why?*" she screamed, her mouth quivering, her face drained of all color.

Nero did not retreat. "Do you and Pallas deny receiving my gift with disgusting arrogance? Don't lie. You were overheard."

"You . . . you would actually dismiss the man who helped make you emperor—because of a *robe?*"

"That was only a tiny token of his insolence and your hypocrisy, Mother. You've both been wearing masks of deceit, conspiring against the best interests of the government—"

"Nero!"

"It's true, and I could say so much more besides. A few people in this vast establishment are loyal to their emperor and they've reported on your incredible conduct, Mother. Your effusive new display of 'maternal love' is sinister, and I saw through it at once. So what are you *really* planning, Mother? Do you want to send me the way of Claudius?" He looked at her with burning eyes. "Well, I don't like mushrooms that much."

"That *won't be necessary!*" she cried. "We'll just send you back to the slums where you belong. At last Claudius will have a *legitimate* successor to replace you!"

"Who?"

"*His own son,* you dunce!" She spat out the words.

"Britannicus?" Nero scowled.

"Yes, Britannicus! He's the *true* heir, not you. He's *worthy* of the Empire. You're obviously not!"

"Careful, Agrippina."

"Aha! You no longer call me Mother. Well, that's fine," she seethed, "because I'd hate to claim you. You'd embarrass anyone."

"Be careful, I said!" Nero was tingling with anger.

"What are you, anyway? Merely an adopted prince, while Britannicus is genuine. The blood of the Caesars pulses through his veins. And what runs through yours? The fluid of the Bronzebeards. That's why you can commit these outrages against your own mother . . . the mother who gave you empire."

"Oh spare me that refrain, Mother. Please do."

"*Ingrate!*" she shrieked. "Get out of the palace! You have no business here!"

"Have you lost your mind?" Nero gritted his teeth.

"I don't care what happens to me: let the whole world learn about the dark deeds in this dreadful house—the poisoning . . . everything. One thing they'll have to give me credit for: Britannicus lives. I'll take him to the Castra Praetoria and we'll let the guards decide. There your cripple, Burrus, and your exile, Seneca, can plead your shabby cause . . . using a maimed arm and a pedant's tongue to claim the government of the world! Ha! But the daughter of the hero Germanicus will present her case. And she will be heard."

"You're dreaming, Mother."

"Dreaming, am I?" she raved, trying to strike Nero while he nimbly dodged the blow. Then she tilted her head upward and cried out in a quavering voice: "Hear me, Divine Claudius! You will be vindicated, finally vindicated, when I put your own son on the throne.

By the shades of all my victims in Hades, I *will do* this!" Her emerald eyes flashed a frightful intensity.

"Get out, Mother! And stay out of my sight!" Nero hissed.

His first impulse was to run and tell Seneca what had happened. But then he checked himself. He really must stop bothering his tutor for advice on every step and start acting like a Caesar. He was shaken, tense, and very frightened, but he was Caesar.

Britannicus in his place? The threat tingled endlessly in the very marrow of his bones. He had always loathed his stepbrother, but recently that fourteen-year-old whelp had been growing obscenely fast. In no time he would assume the toga of manhood. Worse yet, the sullen little ox still had a large following of witless Romans who would support him in a challenge for the throne.

In the days following, Nero cringed to see his mother making a great fuss over Britannicus. But then he learned that she was also smuggling regular messages to the Castra Praetoria, and had even entertained some tribunes of the Guard the previous night at a private reception in her quarters. Smashing a fist onto his desk, he called to an aide, "Summon Julius Pollio!"

Must he spend the rest of his days in a lingering clutch of apprehension? Must he wait for his mother or Britannicus or the praetorians to strike first? Of course not, he told himself. He was emperor. An emperor must sometimes act above the law. Yes, this crisis he would solve himself, and how proud Seneca would be that he had finally learned to take matters into his own hands. He grabbed a wax tablet and began writing.

"Greetings, Tribune," said Nero as Pollio entered. "One of the wisest things I did on my accession was to remove you from service to the empress mother. Now, you still have a woman named Locusta in your custody?"

"Yes, Princeps."

"Bring her this sealed message. Tell her you received it from the hand of Caesar himself. And you're to tell *no* one of your mission. Your very life depends on it."

"Of course, Caesar." He saluted and was off.

When the vial of poison arrived, Nero handed it to one of Britannicus' tutors and told him, "Empty this into the prince's wine. At bedtime, of course, when there's no taster around."

A loyal agent of the emperor, the tutor complied without question.

That night, Britannicus drank the wine and promptly felt ill. But he suffered only a harmless diarrhea and so passed the drug.

Nero told Pollio to bring Locusta before him. When she arrived, he stared at the disheveled hag for several moments and then bellowed, "What were you two trying to do? Make a fool of Caesar? I ordered poison and you gave me a laxative. Your 'victim' is purged and healthier than ever!" He crossed her cheeks with stinging slaps.

Wincing with pain, Locusta said, "Blue vitriol is *no* cathartic, Caesar. But sometimes it acts slowly. I only wanted the death to seem like illness so you wouldn't be accused of a crime."

"Bah! It's likely that I'm afraid of the Julian law against poisoners! I condemn you to death, Locusta. And you, Pollio, will follow her if you can't—"

"Forgive me, Caesar!" Locusta had fallen on her knees before him. "Give me another chance! The next preparation will be a rapid poison which cannot fail. It will cut the victim down like a dagger's steel."

"So you say. But I won't take your word any more, Locusta." He cupped his mottled chin with a hand and then looked up. "Unless you're ready to bring your drugs and prepare the poison here in the palace so we can test it first?"

"Happily done, Master!"

"All right, then. But wear a veil, and don't be seen by anyone. Pollio, help her with her things and set everything up in the room next to my quarters. Here—I'll show you."

Several hours later, Locusta and her baggage arrived. Nero helped them set up the equipment, and, like some apprentice wizard, he watched her heating and stirring the ingredients. When Locusta said the potion was ready, Nero hurried out to fetch a kid that he had tethered inside his bedroom and led the animal in. With the undiscriminating appetite for which their kind are famous, the young goat obediently lapped up the poison and fell over on its side. But it lingered on an agonizing hour before its heart finally stopped beating.

"Like a dagger's steel, Locusta?" Nero grumbled. "It's not strong enough."

"Don't worry, Caesar. We'll distill it several times more."

The stench that rose from the brewing mixture made Nero gag and he stumbled out of the room. Soon he was back, carrying a young pig under his arm. "Are you ready?"

Locusta nodded. They threw some mash on the floor and dripped the poison over it. The pig ambled over, snorted a bit, and began eating the mash. Suddenly it stopped munching, squealed twice, and fell over dead.

"Good," said Nero. "And the poison is colorless too." He took the remaining potion and carried it himself down to the palace kitchen. Then he prepared for dinner.

It was customary for the younger princes to sit with their companions at a separate table in the imperial dining room, while their elders reclined as they ate at the main table. Britannicus was still assigned the children's table, and this evening he was surrounded by other noble youths, including Sabinus' nephew Titus, sitting at his right. Britannicus and Titus had remained close friends at the palace school, always choosing the same sides during Palatine sporting contests.

It was a chilly night, and hot wine was served early in the meal. A butler poured a cup for Britannicus, one of his attendants tasted it, and then passed it on to the prince. "Careful, Master," he warned. "It's good, but it's hot."

Britannicus sipped it, gingerly, then spat it out on the mosaic floor. "Yeccch! Was this piped up from Hades? Burns your mouth. *Water!*"

Another servant hurried over with a silver flagon and poured in some cold water to chill the wine. Nero watched his stepbrother out of the corner of his eye, for the water was saturated with Locusta's poison. Britannicus was cramming a crust of bread into his mouth. Now he paused to take a drink of wine. Several sips and he started sliding down his chair and then collapsed onto the floor, coughing and gasping.

Titus jumped down to assist his friend, and there was commotion at both tables. Nero turned on his side to see what the trouble was. "Oh . . . that," he snickered. "Poor Britannicus has epilepsy. He's had it from birth. Don't worry, the lad will regain his senses soon. Guards! Carry the young prince up to his room."

Titus tried to feel Britannicus' heart. It was fluttering irregularly. Then his gasping stopped entirely, and his skin turned livid. His eyes popped open, unblinking, the pupils fiercely dilated. He was dead.

Titus stood up and made a lunge for Britannicus' cup before the servant who had poured the water could remove it. Snatching a sip from it, he let the tainted wine swish about in his mouth for several moments before spitting it out. There was an unmistakable aftertaste, and he quickly rinsed his mouth from another cup.

Agrippina and Octavia were watching the scene with mounting horror as it dawned on them that Britannicus had been poisoned. Octavia assumed the frozen mask with which she had had to hide her emotions for months, but Agrippina had great difficulty disguising her terror, and her hands began trembling uncontrollably. She forced herself to look at Nero. He was staring at her with a dark glint in his slate-blue eyes, as if to say, "Well, you can't threaten me with Britannicus any longer, can you, dear Mother? What's next?" There was even a challenge in his expression that shouted what remained unsaid, "And as to murder: like mother, like son."

After a brief, shocked silence, they all left the table, each bearing a different personal burden. Octavia cried herself to sleep: she had not had so much as a last embrace from her brother. Agrippina wondered, in horror, how to deal with the son she had brought into the world.

Seneca, profoundly shocked at what his pupil had done, held a hasty conference with Burrus. "The first real decision he made on his own," he said, "and look what he did!"

Burrus shook his head and said, "I always told you Nero had great potential for good—or evil."

And yet Seneca was surprised to find another part of his mind already hard at work, searching for some shreds of justification for Nero's conduct. There was, after all, his mother's wretched example and her threats . . . fratricide was a familiar evil in royal houses . . . Britannicus' comments *had* been quite careless . . . and any joint rule of Rome was impossible: emperorship knew no partnership.

Still, it was hardly enough justification. And would he have to go on apologizing for Nero? Or could he still salvage the good qualities in the young prince?

Britannicus' funeral was indecently hasty. The palace announced his death at midnight, and the rites were held the following dawn. Just as the procession was about to begin, Nero looked at the dead Britannicus and gasped. The body was hideously livid from the action of the poison, a virtual advertisement of his murder. Nero ordered the skin hastily rubbed with whitish gypsum to cover the evidence, and the procession set out. But as they wound their way through crowds of mourners in the Forum, a cloudburst suddenly descended, drenching the lifeless face of Britannicus. Romans recoiled in horror at the sight: a rivulet of chalky water was dripping from the bier, and the ghostly white face and arms of Britannicus were turning a bloated, angry purple. The rumors that had spread through the city were no longer whispered.

Aulus Plautius could not attend the funeral because of the emergency at Vespasian's house on the Quirinal. After Britannicus' poisoning, Titus had slipped away from the palace and made his way across Rome in a gathering delirium, stopping at fountain after fountain in a vain attempt to rinse his mouth of that dreadful, clinging aftertaste. He had absorbed enough poison merely tasting his friend's cup to make him dangerously ill, though he did manage to stagger up to his threshold before collapsing.

When Aulus arrived in the morning, he found doctors hovering over the prostrate youth, who was breathing with some difficulty and seemed to have a slight spasm in his lips. Yet Titus was playing the soldier as only a fourteen-year-old can play it, telling everyone he'd be fine in a short time.

"But *why* did you have to taste it?" Vespasian asked his son again and again, his brow knotted with anxiety. "Anyone would have known it was poison . . ."

"I . . . don't know, Father. I felt . . . I owed it to Britannicus."

"What did it taste like?" Aulus wondered.

"Not very much like wine." Titus made a wry grin. "More like . . . like peach blossoms. Or almonds . . . bitter almonds."

Aulus exchanged a dark glance with Vespasian and the doctors, for this was the most deadly toxin they knew of.

"Don't worry, lad." One of the doctors chucked him under the chin. "If it hasn't gotten you so far, you're safe."

But it would be six months before Titus finally recovered from the last stubborn symptoms of Locusta's brew.

Aulus left the house, wondering darkly about Nero. His early prejudice against the prince seemed justified after all. He wondered, now, why he had spent some of his prime years in that cold and foggy island to the north. Was it to foist on the Britons a "superior culture" that was all but worm-eaten by intrigue and murder on the Palatine? The Roman Republic didn't work, and now the Empire seemed to be failing. What was left?

He would gladly have blamed Jupiter and his clan for what was happening—*if* he thought for an instant they really existed. At times he gave serious thought to emigration, a happy self-imposed exile with Pomponia, perhaps to some Greek island where he would not have to feel embarrassed for his government, and where he could think and write in peace.

13

IN RECENT MONTHS, Plautia seemed to exist for but two reasons: exchanging tender letters with Sabinus in Gaul, and preparing for their wedding. Under other circumstances, the dreadful news from the Palatine would have distressed her as much as it did her father, but she had too many glorious prospects now to be concerned with anything more than Sabinus' safe return.

His brother Vespasian visited them with his ailing Titus to give a more complete account of events at Britannicus' table. But Plautia could only ignore the tragic politics and embrace Vespasian as "darling Sabinus' closest relative." Aulus frowned at the display, but Vespasian for once relaxed his tense features and treated his face to a warm smile.

Even Pomponia seemed to have solved her religious problems, and Aulus thanked the elaborate wedding preparations for that. The Plautii would have only one chance to host a nuptial celebration, and they planned to make the very most of it. The guest list would be lengthier this time, and again the nagging query posed itself: should Nero and Agrippina be invited? Yes, Aulus' closest friends advised, it would be a diplomatic gesture that could do much for Sabinus' career, not to mention the fact that Nero had reinstated Quintus Lateranus.

Aulus listened to all the arguments and then brushed them off: "*Two* poisoners in the house? I wouldn't feel safe at my own daughter's wedding!" No amount of coaxing would change his mind, though he did concede to letting Seneca and Burrus be invited to represent the Palatine. If Nero were offended, they would claim: "The wedding was too modest to expect a Caesar to attend, and the invitation would only suggest that a gift was desired."

Sabinus had promised to finish his Gallic census early in October, but the Ides of that month had arrived, and Plautia still had no definite date for his return. Nor had she heard from him in several weeks, and the wedding was set for mid November. Another week passed without word. A nub of anxiety began gnawing at Plautia, which she tried to suppress in the rush of wedding preparations.

That night—she could not tell when it was—she woke to the sharp crack of a breaking roof tile, followed by a thud in the hallway outside her bedroom. Several floorboards creaked. Lighting an oil lamp at her bedside, she saw, to her horror, that the latch on the door to her room was turning. She tried to scream but fear muted her cry to a hollow gasp.

Slowly the door opened, and in the orange flicker of light she saw the face of Flavius Sabinus. Squealing with delight, she rushed into his arms, and they kissed each other ravenously, trying to make up in moments of rapture the months of separation. At last they managed bits of dialogue, exquisitely broken by further embraces.

"Forgive me for waking you like this, my darling . . ."

"Ohhh, I'm glad you did . . ."

"I rode the final stretch without stopping. Hoped to arrive earlier . . ."

"No matter, my love. But how did you ever get in?"

"I climbed a tree . . . along a branch over the wall . . . and came in through the court. I didn't want to wake the whole household."

"You're here. You're actually here, my darling."

They snuggled together on her bed, kissing and caressing each other again hungrily. Love, the sublime attractor of minds and personalities was rapidly being joined by passion, the flaming blender of bodies. Love and passion was a combination that only the gods could have devised, they thought, but their fullest expression had to be reserved for marriage, Plautia still insisted, even on that night of nights.

"Please, my darling!" he implored, with an urgency she had never heard before. "We'll be married in *such* a short time."

"Soon we'll be one, dear Sabinus. Let's try . . . try to be patient. But do hold me close." He took her in his arms. How very gentle and understanding he was at her refusal, she thought, as she placed herself as close to him as was possible, every part of her body tingling to be in touch with his.

However far in advance they had been preparing for the wedding, the final week proved frantic for the Plautii. While Pomponia laid in vast supplies of food and drink, Aulus was running about the house, developing strategies and issuing commands as if he were at the Thames, not the Tiber. Jabbering servants started a final cleansing of the whole mansion, which now fairly sprouted with flowers, garlands, and greenery. Somehow, the Plautii survived their own preparations.

At dawn on her wedding day, Plautia heard the trumpets from the Castra Praetoria saluting the sunrise. Usually they awakened her, but not today. The first pale tinges of pink filtering into her room had sent her springing out of bed to begin the intricate process of arranging her hair into the traditional six locks of a bride. Soon Pomponia was there with breakfast and a mother's solicitude to help her dress.

Now the whole house was rumbling with activity. Aulus, the last fold of his toga carefully adjusted, was supervising last-minute decorations in his domain. Pomponia was running between Plautia's room and the kitchen, which now resembled the commissary of a Roman legion. "At least thirty more bottles of Setinian from the wine cellar," she ordered. "And fetch more of the pickled squid."

Aulus kept darting outside to look at the sky. There were comforting traditions about rain being a good omen on a wedding day, but he preferred that sort of clear day which was its own happy portent. A cold morning haze lurked overhead, but it was the kind that would burn off by noon, when the guests were expected.

Late in the morning, the litters began arriving, large gilded conveyances swinging their way up the slopes of the Esquiline on the shoulders of hard-breathing slaves. Running footmen surrounded each litter, insulating it from the next in what was becoming a colorful procession. Senators and their wives stepping out of the litters flashed an almost immodest display of purple and jewels and gold.

Some veterans of the war in Britain from the lower ranks of Roman society had also been invited and were now climbing the Esquiline in their best clothes.

The groom arrived and stood next to his attendant, Vespasian. Sabinus was dressed, like Aulus, in a white woolen toga bleached to special brilliance by processing with fuller's chalk. It was the garb of hosts, bridegrooms, and those running for public office (the *candidati* or "white-dressed"). Later they would change to gala dinner costumes, which some of the ultrafashionable senators were wearing in various tones of saffron, azure, and amethyst—still no match for the women, who quite outdid the men in the color and dazzle of their garments.

Plautia, in contrast, was dressed almost simply. When Sabinus saw her enter the crowded atrium from the opposite side, she was crowned with a flower garland and wore the traditional ivory tunic, shoes of white leather stitched with pearls, and a gauzy silken veil the color of fire.

The groom's business partner, Quintus Lateranus, was serving as augur. With a wink at the bridal pair, he grandly uncovered a coop of sacred chickens and fed them some meal—the Senate's method of discovering the day's portents. The chicks, of course, had been carefully starved and now pecked away with gusto. A half smile on his face, Lateranus announced, "*Omina . . . bona!* The omens are favorable!"

"*Bene! Bene!*" shouted the guests, for the ceremony could now begin.

Plautia's matron of honor—her cousin Quintus' wife—led her up to Sabinus, who had moved to the center of the atrium. Plautia thrust her right hand out from under the flame-colored veil and placed it into Sabinus'. Smiling broadly and in a resonant voice, Sabinus looked into her eyes and asked, "Will you be my *materfamilias?*"

"*Certe.*"

Then Plautia asked him, in her lilting tone, "Will you be my *paterfamilias?*"

"*Certe.*"

The guests were pleased. The personal wedding vow had been selected. The traditional "Where you are Gaius, there am I Gaia" always sounded so stilted.

The bridal pair, now joined by Aulus and Pomponia, advanced to a small altar at the center of the hall. The four united in placing a cake of coarse bread on the altar, uttering brief prayers to Jupiter, Juno, and several rural gods—all except Pomponia, who helped place the bread but then bowed her head and said nothing.

"The gods bring luck!" cried Aulus.

"*Feliciter! Feliciter!*" the guests immediately responded, for the two were now man and wife.

A phalanx of relatives and friends converged on the bridal pair and escorted them into the peristyle, where the wedding banquet would be served. Polla, the wiry little mother of Sabinus and Vespasian, was entranced with Plautia. She had never met her before, because Polla hated to leave her beloved Reate in the picturesque Sabine hill country, and she cordially disliked Rome. Now she threw her bony arms about Plautia and thanked her for relieving the Flavii of years of anxiety over "my wayward bachelor of a son who shunned marriage like the very plague." Then she added wistfully, "If only my husband could have lived to see this day."

Vespasian proudly introduced his wife, Flavia, to everyone and presented their children: Titus, who had finally recovered from Locusta's poison, and a younger brother and sister, Domitian and Domitilla.

Everyone reclined at tables flanking that of the bridal party, as a corps of servants brought the appetizers: fresh oysters, crab, sauced egg, and greens, all served on glittering silver platters from which guests hungrily plucked the food with their fingers. Eight courses followed, for this was to be more than a wedding banquet. It would also serve as clan feast, gala, and gastronome's delight, and it would last the rest of the day.

Seneca and Burrus not only came, but they seemed to enjoy themselves enormously. Just before the ceremonies, they had had a few words with Sabinus. No one could hear what was said, but Sabinus' face was cut by a vast grin and he had shaken their hands enthusiastically. They were now reclining with the wedding party at the head table, befitting their imperial rank.

Next to the bridal pair was the other member of the Twin Brothers enterprises and his wife. The bride forbade Sabinus and Quintus to talk business, and they complied for at least five full minutes. After that, there was no stopping them. Using coded signs so as not to flaunt sums before the guests, Quintus signaled the bonanzas he had achieved in Sabinus' absence. "We sold our grain ship for a much larger one," he said, "over 140 feet long—stole it really—and we've registered it in Alexandria."

"Egypt? Why not a port in Italy?"

"Tax advantages."

"Need I have asked?" Sabinus made a wry face. "What's the name of the ship?"

"It had been the *Isis*. Now it's the . . . *Twin Brothers*."

"Need I have asked?" Sabinus repeated, and broke out laughing.

"We did have one reverse, though. We had to sell the pottery works at Arretium. Took a small loss on it."

"Loss? That doesn't sound like you, Quintus."

"Be glad we're out. They're making the same ceramics in Gaul now, undercutting the whole Roman market. The fellow we sold the factory to has to close down, sorry to say."

"Quintus, you have better timing than the Fates themselves. What did you do with the proceeds?"

Lateranus had been waiting half the afternoon for Sabinus to ask. Unleashing a great smile, he asked, "I trust you like what you're drinking?"

"The wine? Naturally, it's Falernian. Oh . . . you mean—"

"Exactly! Vineyards too: five hundred acres down in Campania." Quintus caught the arm of a servant and showed Sabinus a wine bottle labeled GEMINI, with a figure of Castor shaking Pollux's hand. The Twin Brothers, it seems, were now in the wine business, too. Sabinus shook his head in disbelief.

When the feast had reached its final course of pastry and almonds, a towering wedding cake was sliced and served to guests on traditional bay leaves. Sabinus leaned over to his bride and said, softly, "I have *quite* a surprise for you . . ."

"What this time, darling *husband?*"

"It's rather . . . important."

"Tell me."

He leaned over to whisper something to her, but nibbled at her earlobe instead.

"Stop it. And tell me, Sabinus."

"No. You'll find out shortly."

Now it was time for toasts and speeches, the first given by Aulus Plautius in one of his rarest moods. Then he introduced Annaeus Seneca. The philosopher, whose stock in trade was words—spoken, written, whispered, implied—delighted the guests with a witty performance. At the close, he slit the seals on a document from the palace. There were a few indrawn breaths, and Aulus' smile faded.

Seneca read Nero's message of congratulations to the bridal couple and regrets that business detained him in the palace—Aulus was squirming uncomfortably—and he had special praise for the bride's beauty:

> Once, if I recall correctly, I lauded her loveliness perhaps too highly, but a tiny mark on my cheek has cautioned me to mind my manners the better. Forgive my youth, fair Plautia!

The head table broke into a roar of laughter, while the other guests could only smile. Clearly, it was something esoteric. Then Seneca read on:

> Fortune smiles on you, Flavius Sabinus, and so do the Senate and the Roman People. You won triumphal regalia for your valor in the Britannic campaign under an illustrious father-in-law. You were the finest governor Moesia ever had, and for the first time Gaul has had an honest census. Because of your distinguished qualifications, I have appointed you to the high office of *praefectus urbi*, your inauguration to take place this coming January.

Seneca could hardly be heard as he finished Nero's letter, for all the guests were scrambling to their feet in applause and wild cheering. As *praefectus urbi* or prefect of the city, Sabinus would be lord mayor of Rome, the highest office to which a senator could aspire. The post held enormous prestige, and, in terms of actual power, the new ranking in the Roman Empire would be: Nero, Seneca/Burrus, and Sabinus, in that order.

Plautia kissed him proudly, and the other Plautii and Flavii pommeled his back in congratulations, while his little mother had tears in her eyes. Vespasian cuffed him playfully on the shoulder and said, "I always knew you were the man of destiny in our family."

"No, Vespasian," he bantered. "It's just that you crested too early." The brothers had been having a lively political rivalry, and at one time Vespasian was clearly ahead as Sabinus' superior in Britain.

"*Pompa! Pompa!*" someone yelled. The other guests took up the cry, calling for the customary procession to escort the bride to her new home. By now it was dark and a band of veteran comrades, serving as torchbearers, lit firebrands until the vestibule was flaming with a ruddy glow.

"Music!" Aulus called, and a dozen flute-players began piping.

Guests fell into line behind the bridal party and streamed out of the house to join a procession westward across central Rome to the Quirinal. The parading revelers broke into traditional wedding songs as they marched under flickering torchlight, while bystanders at the roadsides shouted cheers honoring the god of marriage: "Talasse! *Io* Talasse!"

Sabinus' town house was ablaze with light as the cavalcade arrived, his domestics standing at attention to greet their new *domina*. To avoid any chance stumble—a dreadful omen—Sabinus gently lifted Plautia over the threshold. Then he placed a cup of water and a glowing firebrand into her hands, symbols of life together. She now produced three silver coins. One she gave her husband in token of the dowry; another she put on an altar in the atrium for the household spirits of her new home; and the third she threw back into the street for the spirits of the roadway.

"The consummation," Plautia's matron of honor now whispered, with a coy smile. She led the bridal couple to the marriage chamber and carefully shut them inside. Guests serenaded them with a final nuptial song, and then took their leave. The wedding was over at last.

It had been an exhausting day—and one they would remember forever. Gathering his bride into his arms, Sabinus bent down to her lips and kissed them with tender passion. "Plautia, *my* Plautia," he whispered, while untying her ivory tunic.

"I love you, *mea vita.*"

"*O summa voluptas!*"

She started breathing heavily and heard a distant roar in her ears. She held onto him even more tightly, hoping in that way to halt the warm and delicious waves of desire that were gently eroding her will. But that very gesture merely inflamed her further, and she could only float out with the roaring tide of their love. She cried softly with ecstasy, and then sobbed with relief and a gladness she had never known before.

Sabinus was engulfed in an exquisite flood of rapture. He thought that if he died the next instant, his whole life would have been lived to the full. The radiant creature who had invaded his senses ever since that day on the Capitoline but seemed so unattainable a dream for so long was part of him now. He slipped off the bed and onto his knees to worship his very goddess of love, pressing his burning cheek against her hand, kissing the ring he had slipped on her finger. No man anywhere, he swore, was happier, luckier, or more in love than he. Or ever had been. Or ever would be.

14

THEIR LOVE was a very private thing, yet it became public soon enough. A popular senator—soon to be city prefect—marrying the daughter of a war hero tickled the people's fancy. Clusters of Romans started gathering in front of their house in hopes of seeing the bride and groom come or go. Their appearances in the city drew plaudits, and the remaining weeks of the year were filled with dinner parties and social engagements in their honor.

The joy of their life together was more than they had dared imagine. Love was rich and various, all-consuming yet all-renewing, and now total too. "Somehow, it's different every time," Plautia would sigh with wonderment.

"Yes. Exactly. Each . . . encounter is unique," he agreed. "I don't see how that's possible, my darling."

To learn his new responsibilities, Sabinus had to spend considerable time at Rome's municipal headquarters, which stood just across the Forum from the Palatine. Saturnus, the retiring mayor of Rome, proved quite cooperative in grooming Sabinus for the post, though he also gave the impression that Rome would never be quite the same after he retired.

"Coming back to you after a day's work is like a shivering man plunging into a warm, bubbling pool," Sabinus murmured, as he brushed aside Plautia's chestnut tresses to kiss her neck. "I know, the analogy isn't very graceful, but the feeling's cozy."

"Sabinus, there's something I want to ask you about your new position," she said, with a slight frown.

"I think I already know what it is."

She hesitated. "About Nero?"

He nodded. "I think you want to know if I'll be working closely with him?"

"Yes, that's it."

In fact, it was the unexpressed question on the minds of all the Plautii and Flavii, the slight shadow edging their bright happiness. It was the reason why Aulus, after congratulating his son-in-law on the new post, had also seen fit to add, with a knowing glance, "You must be very careful."

"It's a legitimate question, carissima," Sabinus conceded. "And the answer is yes and no. Yes, I'll be closely available to Nero if he wants me, just across the Forum from his palace. And if any major decisions have to be made about the city, he, Seneca, and I will have to discuss them. But no, I won't be in daily contact with him. The headquarters of the Empire and of the city are entirely separate, and if I keep things running smoothly in Rome, he'll have little reason to look in."

"Oh, Sabinus"—she frowned—"why did you have to . . . get involved?"

"Why does anyone choose a career in politics, Plautia? High stakes are always involved. I suppose I should say, 'I do it for Rome,' and, believe it or not, that's a large part of the answer. Seneca and Burrus are trying something very noble for the state: to see if Nero can still be groomed as an ideal ruler. And I want to be part of it."

"Is that the whole reason?"

He smiled and shook his head. "No, I'll admit it. I also like . . . the excitement of public life."

On New Year's Day of A.D. 56, Flavius Sabinus was sworn into office. Nero gave a glittering palace dinner in his honor, to which much of the senatorial aristocracy was invited. The dining room held sentimental memories for the newlyweds—they had their first conversations here—but this time Plautia tasted every morsel of food suspiciously, although, actress that she proved to be, she seemed to be having a wonderful time.

Sabinus was combing the crowd of guests for familiar faces when suddenly he felt his stomach tighten. Agrippina had stationed herself as if to have an unobstructed view of the new city prefect and his bride. He had never revealed to the Plautii Agrippina's ominous interest in him and only hoped that the empress had forgotten him entirely during his absence in Gaul.

During the feast, Sabinus carefully avoided looking at Agrippina except for stealthy side glances. But now all his apprehensions were richly confirmed. Not some times, but *every* time, the flaming fluorescence of Agrippina's green eyes were locked onto him with a studied intensity. She could not have been eating much, because her lips seemed continually pursed together in a taunting grimace. He hoped Plautia would not notice the sight, but he was wrong. During a lull, she leaned over and whispered, "That harpy wants you in her claws, Sabinus. She's been consuming you instead of her food."

In the melange of conversation following the banquet, while some of the younger senators were clustering about his wife, Sabinus saw Agrippina advance toward him, smile, and say, briskly, "Congratulations, Prefect! May I have a word with you privately . . . in the alcove over there?"

She turned and walked toward it, assuming that he would follow, mayor of Rome or not. Sabinus thought seriously of ignoring her. Let Agrippina talk to the walls instead, he thought. Let her hear, for the first time, her own imperious, demanding tones and get as disgusted by them as everyone else.

One does not, however, create a crisis at one's own inaugural banquet, Sabinus decided, as he followed her. Predictably, Agrippina had the first word.

"I'll be brief, Sabinus, but you must weigh my words carefully.— No, don't look away.—After your little 'escape' up to Gaul, I *could* have arranged for your . . . sudden illness, shall we say? Yes, Sabinus, even in faraway Gaul. But I didn't. Do you know why?"

Sabinus hated even to think of asking.

"Because I knew then—and I know now—that you and I will share love, Sabinus. If not now, then shortly. No one has *ever* refused me, and what—"

"Empress," Sabinus cut her off. "I'm *married,* and very happily so."

"And what does that prove?" She laughed. "Oh, your bride is a tender little dove—I'll grant you that—but what I'm offering is a rich and *mature* relationship, with untold possibilities. You'll *not* be able to refuse that." She stroked his cheek with a cool hand. "Nor would you want to."

She turned to leave, but he decided to say it now, whatever the consequences. "Empress, this cannot—this *will not*—take place. Not now. Not ever. I love my wife very much."

Her mood chilled instantly. Grasping his wrist so tightly that her fingernails imprinted his flesh, she said, in a very low voice, "What if there will be no wife to love, Sabinus? Or no Sabinus to love her?"

One flash of fear rippled through him, but then anger took its place. "I *don't* like being threatened, Empress," he sliced out the syllables, "and I am not without resources. Threaten me again, and I'll lay the matter before the emperor, Seneca, and Burrus."

"I won't *threaten* you again, Sabinus," she seethed. "I'll *act*."

Sabinus turned about and walked away.

"By the infernal powers, Sabinus, I'll *destroy* you! First those you love. And then you!"

In the weeks that followed, Sabinus mentioned nothing of the scene to Plautia, since she was a more exuberant worrier than he. In fact, he found himself guilty of "moral lying" when she inquired about Agrippina from time to time. He did, though, have a confidential discussion with his chef on matters of security, since Agrippina usually felled her victims by poison. "Don't worry, Prefect," the rotund Sicilian told him, "I'll personally taste everything before it gets to your table."

"But that wouldn't serve you well if it *were* poison," Sabinus objected.

"Bah!" he scoffed, patting his paunch. "I can absorb anything. What would kill other people only gives me indigestion!"

Sabinus did not have much time for worry. The inaugural glitter faded soon enough as he came to terms with his awesome responsibilities. As city prefect, he had to maintain the general good order of Rome with four Urban Cohorts of a thousand troops each under his command. These police were billeted in the Castra Urbana at the north of Rome.

But as an entirely civil, not military, official, Sabinus went to work each day dressed in a regular toga, draped over a tunic banded with the broad purple stripe of the senatorial class. His sprawling suite of offices was composed of a secretariat, a tribunal where he sat in judgment, and the municipal archives. His titular rank was Clarissimus, "most illustrious," and an honor guard of six lictors officially preceded him on the streets of Rome.

His range of responsibilities was almost too wide, Sabinus soon concluded. In his first months of office, he had to deal with traffic problems, scheduling the public games, supervising trade associations, curbing the rising price of food, and dozens of other administrative functions. He was also chief justice of Rome, and while minor cases were heard in lower courts, all important trials arising in the city, particularly those involving capital punishment, were referred to Sabinus and his assessors.

Fortunately, he was assisted by a prefect of the grain supply, and a prefect of the *vigiles,* seven thousand troops who acted as night police and firemen. Several commissions also helped him supervise the streets, the aqueducts, the sewers, and maintain the public buildings and monuments.

Anxious to master his duties quickly, Sabinus was spending long hours at city headquarters, and Plautia voiced her concern. "It's only a matter of learning the office," he assured her. "Once I've figured it out, I'll delegate all my responsibilities and spend my days up here in amorous ease with you."

It was only a pleasantry, he knew, for solving the problems in a metropolis of over a million people continued to consume massive amounts of his time. He was forever having to make instant decisions or immediate rulings. Eventually, though, he discovered the bureaucratic redundancies and petty empire-building of city magistrates and ruthlessly curbed it. His whole staff was put on notice to find ways of making the municipal administration more efficient.

In several months, the effort succeeded, and the improvements were noticed even on the Palatine. Nero wrote Sabinus a note of appreciation for the new directions in city government. But apart from this—and mercifully, Plautia thought—there had been little contact with the emperor.

Early that summer, a crime wave struck across Rome. A large gang, operating only at night, was breaking into shops and causing riots in taverns and brothels. Sometimes there was only horseplay—people stopped in the street and tossed in a blanket—but at other times, they were assaulted and robbed. Anyone who resisted was beaten, or even stabbed to death and dropped into the nearest sewer. Not one of the culprits had been caught.

Sabinus debated the problem with Serenus, the go-between in Nero's romance with Acte, who was now prefect of the night watch. "If your *vigiles* can't seem to catch any of them," Sabinus said, with bite, "can't they at least describe them? From reports of victims?"

"We're trying," Serenus sighed, scratching a scalp full of black curly hair. "The victims say they look like slaves."

"Slaves? That's ominous," Sabinus replied, with a Roman's memory of the Spartacus revolt.

"But that doesn't mean they *are* slaves. They could be disguised. Last week we found a wig lying on the street after one of the brawls."

"Any other clues?"

"Nothing yet. But we're committing most of our men to patrol the streets at night."

"We may have to call in the Urban Cohorts as well. Good luck, Serenus."

With a sickening regularity in the next days, Sabinus had to pin reports of fresh assaults onto his large map of Rome. Here a girl ravished, there a boy molested, a couple beaten and robbed. But Serenus' latest report was alarming: when his men were closing in on a gang of ruffians, the previous night, they were suddenly attacked by what seemed an unidentified *military* force.

"That does it," Sabinus told Serenus. "We commit the Urban Cohorts too." Just then, his secretary came in and said, "Senator Julius Montanus is here, Clarissimus. He urgently requests a conference."

"All right, send him in. Let's confer each day from now on, Serenus. *Vale.*"

Montanus, a sturdily built young senator, stepped in just as Serenus left.

"How are you, Montanus?" Sabinus smiled. "Lately I find myself wishing I'd never left you people in the Senate. But what's that gash over your eye? Haven't been fighting with your beautiful wife, now, have you?"

"Not fighting *with* her, friend. *For* her. Gods, what a *horrible* mess I'm in."

"Sit down and tell me about it."

"Maybe I should go into exile immediately," he muttered wearily, as he sank down on the proffered couch. "The Father of the gods knows my life isn't worth very much now."

"What happened? From the beginning."

"It was last night. My wife and I were returning from a banquet with some friends when we were attacked by a gang of thugs on the Via Lata. Well, we gave back what we got, and it . . . was a pretty good fight. But while we were brawling, I heard my wife scream. One of the ruffians—he had a thick neck and spindly legs—was dragging off my wife. I caught up with them and pounded his ugly face bloody. I . . . I really mauled him, I think. Anyway, with one of my punches his . . . his hair seemed to slip off—it was a wig!—and in the torchlight I saw his real hair. It was blondish, and . . . oh, sweet Mother of the gods . . . you know who it was."

"No, I don't. Who was it?"

"Nero."

Sabinus' head jerked backward. "How do you know it was Nero, Montanus?"

The senator looked up in surprise. "Don't I know what Caesar looks like?"

"The light wasn't good. There are a million people in Rome—a few must look like Nero."

"Don't you think I've thought of that? But how many of those few also talk like Nero? Have his pot belly? His pock-marked face? His bull neck? Oh, it was Nero all right. I also recognized several of his friends, I think . . . Otho for sure."

Sabinus felt his pulse quicken, and asked, "What happened then?"

"As soon as I recognized him, I held back, of course. And then they all ran off, hooting and yelling and laughing."

"Assuming for the moment that it *was* Nero, what do you plan to do now?"

"That's why I'm here. I figured only the 'Lord Mayor of Rome' would have the answer to that riddle," the senator said, with a grim smile.

"Does Nero know you? And did he seem to know it was you?"

"No question. I heard one of them mutter 'Montanus' as they left."

"All right, now the big question: did Nero *know that you knew* it was he? Think carefully."

"I'm not sure. I . . . I don't think so. I didn't mention his name. I just quit beating him when his wig fell off and I saw his face in the torchlight. Right after that, they all ran off."

"All right, then. The matter's solved."

"What should I do?"

"Nothing."

"Nothing?"

"Absolutely nothing. If Nero *were* out on that mad escapade, he should have had sense enough to realize that any Roman would defend his wife. It would have to be part of their crude game to expect blows in return."

"Shouldn't I apologize? What if he did think I recognized him?"

"That's just the point, man: by not apologizing, you show you didn't know it was Nero. If you do, you admit that you beat up the lord of the world, and *that* he couldn't stand. And if your attacker were *not* Nero, you'd make new trouble for yourself."

Montanus thought for some moments. "Maybe you're right, Sabinus," he said slowly. "I . . . I appreciate the help, friend."

In a kind of haze, Montanus left the office, but in a moment he was back. "You keep saying 'if it really were Nero.' Do you still doubt it?"

"I'm afraid I do, Montanus. It's really rather preposterous, isn't it? The richest man in the world stealing? The most powerful person getting bruised and beaten?"

"He's young, Sabinus. He does it for excitement. And if you don't believe me, I suggest you try to see him today or tomorrow. If his face isn't worse than mine, you can thank the palace physicians for that."

"That *would* be proof." Sabinus smiled. "But relax, Senator. *Vale.*"

Sabinus tried to get back to his work, but he was too preoccupied by the visit from Montanus. If Nero and his comrades *were* behind the string of disorders in the city, it would easily explain why they were rescued by unidentified guards. He got up from his desk, hurried across the Forum, and climbed several colonnaded staircases to Burrus' office at the base of the palace, where he found the praetorian prefect at his desk.

"Hello, colleague," Sabinus said hurriedly. "Sorry to bother you, but have you seen Caesar today?"

"No, Sabinus. He's not seeing anyone right now. Says he isn't feeling well, I understand."

"This is important. Can you think of some excuse to see him—even for a moment? I just want you to tell me what his face looks like today."

Burrus cocked his head askew. "What his *face* looks like?"

"Trust me, friend. I'll wait here and explain the moment you return."

"Well . . . all right. I'll have him sign several of these documents for Egypt."

Burrus left his office and returned some fifteen minutes later. "Well, how did *you* know anything was wrong with him? By Neptune's soggy beard, he's a mess, he is . . . eyes all purple and black, welts across his forehead . . . puffy cheeks."

The color drained from Sabinus' face. "Did Nero offer any explanation?"

"Mumbled something about an accident while running his horses . . ."

"Did he, Burrus? *Did* he work out with his horses yesterday?"

Slowly Burrus shook his head. "I don't think so."

"And what does Caesar do with his evenings lately?"

When this brought no response, Sabinus snapped, "Well, I'll tell you then." And he launched into a furious recitation on the cause of Rome's recent crime wave.

Burrus interrupted him several times, suggesting he lower his voice, but finally he nodded in agreement. "All right . . . yes, we know all about it, Sabinus. Gods, he even tries to sell the loot to our palace staff! Seneca and I have been trying to stop him, but he has his own tight circle of revelers. All right, I'll see Seneca and we'll *have* to figure some way to put a halt to it."

"*Immediately*, I trust?"

"Yes, Sabinus." Then he added, "All in confidence, Prefect?"

"How else?" Sabinus shrugged his shoulders.

Rumors spread through Rome that Nero and his roistering companions were, in fact, behind the recent disorders in the city, and the fact that they were beyond arrest gave criminal elements in Rome an ingenious idea. Turning their own gangs loose on the city, they gave warning shouts of "Caesar! Caesar!" if any of the night watch tried to arrest them, leaving the police puzzled about whether to give chase or not.

But what destroyed Sabinus' patience was a very tragic bit of news: Julius Montanus, unable to stand the uncertainty, had dispatched a letter to the palace anyway, apologizing for the "accident" and craving the emperor's pardon. Nero, who had thought Montanus' blows normal enough, now read the letter with surprise and remarked, "So! He *knew* he was striking Nero, did he?" Then he issued orders. Montanus committed suicide.

Sabinus slumped down in his chair at the report, strangling an ink well until his knuckles whitened. "*Why* didn't poor Montanus keep his head?" he muttered to himself. But the more appropriate query then posed itself: what had become of Rome when a senator had to apologize to a felon for defending his own wife? And then had to take his own life for his pains?

Sabinus immediately ordered his Urban Cohorts into the streets, and soon Rome was crawling with so many troops it resembled a captured city. Next, although they outranked him, he summoned Seneca and Burrus down to a conference at city headquarters. They were not offended, for here they could converse in the kind of privacy denied them up on the Palatine.

Embarrassed and almost despairing, Seneca threw up his hands and admitted, "It's all we can do to *try* to control him, Sabinus. He now knows, unfortunately, that he's lord of the world. And all his young friends are filling his ears with slogans like, 'Is Nero a slave to Burrus and Seneca? Show them who's master of Rome!'—that sort of thing, and, for the moment, he's taking their advice. But I don't think we've lost him. He's going through a period of his life in which he craves adventure and danger."

"Granted," said Sabinus. "But meanwhile, Rome's being torn apart by street gangs. We're in the worst crisis since the 'municipal wars' of Cicero's time."

"I know. We'll have to act now. I'll tell Nero that criminal gangs are copying his escapades, and it just *has* to stop. I think he'll listen."

"All right," Sabinus replied, "but if he doesn't take your advice, I want you, Burrus, to send an agent to follow Nero's retinue at night and alert us where they're headed. We'll have police ready and waiting."

"Good," said Seneca. "And when these nightly exploits get less rewarding for Caesar, he'll soon tire of them. Meanwhile, I'll try to deepen his interest in literature and the arts. If that fails, there's always sports, the races—*anything* to get his mind off this . . . this pillage."

The strategy eventually succeeded. After several run-ins with Sabinus' police, Nero grew weary of his mad lust for nocturnal adventure and abandoned the escapades. In the meantime, Sabinus had restored order in the city. Rome was civilized once again.

15

AULUS' MEMOIRS of the campaign in Britain—the project forever interrupted by Rome's political turbulence—were finally completed. Finding a publisher was simple enough. Several had even
approached Aulus, though everyone knew the manuscript would
finally go to Atticus House. The firm had been founded by T. Pomponius Atticus, Cicero's close friend, who happened to be Pomponia's great-grandfather, and her relatives were still in charge.

The publishers invited the Plautii to pay them a visit on the great
day when production of the book began. The author and his wife
were there, as were Sabinus and Plautia. "They're already beyond
your introduction," the director told them. "And I also have a happy
surprise for you, Senator. Atticus House will publish . . . *one hundred* copies in the first edition."

"That many?" Aulus seemed staggered by the news.

"How will you ever sell them all?" Pomponia wondered, until she
saw her husband glaring at her.

"Oh, we're not worried." The director smiled. "Of course, the Britannic War was fourteen years ago, and we do wish we'd had the
manuscript earlier. But the name Aulus Plautius is still revered in
Rome. Here we are. Step inside, please."

A hundred scribes were seated at rows of oblong tables, writing on rolls of papyrus coiled at both ends. At the front of the hall on a raised dais sat a reader with Aulus' manuscript. Aulus heard his own words being enunciated loudly in a monotonous but precise voice, while the corps of scribes busily copied it all down word for word. Hands were occasionally raised when scribes wanted to know the spelling of a difficult British name or term.

The director walked over to the nearest scribe and showed Aulus the quality of the papyrus he had chosen. "It's *hieratica,* Senator, Egypt's very best."

Several weeks later, the publisher personally delivered four sets of author's scrolls at the Plautius residence. Each book comprised three scrolls, wrapped in a parchment cover marked with the author's name and the title *De bello Britannico* (*On the Britannic War*) in large red letters.

Smiling, and with the immense pride of new authorship, Aulus carefully unrolled the first scroll and showed his wife the dedication:

> For my magnificent
> Pomponia Graecina,
> *sine qua non*

She had known nothing about it. Several great tears filled her eyes, and she pulled Aulus' leathery cheek down to her lips.

Over the next weeks, enough colleagues in the Senate stopped Aulus to comment on passages of his work to assure him that his lines were circulating in fact. But it was on such a day that a shattering blow struck the Plautii.

Aulus would never purge himself of the bitter, corrosive memory of that morning in the Senate. The consul had just called for new business, when chubby little Cossutianus Capito stood up to deliver a prepared statement. Capito was a minor senator known for disreputable dealings, and one of the most feared informers in Rome. Stretching out his right arm, he began in a shrill, piping voice, "I regret to detain you, Conscript Fathers, with a charge against the family of a colleague, but the matter must be made public if we are to maintain the sanctity of Rome and her gods. I herewith accuse the Lady Pomponia Graecina, wife of our illustrious Aulus Plautius, of practicing a dangerous and alien superstition."

A hubbub arose in the august chamber. Aulus, who sat bolt upright at Pomponia's name, clutched the cold marble slab on which he was sitting and stared at the accuser. Capito continued in his strident, abrasive tone.

"The Lady Pomponia has become a devotee of a weird and noxious cult, somewhat related to Judaism but quite different from it. The cult has been illegal at Rome ever since the Divine Claudius expelled its members eight years ago after the Trans-Tiber riots."

Immediately Thrasea Paetus was on his feet to interrupt. "The *Senate* decides whether a cult is legal or illegal at Rome, and I know of no senatorial decrees on this matter." Gray-haired and mid-sized, Thrasea was the most independent, fearless, and candid member of the Senate, the non-compromiser among colleagues, many of whom were toadies. He continued in a cool, contained tone, "What is the name of this cult, Senator Capito?"

"I wish I knew! Like Hercules slaying the hydra, it comes up in many new places with as many new names. First its members were called 'Followers of the Way,' then 'Nazarenes,' and now, as I understand it, the term is 'Christiani.'"

Aulus' palms were clammy and his mood equally divided between anger and embarrassment. Half the Senate was glancing in his direction. But his nephew Quintus Lateranus loyally hurried over to sit beside him.

"The Lady Pomponia," Capito continued, "in order to worship with this cult—and who knows for what other, perhaps illicit, purposes?—makes secret visits by night to the house of a Jewish Christianus named Aquila on the Aventine, and—"

"You *dare* impugn the honor of Senator Plautius' wife?" Lateranus stood up and shouted in a rage.

A great commotion arose, and the consul rapped for order. Then he recognized Thrasea. Fixing an icy glare at the smallish accuser, Thrasea measured his words. "It is not enough that our unworthy colleague has seen fit to invent edicts of the Senate—for whatever tawdry purposes of personal aggrandizement. He must also try to besmirch one of the great families of Rome, particularly the wife of the man to whom the Empire remains in debt. Since it is now a question of her good name and family honor, I move that we follow the ancient custom and refer this case to her own family tribunal. In this way, our ears need not be assaulted by what will doubtless prove to be a worthless and self-serving accusation."

"*Euge! Euge!*" the shouts rang out. "Well said! So be it!"

Capito tried to reply. "But this is a matter of grave—"

"*Order!*" the consul cried. "There is support for Senator Paetus' suggestion, and we shall vote on it." He glared at the accuser. Then he announced, "All those in favor of committing this charge to the family tribunal of Senator Aulus Plautius, move to the right. Those opposed, to the left."

The vote was a magnificent demonstration of support for Aulus: 320 in his favor, 24 opposed. Immediately he asked for the floor. In a remarkably steady voice for one whose emotions were churning, he said, "Thank you, my colleagues. But I must assure you that, in conducting this trial, I shall set before me the example of the first Brutus, who judged and condemned his own sons when he found them guilty. I shall also request that one of the clerks of the Senate record the entire proceedings and make them available to you. And you are all welcome at the hearing, which I shall conduct tomorrow morning."

"*Euge! Euge!*"

When they left the Senate chamber, Aulus and Quintus headed directly for city headquarters. Five minutes later, three men were seen crossing the Forum and climbing the familiar route up to the Palatine.

Seneca and Burrus seemed as disturbed as Aulus. "First of all, you should know that Nero had nothing to do with this," Seneca advised, "and we just found out who did. Can you guess?"

"No," Aulus snapped.

"The empress mother."

"Agrippina?"

"Yes, she's calling it a 'patriotic gesture' to expose one who might corrupt the state with a new religion. Probably she also has something against your Pomponia—what, we don't know. At any rate, she's been having her followed."

Sabinus seemed to hear a voice saying, "First those you love . . . and then you." He interrupted the dialogue, "Gentlemen, I hadn't wanted to trouble any of you with my personal problems, but the time has come." He went on to reveal the threats Agrippina had made at his inaugural banquet. All four looked at him with astonishment.

"But the important thing is this," Seneca commented. "Nero,

evidently, isn't interested in the matter. So don't let him be, Aulus. The 'domestic tribunal' idea is superb."

"Thrasea has a great mind," Burrus observed. "So simply acquit Pomponia and have done with it, my friend."

"Not so fast," Aulus responded. "If Pomponia *is* guilty, I'm not going to dismiss the case."

Seneca looked at him curiously and then smiled. "You know, Aulus, you *are* one of the last of the old Romans . . . you and Thrasea. I really think you *would* condemn her."

"But who are these Christiani anyway?" Sabinus wondered.

Burrus and Seneca shrugged their shoulders. Aulus related what he knew about the Christians, and since Aquila figured so prominently in his report, Quintus said, "I'll go over to the Aventine and question him. That will help me in preparing the defense."

"*You'll* defend her?" Aulus asked.

"Could I do less for my favorite aunt?"

Aulus spent the rest of the day summoning relatives and witnesses, and preparing for the trial. That evening he had a long talk with Pomponia. Some of the accusation was substantially true, and both knew it. In recent months, Pomponia *had* made frequent trips to Aquila's, for a congregation of the Christians assembled there each Sunday night. No, she had not formally joined them through a certain washing rite of theirs, but she had not kept her interest in them secret from Aulus. For his part, he had tried to dissuade her by every means short of outright quarantine, but Pomponia was a free woman and could come and go as she pleased.

Before falling asleep that night, Pomponia reached over to touch her husband's arm. "Are you sorry you married me, Aulus?" she asked. There was a silence longer than she had feared before Aulus managed a quiet "No."

"That's not very convincing," she sighed. "Though I can't really blame you. I . . . . I never wanted any of this to happen. *Why* can't I believe as I wish? Quietly? In my own way?"

"You could have, I suppose, if it hadn't become public knowledge."

"Rome has dozens of different religions, hundreds of philosophies. Why should they be so concerned about the Christians?"

"It's not that so much, Pomponia. It's Agrippina and her vendetta against us. Besides Sabinus rejecting her, she learned about your remark at the betrothal: 'These delicacies are more reliable than Agrippina's.' Somehow, it got out."

"Well, why not explain that to the Senate, then?"

"Ha!" Aulus huffed. "Attack the emperor's mother in public? Besides which, your . . . beliefs are now a matter that must be decided in court, whatever motives were behind the suit."

She was silent for several moments. Then she said, quietly, "I know you, my love. You *could* find me guilty, couldn't you?"

"If the evidence warrants it."

"What would the punishment be?"

"Probably none, *if* you rejected this superstition immediately." He said it with obvious animus.

"I don't believe I could do that, Aulus."

"Then I'd probably have to stand by Claudius' precedent in the case of illegal religions."

"What's that?"

"Exile from Rome."

There was another silence. "So? You'd exile your own wife?" she finally asked.

"I'd *have* to, Pomponia. There would be no other way. No other honorable way. Can't you see that *I'll* be on trial tomorrow too? As judge?"

Turning away from him in bed, she let the dreadful impasse finally register on her emotions. She started crying very quietly, hoping he would not notice.

Aulus reached over to stroke her hair. "Don't worry, carissima," he said. "I'd join you . . . wherever I had to send you. It might even be the excuse I need to leave Nero's cesspool."

Before falling asleep, Aulus suddenly realized the extreme irony of it all: the Christians *were* going to have a test case for themselves anyway, and right under his own Roman's nose! Thrice-cursed the day that cursed tentmaker ever set foot in his house!

By midmorning, their atrium was filled with solemn-faced relatives and friends who were milling about nervously and conversing in muted tones. Thrasea and a number of senatorial colleagues were there, as well as all Plautii who could be reached in time, for the honor of the family name required it. Sabinus and Plautia had arrived earlier, while the prosecution, represented by Cossutianus Capito and several of his aides, stood off in a corner by themselves.

Capito was furious that the trial had been remanded to Aulus' family tribunal—a legal throwback to Republican Rome—and he would not have bothered pursuing the case further had the empress mother not insisted on it. Aulus' natural bias in favor of his own wife would at least be tempered by the Senate's interest in his impartiality, Capito knew, for the clerk of the Senate was there to record the proceedings word for word.

Pomponia now appeared, clad in the customary dark mourning garments of one about to face trial. The excited babble stilled to a sympathetic hush as she walked through the atrium into the peristyle, followed by the whole assembly.

At the center of the hall, Aulus sat down on an ivory curule or judge's chair, a memento of his own consulship. His wife took a seat directly in front of him. To her right was Quintus Lateranus to conduct the defense. To her left, a suspicious-looking Capito took his place, along with his aides, while the assembly seated itself through the rest of the mansion.

Aulus looked up and said, "At the request of the defendant, this court will dispense with the taking of omens at this time"—a sudden mumble vibrated through the hall—"because as judge I took them earlier this morning, and I assure you they were quite favorable." Sabinus thought he detected a low smile on Aulus' face.

Then, turning to the prosecution, he said, "Yesterday in the Senate, you brought two charges against the defendant. In essence, they were: first, that she is a follower of the Christian cult, which may be illegal in Rome; and second, that she may have gone to the house of one Aquila for immoral purposes."

Capito stood up at once. "If it please the court, I should like to withdraw the second charge entirely. It was . . . totally unwarranted."

"I shall allow you to withdraw it only upon your apology for an unnecessary and malicious blunder, for which I could hold you personally liable."

Capito looked down and made what he hoped was a suitably abject apology. He had meant only that some of the Christian practices were immoral, he said.

"That will be determined in the course of this hearing," said Aulus. "Proceed with your accusation."

Capito began deliberately. "I shall attempt to prove, by the testimony of several witnesses, that the defendant did indeed frequent the house of one Aquila on the Aventine hill for purposes of cultic worship, and that this sect of the Christiani so-called is illegal, subversive to the state, and a foreign superstition of the worst kind."

Lateranus stood up. "If the honored judge will permit, the defense would like to simplify this hearing by agreeing to one of the charges: Pomponia Graecina *did* in fact visit the house of a couple named Aquila and Priscilla on the Aventine for purposes of Christian worship."

The peristyle broke into a low rumble of surprise.

"Order!" Aulus called out. Then, looking at his wife, he asked, "Pomponia Graecina: *did* you frequent the house of Aquila, as charged?"

"I did," she replied, her eyes fixed on the tessellated floor over which she had walked so many times.

"Was the cult of the Christiani practiced at this house while you were there?"

"Yes . . ."

"Are you a member of this cult?" Aulus continued.

"Well . . . no. No, I am not."

"But do you share their beliefs? Their practices?" Capito interposed.

There was a tomblike silence while everyone cocked an ear to hear her reply. Pomponia said nothing for some moments. Then she admitted, "Yes. I do."

Again the undulating ripple of surprise, as relative nudged relative and stole glances at the city prefect and his wife sitting just behind the accused.

"Very well, then," said Aulus. "It remains for this hearing to determine whether the Christians practice a *religio licita*—a legally accepted religion—or not. If they do, the defendant is not guilty. If not, she has committed a crime. Do you accept this as the remaining purpose of this hearing, Senator Capito?"

"Yes. Yes indeed."

"And do you, Senator Lateranus?"

"Well, not quite, honored Judge. What would happen, for example, if it could be demonstrated that the Christians, while not yet possessing the status of *religio licita*, might still cherish harmless beliefs and practices not at all dangerous to the state so that they could be accorded legal status in the future? In that case, it would be morally wrong to condemn the defendant."

Aulus pondered the objection for a moment, but then replied, "That would be for a future senatorial hearing to decide. But in any case, the defendant would be guilty of practicing an illegal religion in the present."

The boyish, handsome features of Lateranus lifted in surprise. Sabinus turned to Plautia and whispered, "He's making the first ruling against his own wife!" Pomponia raised her eyes to explore those of her husband.

Turning to the prosecution, Aulus asked, "What evidence do you have to support your charge?"

Capito stood up to corroborate his indictment, and it was clear that this time he was much better prepared than in the Senate. Beginning with the "Chrestus" riots in the Trans-Tiber, he showed how Claudius had banished the Christian leaders and added his rescript against grave robbery, the hoax on which the new cult was building itself. The fact that the Christians had returned in the meantime was due to the generous oversight of the new government, but such laxity must no longer continue.

"This is a very dangerous cult," Capito argued, his high pitch escalating in excitement. "Their secret assemblies witness a nauseous rite in which they eat the body and drink the blood of their god—not really, of course. Like the Druids, they probably get their ingredients from people whom they kidnap and then sacrifice." He paused and noted with satisfaction the look of horror on everyone's face. "But I've heard another and even worse report: they set a large, oblong wheat cake before their initiates and tell them to carve it up. They do, but the cake screams! For inside is a little sleeping baby . . . who is then murdered . . . drained . . . and eaten."

"All this is a *lie!*" Pomponia shouted, rising from her chair. "A horrendous *falsehood!*"

"You'll have your chance to testify later," Aulus admonished her. "The prosecution may continue."

"Some of their rites are more enjoyable, I understand," Capito said with a leer. "The men and women meet for a very special kind of worship. They enter a room, where only one lamp is burning . . . on the floor in the middle of the chamber. Then they select one another in the flickering light, sometimes even brother and sister. Finally a little dog is let loose in the chamber, and it dashes for a bone that is tied to the lamp, toppling it over. The room is plunged into darkness. Aha! And then—"

"Disgusting *fabrications!*" Pomponia cried, against a background of astonished whispering.

"All right, all right. Let me spare you any of their other lurid rites. Their beliefs are equally revolting to civilized Romans, for they hate the world and the people in it. It's not good enough for them, and they look forward to a . . . a mythical paradise at the end of life. Their faith centers on a convicted criminal who was crucified by one of our governors. They seek to overthrow the state. They despise the emperor. They practice sorcery. They reject the gods of the Senate and the Roman People. For this reason, and many more, this is a most dangerous and vicious cult that will destroy Rome if it is not halted now . . . today . . . at this very tribunal."

Then, looking at Aulus, he concluded, "Some have thought me a fool to prosecute this case, honored Judge, before one so closely related to the defendant. I replied, 'You do not know Aulus Plautius. This is a man who puts Rome first in his mind, in his heart, and in his judgment.' Relying on your patriotism and sense of justice, I rest my indictment."

Aulus found the final flattery especially galling, because it raised again the tender issue of his impartiality. "The prosecution," he announced, "has made many charges, some of them new. But I must ask again: what *evidence*, apart from rumor and hearsay, do you have that the Christians believe and practice all these things?"

"Oh, this is very simple." Turning to the defendant, Capito asked, "Lady Pomponia . . . *do* you believe in that Christus who was crucified as a criminal by our governor of Judea?"

"Yes, but—"

"And you do *not* believe in Father Jupiter, Mother Juno, Minerva, the divine Venus, and the other Olympian gods and goddesses, do you?"

"No . . ."

"And in your solemn rites, do you not claim to eat the body and drink the blood of your founder?"

"Well, yes, but this is—"

"And aren't little children also involved in your worship?"

"Certainly, but not in the way that—"

"By her own admission, then, the Christians believe substantially as I've indicated, even though I don't claim to have every detail accurate. And here is the rest of the evidence: written depositions from my infor— ah—aides who witnessed the defendant's presence at the house of Aquila."

Aulus took the testimony in hand and thumbed through it. "Before this hearing can continue," he announced, "I must have the opportunity of reading the depositions. This court is adjourned for two hours."

When the hearing resumed, Aulus handed the documents to the clerk of the Senate and said, "Let these be entered in the record of this hearing. But I must inform the prosecution that a great amount of rumor is included in these lines, not hard fact. They prove little more than the defendant's presence at meetings where there were readings and prayers and hymns. And the consumption of a little bread and wine."

"But this is such a *new* cult," Capito protested. "It's difficult to get decent information about it."

"Which is exactly what we must have. Perhaps the defense can supply it. Senator Lateranus?"

Quintus stood up and made a flowery little introduction that achieved little more than loosening his vocal cords. But when he focused on the charges, he became more effective. That Claudius had dismissed the leaders in *both* factions of the "Chrestus" riots proved nothing, he argued, because Jewish leaders had also been exiled, and Judaism was certainly a legal religion. Labeling the claims of human sacrifice "an absurd misunderstanding," Quintus did his best to disentangle the rites of what the Christians called "communion" and "baptism."

"Children are involved," he said, "but only to receive a sacred washing, *not* to give their blood! And those ridiculous rumors about indecencies in dark rooms probably grew out of their practice of greeting each other with a simple kiss as a 'brother' or 'sister' in their faith. Really now, that's rather harmless, isn't it, Senator Capito? Only a filthy mind would draw worse conclusions."

Capito flashed him an ugly scowl. Sabinus whispered to Plautia, "Don't worry, dear. My twin seems to have matters well in hand."

"It's true that the Christians reject the gods of the state," Quintus conceded. "But again, this doesn't make them guilty of practicing an illegal cult. The Jews also reject the Olympian deities, yet Rome, in its tolerance and maturity, permits such diversity in matters of religion. In fact, this is one of the glories of the Empire.

"But far more serious are the charges that Christians hate the state, seek to overthrow it, and despise the emperor. I call to witness the husband and wife known as Aquila and Priscilla."

Immediately all heads craned to get a glimpse of the pair who were most responsible for getting the clan into legal difficulty. What they saw disappointed them: a simply dressed couple who stepped before Aulus' tribunal and seemed not at all threatened by the possible hostility about them. Priscilla was a composed, dark-haired woman of middle age with soft, cream-colored skin and nut-brown eyes. She was clutching a scroll under her arm.

Aulus gave them both a look of ill-disguised scorn. This was the pair that had caused the present family torture.

"Are you both Christians?" Lateranus asked them.

"Yes," each replied.

"But aren't you Jews too?"

"Yes," replied Aquila. "The two are not exclusive."

"This is a point to which we must return. But for now, give us a brief summary of what you Christians believe. Perhaps your wife might do this, since the defendant is also a woman."

Priscilla explained her beliefs in simple, direct language, but her mention of some salvation concept with its promise of a resurrection after death was difficult for the hearers to understand. Then Quintus questioned Aquila about the Christians' attitude toward the Roman state. His reply was in such marked contrast to Capito's charges that the prosecutor leaped to his feet, objecting, "How do we know he's telling the truth? Suddenly, these cultists seem to have become patriots!"

Lateranus frowned. "If you call his veracity into question, does the name Paul of Tarsus mean anything to you?"

"Yes, he seems to be the chief troublemaker in this sect. He goes from place to place in Greece and Asia, trying to make Christians of the whole Greek world."

"Then Paul of Tarsus would speak with some authority for this sect?" Quintus asked.

"Yes. Why do you ask?"

"Aquila, please read several excerpts from the letter that your people in Rome just received from this same Paul of Tarsus."

"But it's written in Greek, Senator," he replied.

"No problem. Most of us here are educated enough to understand Greek. I'll translate for the rest."

Priscilla handed the scroll to Aquila, opening it to a marked section. He began reading from the thirteenth chapter:

Let everyone be subject to the governing authorities. . . .
Pay them your obligations, taxes to whom taxes are due, tribute
to whom tribute, respect to whom respect is due, honor to
whom honor.

Owe no one anything except to love one another, for he who
loves his neighbor has fulfilled the law. The commandments,
"You shall not commit adultery, You shall not kill, You shall
not steal, You shall not covet" and many other commandments
are all summed up in this sentence: "You shall love your neighbor as yourself". . . .

"Thank you, Aquila," said Quintus. Then he gave a loose translation in Latin and commented, "Now it seems, Senator Capito, that the official teachings of this sect are quite the opposite of what you have suggested."

"That still doesn't make it a legal religion," Capito objected, taking his cue from Aulus' ruling.

"We shall now deal with that issue. In your friend Paul's letter, Aquila, there was reference to various 'commandments.' Are these not the same as the famous Ten Commandments of the Jews?"

"Yes. Certainly."

"Do you regard yourself as a Jew? I mean, not only in origin, but in belief?"

"Yes . . . but there are various kinds of Jews, of course."

"Precisely. And your friend, Paul of Tarsus. Is he a Jew?"

"Yes."

"And Jesus, the founder of your sect. Was he a Jew?"

"Yes."

"And his followers in Judea—Jewish?"

"Yes, mostly."

"But Gentiles may also become Christiani?"

"Oh, yes. The faith is open to everyone."

"At this moment among your Christians, are there more Jews or Gentiles?"

"Jews."

"Thank you, Aquila. You may be seated." Quintus now turned to the defendant and said, "Lady Pomponia, the questions I shall now address to you are very important. Please consider them carefully before answering. The first is this: do you believe in one God, the God of the Jews?"

Pomponia replied, "Yes, I do."

"Do you believe in the Ten Commandments of the Jews?"

"Yes."

"Do you believe that the Scriptures of the Jews are their God's revelation?"

"Yes."

"Well, then, distinguished Judge, Senator Capito, honored friends and relatives, we must come to the quite obvious conclusion which has been implicit all along: the Christiani are merely a sect *within Judaism*—no more, no less—and as such they are indeed members of a *religio licita*, which is protected by our Law of Associations."

Excited murmuring broke out. Capito was on his feet, objecting, "If they're all Jews, how come they rioted against each other in the Trans-Tiber?"

"Everyone knows the Jews have many factions. I understand there are Pharisees who believe in a resurrection and Sadducees who do not. Yet they're both good Jews. There are Essenes and Christians. There are Greek Jews, Egyptian Jews, Roman Jews. Their customs differ but they all believe in one God and his commandments. That's what makes them Jews."

Capito countered by insisting that the Christians had a different enough faith to be a wholly different cult. Quintus rebutted by asking what was more basic than belief or non-belief in an afterlife, and yet no one doubted that Pharisees and Sadducees were both Jews. Clearly, he had been well schooled by Aquila.

Both prosecution and defense delivered their summations. Finally Lateranus concluded, "Since the defendant seems to believe everything the Jews believe—so what if it is *more* than they believe in the case of the prophet Jesus—and since the founder, the first followers, the present leaders, and most of the members of this faction were or are Jews, it *is* a Jewish sect, pure and simple. Therefore the Lady Pomponia is *not* guilty of practicing a foreign superstition, as charged, but a legal religion, recognized by Rome and protected by our Law of Associations. We rest our case."

Aulus adjourned the hearing while he pondered his decision. Sabinus badly wanted to talk to him as he walked for some minutes alone out in his garden, but he thought better of it. He had nothing but the profoundest sympathy for the turmoil that had to be boiling inside Aulus' mind. Whatever his decision, Quintus had done extremely well, Sabinus thought, and he told him so.

Presently, Aulus stepped back inside. After a final check of depositions and a brief conference with the Senate clerk, he again mounted his tribunal. For several moments he glanced down at his wife with a sad expression, so sad, in fact, that it frightened the Plautii. At last, he announced, "I must pass this judgment with keen personal disappointment that *any* member of our senatorial order—the fact that she is my wife is incidental—should have become converted to Judaism in any form. But by participating in the rites of the Christian sect of Judaism, the defendant has not exceeded the bounds of what is legal. I therefore find the defendant, Pomponia Graecina, not guilty."

Plautia ran over to her mother and twined her arms about her neck, crying with relief. Sabinus walked over to Quintus and fairly pounded his shoulders. Aulus would later congratulate Lateranus on his defense strategy, but for the moment he had to continue pursuing a neutral posture. He was moved, though, when Thrasea Paetus walked over, shook his hand with a broad smile, but said absolutely nothing. Aulus did not feel in a mood to be congratulated.

Capito, meanwhile, had hurried over to Aquila, barking the question, "Is your conscience entirely clear, *worthy* tentmaker?"

"Yes. Why do you ask?"

"Taking refuge under the protective blanket of Judaism? Are you Christians *really* Jews?"

"Yes, in all the senses brought out in the trial. In fact, we call ourselves 'the true Israel.' And we hope and pray that all Jews will become one with us."

"Hmmmm. I wonder what the Jewish leaders in the Trans-Tiber would have to say about that."

Before Aquila could reply, Capito and his aides took their leave in something of a huff. But the Plautii, of course, were obliged to host their vast clan for dinner.

When Aulus returned to the Senate the next day, only a few made the error of congratulating him on his conduct of the trial. Most of his friends—those who really knew the man—simply treated him as if nothing had happened, for, in their opinion, nothing had.

Aulus hoped they were right, but he was not entirely convinced. He felt that he could never share his wife's new religious interests, and the fact that she believed something which he did not bothered him more than he cared to admit.

16

"WE NEED a closer link between the city and the Empire," Seneca told Sabinus during a chat at municipal headquarters. "So Burrus and I want you to attend our conferences with Nero each Friday in the palace. Caesar admires you, and your presence would do much to help our cause."

Sabinus listed a half-dozen reasons why he did not especially favor the idea, but Seneca brushed them aside in the name of Duty. Duty was deity in Rome. The sure way to bend any Roman statesman to your cause was to invoke that quasi-magical term Duty.

Sabinus now met with the emperor, Seneca, and Burrus around a black marble table in Nero's office suite each Friday morning. This was the council of state that governed the city and the world—*urbem et orbem*. More casually, Sabinus called it his weekly "Date with Fate," for the decisions made by that foursome usually produced repercussions across the entire Mediterranean.

Seeing Nero regularly, and at close range, Sabinus was pleased to note some maturity, finally some improvement in the young emperor's approach and bearing. The way he reacted to the aftermath of Pomponia's trial, for example, was almost heartening. No sooner had Sabinus arrived one Friday than Nero told him wryly, "The Lord Mayor of Rome may be delighted to learn that Cossutianus

Capito, who prosecuted his mother-in-law, has just been indicted by the Senate for extortion, and I've given him a week to get out of Italy."

Sabinus' smile was so enthusiastic that it brought chuckles from the other three. Seneca went on to explain, "Last year, you'll recall, Capito was governor of Cilicia?"

"Yes . . ."

"Well, our good friend Thrasea Paetus helped a delegation of Cilicians indict him for extortion. Thrasea did such a noble job of it that Capito didn't even try to defend himself. He simply threw up his pudgy hands and waddled out of the Senate."

Nero looked at Sabinus and frowned. "I ought to be embarrassed about all this, you know, since it was my own mother who egged Capito on in that suit against dear Pomponia."

"Oh?" Sabinus responded, as if it were fresh news. He looked with some concern to Seneca and Burrus.

"But then"—Nero cleared his throat—"it's not the first time that Mother and I have disagreed on something." Nero's smile broke the tension and gave Sabinus some relief from his gnawing concern about Agrippina and her threats. Perhaps this major reverse would keep the harpy at bay.

Seneca's tutoring, his calculated gamble might yet pay off, Sabinus reflected. The twenty-year-old Nero was now expressing himself well at their council meetings, while classical culture seemed to have taught him restraint. When the four approved plans for a new amphitheater in Rome, Nero humanely decreed that no combat there be carried to the death. Greek games, which were bloodless athletic contests, had inspired him.

When Sabinus returned home that Friday, he told Plautia of the favorable signs in Nero. "Is it possible?" she responded. "Can we really hope that it will still work out, Sabinus? That violence and murder in the palace are all history now?"

That evening, Nero had dinner with his close friend and comrade-in-escapade, Marcus Otho, a fashionable young dandy who had become the emperor's alter ego. Of medium size, like Nero, Otho was slightly bowlegged and splayfooted, but he had a woman's concern for the rest of his appearance. He depilated his body and drenched his feet in scent. No one, not even Nero, knew that he wore a well-fashioned hairpiece.

When they had finished supper, Nero suggested an evening fling, but Otho begged off with a simple, "I have to get home."

"What is it, friend?" Nero frowned. "Nothing's come between us, has it?"

"Perish the very thought, Caesar," Otho apologized. "It's just that—"

"Lately I almost have to *order* you to join us for a night on the town. And the women we find—you take no interest in them. What's the matter with you, man?"

"The simplest reason in the world," Otho chuckled. "I'm in love."

"Good for you," Nero smiled. "Who?"

"Poppaea Sabina, of course."

"But that's your own wife, Otho."

"It *is* a little unique, isn't it?" He smirked. "But that girl's making me . . . deliriously happy. She eclipses everyone. She's—well, Poppaea is the most serenely beautiful creature in all Rome. No, in all the Empire."

"Rather extravagant claim, isn't it? Of course, I've never seen the girl without that veil of hers."

"She still wears it whenever she goes out in public. Has to, in fact."

"Why?"

"She'd disrupt the city if people saw her. Too striking. Too extraordinary."

"Enough of that, Otho!" Nero laughed. "It's sweet and old-fashioned for a man to be proud of his wife, but let's not carry it too far."

"No, that girl is Venus herself. And she has a mind too—enough wit to keep a philosopher on tenterhooks. After we . . . after our embraces, it's actually fun just to *talk* with Poppaea."

"I know. That's the way it is with Acte."

Otho made no comment, for comparisons were decidedly not in order here. But he was telling himself, "No contest." Then he smiled and rose from the table.

"Where are you going? Home?"

"Of course. And forgive me, good friend"—Otho sighed extravagantly—"I'm returning to that treasure for which all men pray . . . but which I possess."

"Come now, Otho! You sound like a slave auctioneer. Or a pander."

"Or a supremely happy husband. You'd agree if you saw her, Caesar."

"Well, let me see her then. Bring her to dinner here . . . to make up for my missing your wedding."

Otho thought for a moment, then nodded. "Why not?"

"When? Is tomorrow night all right?"

"Should be fine."

"But fair warning: I'll give you my candid opinion—privately, of course—and you mustn't take anything amiss. We'll still be friends?"

"Always!" Otho smiled.

The next afternoon, Nero ordered a private dinner for three and waited for Otho and his wife with rising interest. He had spent an abnormal amount of time getting himself dressed and groomed, and was now redolent of his favorite Arabian perfume. He glanced into a large mirror and tried, for the first time, to look at himself objectively. As an emperor he had no limitations, of course. But as a man? His height? Average. His appearance? A few detestable spots and pimples still marked his skin, but they were well covered this evening. His darkening blond hair, set in rows of curls, his deep blue eyes, and handsome features more than compensated for his skin problems, he thought.

Nero was satisfied. And no one would have dared complete his physical description, at least not to his face. But his perfumes never quite disguised his problems with body odor. His features were effeminate rather than handsome. His eyes were a weak slate blue— hardly the royal blue he imagined. And a thick, squat neck, protuberant belly, and spindly legs completed the bodily ensemble of the man behind the emperor.

Finally Otho and Poppaea were announced, and Nero rose to greet them. Poppaea was wearing a thin aquamarine stola, with gilded jewelry to set off tresses of the same golden amber hue. Her hair, the blondest Nero had ever seen, was combed back and fastened. But everything below her eyes was covered with a gossamer veil. Ridiculous conceit!

Said Nero, "Forgive me, fair Poppaea, for not having asked you to the palace before this."

"Caesar needs beg no one's forgiveness"—she smiled—"simply because he is Caesar."

Nero admitted to himself that the vain thing did have beautiful skin and entrancing greenish-blue eyes. And she knew it. More the pity.

A butler brought in a flagon of wine and three jeweled cups. "A bit of Falernian to whet the appetite?" Nero asked, chuckling inwardly at what would follow: the little minx would have to remove her precious veil to drink the wine.

Poppaea shook her head. "I'd prefer mine with dinner. I want to relish every moment of the evening, Caesar, and I fear your Falernian would dull me a bit."

Nero looked at her lamely, trying to control his impulse to reach over and tear her precious veil to shreds. Poppaea, evidently, was fully aware of the impression she was making on him if those laughing eyes were any indication. Presently, they all reclined for dinner.

Nero never saw her take the veil off, but when next he looked at Poppaea, she had removed it and was smiling at him with lips parted slightly to reveal teeth of flawless white. The rest of her face easily fulfilled what was promised by the forehead and eyes. Poppaea *was* striking. In fact, she was a masterpiece, Nero thought, as he took in her exquisitely chiseled features. Small wonder Otho was so dazzled, the lucky fellow. And she proved an extraordinarily good conversationalist at dinner as well.

Later on, when they prepared to leave for the evening, Otho pulled Nero aside to gauge his reactions. "Well—what do you think?" he probed.

"Love to twist your nose a bit"—Nero grinned—"but . . . forget it. Yes, she *is* a splendid girl. And what's more, you don't deserve her, you scoundrel."

"I know," Otho sighed. "But I'll try to make the best of it."

Poppaea's thanks seemed warm and very genuine, and again her fascinating eyes seemed to pierce into Nero's soul. Was he imagining a slight extra pressure in her handclasp as she said good-bye?

He must *not* play the fool, Nero solemnly decided after they left, giving way to a hasty infatuation like some smitten schoolboy . . . embarrassing . . . not fair to Acte . . . or Otho, for that matter . . . He certainly mustn't fall in *love* with the girl, for what if she were really aiming for power? . . . Or maybe she only wanted the satisfaction of turning a Caesar's head . . . Or maybe she wasn't interested in the least. But *such* a striking creature!

The next morning, a courier delivered a note in small, cursive lettering:

Poppaea Sabina to Nero Caesar, greeting. Last night was a delight, thanks to you, though I do apologize for my coy performance with the veil. (Will I ever reach maturity?) I am, however, old enough to set a good table, and Otho and I would like to invite you to dinner a week from today, if Caesar will not find a visit here demeaning. Farewell.

"I have to wait a whole *week?*" Nero moaned, until he realized that the messenger was still standing there, waiting for a reply. "Tell your mistress that I'll be delighted to come."

After a week in which he maundered in distraction about the palace, Nero arrived at Otho's house on the appointed evening. Poppaea greeted him heartily, her hypnotic eyes burrowing into him once again. She was dressed in a diaphanous saffron house tunic that set her figure off to much better advantage than the smothering folds of a stola.

"Where's Otho?" Nero wondered, gazing for a moment at the entrancing twin hillocks of yellow gauze that crowned Poppaea's chest.

"I have another apology to make," she said, with a sly little smile. "I should have sent a message, but it was getting too close to dinner. Otho, unfortunately, has urgent business down in Antium and won't be back till late tonight. But I hope you'll still have dinner with me?"

Through a light, tasty supper of five courses, Nero barely noticed what he was eating, for Poppaea's animated dialogue ranged over many subjects, betraying a quick and versatile intellect. Like himself, she was a restless soul, trying to break free of the ordinary, the expected, and the customary. She was entranced with art and drama. She toyed with astrology. She was fascinated by the eastern cults, and even admitted to a certain admiration for Judaism. No, she was not a proselyte, but the idea of believing in one supreme deity seemed appealing to her.

Nero agreed, but then, he was so captivated by the alluring girl he would have agreed to anything. Radiating her sensual charm all the while, Poppaea seemed even more beautiful than during her visit to the Palatine, probably because her honeyed strands of hair were not tied back but cascaded over the edge of the couch, glistening in the soft amber glow from the solitary candelabra on the table.

They had finished dinner, and the servants had retired. But they were still reclining at the table. Nero edged closer to Poppaea, his heart throbbing, and he brushed her cheek with a kiss. She turned the other way for a moment or two. But then, holding out both her arms, she slowly pressed her lips to his forehead, cheeks, and mouth, until he was groaning with anticipation. Her approach had been emboldened by the messenger's detailed report of Nero's reaction to her invitation.

"No, Nero," she said, suddenly holding him off. "First you have to know the whole truth about me."

"It can wait," he said in a husky voice.

"No. Else you'll think the worse of me later—a shameless girl who gives herself lightly."

"I won't. I promise."

"What I'm trying to tell you is this: my love for you isn't something sudden. I've seen you on many public occasions, and—I know it sounds impossible—but I . . . I think I fell in love with you even at a distance. I told myself it was madness, and I tried to forget you. But now, Nero, you must hear this confession: do you know why I married Otho?"

"Well, he's a grand and very handsome fellow . . . probably my closest friend."

"Yes—that second reason."

"What?"

"Simply *because* he was your closest friend, I knew someday I'd get to meet you. It's madness, isn't it? Sometimes I hate myself for using Otho that way. But . . . what choice does a woman have when she's so . . . *completely* in love?"

Nero had broken into a rapturous smile. "Darling, darling Poppaea," he whispered, touring her cheeks with burning kisses. "I had no idea. These are . . . the most wonderful words I've ever heard."

"You won't think badly of me?"

He shook his head emphatically.

She parted her lips and let him kiss her deeply. "This really is a . . . a culmination of a long romance, then, isn't it?" she whispered.

"Sweet Venus, how I love you," Nero crooned. Then he moved closer to her, kissing and caressing her until they were both smoldering with flames of desire. Moaning with quiet ecstasy, they embraced with reckless, heedless passion.

Nero had never known such joy. Sex he had sampled, almost to satiety. Love he had ventured with Acte. But Poppaea brought him the most intense blend of the two he had ever known. From that moment on, she would have to be part of his life, Nero vowed.

The problem of Otho posed itself immediately, of course. Nero was ashamed of himself for taking the wife of his best friend as mistress, but everything was now subordinated to his love for Poppaea. Otho, meanwhile, was trembling with outrage, cursing the day he had so stupidly boasted of Poppaea in front of the man he had thought his friend. However, there was little he could do now but play the bitter role of cuckold. Perhaps Nero would tire of her. Or she of him.

It was not to be. Nero grew hopelessly enthralled with Poppaea, but she complained that their love was hardly being expressed on an honorable level. "It . . . simply can't go on this way, Nero," she told him one night. "I come from too noble a family to be anyone's mistress, even Caesar's. Otho can't tolerate it any longer, of course. And sometimes I think we live better than you do here on the Palatine."

"How do you mean?" he scowled.

"I mean, Otho and I live as husband and wife. It *is* rather normal, isn't it? But you keep your own wife in a closet while you're enslaved to a slave—or an ex-slave, at any rate. Yes, I know you continue to see Acte. I suppose I'm jealous of every moment someone else spends in your arms, Nero."

"I despise Octavia. And I love you *far* more than Acte, *carissima optima.*"

"Well, as I said, it just . . . can't go on this way. Much as I love you, I'd sooner be wife to Otho than mistress to Nero."

Nero lost control of himself. He slammed his fist on a table of fretted ivory, cracking it neatly in half. Then he fired a salvo of abuse at Poppaea, followed by remorseful weeping. She let him vent a maelstrom of emotions without saying a word. Then, preparing to leave, she placed a good-bye kiss on the bared imperial neck, slumped over in dejection. Nero suddenly looked up and asked the question she had waited so long to hear: "You said you'd rather be Otho's wife than Nero's mistress, Poppaea. But what if you were to be . . . Nero's *wife?*"

She uttered a cry of joy and kissed him exuberantly. It would all be a lengthy process, he admitted, and he could promise no dates or schedule, but he would not rest until she were empress. Meanwhile, no matter where her husband was sent, she was to remain in Rome with him. Happily, she agreed.

Nero appointed Otho to the high post of governor of Lusitania.* For all intents and purposes, it was at the end of the world. Sadly, Otho packed his things, closed that chapter in his life entitled "Poppaea," and sailed to the far west. For the next decade, Lusitanians would find him a surprisingly able and honest governor. Apparently, he had left all his flaws of character back in Rome.

Just after Nero left at the close of one of their Friday conferences, Sabinus huddled with Seneca and Burrus for strategy. Poppaea was a powerful new force that had to be taken into account in the delicate balance of Roman statecraft. All three wondered anxiously to what extent ambition was fueling the fires of her love for Nero. Seneca had more information on her background, and he confided, "Poppaea is a less political girl than, say, Agrippina, but if Nero is determined to marry her, there could be danger."

"*Could* she become empress?" Sabinus asked. "I mean, is there legal precedent?"

"That's the problem we *didn't* have with Acte," Seneca responded. "As a freedwoman, Acte could never have aspired. But Poppaea is a daughter of the nobility. If Nero divorces Octavia, he certainly could raise Poppaea to the throne."

Burrus was shaking his head. "But if he divorces the daughter of Claudius, he severs his claim to empire," the praetorian commander warned. "The people won't stand for it. At least my praetorians won't."

An aide entered the room, whispered a long message into Seneca's ear, and then withdrew. The philosopher's brow knitted with concern. "We have a *major* problem, gentlemen. You know, of course, that Caesar moved his mother out of the palace some months ago into her own town house, but lately they seem to have become reconciled. Agrippina spent last night at the palace, and this noon she's having a private lunch with Nero."

"So?"

* Today called Portugal.

"You also know that she's *seething* over his affair with Poppaea—she's always been jealous of anyone coming between herself and Nero. Well, the palace maid who attended her this morning reported that while she was preening herself in front of a mirror, Agrippina talked to her reflected image and said, 'I'll never let that blond harlot have you, my son. I'll *get you myself,* first.' "

"What in the world is *that* supposed to mean?" Sabinus wondered.

"I have no idea. But to me it sounds threatening. Very threatening."

Burrus, in charge of palace security, suddenly came to life. "All right. I'll have the usual taster on duty in case she tries poison. And I'll also hide inside the observation cubicle in the dining room."

"What's that?" Sabinus asked.

"Claudius had it installed during one of his paranoid periods," Seneca explained. "It hasn't been used since. Nero doesn't even know it exists."

"Come to think of it," Burrus added, "if any infamy were attempted, I'd need witnesses. You both had better join me."

It was easily the most boring hour Sabinus had ever spent. He, Seneca, and Burrus were ensconced in a small closet peering into the palace dining room through a long slit cut into the wall. Nothing unusual transpired at the luncheon, other than that Nero was drinking more than usual. In fact, he was half intoxicated by now, and waved the taster out of the room. Burrus tensed at that point. Since Agrippina had been drinking hardly anything, her befuddled son was now more vulnerable than ever.

Three pairs of eyes watched as Agrippina moved closer to Nero. Burrus was breathing heavily, his hand clasped on the dagger at his side. Agrippina now removed her stola until only a sheer tunic of briefest dimensions hugged the still-lush contours of her body. Nero turned to look at her. For a moment, his eyes widened in surprise, but then his thick, wine-stained lips curled into a smile. She snuggled over next to him as they reclined at the table and took him in her arms in a motherly sort of way. But her maternal caresses suddenly grew wanton as she lavished kisses on his ears, and her fingers started probing forbidden regions. The drunken Nero began breathing heavily and reciprocating.

"By all the Olympian *gods!*" Sabinus whispered. "So *that's* how she's going to 'get him'!" He felt physically ill and nauseous.

Seneca had already hurried out of the closet in a quiet panic. Several minutes later he pushed Acte into the dining room; she rushed over to Nero and fell in a huddle at his feet, weeping and clutching at his knees. "*No,* Master!" she cried. "Not *that* crime . . . not incest! Rumors are already circulating about you and your mother."

"Wha' rumors?" Nero sat up.

"About what your mother just tried to do. I'll tell you this: the praetorians will *never* follow a Caesar guilty of . . . of such an outrage!" Then she shook with sobs.

Agrippina quickly refastened her tunic, beaming waves of cordial hatred at Acte. Then she rolled off her couch and flew out of the room in a rage.

Nero stroked Acte in consolation and tried to get up. But he was tipsy and lurched to one side. She had to help him out of the dining room.

As they left the closet, Sabinus debated whether or not to tell Plautia of the revolting scene. Was she old enough, or would she even understand the shabby story? Before leaving the palace, he asked Seneca what would happen if Poppaea learned, but the philosopher gave his shoulders a sad and vacant shrug.

The answer came later that day. Poppaea stormed into Nero's suite and fulminated, "And how is our darling Oedipus this evening?"

"I was drunk, Poppaea," he growled.

"Talk about my rivals!" she hissed. "I used to think a slave-girl was bad. Now, by all the gods, it's a *mother* too! Of course, incest's an old habit with her, and dear Uncle Claudius wasn't the first. How old was she when her brother Caligula first seduced her? Twelve?"

"I told you I didn't know what I was doing. And if it's any consolation to you, I . . . I'll never forgive Mother for *this.*"

"Oh yes you will! Just like all the other times. She threatens you, and you forgive her. She plots against you, and you forgive her. She defames you behind your back, steals from you, intrigues against you. And now, to cap it all off, she tries to seduce you too." Poppaea ranted on, knowing that she had to break the power of Agrippina forever if she were to marry Nero. Never again would there be an opportunity like this.

"Trust me, my darling," said Nero softly. "Leave it to me."

Nero banned his mother from the Palatine. Then he had friends start harassing her with petty lawsuits to keep her on the defensive. When she took a trip down to her country estates, he praised her for courting repose, implying that she would do well to stay away from Rome permanently.

But the steel-nerved, resilient woman had as much foolhardy courage as an army of the opposite sex, as much stamina as a troop of gladiators. She returned to Rome and tried to rebuild her power base once again through secret interviews with key members of the nobility and the military. She amassed a treasury, and, putting a brave front on it all, she told Nero quite scorchingly what she thought of him and his lawsuits. Rumors also surfaced that she was bypassing the Praetorian Guard and establishing touch directly with the legions.

So it was that Nero pondered a final solution to his maternal problems. He did first weigh other alternatives. Banishment from Rome and Italy? Perhaps. But, knowing his mother, she would be busily plotting, whatever her Mediterranean island of exile. Imprisonment? Never. It would not look proper for an empress mother, and she would attract public sympathy behind bars. There were, then, no other alternatives, Nero decided.

But one. He wrote Locusta at the toxicology academy he had set up for her, and received several samples of their latest research. But he finally decided against poison. His mother now knew nearly as much as Locusta, and had been adding antidotes to her diet for months. Were there other ways of inducing the necessarily "accidental" death? Should he discuss it with his council of state? No, this was Caesar's business.

One evening in early spring, Sabinus was returning from a pleasant stroll across the Quirinal with Plautia when a figure accosted him from behind some shrubbery near their door.

"*Who* in the—" Sabinus was startled. "Oh, it's you, Hermes."

"Ssshhh! Forgive me, Clarissimus," whispered the face in the shadows, "but I have to see you on a *very* urgent matter. Privately."

"Inside then. The library."

Plautia recognized him as the Syrian contractor who had helped build her father's outdoor study. Sabinus had been impressed with the little Syrian and taken him into the city engineering staff.

"Why so secret?" Sabinus asked the raven-haired Levantine once they were alone inside. "Are you being followed?"

"I hope not, but I didn't want any witnesses to my being here. Now, Clarissimus, do you remember when Caesar wanted some carpenters from our staff and you sent me over to the Palatine in charge of a detail?"

"Yes . . ."

"Well, we didn't stay at the palace. We were sent to Agrippina's house instead. She was off to one of her country places, and while she was gone, we were ordered to—oh, gods, why am I telling you this?"

"Go on, Hermes."

"We were ordered to install a . . . a collapsible ceiling in her bedroom."

"A *what?*"

"A collapsible ceiling. At the pull of a lever, huge concrete panels will dislodge and drop down on her bed—"

"Sweet Jupiter! Heavy enough to kill her?"

"Yes. Yes of course."

"Did you actually do it?"

Slowly he nodded. "We had to. Nero's personal orders."

"Is the ceiling . . . operative now?"

"We finished it this afternoon. Before we left, Nero himself came over to test the mechanism. Only we propped up the panels so they wouldn't fall out and cause a mess. It'll work, all right. Then he looked the four of us in the eye and threatened us with death if we told anyone a word about it. Plus a big reward if it works as planned."

Sabinus sank back into a chair, a fist supporting his large, square chin. For some moments he said nothing. Then he asked, "Why did you come here and tell *me* all this, Hermes?"

"I . . . I didn't know what to do. I really despise the empress mother, you know, but I couldn't just . . . let her die like that. Oh Hades, I might just as well admit it, Prefect: I think I'm becoming a Christian—that Aquila is *quite* persuasive, you know—and we're supposed to love our enemies."

"You too?" Sabinus smiled. "I thought that sect was just for mothers-in-law." Then he frowned. "Well, thanks Hermes," he said sardonically. "Now you've placed the matter squarely in my hands while you're free of it. By the way, when is Agrippina supposed to return?"

"Tomorrow afternoon."

"Oh, splendid." Sabinus shook his head. Then he saw Hermes to the door and advised, "Say nothing. Do nothing. We never saw each other tonight, right?"

"Right." Hermes slipped out furtively.

Let Agrippina die, Sabinus thought, and all her vile threats with her. She aims to destroy us . . . A faulty ceiling would finally free us all. She tried to ruin Aulus and Pomponia. Let her die. She's a cancer on the body politic. Besides, anyone warning her would endanger his own life. Yes, let the overambitious, murderous, incestuous harpy die.

He went to bed. Plautia was sleeping, fortunately, so he did not have to answer a fusillade of questions. But sleep did not come to him, and he tossed about for several hours. Finally he got up and went to the lavatory. It was there that the idea occurred to him. "Yes," he said to himself, "she must use the privy."

Before returning to bed, he wrote a note in small block lettering but carefully left it unsigned.

The litter ride back to Rome had exhausted Agrippina, and she was now preparing to retire early. On the table near her bed stood a stack of correspondence that had accumulated while she was gone. She would glance through it tomorrow.

She shut her eyes and was nearly asleep when her mind's eye looked again at the pile of mail and saw something unusual. She sat up in bed and stared at it, a small scroll tagged with purple. She broke the wax seal that strangely bore no monogram, and read the note. Cringing with disbelief, she jumped out of bed and climbed onto a chair for a closer look at the ceiling. She noticed the telltale alterations—a series of parallel cracks between panels of fresh plaster —and was horrified. Obviously, the unsigned warning did not come from a crank. Almost helpless as her nerves caught fire, she did exactly as the note suggested. She made a pallet on the floor of her adjoining lavatory and tried to sleep on it.

In the dead of night, a thundering clatter shook the house. By the light of a half moon streaming in through the windows, Agrippina saw the jagged scene of devastation that had been her bedroom. Her bed itself was smashed beyond recognition, and a powdery substance had coated everything. Coughing from the plaster dust, she climbed over the wreckage and hurried into the hall to see if she could catch anyone who might have tripped the mechanism. But she saw no one until her whole household staff came running to assist her. She was about to announce that one of them had just tried to murder her, but she shrewdly checked herself. Otherwise Nero would know she knew, and her life would be snuffed out. "A terrible accident!" she cried. "Luckily, I was out in the lavatory at the time."

What should she do now? Driven by the fiercest hatreds for her "monster son," Agrippina spent the next days deciding whether to try to poison Nero, or cast herself on the mercy of the Senate and implore the Fathers for asylum. Or should she flee north to the legions?

Sabinus, with the rest of Rome, publicly marveled at Agrippina's luck in avoiding catastrophe. Privately, he hoped Nero was having second thoughts about murdering his own mother. Should he tell Seneca and Burrus of his role in the matter? Under any other circumstances, yes. But it was just possible that one or the other had condoned the matricide.

Nero was beside himself with fury and yet fright at the failure of his collapsible ceiling. He was not sure whether to believe his mother's explanation of her escape or not. If she suspected him, his own life was in danger, and in any case he must act at once, and successfully. His every morsel of food now twice tasted, he conspired with the one man who hated his mother as much as he did, Anicetus, commander of the Roman fleet. Anicetus had been Nero's boyhood tutor, and his violent quarrels with Agrippina had left wounds that only festered with age.

"What's simpler than an accident at sea, Princeps?" Anicetus suggested. "At a play the other day, there was a ship on stage with a hull that opened up to let out some wild animals and then snapped shut again. We could adapt the idea to . . . eject a beast of another kind."

Nero pondered the plan for several moments, then smiled. "Why not, Anicetus? But nothing at Ostia—too near Rome."

"Here's what I had in mind. You're going down to Baiae for the Feast of Minerva, aren't you?"

"Yes, we'll spend about a week down there." Then he grinned. "Of course, you . . . scheming son of a satyr."

"So. Now, of course, you must do everything possible to stage a 'reconciliation' with your mother and invite her along."

"And no one will outdo me in shedding filial tears after the accident." Nero spread his arms. "There will be temples and shrines in her honor."

While Anicetus went down to the Bay of Naples and devised a collapsible ship, Nero carefully reversed tack and started begging his mother's forgiveness for the dark thoughts that had been brewing in his mind. At first Agrippina was extremely suspicious, but some of the lines in his almost pathetic letters had a ring of truth about them:

> . . . Of course, you've done your part too, Mama, in nourishing our quarrels. You can be quite a formidable antagonist! But children should bear with the irritability of their parents and be first to show a spirit of forgiveness. . . .

A hypocrite would have been only apologetic, she thought. Besides, rumors trickled down from the Palatine that Nero truly wanted a reconciliation. And then his cordial note arrived, inviting her to spend the holidays with him down at Baiae. "The family should be together at the Feast of Minerva," he added, in a pious touch. It *had* to be true then, she thought. Reconciliation!

The Gulf of Baiae, the most northwesterly inlet in the great outspread arms of the Bay of Naples, was a favorite resort of the emperors and a fashionable watering place for Roman nobility. Agrippina and her escorts sailed down the Mediterranean coast to Baiae in mid-March of 59. Exuding smiles and cordiality, Nero met them at the dock and escorted her up to a country villa where she and her party would stay. The villa lay on the coastline north of Baiae and was separated from it by a cove of water several miles wide.

The following evening, Agrippina and her attendants sailed across the cove for a great feast of reconciliation at Nero's villa. Again he stood at the wharf with widespread arms, and was gallantly helping her up the steep path leading to his villa when they heard a splintering crash from below. Turning about, they saw that a ship had rammed into Agrippina's galley as it was docked, damaging its stern. Nero was furious. "Is that you, Anicetus?" he shouted.

"I'm afraid it is, Caesar. Forgive our clumsiness!" he wailed. "We'll start repairs immediately."

"You'd better, you blundering idiot! Unless you want to see a new fleet commander here!—Come, Mother."

Nero's banquet disarmed any remaining doubts. Only those members of the imperial party who were friendly to Agrippina had been invited, and she herself reclined at the place of honor. In high spirits, Nero bubbled, "This merely symbolizes your return to highest favor, dear Mother. And I have some happy news for you: your beautiful profile will soon be next to mine again on our coinage."

Agrippina was exuberant. Her spirits surged. But she had never seen Nero so unmatched in his moods. One minute he would chatter playfully and poke fun like a boy; the next he seemed overcome with an air of constraint, as if his thoughts were miles distant. Most of all he wanted to talk about the past.

In the middle of the feast, he seemed to have remembered something, for he leaned over to whisper, "One thing we've never cleared up, dear Mother. You once told me that when I was born, astrologers made some sort of dreadful prediction about me. What was it?"

Surprised by the query, Agrippina shook her head. "No, darling son. This isn't the time to talk about anything like that."

"Oh, but it is, Mother, it is." It was time indeed to ferret out any secrets. "In a true reconciliation, nothing is concealed."

She frowned and hesitated. "Well, if you insist," she gave in. "Yes, maybe it *is* a good time. Let it be a token of my great love for you. It was Balbillus who cast your horoscope and said, 'Your son will be emperor one day, but he will also . . . kill his mother.'"

Nero, who was swallowing an olive, choked on it and coughed violently. Then he cleared his throat and asked, "Is that it, Mother? Anything else?"

"Yes . . . my reply to him. I said, 'Let him kill me, then, *provided he is emperor!*'"

Nero flushed. "Such . . . great love, dear Mother. But what a ridiculous horoscope. Astrologers *are* a pack of deceivers and scoundrels!" He grabbed a cup of wine and drained it, hoping Agrippina would not notice his sweat and agitation.

About midnight, after the feast, Nero escorted her down to the dock. It was a magnificently warm night for early spring, with thousands of stars hanging in the heavens. The sea was calm, barely ruffled by a fragrant, pine-scented breeze that seemed to be blowing up from Capri.

At the dock, an apologetic Anicetus greeted them. "I'm sorry, Caesar. It'll take another day's work to repair the galley."

"Dunce! Why didn't you ever learn to sail?" Then he softened. "Well, no great problem. Here, Mother, use one of my ships. Do you suppose you can sail this one without smashing it, Anicetus?"

The fleet commander merely hung his head in shame. Nero then bade his mother good-bye with a lingering embrace, straining her to his breast and kissing her eyes and hands. "Strength and good health to you, Mother," he said. "For you I live, and because of you I rule."

"Good-bye, dearest son," she said, slurring her words a bit from the quantities of wine she had consumed. A male aide helped her onto the ship, while a girl attendant, Acerronia, followed. Anicetus and his crew now cast off as mother and son continued waving good-bye to each other across a widening strip of water.

Agrippina went below to stretch out on a couch inside the cabin, while Acerronia jabbered joyfully at her feet about the glories of reconciliation. Ten minutes later, Gallus, the male aide, stepped inside to check on the comfort of the empress mother. Someone topside yelled, "*Now!*" Instantly, heavy lead ingots crashed down upon them from the cabin ceiling. Gallus' head and shoulders were crushed, and he died instantly. But the women were saved by the high oaken sides of the couch which were too solid to give way and held up their share of lead bars.

"Pull the *other* lever!" Anicetus barked. It was supposed to open the hull.

"*Won't budge!*" someone else shouted and then swore. The hull panel, which had opened easily in dry dock, was held shut by subsurface water pressure.

"Capsize the cursed ship, then!" the commander yelled. "Everybody to the starboard rail! Then to portside! Get her rocking!"

But now Anicetus paid his price for secrecy. Only the officers had been alerted to the true purpose of the voyage. The crew, who thought their commander had suddenly gone mad, resisted all efforts to capsize. When the officers ran to one rail, they dashed to the other, stabilizing the roll.

"No, idiots! Help us *sink* it!" Anicetus shouted, as he and the officers plummeted over toward the crew, who just as quickly threaded through them to the opposite side. Sounds of confusion and cursing filled the night air.

Agrippina, meanwhile, managed to salvage a plan of action from her soggy senses. Creeping out of the cabin, she slipped quietly over the side of the ship into the water. At the same time, Acerronia stumbled onto the deck shouting, "Help me! Help the empress mother!" Swimming away from the ship, Agrippina watched in horror as officers clubbed her attendant to death with oars, her crumpling tunic yellow orange in the ship's running lights.

Was Acerronia trying to save herself or cover her escape, Agrippina wondered, as she swam farther away from the ship toward lights on shore. She felt a stab of pain in her right shoulder—somewhere in the melee, evidently, she had been wounded after all. She counted one hundred breast strokes and was starting to weaken when a flotilla of small oyster boats returning to shore glided past her. She screamed for help. They hove to and pulled her out of the water. When the dumfounded oystermen learned that they had rescued the empress mother of Rome, they reverently delivered her to the villa on shore—miserable, enraged, exhausted, but alive.

First she must dress her wound and sleep, Agrippina thought. Then she would decide how to outwit the murderous beast she had spawned and save her life.

Two men had been watching the ship in distress out on the gulf. One of them, Nero, stood on a hill by his villa until he heard the shouts and screams. Then he smiled and went back inside.

The other was a ship's passenger, who was watching the scene from the portside gunwales of a large Alexandrian merchantman named *The Twin Brothers,* for its figureheads were Castor and Pollux, carved to bear an uncanny resemblance to Sabinus and Quintus Lateranus. The vessel was approaching the great harbor of Puteoli after wintering in Malta. The passenger, a short, slightly built Jew, had stayed up to see the ship glide into the Bay of Naples, and he now heard the shouting and screaming, apparently from the small vessel with running lights a mile or so to the west. Peering into the night, his balding gray locks and pointed beard ruffled by the breeze, the Jew alerted a Roman centurion on board, but when the soldier peered out to see what was wrong, the shouting had ceased, and everything seemed normal. The centurion seemed to be a friend of the Jew. In fact, however, he was his imperial guard, conducting him to Rome for trial before Caesar. And the Jew was named Paul of Tarsus.†

  † Lest this be deemed too great a coincidence, please see the Notes.

17

SLEEP PROVED IMPOSSIBLE for Agrippina. Her mind was painfully alert, searching feverishly for a way out of mortal danger. First she must escape imminent assassination. Later she would flee to the Senate chamber in Rome and denounce Nero for the monster he was. Nero, of course, would now be learning that she may have survived. If he thought she knew it was attempted murder, he would be forced to kill her. He *must*, therefore, be led to believe that she thought it all an accident, like the other times.

"Agermus!" she called to her freedman. "Go to Caesar—immediately—and deliver this message, exactly as I word it. Tell him: 'By heaven's favor, O Caesar, the empress mother—no, *your* mother—has escaped a terrible accident. She knows you'll want to come over and inquire after her health, but she begs you to put this off, since she's well and needs nothing so much as a little sleep.' . . . Yes, that's it. Can you remember it?"

"Certainly, mistress."

Nero had been waiting nervously in the dead of night for Anicetus' return. When he did appear, the fleet commander was a little defensive. "We think she's dead, Caesar," he said. "Her attendants are dead for sure—we saw to that—and she was clubbed too and must have drowned afterward. That would be *some* swim!"

"Sweet Neptune!" Nero wailed. "You don't know my mother! What happened out there?"

Anicetus was giving a detailed report when a guard raced in from the beach and cried, "Caesar! Some oystermen found the empress mother out in the gulf, swimming for her life. They rescued her. You'll be glad to know she's back in her villa with a slight wound, but nothing serious."

Nero threw his hands over his face and cried, "Oh . . . gods!" while slowly collapsing onto a couch. The guard thought it a touching display of filial affection and withdrew.

"She's . . . she's immortal, I suppose," Nero whimpered. "That woman . . . just won't die! By all the flames of Hades . . . how *do* we help her across the Styx? *How*, Anicetus?"

The fleet commander said nothing.

"Oh, but we're dead men, we are. She'll be here in a moment, breathing fire. She'll kill me. She'll take over Rome."

"I doubt that, Caesar," Anicetus said. "Why don't you summon Seneca and Burrus for some . . . ah . . . advice in—?"

"Yes, yes, *yes!* Get them. Get them at once!"

Both men had been part of the imperial entourage spending the holidays at Baiae, but they had not attended the reconciliation banquet and were not informed about the collapsible ship. It took Nero some embarrassed minutes to explain to them why he had plotted his mother's death, and why the attempt had failed.

"Does she know it wasn't an accident?" Seneca asked, with an anxious frown shared by Burrus.

"She couldn't *help* but know," Anicetus muttered, staring at his sandals to avoid meeting anyone's eyes.

"Oh yes. Mother's very bright about plots . . . especially on her own life," Nero groaned. "But you two are here to tell me how to save my life, because"—he faltered, with the look of a cornered, maddened animal—"because she'll get us all otherwise. She probably has messengers going at this moment to the Senate. She'll do anything. She'll arm the slaves. She'll get the Guard to defect. O immortal gods!" He broke down and cried. "What should we do?"

Seneca looked down to the mosaic floor and said nothing.

Burrus shifted uneasily from one foot to the other, rubbing his stubbed arm but saying nothing, though he was trying to catch Seneca's eye.

"Help me!" Nero finally howled. "You're my advisers, aren't you?"

"Give us a moment, Princeps," Seneca snapped. "This is all very sudden for us." Then he paced about the room, chin in hand, thinking of all the alternative courses of action. His Stoic conscience told him he must try to save Agrippina, enemy that she was. "What if we were to arrest your mother and send her into exile?" he asked.

"*Impossible!*" Nero cried. "After this, she'll not rest until she kills me. And you too. The whole Empire isn't big enough for both of us. You ought to know that."

There *was* another alternative, Seneca thought to himself. If Agrippina were not crushed, Nero might indeed perish. Rome would be rid of its tempestuous and unpredictable young emperor. Yet that alternative was equally grim, or worse: Agrippina triumphant and reigning as empress? His own life would be snuffed out shortly after Nero's. No, at this point in the incredibly bungled state of affairs—and despite any philosophical principles—Agrippina would have to go . . . if, indeed, she could still be caught. Looking up at Burrus, Seneca asked, "Well . . . who gets the fatal order, then? The guards?"

Burrus shook his head. "Not the praetorians. They're pledged to protect the whole family of the Caesars." Then he looked over to the fleet commander and said, "No, let Anicetus finish what he set out to do. The army respectfully defers to the navy."

Nero looked up and nodded. Anicetus bowed and left the room. He had a reputation to clear.

A guard entered with news that Agermus had arrived with a message from his mother. Nero's eyes darted to Seneca for advice, but then snapped back again. He was Caesar. After his emotional and childish performance he and he alone must decide what to do next. "Bring him in," Nero commanded.

Agermus was ushered in and he delivered Agrippina's statement almost word for word. For an instant Nero wondered if his mother really *did* think it was all an accident. He could still recall Anicetus and halt her murder. He would not be accused of matricide. But . . . oh, gods, he quailed inwardly, what if it were just another of her stratagems to save her life now for revenge later? He must make an instant decision. Self-preservation. Yes, for an emperor, self-preservation always came first. His mother had to die. To justify his action in Rome, he must now frame her for an attempt on his life.

Nero instantly pulled out a dagger and threw it at Agermus' feet. Then he shouted, "*Guards! Guards!*" until several praetorians came rushing in. "Arrest this man for treason! Agrippina sent him to assassinate me! See the dagger? Clap him in irons!"

Meanwhile, news had spread about the empress mother's injury from shipwreck, and the beach about her villa was now ablaze with the flickering torches of concerned coastal folk and groaning with prayers for her recovery. But suddenly an armed company of marines wedged through the crowds, trotted up to the villa and surrounded it. Anicetus drew his cordon a bit tighter, then broke through the entrance and marched to the master bedroom. Kicking the door open, he saw Agrippina lying in bed, being tended by a terrified slave girl.

Agrippina stared at Anicetus and his marines in terror. But, preserving her dignity, she said calmly, "If you've come to visit a sick woman, take back word that I'm recovering."

Anicetus said nothing. He merely gazed at her in contempt.

"But if you're here to . . . to commit a crime, the blood will be on *your* hands. My son couldn't possibly have ordered you to murder his own mother."

Armed marines surrounded her bed. "Now?" the captain asked. Anicetus nodded.

The captain raised his club slowly, then brought it down on her head.

Stunned with a flood of intense pain, Agrippina saw another marine drawing out his sword. She opened her mouth but no words came out. Drawing on her powerful will one last time, she finally screamed, "Strike here!" and uncovered her abdomen. "Strike my womb, for it bore Nero!"

The sword came down repeatedly. The green of her eyes assumed a last, fearful fluorescence and then faded in death.

Nero had to see for himself that his mother was truly dead. He went to her villa, and then had her body carried outside on a couch and cremated in a mean and hasty funeral.

Returning to Baiae, he slowly began to absorb the enormity of his deed. Befuddled by events, terrified by sounds and shadows, he wandered about the villa, dreading the dawn and yet waiting impatiently for it. Haunted by the scene of his crime, he left Baiae for Naples several days later.

When he had finally gathered his wits, he dictated a letter to the Senate, telling how Agrippina's chronic plotting had finally led to her suicide when the assassination she had planned for him failed. Seneca edited the letter, appending a list of her crimes ever since Claudius' time.

But the true story of Agrippina's death followed, by word of mouth, hard on the heels of the official story. Romans had little trouble deciding which to believe, and a fresh rash of graffiti on the theme of matricide was daubed on the walls of Rome.

Sabinus was not particularly shocked by the news from the Bay of Naples, since he guessed it was only a matter of time before Nero would strike again. But it was sad, he thought, that someone's death should spell relief for himself; yet relief he felt, in every fiber of his being. He wondered how Aulus was reacting to the news.

At the other side of the Forum, Nero's explanatory letter was being read aloud in the Senate. The Fathers showed disgust with Seneca for having added his rhetorical flourishes to such a message— no one believed the dagger story—and yet they knew their actions would be reported to Nero in detail. So they took the easy, docile, obsequious course and vied with one another to introduce decrees declaring Agrippina's birthday inauspicious in the calendar and offering thanksgiving for Nero's deliverance.

Aulus Plautius had suffered directly at Agrippina's hands, but the sham unfolding in the marbled chamber nauseated him. He stood up and walked out of the Senate, joined by his friend Thrasea Paetus, who had taken the same route. Aulus asked him with a wry smile, "Why didn't you express yourself inside on Nero's letter?"

"I couldn't say what I would. I wouldn't say what I could."

Aulus nodded. "Do you think we'll get into trouble?"

"Nero can kill me, Aulus. But he can't harm me."

Aulus smiled and said, "It would take Seneca a whole treatise on Stoicism to say the same thing. Soon I'll have to have a talk with my son-in-law. I really wonder if Sabinus wants to . . . stay in this regime."

On that fateful night in the Bay of Naples, Paul of Tarsus had disembarked at Puteoli, where he was met by a small group of Christians. They urged the great missionary to spend a little time with them in the port city. Paul turned to his guard and asked, "Would it cause you any problems, Julius? Delaying our trip to Rome for several days?" His voice had an unexpected depth and resonance for one with so slender a build.

The ebony-haired centurion, dressed smartly in the uniform of the Augustan Cohort, shook his head. "Sorry, Paul. That's just not possible. Military regulations." But then he burst out laughing. "On the other hand, we're merely five months overdue anyway, so what's another week! Yes, take a week. Long enough?"

"Certainly. And thank you, Julius."

"Besides, the emperor's mother just died, so the road to Rome must be clogged with traffic. We'll do better to avoid it."

When they set out a week later, spring had fully splashed across the Italian countryside. The hills were lush green, and the breezes fragrant from the legion of wildflowers standing sentinel along the roadsides. Now Paul and his traveling companion, a Gentile physician named Lucanus, easily forgot the terrors of their voyage from Palestine, which had ended in shipwreck on the coast of Malta, winter there, and transfer to the ship that had brought them to Puteoli.

They traveled up the Appian Way to a halting place called Three Taverns on the thirty-third milestone from Rome. A large cluster of people seemed to have gathered at the village crossroads here. Suddenly someone shouted, "There they are!" and a couple rushed out into the roadway and into Paul's arms. The apostle's eyes filled with tears as he cried, "Priscilla! Aquila!"

"Seven years, Paul," said Aquila. "It's been seven *years* since we were in Greece together!" His face blooming with a great smile, Aquila proudly introduced Paul and Lucanus—or Luke, the more affectionate form his friends preferred—to the welcoming delegation of Roman Christians.

"My brothers and sisters," said Paul, beaming, "most of you I know only by the names I wrote at the close of my letter to the church in Rome. But seeing you gives me courage, for, as you know, I must stand before Caesar." Then he introduced his guard to them. "And my case has begun very well indeed, for I'm in the custody of a distinguished centurion. Julius, meet the Christians of Rome."

"Oh, but there are many more," said Aquila.

"I should think so." Paul smiled. "I'd hoped that you would have had Caesar himself converted by now!"

They all laughed, relieved to find Paul a very human sort, not that larger-than-life saint of God who seemed to command a prestige in the church second only to that of Jesus himself. Luke they also found impressive, though in a different way. He stood a head taller than Paul, and his dark brownish hair and cultured beard, clipped close to the edge of his jaw line, set off a very Hellenic visage in contrast to the Semitic cast of Paul's face, fringed by its gray and pointy beard.

Together they traveled the final leg of their journey, and the black stones of the Via Appia seemed to have a destination at last. In the distance lay Rome, her red brick walls pierced from all directions by gracefully arched aqueducts, a vast, living hub for the network of roads that seemed to be breathing in and exhaling traffic at the same time. It was the greatest city even the much-traveled Paul had ever seen, and, as with any tourist, his eyes widened to gather its wonders.

Julius led them across town to the Castra Praetoria, where he turned Paul and several other prisoners over to the camp commandant.

"Here are the documents of indictment on these men," Julius told the commandant. "They're to stay in irons until their punishment is decided. But this one here—his name's Paul of Tarsus—he gets free custody."

"Free custody?" the commandant asked, arching his eyebrows. "Why?"

"He's a Roman citizen. He's waiting for Nero to hear his case."

"He appealed to Caesar?"

"I did," Paul interrupted.

The commandant shrugged his shoulders. "Must be important. You'll have to have a guard anyway, Paul of Tarsus, since you're not from Rome."

"I understand."

"Ah, Commandant." Julius drew him aside. "If possible, I'd like every courtesy extended to this prisoner. We've just been through a voyage that . . . was designed in hell. And, by all the Furies, if it weren't for this Paul, we'd be at the bottom of the Mediterranean. Besides, I think he's innocent."

"That's for Caesar to decide . . . if he hears the case." Then, turning to Paul, the commandant said, "If you can manage to find lodging near here, we'll send over a praetorian each day to . . . ah

. . . to keep you company. Rome pays for the guard, but you'll have to rent the house. Do you have the funds?"

"Yes. But will my friends be able to visit me?"

"Why not? And you'll be able to get out too, if your guard doesn't mind. But he has to be with you at all times, and you can't leave the city."

Aquila and Priscilla found a house for him on the Viminal hill near the Castra Praetoria. Aquila's congregation helped Paul and Luke get settled, and they brought them furnishings and enough food supplies to last for several months. Soon they were more comfortable than they had dared hope, despite the constant presence of a guard.

Aquila gave them a full report on the progress of the Faith in Rome, including a word-for-word account of the trial of Pomponia Graecina. Paul strained to catch every syllable.

"But now I wonder if what we did was justified," Aquila fretted, "staking our defense to Judaism. Was it honest? Letting our fellow Jews protect us?"

"You're a Jew," Paul replied. "I'm a Jew. And if our faith isn't the fulfillment of Judaism, it's nothing." He paused several moments, then resumed. "You know the pattern I've followed in all of my missionary journeys: 'to the Jew first and only then to the Gentile.' The same holds for Rome."

Several days later, Paul invited the leaders of the Roman synagogues to a reception at his house, where they had a free and lively discussion on any topic they chose, for they were alternating between Hebrew and Aramaic, while the bored guard—to whom Paul was attached by a long chain—knew only Latin.

"Brothers," said Paul, "I did nothing against the customs of our fathers, and yet I was delivered into Roman custody. Two governors of Judea examined me, and both wanted to set me free. But some of our brothers objected, and I was forced to appeal to Caesar to save my life. Hence my trip here. I wanted to see you and talk with you, since it's because of the hope of Israel that I'm bound with this chain."

When Paul had finished explaining his view of the "hope of Israel," one of the rabbis stood up and said, "I haven't received any letters from Judea about you, Paul. Has anyone else?" There was no

response. "But you're an interesting man, Paul of Tarsus. A Pharisee, aren't you?"

Paul nodded. "Yes, from the Tribe of Benjamin. I studied under
Gamaliel."

"And yet you're clearly one of the Nazarenes. That sect, of
course, is being spoken against everywhere. But we'll still encourage
our brothers to give you a hearing. Shall we set a date, gentlemen?"

True to their word, the rabbis appeared two weeks later with a
large number of members from their synagogues. "Now I know why
you insisted on a house with an atrium and peristyle," Aquila commented to Paul.

The meeting lasted a whole day. In the morning, Paul expounded
his view that Christianity was fulfilled Judaism—that Jesus was the
Messiah predicted in Hebrew Scriptures. In the afternoon, there was
much debate over this claim. Some were convinced and, in fact, later
joined the Christians. But the majority were not.

"It's the great *Shema*, Paul," said one of the rabbis. "Your eleva-
tion of Jesus challenges it: *Shema yisroel, adonai elohainu adonai
echad.*"

"True," Paul agreed. "Hear, O Israel: the Lord our God, the
Lord *is* one!"

"Not two."

Paul then tried to explain why Christians had no quarrel with
that Scripture. But later it seemed clear to him that he would have
to carry his message also to the Gentiles of Rome.

Flavius Sabinus virtually ruled Rome in the months following
Agrippina's murder, since Seneca and Burrus were staying near
Naples with Nero, who was afraid to show his face in Rome. The
city enjoyed a calm and pleasant summer under Sabinus, because
Nero, always the chief troublemaker in town, was absent.

Sabinus' docket was crowded with the usual trials, some petty,
others serious. There was one case of considerable interest that
struck close to the family, but he could not adjudicate it since his
was the wrong court. It concerned the recently arrived Jew, Paul of
Tarsus. Sabinus remembered the name from Pomponia's trial, and in
fact it was she who brought the case to his attention.

As a favor to her, Sabinus had Paul come down to city headquarters to see if he could assist in his defense. But ten minutes' discussion with the man convinced him that it was a religious case, so

he arranged for Paul to meet with him at Aulus Plautius' place, "since the senator is a better judge than I in such matters," he said with a wry smile.

Aulus winced when he learned of Sabinus' comment. But Pomponia seemed so enthusiastic at the prospect of meeting Paul that he could not deny her. Plautia was also visiting her parents the evening the manacled apostle and his guard arrived on the Esquiline.

Sabinus turned to the guard and asked, "Do you have the key to his chain with you?"

"Yes . . ."

"Unlock him, then. I'll be surety for him."

"But . . . this isn't permitted."

"When the city prefect tells you to do something," Sabinus growled, "you'll *do* it! Immediately!"

"All right, Prefect. Sorry." He dropped the chain from Paul's wrist.

"That's fine. Now leave us and go get something to drink in the kitchen."

They moved into the peristyle and sat down. Sabinus began. "You should know, Paul, that our interest in your case stems only from our love for Pomponia here, who wants us to help you in any way we can. Now suppose you tell us . . . well, yes, your whole story."

It proved to be an extraordinary saga, consuming much of the afternoon. Paul started with his young days as a persecutor of the Christians in Jerusalem, and then told of his conversion on the Damascus road, his various missionary travels, the circumstances of his arrest in Jerusalem, his appeal to Caesar, and finally the shipwreck voyage to Rome.

When they learned that Paul had sailed the final leg of his voyage from Malta on *The Twin Brothers*, everyone exploded with surprise at this stunning coincidence, especially Sabinus. The apostle was puzzled until Sabinus explained the nature of Twin Brothers Enterprises.

Paul smiled to himself, wondering whether this "coincidence" had a higher purpose. Throughout his presentation, his hosts reacted in different ways to his story. The women were held spellbound. Aulus too thought it a remarkable tale—and told with sincerity—but he still wondered how this slight, balding, bandy-legged Jew could have had such an influence among members of the new sect. Sabinus merely jotted down notes from time to time, trying to frame his suggestions for legal procedure.

As Paul finished his story, he added, "One comment at the Castra Praetoria I didn't understand. The commandant said something about '*if* the emperor hears' my case. Surely he will, won't he?"

"That's just the point," Sabinus replied. "It's by no means definite *where* your hearing will take place. Not many appeal directly to Caesar. Claudius, of course, always heard such appeals personally—"

"And zealously, too," Aulus interposed. "Poor man. He had so many cases that lawyers sometimes found him nodding at the tribunal. Then they'd suddenly shout, '*If Caesar agrees* . . .' He'd wake with a start and continue listening."

"But since Nero was so young when he acceded," Sabinus explained, "he usually delegated appeals to senatorial friends and confirmed their verdicts afterward. Generally, he still does."

"What about the prefect of the Praetorian Guard?" Paul inquired.

"Burrus? Sometimes he'll take a case for Nero, but usually he serves only as one of the assessors—advisers—in the imperial court." Then Sabinus smiled. "And of course, if only you'd committed your 'crime' here in Rome, Paul, can you guess who would have judged you?"

"You?"

"Yes indeed. And you'd be a free man by now." Then he shook his head. "But you're on record as appealing to Caesar, so he—or Seneca and Burrus—will decide if he hears your case or someone else."

"When will they decide this?" Paul wondered.

"After the prosecution registers its formal charges."

"The prosecution? From Jerusalem?"

"Oh yes. Under Roman law, no trial can take place until a plaintiff lodges his indictment."

"But aren't the *literae dimissoriae* enough?"

"No. The documents of indictment simply show basis for imprisonment while awaiting trial."

"But what if the prosecution doesn't choose to make so long a trip here?"

"That's a sticky point. And I must confess that our law code doesn't really allow for such a situation. This hardly ever happens, you see. The burden of our law is to *compel* a plaintiff to carry through his charges to public trial, and to penalize him if he does not. But there's no provision for freeing the accused in the meantime."

"But that's . . . unfair." Paul frowned.

"It certainly is," Pomponia interposed.

Paul had bitter memories of his two-year imprisonment in Caesarea, and he had hoped his case would be resolved quickly in Rome. He also feared that, having failed to secure a conviction in Palestine, his prosecutors might not bother making the lengthy trip to Rome.

"Of course, if your prosecution doesn't appear, we'll do what we can to compel some kind of hearing," Sabinus said. "But tell me, Paul: *why* did you ever appeal to Caesar? Once you did, you got yourself inextricably enmeshed in our Roman legal machine."

"I *had* to appeal. After your governor, Felix, heard my case in Caesarea, he wanted me to bribe him for my freedom, but I wouldn't do that."

"Felix, the brother of Pallas?" Aulus inquired.

"Yes."

"Of course!" said Aulus, with a smirk. "Any brother of our retired Pallas would want money."

"Then Festus, the next governor, was trying to conciliate the prosecution, so he suggested sending me back to Jerusalem for trial. Since that would have meant certain death, I appealed to Caesar. And I later realized that God had intended me to do exactly this, so that I might preach the Faith here in Rome also."

"Yes, yes. But—well, for obvious reasons, please keep our next remarks utterly confidential. Why do you seem so eager to have the . . . the present Caesar hear your case? He's still quite young. He'll hardly understand the religious depths in the matter. He's unpredictable, and—we all hate to admit it—he's also quite dangerous."

"It's not that I'm so *eager* to stand before Caesar, Prefect. It's just that I *know* I'll be facing him, regardless of—"

"How do you know that?" asked Sabinus.

"During our terrible voyage, when all hands had abandoned hope, I had a vision or dream during the night of the worst storm. A messenger of God spoke to me and said, 'Don't be afraid, Paul. You must stand before Caesar. And God has granted you all those who sail with you.' And, as you know, not one of the 276 lives was lost."

Sabinus smiled. "Do you *really* think you had a message . . . from your god, Paul?"

"Yes. I do. It was such a vision on the road to Damascus that transformed my life a quarter-century ago."

Sabinus looked at the intensity in Paul's bluish-gray eyes—and shook his head in wonder.

18

IN SEPTEMBER, Nero hesitantly returned to Rome. But his flatterers were right: he need not have stayed away for fear of the people. Privately they might call him "matricide" and now also "coward," but a dead Agrippina was no basis for revolution. His return to the city, in fact, was greeted by more enthusiasm than even his lickspittles had promised.

For the first time in his life, the twenty-one-year-old emperor felt truly free. "At last I can do whatever I like," he told himself. "Great Jupiter, I can even kill my mother and they cheer me!" Now he could fly into Poppaea's arms without worrying about whether Agrippina were looking on from some palace balcony.

As a man of age, he could also do with less advice from Seneca and Burrus. "It doesn't suit the emperor of Rome to be seen racing horses," they had told him. But Nero craved the excitement of standing in a lurching chariot, grasping the reins behind four snorting steeds while careening around a curve of the circus. Now he would simply do it. Seneca and Burrus gave up any hope of restraining him, but Sabinus saved the day with his suggestion: have Nero manage his horses out of public view across the Tiber in the Vatican valley, where there was a hippodrome that Caligula had begun but never finished. Nero was pleased with the idea and spent several hours here each day running his horses.

Busy as he was with other pursuits, Nero started absenting himself from the Friday councils of state, which gave the other three remarkable privacy in their conferences. Seneca's morale was drooping. "All I can do is try to cushion Rome from the worst shocks," he told Sabinus and Burrus. "Last week, the idiot palace astrologer had his planets mixed up and told Nero some ugly portents lay in his path. The charlatan also told him he could escape if he diverted the impending evil onto others. So he actually prepared a long list of victims until I looked over his shoulder and said, 'Forget the astrologers, Caesar—they're deceiving fools—and no matter how many people you cut down, you could never kill your successor.' "

"Bravo, Seneca!" Sabinus smiled. "What did he say?"

"He agreed, thank the Fates, and crumpled up his list."

"Why not throw that star-gazing fraud out of the palace?"

"I'd love to, but Poppaea wouldn't have it.—At other times, my friends, the crime is committed *before* I can stop it. You know Nero's aunt, Lepida, who was sick in bed with constipation before she died? When Nero visited her, she stroked the fuzz on his cheeks and said, 'As soon as I receive your first shavings as a man, I'll gladly die.' Nero turns around and tells her doctors to give her so much laxative she'd never need any more."

"But why?" Sabinus asked, in anger.

"So he could seize her properties now rather than later. Lepida was *very* rich. No, Nero has other plans for that golden gristle on his face. He wants to shave it off at a great public festival he's originating—the Juvenalia. Everybody is to help celebrate Nero's manhood in a huge ceremony. We're all going on stage, it seems."

"You *are* joking, Seneca," Sabinus countered.

"I wish I were. Here. These invitations are just going out to all the patrician families of Rome."

Sabinus read the parchment and his skin tingled. The last two sentences he read aloud: "Act, sing, dance, do a mime—anything that will set off your skills to best advantage. But you *must* attend, even if only to sing in the choruses." He paused and looked up. "That's ridiculous. No, it's disgusting. Our nobility won't walk on stage—the plebes would hoot us out of the theater."

"We know that," said Burrus in a tired voice that broke his long silence. "But what can we do?"

High on the Esquiline, Aulus Plautius read the imperial invitation, crumpled it in disgust, and threw it away. "It's obvious what Nero's doing," he told Pomponia. "He desperately wants to go on stage himself. But Seneca tells him—and correctly—that as emperor he simply can't."

"So if members of the nobility perform first," Pomponia commented, "the precedent will have been set. What shall we do, Aulus?"

"Nothing."

"Couldn't we take a trip to the south and say we didn't receive the invitation in time?"

"We'll do nothing."

Sabinus and Plautia wished they could have taken the same course, but Nero insisted that they join him in the imperial box at the festival. Sabinus agreed, but only on condition that they not be expected to perform. Nero concurred, although he was not especially pleased at the diffidence of his city prefect.

The marine theater of Augustus, just across the Tiber, was packed for Nero's command performance. Sabinus and Plautia were seated in the center orchestra with the imperial party, and at high noon cornets blasted out an opening fanfare. Slowly, dramatically, Nero stood up and faced the expectant crowd.

A slave solemnly daubed his jaw and cheeks with oil. Nero then reached for his razor. Its handle was of gold, studded with precious gems, and he held it up for all to see. Looking into a small hand mirror, he gingerly severed the amber-red stubble that had erupted along the lines of his jaw and chin. Another slave carefully held a towel under the emperor to catch any severed hairs and to receive the precious wipings from his blade. When his cheeks were suitably smooth, Nero gathered the shavings and placed them inside a small golden globe, which he now held up triumphantly. "To Jupiter Capitoline!" he shouted. Applause flowed down the tiers of the theater, and the Juvenalia could now begin.

A herald walked out onto center stage. "Look who it is!" Sabinus nudged Plautia. "It's Gallio, Seneca's brother—the one who set Paul free in Corinth." Sabinus winked at Seneca. The philosopher returned a wan smile and a slow shake of the head.

Gallio now announced grandly, "Only the highest quality of entertainment will grace this occasion. Therefore, our performances today will be given exclusively by families of Roman nobility."

He went on to announce each family act, the great names from Rome's past re-echoing across the theater, followed by their amateurish performances. Some played the flute or sang to the lyre. Others, acutely embarrassed, tried to dance in mimes or give exhibitions of prowess in hunting, although several of the performers showed hidden talent and even seemed to be enjoying themselves.

"See, Sabinus," Nero leaned over and smirked. "There's a bit of the mime in every one of us, and it was left to me to bring it out. So maybe next time you won't be so . . . condescending about my arrangements."

Sabinus saw, even felt, Nero's smile fading into a chilling stare. Plautia reached for her husband's hand.

After several more performances, Sabinus looked over to see if Nero were still relishing his spectacle, but he had disappeared. Then Gallio stood up to declare, "Caesar has often told us, 'Hidden talent counts for nothing.' Nor does he exempt himself from his own advice. Although Rome is 812 years old, and never in her history has the chief of state deigned to give a public performance, Caesar loves you too much to be shackled by past traditions."

A droning buzz of excitement in the crowd almost drowned out Gallio's climax: "Fellow Romans, our last performance today will be given by . . . Nero Caesar himself, singing his own verses!"

Happily washed by waves of applause cascading down on him from the galleries, Nero walked to the center of the stage, clad in the simple tunic of a lyre-player. Holding up his hands for silence, he nervously bent over his instrument, tuning it with care. He gave each string a final, testing twang, looking into the wings for a signal from Terpnus, his music tutor and the leading lyrist in Rome.

When Terpnus nodded his approval, Nero smiled and called out, "My lords, of your kindness, lend me your ears," the performer's traditional opening. "First I shall sing a poem I composed about Cybele's lover, entitled *Attis*, and then a . . . a more rousing piece of mine called *The Bacchantes*."

The thousands stilled to a hollow hush. Nero strummed several notes and then began singing. But his throaty bass was muffled, hesitant, indistinct. "Louder!" Terpnus advised in a shouted whisper. "More body!"

The instructions confused Nero, and his playing and singing became unsynchronized. Laughter and then even hissing broke out in various pockets of the audience. Sabinus glanced at Plautia, who had thrust a hand over her open mouth. Seneca was cringing in a hot pool of embarrassment. Nero stopped, started over, and finally blended music and lyrics.

After finishing his breathy *Attis*, he launched with more spirit into *The Bacchantes* and gave a better performance. When it ended, the Augustiani, Nero's hired claque, rose as one man in wild jubilation and cheering. Soon the entire crowd learned the proper way to receive an imperial recital, and joined in the acclaim.

In his exhilaration, Nero invited the imperial party and all the Augustiani to an evening feast, and it was midnight before Sabinus and Plautia returned to the Quirinal.

"Well, what did you think of Nero's music?" she asked, as they were preparing for bed, since he had dropped no comment whatever.

"I think Nero's voice would improve remarkably if he shared the fate of the Attis he sang about."

"Oh? What was that?"

"Attis was castrated."

The next morning, Nero summoned Terpnus for a frank critique of his performance. The master lyrist came into the emperor's suite and found him on the floor, almost suffocating under two massive sheets of lead strapped across his chest.

"Don't overdo it, Caesar!" Terpnus warned. "I told you *one* lead plate would be quite enough to build up your wind."

"Well, how can I develop—aahh—my diaphragm otherwise?"

"Have you been purging yourself as I instructed?"

"Aahh—yes, enemas each time I eat too much."

"And disgorging?"

"Oh yes—aahh—always the feather."

"Have you been eating fruit? Apples? Anything else harmful to your voice?"

Nero shook his head. Then he looked up at Terpnus and asked, "Huuhh—how did I do last night?"

"Rather splendidly, Caesar, considering . . ."

"What?"

"That you have a rather weak and husky voice, dear boy. But it's improving . . . improving remarkably. So let's consider last night's performance something of a dress rehearsal. With patience, you'll soon be able to give your first concert. Oh, and you'll also have to work on your poetry if you want to use your own material." With that, Terpnus patted Nero's cheek and whisked himself off.

Nero doggedly continued his labored breathing for a half hour more. Then he unstrapped the lead plates and called for Seneca.

"Now don't complain about last night," Nero said, as soon as the philosopher came into view. "Terpnus said I did just splendidly."

"He's . . . a better judge than I in such matters."

"Yes he is." Nero frowned. "But I have some good news for you, Seneca. I think I *will* take your advice about broadening myself. You see, I don't want to be known only as a lyrist or an actor. I want to write more verse. I want to try painting and sculpture. Even philosophy."

Seneca could scarcely believe his ears, but he quickly organized a working circle of poets that met regularly with Nero on the Palatine. The emperor spent many hours on some of his verses, but when Seneca saw the polished versions, he was impressed. He was also certain that Nero had assistance, until one day he saw his worksheets. Unquestionably, the poems were his own—so heavily had the early drafts been crisscrossed with lines and arrows, and the wording erased. Nero also encouraged philosophers to come debate with Seneca after palace banquets, and he actually seemed to enjoy the intellectual wrangling that took place.

Might Nero choose the better path after all, Seneca wondered.

Late that spring, Pomponia had a slight edge to her voice as she reminded her son-in-law that Paul of Tarsus had been in Rome a year now, with prospects of his trial no nearer than when he arrived. But Sabinus had not been idle. Months before, he had given Burrus a full briefing on Paul and wondered if he could devise a legal means of quashing the case, since the prosecution still had not appeared.

As a favor to Sabinus, Burrus promised to do what he could. He laid the matter before Nero, though without mentioning the special interest of the Plautii. Had he chosen the wrong time, Burrus wondered, or was the emperor suddenly trying to play the legal purist? For Nero merely replied, "We'll wait for the prosecution to arrive in this case."

To help soften Paul's disappointment, Sabinus personally took him word of Nero's decision. While approaching Paul's lodging on the Viminal, he heard the missionary's voice through the open windows, apparently dictating some correspondence:

> . . . I want you to know, brothers, that what has happened to me has really served to advance the gospel, for it has become known throughout the whole Praetorian Guard and elsewhere that my imprisonment is for Christ. . . .

Poor man, Sabinus thought. As if the praetorians really cared about him! Here he was, trying to convert detention into some kind of success.

Sabinus knocked on the door. Inside, Paul and Luke welcomed him happily and then introduced a young, slender Greek with soft features named Timothy, who was sitting at a desk, taking Paul's dictation.

When Sabinus reported Nero's decision, Paul seemed not in the least dismayed. "I had no idea free custody would be this favorable," the apostle confessed. "I'm able to teach unhindered. Anyone who wishes to see me, can. And many, many come. Luke and I have a busy correspondence with our congregations in Greece and Asia. And the church here in Rome is *growing*, Prefect, more than we dreamed. Your dear mother-in-law finally asked to be baptized. Several of my guards are now converts, and they're carrying the 'good news,' as we call it, to comrades at the Castra Praetoria. Even in Caesar's household there are enough Christians for them to hold their own worship in the palace."

"There *are?*"

"Oh yes, especially among the group of servants who once belonged to Narcissus."

"Does . . . Caesar know about this? I don't believe he'd take kindly to news of Christians increasing their numbers in Rome."

"Why?"

"Paul . . . you just don't understand Caesar. If you did, you might even hope the prosecution would never arrive."

"I'd be glad enough to have things go on this way indefinitely." Paul smiled. "But I will, of course, have to stand before Caesar eventually."

"I don't know. We'll try to quash your case somehow."

"No, Prefect," Paul remonstrated, tugging more slack into his chain. "You must *not* try to do that, much as I appreciate your good will. I *must* stand before Caesar."

"Why? Oh, that vision of yours?"

"Yes, and—"

"I'm finally beginning to understand you, Paul of Tarsus. You really *want* Caesar to hear your case so that you can convince him to rule Christianity a legitimate religion. Pomponia's hearing was not enough to determine this. Your trial will be?"

"I don't know, my friend. There *is* some wisdom in what you say. But I'm merely heeding the words told us by the Christ: 'You will be dragged before governors and *kings* for my sake, to bear testimony before them and the Gentiles.'"

Several days later, Sabinus realized that he would no longer be in any position to give Paul official help. He read it several times before really believing it—that curt note just delivered from the Palatine. It bore Nero's official seal, but the rest of the message seemed hasty and informal. He read:

> Nero Caesar, *Princeps et Imperator*, to T. Flavius Sabinus, greeting. I hope you are in good health. I also am well.
>
> Rome has appreciated your performance as city prefect for the past five years. But I have decided to terminate your services as of July 1. Your successor will be L. Pedanius Secundus. I trust you will show him every courtesy in helping him learn the responsibilities of your office. Farewell.

Later in the day, Seneca and Burrus paid a visit to city headquarters to explain. "Obviously, we had nothing to do with it, Sabinus, but here's the reason," Burrus led off. "Or, there really are two reasons. One, Nero was angry about your attitude at the Juvenalia—which was ours too, of course, though we concealed it better." He smiled wryly. "The other reason is—well, do you know that Sicilian who sells Nero his racehorses?"

"Tigellinus?"

"Yes. He and Nero are getting *very* friendly, and he doesn't seem to like you."

"Small wonder!" Sabinus smirked. "I once saw him rubbing Nero with . . . with *boar's dung!* He said it was 'a charm against injury,' so I called him a simpering, superstitious fool. To his face!"

Burrus and Seneca chuckled briefly, then returned to their task of consoling Sabinus over the loss of his position. By now, however, his mood had changed abruptly, and he was smiling. "Enough, gentlemen!" he said. "Will you believe that I was nearly at the point of resigning anyway? And that the longer I dwell on Nero's note the happier I become?"

Seneca, who was only momentarily surprised, nodded slowly and sighed, "How many times have I said almost the same thing, Burrus?"

"And I, too. Well, you're the lucky one, Sabinus: now you're *able* to quit. But we'll miss you . . . more than we can say."

When Sabinus told Plautia about his dismissal, she looked at him for several moments in shock before screaming with delight and throwing her arms about him. "I'm so *very* happy, Sabinus," she cried, "so relieved, so—"

"That's hardly the way to talk to someone who's just lost his job!" he trifled.

"Oh, *good riddance* to that awful job! Think of it, darling: now we can get away from *him*. That fearful, flabby face of his and those puffy eyes won't be leering at us any more."

His smile quickly faded. "But what am I supposed to do with my life now, Plautia?"

She drew back and looked at him curiously. "Your income? Money's not the problem, is it, Sabinus?"

"Hardly," he laughed. "The Twin Brothers are doing *ridiculously* well, thanks to your cousin Quintus and his Midas touch!"

"Well, you could always take a more active role in the partnership."

"Perhaps. But I think the Senate would be more challenging . . ."

"Don't, Sabinus. Don't resume your seat there."

"Why not?"

"Please, darling, can't you stay clear of *all* politics? I . . . I might as well tell you. For months, now, I've wondered if I shouldn't have married some pleasant, unassuming man rather than someone so much in the public eye. I'm *weary* of all the anxieties. Yes, Sabinus. At this point, I'd prefer being a . . . a milkmaid somewhere in Apulia, as far away from Rome as I could manage." She paused and smiled. "But only if *you* were the peasant down there beside me." Then she pulled his face down to hers and kissed it.

Over the next weeks, Sabinus patiently groomed Pedanius in the tasks of city administration and found him capable enough. The wealthy senator was slightly embarrassed by his role as successor, though he could hardly disguise his pleasure at reaching the summit of senatorial privilege.

Without fanfare on the first of July, Flavius Sabinus quietly retired from office. He even declined Nero's offer of a farewell dinner, fearing that he might also supply the entertainment. Happily, he would now be able to see much more of Plautia. And appropriately, for she was gloriously pregnant.

"Congratulations on your timing, carissima mea," he said, stroking her hair upon learning the news. "You let us have a five-year honeymoon before starting the family."

"Disappointed, my darling?"

"Yes . . . I have to wait several months yet until I hold our son in my arms."

"You're sure of that, aren't you?"

"Of course."

Several weeks before the birth, Mother Pomponia moved into their Quirinal residence. Aulus made the traditional protests at losing a wife, but, all things considered, the aging new bachelor managed rather well on the Esquiline—with a corps of servants to assist him.

It was in the hottest part of August that Plautia chose to deliver. At the first symptoms, Sabinus nervously summoned the doctor. It was not an easy labor in that stifling, fervid atmosphere. Fretting and anxious, Sabinus had servants continually fanning Plautia, but Pomponia, sensing the time had come, finally ordered him out of the room. Not long afterward, Sabinus heard the cries, vaulted inside the door, and stared at the infant—a flushed pink, scrawny, dark-fuzzed, bawling bundle. "It's . . . it *is* a boy, isn't it?"

"What do you think?" Pomponia laughed.

Sabinus roared his approval, then hurried to the bedside. Pale and perspiring heavily, Plautia could still manage a serene smile as Sabinus covered her face with adoring kisses. Then he ran out into the atrium, cupped his hand in the central fountain and sent water splashing across the floor. "*I have a son!*" he shouted. An oversize laurel wreath was hung on his door, announcing the glad news to the neighborhood.

When Grandfather Aulus arrived, Pomponia made him promise to keep the exultant new father out of the bedroom. The men sat down to compose a list of those who should be notified of the birth and the grand *lustratio* nine days later.

Babies were unnamed the first eight days, lest they die and carry off a precious family name with them. But then the *lustratio*, or naming-day, arrived, and Sabinus' house was thronged with a merry mélange of guests. At noon, a nurse walked into the hall, cradling the infant and bowing to all the guests. She then approached the new father himself and gently laid the baby at his feet.

Solemnly, Sabinus bent over and lifted his tiny son off the floor. The guests burst into applause and cheering, for the act of "lifting up" declared the baby legitimate, a member of the Flavian gens, and entitled to all the protection of Roman law.

Sabinus formally announced, "Let the child be called Titus Flavius Sabinus!" Such a name was fully expected for a firstborn, though later they would start calling the baby Flavius to avoid the confusion of two Sabinuses in one house.

Relatives came forward and strung cords about the infant's neck with little metal toys attached: tiny dolls, animals, and tools, all designed to rattle and amuse the baby. Sabinus himself added a golden amulet which little Flavius would wear until the day he grew up and donned the toga of manhood.

The fall, winter, and spring that followed were months of pure discovery for Sabinus and Plautia. In that magnificent recapitulation of the life process called rearing a child, they watched their baby shed his blotchy infant features and look more like the human species. Their exuberant love—serene yet exciting, mature yet ever-fresh —now seemed to find a more profound basis for itself. Perhaps fame or wealth or power or adventure was not really the *summum bonum* in life, but this: the love of a man and a woman, the begetting of a child.

Pedanius was giving an adequate performance as city prefect, although members of his staff wished, a little wistfully, that Sabinus were back at his post. "Pedanius doesn't have your touch," they told him. "There's no group approach to problems, and he even has trouble in his own house, we understand." Sabinus appreciated their loyalty, but he was careful not to criticize his successor. New magistrates had a difficult enough time, he well knew.

No longer bound by the daily responsibilities of office, Sabinus took Plautia on a trip away from Rome. They both needed the change, and they were also searching out "the most pleasant spot in Italy" to build their country villa, a refuge from the noise and congestion of Rome. They visited Capri and the Bay of Naples. They were shown luxurious properties along the west Mediterranean coast of Italy. But the section that finally lured them was the picturesque, olive-groved Apennine foothills near Tibur (later, Tivoli), an enchanting resort area fifteen miles east of Rome. The place bubbled with hot springs and crystal fountains, and was shaded by fragrant groves full of exotic flowers and wildlife.

The captivating countryside seemed to return Sabinus to boyhood, and he romped up and down the hills and valleys at Tibur with tireless exuberance, as he had years earlier up in the Sabine country. He and Plautia bought acreage and selected the site for their villa, which lay very near Horace's fabled Sabine farm. Sabinus drew up his own plans, and presented them to his builder—who but Hermes? The Syrian later claimed he lost all his profits commuting each day from Rome with his detail of carpenters. He also admitted that building the villa was the most delightful project he had ever undertaken. The only engineering problem he encountered was the overzealous ex-Lord Mayor of Rome, hovering about to supervise the driving of each nail in the structure.

Late in the fall of A.D. 61, the villa was finished. Set into the brow of a hill, its peristyle overlooked a lush valley at Tibur on one side, and a trellised garden covering a sloping hillside on the other. Plautia wanted to move into the place permanently. They were to spend some of the happiest hours of their marriage here. They could not know that others would shortly spend some of their saddest.

19

"IT'S BEEN OVER TWO YEARS, Burrus," Sabinus told the praetorian commander. "I think Paul of Tarsus has waited long enough. The prosecution just hasn't arrived. I doubt they ever will."

"Why not?" Burrus frowned. "Any idea?"

"Paul tells me it was the chief priests at Jerusalem who indicted him—specifically, the high priest Ananias. But he's been deposed. So why should he, or anyone else, bother making the trip here merely to accuse one man who no longer troubles them?"

Burrus nodded.

"In any case, there seems to be no prosecution against Paul. But what happens to him, then? Is he to grow old and die under house arrest?"

Burrus scratched his russet scalp for several moments. Then he said, "All right. I'll press Nero to open the case. And I'll suggest that he follow Claudius' precedent: if the prosecution failed to appear, Claudius would dismiss the suit."

"Thanks, Burrus." Sabinus squeezed his shoulder in gratitude.

"Ah, Sabinus . . . what's your special interest in this case? You wouldn't be . . . turning Christian, would you?"

"Hardly!" Sabinus laughed. "It's my mother-in-law. Dear Pomponia's been hounding me. Though I will admit that Paul's a good and harmless sort."

Later that day, Sabinus sent Paul a message with the promising news. The apostle read it with a broadening smile. "At last, my brothers!" he cried. "My case will soon go before Caesar! And it looks favorable."

They cheered and embraced Paul.

"And Luke," he said, "this part involves you. Flavius Sabinus suggests we prepare in writing our version of what happened at Jerusalem in case it's needed. An excellent idea, I think. But why not begin it earlier? Yes, perhaps with my appearance before Gallio in Corinth."

"The first time you faced a Roman judge?"

"Exactly." Paul smiled.

"I'll cast an outline of the material today."

The next morning, Sabinus found Burrus at his door. "I'm sorry, friend," he said, "but Nero won't quash the case. He insists on hearing it personally."

"But who will serve as prosecution?"

"I don't know. He may just use the documents of indictment from the two governors of Judea: Felix and Festus."

"Felix *is* in Rome, isn't he? Maybe we should summon him as a witness."

Burrus shook his head emphatically. "I don't think I would. Felix finished his term in disgrace. In fact, Nero was wondering where to banish him when Pallas suddenly crawled out of retirement and worked his magic once again. He pleaded in his brother's behalf and Nero gave in."

"Ha! Using Felix *would* be a misstep, then. But tell me this, Burrus: would it prejudice Paul's case if *I* conducted his defense? After all, Nero dismissed me from office . . ."

"I wonder . . . No, I don't think so. Nero's not too happy with Pedanius. I recently heard him say that he lost a good man in you."

"Then he's forgotten about my . . . opinion of his recitals?"

"Let's hope so." Burrus smiled.

In November of 61, Paul of Tarsus was summoned to the Palatine. His close companion-secretary, Luke, accompanied him, as did, of course, the guard to whom he was chained. Luke was carrying a

new scroll, his record of Paul's activities ever since the days in
Corinth.

Inside the palace, Sabinus met them, also carrying a sheaf of
scrolls. His eyes were narrow with concern. "I've some bad news for
you, Paul," he said. "Caesar's going to make a case of this anyway,
and a certain Ofonius Tigellinus will serve as your prosecutor. Have
you heard the name?"

"No."

"Well, he's something new on the political scene here. Not a very
happy record. He's a Sicilian who took his first step in politics . . .
into Agrippina's bed. Then he was exiled to Greece, where he
turned fishmonger to stay alive. Claudius let him return only if he
promised to stay out of sight, so Tigellinus bred racehorses in southern Italy. That's how he came to Caesar's attention, and now they're
close friends."

"Don't worry, Senator," Paul reassured Sabinus. "My life is not in
Caesar's hands. If I have further work to do, God will deliver me
and I'll surely be acquitted. If not—if my task is finished—I'll gladly
depart to be with Christ, which is far better."

Sabinus shook his head. "I can't believe your serenity, Paul. But
you'd better make a strong defense for yourself. If you don't—if
you're passive as that Jesus of Nazareth was, you'll surely be condemned."

"He was determined to die for us, as part of God's plan. But certainly I'll testify in my defense."

By now they had reached the forest of columns that was the imperial hall of justice, refulgent in the rays of the morning sun. Overlooking the Forum, the hall was lined with precious red marble from
Egypt and domed in blue-glazed tile spangled with golden stars to
represent the sky. At the far end was the imperial tribunal, where
toga-clad figures were slipping into benches on both sides of the emperor's dais.

"The men filing in behind the tribunal will act as Caesar's assessors—assistant judges," Sabinus explained to Paul. "See, there's Annaeus Seneca. And Burrus. And the other three are senators."

"Are there always five assessors?"

"Oh no. There may be as many as twenty for important cases. Ah
—excuse me, but—"

"I understand." Paul smiled and took his place in front of the
dais, Sabinus at his side.

At last, Nero himself entered the chamber, followed by a tall, middle-aged man with broad shoulders and tanned, swarthy skin whom Sabinus identified as Tigellinus. But Paul stared far more curiously at the blond-haired young man in the amethystine toga who ruled the world. Everyone rose to salute the emperor as he seated himself in an ivory magistrate's chair on the raised dais. Bidding the court be seated, Nero leaned over to converse with his colleagues on either side of him. Then he glanced at the prisoner in chains before him, clearly less than impressed by what he saw.

"Are *you* Paul of Tarsus?" he asked, with obvious emphasis.

"I am, Caesar."

"And you claim to be a Roman citizen?"

"I *am* a Roman citizen, Caesar."

"Can you prove it? How did you get it, by purchase?"

"No. I was born a citizen. My father was awarded citizenship by the governor of Cilicia for his services to the city of Tarsus. My name is on the censor's list in Tarsus and may be checked by any of your agents in the East. Certainly I would not have dared appeal to you unless my citizenship could be attested."

"All right," Nero nodded. "This court is now in session in the case of . . . ah"—he snapped his fingers and a secretary came running with an inscribed tablet—"in the case of Ananias, former high priest of Jerusalem, versus Paul of Tarsus. I understand that Ofonius Tigellinus will serve as prosecutor, and T. Flavius Sabinus will conduct the defense. Is that correct?"

Heads nodded. And no eyebrows were raised at two prominent Romans pleading the case of an obscure Jew, for similar instances were common.

Nero opened, "If this were a civil case on appeal from the provinces, I, like my divine predecessors, would have delegated it to a senator of consular rank. But since it involves a criminal charge, I've decided to hear it personally. However, I must regret, my colleagues" —he turned to the assessors—"that a regular prosecution did not appear. Still, lest it be said that Caesar awarded a case by default, Tigellinus has kindly consented to serve as prosecutor. You may proceed." Nero nodded to his tall friend, who now arose.

"Noble Caesar, honored assessors," Tigellinus began, in a deep voice. "I have informed myself on this case from various sources, including these documents of indictment compiled by our governors in Judea, Felix and Festus."

"Ah . . . pardon me, Tigellinus," Nero interrupted. "Would you show me those scrolls for a moment?"

Tigellinus handed the documents to Nero, who unrolled them and then became irritated. "I've never in my life seen an uglier pair of scrolls! The papyrus is stained. The ink runs. They're wrinkled and smell too, musty as a sewer! What's the matter with our governors . . . sending in something as disgraceful as this?"

"True, Caesar." Tigellinus smiled. "But the documents were saturated with seawater, I understand, in a shipwreck off Malta. Is that correct?"

Sabinus and Paul nodded.

"Oh," said Nero. "Continue, then."

"It was before Felix in Caesarea that the Jewish high priest and his colleagues indicted the defendant on three charges. We herewith reiterate these charges as our own formal indictment: first, that this Paul is a pestilent agitator, who is causing disturbances among Jews throughout the Empire; second, that he is a ringleader of the sect of the Nazarenes—"

"What in the world is that?" Nero frowned.

"In Rome we call them Christiani, Caesar."

"Oh . . . them. Yes, I've heard of them. Continue."

"And third, that Paul tried to desecrate the temple in Jerusalem. Indeed, he was seized in the very act. Now, as to—"

"*Were* these the charges, Paul of Tarsus?" Nero again interposed.

"Yes, they were, Caesar."

"Continue."

"As to the first charge, there is no question but that disorder and rioting erupt wherever this agitator goes. He has undertaken three long journeys in Asia and Greece to gain adherents for the Christian sect, and just as sickness follows exposure to the plague, so violence follows this man. He was driven out of Antioch, attacked in Iconium, and stoned in Lystra. Then he carried the disease to Europe! He enraged the merchants in Philippi, raised turmoil in Thessalonica, and set off a riot among the Jews of Corinth and the silversmiths of Ephesus. He created his *final* uproar, thank the Fates, in Jerusalem, where he was arrested."

Nero's eyes were widening on the defendant. "This *one man* did all these things?" he asked.

"Yes, and much more, Princeps. The Empire hasn't had such a treasonable troublemaker since Spartacus himself!"

"What proof do you have for this charge?" asked Nero, in the standard formula.

"If Caesar pleases, I thought I would expand on the other two charges first, and then present the proofs."

"No, no, no. I like to exhaust each charge—hearing both the accusation and defense on it individually—before moving on to the next."

"An excellent procedure, Caesar"—Tigellinus bowed—"and one our courts would do well to follow. Very well, then. I have here depositions from Asia and Greece testifying to these riots." He handed them to Nero.

The emperor studied the documents for some minutes. Then he passed them on to his assessors. "Continue."

"I call as witness Senator Lucius Junius Gallio, the brother of our esteemed Annaeus Seneca."

Gallio, whose presence had been desired by both sides in the case, rose to take his place before the tribunal. He looked at the defendant a little curiously, then nodded. Paul, in turn, smiled a greeting at his former judge.

"Senator Gallio," said Tigellinus, "you were proconsul of Achaia in the city of Corinth?"

"I was. Ten years ago."

"Have you ever seen the defendant before?"

"Yes. Some of the Corinthian Jews indicted him before my tribunal."

"Could you tell us what happened?"

Gallio reported the case as best he could remember, admitting that there had been a riot. But he defended his decision in dismissing the suit: "Obviously, it was an internal matter concerning the Jewish religion."

"Not so obviously, Senator," said Tigellinus. "But we shall discuss that point later on. However, this testimony proves, noble Caesar, that the defendant is in fact an agitator who touched off rioting in Corinth. And the depositions from our magistrates elsewhere prove the same for the other cities. I rest my evidence on the first charge."

"As well you might," commented Nero. "This is a serious business. *Very* serious indeed! I had no idea a man so small could cause so much trouble."

Sabinus winced at this display of partiality, which was adverse to Roman legal procedure. Clearly, Nero was not very practiced at the bar. Yet he was glad that Tigellinus had raised this charge first, for, by all odds, Paul was most vulnerable on this point.

Nero conferred with his assessors. Then he looked at Sabinus and said, "We will now hear the defense on the first charge."

Sabinus stood up and said, "The prosecution has ably listed the altercations that sometimes arose when the defendant taught the beliefs of the Christiani, although comparing him to the bloody rebel Spartacus was both inept and false. More than anything else, Caesar, we are dealing here with the Eastern—not Roman—mind. We in the West are a tolerant, practical people who are not swept up into such furious partisanship for or against a new philosophy or religion. But the Greeks, as you know, will wrangle endlessly in the Athenian agora and even come to blows over some minor point in logic. But when they discuss religion and the gods—well, we all know what happened to Socrates."

"Oh, I don't know about that," Nero broke in. "We in Rome also debate philosophy, and I saw one of Seneca's opponents once leap for his throat after he'd nicely cut his arguments to shreds," Nero chuckled. "Eh, Seneca?"

The philosopher smiled and nodded.

Nero was swallowing his bait, Sabinus grinned to himself, or at least seemed to be mellowing a bit. He resumed, "Now as different as the Greek genius is—or seems to be—from the Roman, so the Jewish mind is *much* different again. To the Jew, statecraft is not important. Neither is the military. Nor is philosophy, or art, or sculpture, or science. Only *one thing* has ultimate significance for the Jew, and that is his religion, his belief in one God. He will hold to this with a furious tenacity that dare not be tampered with."

"But your defendant *did* tamper with it," Tigellinus exclaimed, "and so caused—"

"Please don't interrupt." Sabinus scowled and then continued, "Now the Jew has another trait: call it his 'priceless individuality' if you please. He is quick and bright, and he has his own opinions about everything—especially religion. We all know the expression: 'Two Jews, three opinions.' So it's not surprising that when a very religious people is also very opinionated, disturbances are *bound* to result. The defendant, therefore, is merely the latest teacher to cause what is almost normal controversy within Judaism."

"But Gentiles rioted too—"

"Only when Paul's teaching rubbed against some vested interest.

In Ephesus, it was the silversmiths, who feared that worshiping an invisible god would halt sales of their little silver statuettes of Diana."

Seneca began chuckling at this point, but he stopped when Nero turned to him with raised eyebrows.

"I now call the accused himself as witness for the defense," Sabinus announced.

Paul, who had been listening to the trial with extreme interest, almost as if it concerned someone else, now stood up.

"Would you care to add anything to what has been said so far?" Sabinus inquired.

"Yes, I would. First this. In every city we visited, we made it a practice to teach *both* the Jews and the Gentiles as well, for faith in the Christ is not limited to one or the other. Everyone is welcome."

"Aha!" Tigellinus stood up. "That proves, then, that the Christians are *not* a sect of Judaism: Jews do not wish to make converts of Gentiles. Christians do."

"It proves nothing of the sort," Sabinus rejoined. "And you are misinformed, Tigellinus, for Jews certainly *do* make converts among Greeks and Romans."

"I'm afraid they do," Nero smirked ruefully. "Even my . . . or, ah . . . the Lady Poppaea is interested in them. Though she's not a proselyte. They call her a 'god-fearer' . . . whatever that means. But let the defendant continue."

"I would also like to emphasize that I have never incited anyone to riot anywhere. And I have never been judged guilty of anything before any tribunal—Judean, Greek, or Roman—and I would beg this court to remember that fact."

"Well said, Paul," commented Sabinus. "Would you care to cross-examine the witness, Tigellinus?"

"I would. In essence, the defense argues that Jews are prone to factionalism, and this is only more of the same. What, then, are the other factions among the Jews?"

"Some are Sadducees, who do not believe in a resurrection," Paul replied. "Others are Pharisees, like me, who do. Again—"

"You're a Pharisee too?"

"Yes. To continue, a third Jewish sect is that of the Essenes who lead an ascetic life near the Asphalt Lake in Judea. A fourth would be the nationalistic Zealot party. A fifth is—"

"But none of these factions quarrel among themselves or cause the sort of rioting that follows your preaching."

"On the contrary. Sometimes it's much worse, with bloodshed too." Paul frowned and cited several recent examples.

"So, then, are you really claiming that you Christians are merely a Jewish sect? Tell me honestly, Paul." Tigellinus stared directly into the apostle's eyes.

"No, not 'merely a Jewish sect,'" Paul replied. "The Faith considers itself the *fulfillment* of Judaism because it centers in the Christ or Messiah foretold in the Hebrew Scriptures."

"I see. But isn't it possible that the Christians and the Jews will *separate* from one another in the future, since they seem to be at such odds?"

"Yes," Paul sighed. "I regret that this *is* possible, though it's not the ideal we seek."

"Indeed. Has this separation not already taken place?" Tigellinus probed, a gleam in his eye.

"Yes. It has in certain places. Some of the synagogues have become Christian. Many have not."

"So! We've proven, then, noble Caesar, that the Christians are *separate* and *distinct* from the Jews, so they dare not claim legitimacy by hiding behind our generous laws favoring the Jews! I have no further questions for the witness."

"Then you may continue, Senator," said Nero.

Sabinus was nettled. "The prosecution must *not* vault over to unwarranted conclusions," he said. "The fact that Jews and Christians may now be separating or will separate in the future proves, in fact, that they were *not* separated in the past, when Paul did his preaching! Indeed, the founder was Jewish and so were his twelve closest associates. So is much of the membership. The chief Christian in the city of Rome—this Aquila sitting over there with the red beard," he pointed, "is Jewish. The defendant is Jewish. So if this is not a Jewish quarrel, what is? And such religious debate *is* permitted to Jews under our Law of Associations. The defense rests on the first charge."

Nero conferred with his assessors for several minutes. Then he looked to Tigellinus and said, "We are ready to hear the second charge."

"The next accusation against Paul of Tarsus," said Tigellinus, "is that he is a leader of the sect of the Nazarenes or Christians. Now this charge is so obvious that—"

"If it please the court," Sabinus interrupted, "the defense agrees that Paul of Tarsus *is* a leader of the Christians. But we wonder why this is called a 'charge'?"

"Because the sect is illegal: Christians are not protected by the Law of Associations."

"The sect is legal," Sabinus rejoined. "Christians, as Jews, *are* so protected."

"I see we're back to that point again. But let me go on to sketch some of the crimes perpetrated by this cult, patient Caesar, and you'll see why Christians cannot be tolerated in the Empire." Tigellinus then opened his bag of vicious rumors about Christians and sorted out the lurid contents.

"Objection!" Sabinus cried. "I let the prosecution speak on to see if the ridiculous lies about the Christians would actually be used in this court. We're after truth here, not fantasy. These are tired old calumnies, Caesar, and they have no more basis in fact than the shopworn tale of Augustus' wife smearing poison on his figs to make herself a widow. Do you recall the trial of Pomponia Graecina four years ago?"

"Yes, but not the details," Nero replied. "She also was accused of being a Christian, wasn't she?"

"Yes, and her case is so relevant to the present charges that I've taken the liberty of preparing copies of the Senate's transcript of that hearing for you and your assessors."

"Do you really think it would be germane, Senator? This trial of a wife by her own husband?"

"It would, Caesar. And it would save us all much time in the present case." At that point, Sabinus noticed Tigellinus giving him a particularly malicious frown.

"Well, we've sat long enough this morning anyway." Nero yawned. "We'll adjourn court until tomorrow morning at the same time. Meanwhile, my colleagues, we can all read what happened to dear Pomponia," he added, with a wry smile.

Before leaving, Sabinus reviewed strategy with Paul and Luke, and then returned to the Quirinal, where he related everything to Plautia. Certainly the most difficult part of the trial was past, and Nero had taken it in rare good humor. With his new boon companion as prosecutor, however, this proved nothing.

Then he recalled something. There was a *reason* for Tigellinus' scowl over the transcripts of Pomponia's trial. Yes indeed! It was Tigellinus' *own son-in-law*, Cossutianus Capito, who had served as bungling prosecutor at Pomponia's hearing! Unquestionably, Sabinus sighed, he—and the Christians—now had a powerful enemy.

The next morning, Nero opened deliberations by commenting, "We have read the transcript of Pomponia Graecina's trial. And I must say, *some* of the things for which the Christians are accused would make them quite an intriguing sect indeed." He paused to leer at his assessors.

"Now as I see it," Nero continued, "we have three alternatives in this case. One, to regard the Christians as a sect of Judaism and therefore protected by law; two, to regard them as different from Judaism, but harmless enough to be similarly protected; and three, to regard them as a noxious sect which must be eliminated. The defendant would be declared not guilty if either of the first two were established, but guilty if the third were. Is this a proper summary?"

While Tigellinus hesitated, Sabinus nodded his agreement, delighted that Nero had been fair enough to consider the middle alternative.

"But before this can be done," Nero continued, "we must have more information about the defendant." He stared at Paul for what seemed like a long time, then asked, "*Why* have you decided to dedicate your life to spreading this new message?"

"It was a direct commission, Caesar. To me it was as clear and definite as your assigning a governor to some overseas province."

"Who commissioned you?"

"I'll be happy to explain. Originally, I was hostile to the Christians. I even traveled to Damascus to arrest any I found there and return them in chains to Jerusalem for trial. But just as I approached Damascus, an intense light from heaven overcame me and I fell to the ground. I heard a voice saying, '*Saul*'—for that was my former name—'*Saul, Saul, why do you persecute me?*' I replied, 'Who are you, Lord?' And the voice said, '*I am Jesus, whom you are persecuting. But rise and enter the city, and you will be told what you are to do.*'

"The men who were traveling with me stood speechless, hearing the voice but seeing nothing. Then I stood up and opened my eyes, but all was darkness. I was blind. I had to be led into Damascus by hand. For three days I was in that condition, but then a leader of the Christians came to the place where I was staying and said to me, 'Brother Saul, Jesus who appeared to you on the road has sent me to restore your sight.' He put his hands on me, and . . . I could *see* again! Then he baptized me and said, 'The Lord told me that you are his chosen instrument to carry his name before the Jews and the Gentiles and the rulers.' Then, after months of intense study, I came to see that Jesus is indeed the promised Messiah, and that one day I would stand before even you, Caesar, to testify that there is only one God, who created this world, and that he saved it through Jesus the Christ, and that one day he will also judge it."

Nero shifted uneasily in his ivory chair, while Seneca, Burrus, and the other assessors were staring uncomprehendingly at Paul. Any reference to the supernatural was something ominous and uncomfortable to superstitious Romans.

But Tigellinus started laughing. "Really, Caesar, are we to take such weird tales seriously? This Paul must be a fanatic. Or mentally unbalanced. Only wild men conjure up such visions for themselves."

"I call Paul's associate, Lucanus, as witness," said Sabinus.

When Luke had been identified, Sabinus asked him, "Besides serving as the defendant's secretary and—as I see from your record—historian, do you have another profession?"

"Yes. I am a physician."

"Did the defendant ever manifest symptoms of mental illness?"

"No."

"Or of the falling sickness—*epilepsia?*"

"No."

"What is his medical condition, then?"

"Fine, except for some squinting, due to nearsightedness."

"Bah!" Tigellinus huffed. "Anyone who has to have a personal physician traveling with him must be quite sick indeed."

Luke smiled. "I wasn't accompanying Paul in that capacity. And I will swear to the fact of his health."

Nero was beginning to lose patience. "Enough! Let's finish with this. Sweet Jupiter, why are religious matters always so complicated and mysterious? That's why I'm not a religious man myself." He turned to Paul. "But continue. What did you do after that . . . weird vision of yours?"

Paul resumed with an account of his missionary journeys, with some emphasis on his hearing before Gallio in Corinth. At that point, Sabinus called Gallio as witness, and he repeated his testimony, adding, however, that Paul had not seemed a seditious sort, and that his opponents had caused the confrontation.

"All right," said Nero. "We're ready to hear the final charge."

Tigellinus stood up and said, "The third charge is that the defendant desecrated the Holy Temple in Jerusalem by bringing a Gentile inside its sacred limits. Surrounding the Jewish temple, noble Caesar, are thirteen columns, each of which bears the following inscription:

> Let no Gentile enter within the balustrade and enclosure surrounding the sanctuary. Whoever is caught will be personally responsible for his consequent death.

As you know, Rome has granted Jews the privilege of administering the death penalty in *this instance alone*. The defendant, then, is worthy of death."

"And the proof for this charge?"

"The trial documents show that he was arrested in the very act."

"The defense?"

Sabinus was smiling. "I'm happy to say, Caesar, that this is the easiest charge of all to disprove, for no Gentile was ever involved. Again I call the defendant to witness. Please tell us what happened that day, Paul."

"I went up to the temple with four other Jewish Christians to perform a vow. But several of my opponents who had previously seen me *outside* the temple with a Gentile Christian named Trophimus now assumed that he was one of the four who were with me inside, but this was false. It was this misunderstanding that led to my arrest."

"And the evidence for this defense?" Nero asked Sabinus.

"Depositions from the four Jews and from Trophimus were laid before both Felix and Festus, as their documents indicate." He handed a copy to Nero.

Scanning the material, Nero passed it on to his assessors and said, "Now hear me, gentlemen. I'm getting very *tired* of all this . . . it's much too quibbling for my bones. In fact, I *despise* all religious cults because they take normal men and women and turn them into fanatics. I don't believe *any* of them!—Oh, once I had some faith in the Syrian Magna Mater, but I finally uri—ah—relieved myself on her image too.—So, gentlemen, we really must finish this. Please deliver your summations, and I pray you: *keep them brief.*"

Tigellinus now delivered a brilliant summary of the charges against Paul. The man *could* do more than breed horses after all, Sabinus admitted to himself. When a quarter hour had passed, he closed ominously: "If the defendant had caused only one or two disturbances, we might overlook them. But we have here a long and ugly list of civil disruptions, and if 'no slander is without some foundation,' imagine what a structure of evil is building from his efforts. What this man preaches is *not* Judaism—mark my words, it will become separate from Judaism—and it must *not be given a legal basis* in the Empire. I ask you, noble Caesar and distinguished assessors, do we really want a new and noxious eastern cult in Rome? Do we need another Isis and Osiris, a new Magna Mater, a fresh Cybele or Mithras, an occult astrology that gives its leaders a sunstroke? Or, for that matter, a different and more poisonous Judaism? Don't we have enough trouble with these religions that compete against the gods of the state? Because *if* you release this man, you will be giving his religion legal precedent in Rome. In the name of the gods who made Rome great, I plead that you take on to yourselves the courage of our ancestors and *condemn* this man! To death! I rest my case."

"Bravo, Tigellinus!" Nero stood up to applaud his friend. "Well spoken! Well spoken indeed!" The emperor's clients and friends took their cue and began shouting similar approval from the sides of the hall.

Sabinus cringed at this display, trying to maintain an inner calm in the face of Nero's blatant partiality. He noticed that Seneca's face was as rosy as he had ever seen it.

Now he stood up to deliver his summation, first refuting Tigellinus' "specious suggestions" that Christians were eastern cultists with a gore-saturated worship like Cybele. Had Pomponia Graecina become some raving devotee? Then he concluded:

"There is no question but that Paul of Tarsus is innocent of all charges brought against him. Perhaps Senator Gallio here was the wisest of all: he saw that it was merely a religious dispute, and so he dismissed the case. And at every Roman tribunal since that time, Paul was, or would have been, acquitted. In Philippi the magistrates apologized to him. In Judea, Felix knew he was innocent but wanted a bribe for his release. On Cyprus our proconsul Sergius Paulus befriended him, and on Malta he healed the father of Publius, our governor there, as he has many others. The centurion Julius who accompanied him testified to his great assistance during their shipwreck. Here in Rome he has lived for two years, doing nothing more or less than what he had done in the ten years previous: telling people about what he calls 'the good news.' And there have *not* been any riots.

"Finally, I would ask you to remember that the greatness of Rome lies in her tolerance of many diverse opinions. Rome has learned what Athens forgot at the trial of Socrates: that ideas are, and must remain, *free*. I beg the court not to reverse what has become our glorious tradition. If the defendant had truly sought the overthrow of Roman government, as a senator and former magistrate, I would never have undertaken his defense. But, as you know, Paul of Tarsus has advised his Christians that they are to pray for you, Caesar, and obey the imperial government. The defense rests."

Pockets of applause arose as Sabinus returned to his seat.

"Very well," said Nero, holding up his hands for silence. "My assessors and I will retire to prepare our verdict."

While they withdrew to an anteroom of the great hall of justice, a knot of excited people surrounded Sabinus. "You were *marvelous*, darling!" Plautia said adoringly.

"When did *you* get here? I thought you were—"

"Back home? I couldn't stay away. Mother and Father would have been here too, but she's preparing a celebration for Paul tonight."

"A *celebration?* That's what I call faith."

"Your lovely wife was escorted, partner, and I had the privilege," said Quintus Lateranus. "Not a bad job, Sabinus. You could have been a pleader."

"Well . . . there was this proven defense strategy some amateur used at Pomponia's trial . . ."

"I know, I know," he laughed.

Minutes passed as they waited for the verdict. Then a half hour. A wisp of apprehension tingled inside Sabinus. He had hoped for a quick and favorable decision. He saw that Tigellinus, on the other hand, seemed to have no concerns whatever. And why need he have had any? He had conducted the prosecution as a favor to Nero and without the presence of plaintiffs.

Sabinus tried to assess the assessors. He *hoped* Seneca and Burrus were in his camp, but he could not be entirely sure, especially if

Seneca had taken a philosophical dislike to Paul. And the other three were very questionable. Two of the senators were ominous: known parasites of Nero and Tigellinus. The third was honest, but his old-school republicanism might, like crusty old Cato's, be opposed to importing any more "foreign superstitions."

Almost an hour had elapsed, and now everyone was concerned. The lively conversations in the hall had muted into strained and whispered comments. Sabinus looked for Paul, and noticed that he and the guard had wandered off to a corner. The apostle seemed completely lost in thought—or was it prayer?—as he paced back and forth with his eyes closed, his manacled wrist rubbing against his free hand.

Nero and his assessors reappeared at last, and solemnly reseated themselves. When all was quiet, Nero declared: "I need not tell you that this has been a *very* difficult case for us to decide. And first I must commend Ofonius Tigellinus for undertaking the prosecution. In view of the circumstances, he has done magnificently. And it was also generous of you, Flavius Sabinus, to devote your time to the defense. Because of both your efforts, I wish it were possible for this court to decide here and now the legal status of the Christians. If this were the Senate, and if the Fathers were minded to deal with such religious intricacies, and if all plaintiffs were present—if, if, if . . . there are too many ifs in this case—but *if* all these conditions had been met, then a senatorial court might well have decided to legalize or proscribe the religion of the Christiani.

"This court, with its limited evidence, is clearly unable to do that. However, the case of one, Paul of Tarsus, must certainly be resolved, and we shall resolve it. But his condemnation or acquittal must *not* be regarded as setting a precedent in any sense for other Christians, in view of the difficulties cited. Is this understood?"

Tigellinus nodded, but Sabinus looked disturbed. Paul seemed particularly crestfallen and was on the point of trying to say something.

Nero cut him off. "I would remind the defense that this is the unanimous opinion of the assessors, and the best you can expect for now. It may even work to your advantage—if Paul is condemned, the Christians of Rome need not follow him."

Sabinus looked up and said, "Certainly, Caesar. We accept this decision . . . and, of course, the verdict, whatever it may be."

"Very well, then. We will vote in the Augustan manner. Each

assessor has received the usual three voting tablets, marked with an A for *absolvo*, C for *condemno*, and NL for *non liquet*."* Then, turning to each side of him, Nero said, "I will cast my vote only after totaling yours, my colleagues, since I intend to abide by the will of the majority. Leave your tablets face down in front of you. When your decision is reached, place the appropriate tablet into the voting urn."

Seneca was the first to rise. He walked purposefully to the urn in front of Nero and dropped his tablet inside. Following him, Burrus did the same, and the three senators after him.

Nero now carefully retrieved each tablet. He reached into the urn, picked one out and announced, for the benefit of the court secretary, "*Condemno.*"

Perspiration broke out on Sabinus' forehead.

Nero plucked out a second tablet. "*Condemno,*" he declared.

A jab of anxiety pierced Sabinus' stomach. One more condemnation and Paul could not possibly be acquitted. He looked over at Tigellinus and saw a triumphant smile breaking across his face. Paul seemed strangely passive, though his intense eyes never left Nero.

"*Absolvo,*" said Nero, holding up the third tablet.

Again his hand reached into the urn and withdrew another tablet. "*Absolvo,*" he announced.

The entire hall now held its breath for the final, tie-breaking tablet. Even Paul straightened a bit and moved ahead in his seat.

Nero pulled it out, and his forehead wrinkled with disgust as he let the words drip out of his mouth: "*Non liquet!*"

For some moments, a mortal silence hung over the hall of justice. The five assessors—their number intentionally odd—had still managed an even split.

"So, as always, Caesar must make the ultimate decision," Nero almost whimpered. "And this is one I'd hoped not to have to make." He looked at Tigellinus and saw a smile that all but shouted, "I know how you'll vote, *amicus meus.*" Then he glanced at Seneca and saw eyes pleading for clemency. There was no question of how Seneca had voted: a philosopher, secular or religious, must always fight for freedom of expression.

Then Nero looked at Paul, who had stopped squinting and now

---

* "Not proven," the equivalent of abstention.

gazed at him with a penetrating serenity. Nero heard himself say, "The prisoner will rise to receive the verdict."

He stared at the manacled figure for several seconds more, and then started constricting the back of his palate for the hard C sound of *condemno*. But he stopped abruptly and murmured, "*Absolvo*."

"What was that?" the clerk inquired.

Nero cleared his throat and repeated, in a strange voice, "*Absolvo*."

A shocked silence was cut by cheering as friends joyfully surrounded Sabinus and Paul. But Paul and Nero continued looking at each other almost hypnotically, the apostle's smile of gratitude finally breaking the spell. Later Tigellinus would ask his friend what had happened and why he decided as he did, but would get no clear reply.

Nero now came out of his trance and held up his hands for silence. "Guards, remove the chains from the prisoner. But I must remind the court again that *no precedent whatever* has been set for the toleration of Christians in the Roman Empire. This movement is on probation . . . at best." Then his eyes shifted back to Paul, and he clipped his words. "We Romans don't wish to become Christians, Paul of Tarsus. For the time being it seems you are not leading a seditious movement, but you would do well to leave our city and stop your preaching here."

"I do indeed plan to leave Rome, Caesar."

"Very well, then. This court is adjourned."

Paul's first sensation was a left wrist that was cool and free—that joint which had been encased in metal, warmed by his perspiration, for more than two years. The next was a chorus of congratulations. Gallio grasped his hand to remark, with a chuckle, "I *told* them they should simply have followed my precedent in Corinth." But it was Gallio's brother Seneca who surprised Paul by stepping down from the dais to come over and greet him.

"I'm somewhat intrigued by your beliefs," said Seneca, "what little I could learn of them from this trial. Perhaps we could discuss them before you leave Rome."

"Indeed. And I've been much impressed with your treatises, esteemed Seneca. Of all the 'pagan philosophies,' as we call them, none approaches Christianity more closely than your Stoicism. You believe in a supreme god—and so do we. You stress the equality of all men, be they slave or emperor—so do we. And your famous statement, 'Treat those below you as you would be treated by those above you' is quite similar to something Jesus taught us."

"Amazing." Seneca looked incredulous. "And where will you travel after Rome?"

"Eventually I'll pay another visit to our new congregations in Greece. But first I plan a brief trip to Spain. I've always hoped to travel that far west, and our teaching must be heard in all the world —so the Christ said."

"By all means, *do* get to Spain. Iberia's a very different country, but very beautiful. And please greet the good people in my home town of Corduba."

Pomponia's faith had not been misplaced. That evening, she gave a victory celebration for Paul. Their door had been crossed with palm leaves to salute the legal triumph, and even Aulus shared the gladness because of the way his wife brimmed with joy at Paul's release. The apostle publicly thanked God—and Sabinus—for their efforts in his behalf. He also told them that Simon Peter, the leader of the apostles, would soon be arriving in Rome, and he hoped they would give him as warm a reception as he had enjoyed.

"But for now," he said, a little wistfully, "my mission in Rome has ended, and the Lord clearly has other work for me to do. Perhaps we shall never see each other again. Perhaps we shall—I hope so. Meanwhile, farewell and thank you, my beloved friends." Then he raised his hands for the blessing: "The grace of our Lord Jesus Christ, the love of God the Father, and the fellowship of the Holy Spirit abide with you all."

"Amen," they responded.

Late that night, back at their lodging on the Viminal, Paul paced the floor restlessly. Luke asked him what was the matter.

"If only mine *had* been a . . . what they call a 'test case,'" said Paul. "I was so certain that my appeal to Caesar would result in a decision favoring the Faith, not Paul of Tarsus. It would have made everything so much easier for us . . . everywhere in the Empire."

"Perhaps the Faith isn't supposed to grow so easily," Luke observed. "Didn't Jesus say, 'If they persecuted me, they will also persecute you'? Maybe it must grow through hardship and challenge."

"And pain. And blood. And persecution." Paul nodded. "And not merely, as now, through quarreling and division and schism. Whenever our powerful friends ask about our progress, we smile and say the cause grows mightily. And it has. But oh, the *inner* troubles!" he sighed. "The factions, the bickering over how much of the Hebrew law still applies, the party spirit, the loveless strife—it's *not* supposed to happen among us, but it does. Jewish Christians and Gentile Christians suspicious of each other, the orthodox versus the freer-minded, the Greek faithful versus the Roman faithful, jealousies, disputes, resentments, mistrust."

He turned to Luke with a smile. "I'm sorry that your record of our travels didn't get presented in court. They're very well written, Luke. I wonder if they would have made the difference."

"I doubt that. Nero was getting impatient with all the depositions as it was."

"But your work isn't in vain. The church will need a record of her early years. Why not take your document and add to it? Tell the whole story—long before Gallio. Start with the birth of the church. Tell about Peter. Tell how I began as a persecutor. Tell about poor Stephen, and carry the story forward. Perhaps you might even call it the 'History' or, no . . . the '*Acta* of the Apostles.'"

"How far shall I carry it?"

"Up to the present, of course."

"But I broke off with this statement . . . here"—he reached for the scroll—"I'll show it to you." He unrolled the document to the final lines:

. . . And Paul lived in Rome two whole years at his own expense, and welcomed all who came to him, preaching the kingdom of God and teaching about the Lord Jesus Christ quite openly and unhindered.

"Fine. End with that."

"But your trial? Your release?"

"If Caesar had declared the faith legitimate, it would have made a glorious ending to your record. But he did not. That only I was spared is disappointing, and I don't want you to close on such a personal note. Christ is important, not Paul."

"What about your ministry from now on—the work in Spain? Or the East?"

"Perhaps a separate scroll, Luke—if God permits. But the most important part of the story will already have been told."

BOOK THREE

THE BLAZE

20

ROME woke to the horrifying news on a morning in late summer. It jolted Nero out of bed and sent the Conscript Fathers scurrying into their togas for an emergency meeting of the Senate. Pedanius Secundus, Sabinus' successor as city prefect, had been murdered by one of his own slaves. Caught soon after the act, the slave admitted his motive: Pedanius had agreed to sell him his freedom for a certain price but then refused when the sum was handed him. It was too much for the slave, who lost his head and stabbed Pedanius to death in his bedroom.

But what made this murder so unprecedented an outrage was the ghastly law the Senate had passed to keep Rome's growing army of slaves terrified into proper submission: if any Roman citizen were murdered by one of his slaves, the law required that *all* slaves in his household ("living under the same roof") were to be dragged off to execution. It was hoped that the law would be totally preventative: to save their lives and families, slaves would certainly alert their masters to any word of conspiracy in their ranks.

Now, however, the law would have a grisly test. Pedanius presided over one of the largest household staffs in Rome, as well as the corps of slaves attached to city headquarters. In the eyes of the law, *both* groups of slaves were implicated—the murderer also served in the urban administration—and they numbered no fewer than four hundred men, women, and children.

News that four hundred would have to die for the crime of one horrified the people of Rome—and many inside the Senate, too, where the session was stormy and raucous. Opinions, epithets, threats ricocheted off the marble walls.

"Four hundred didn't kill Pedanius! *One* did!" cried Quintus Lateranus. "What about the innocent women and children? Think of your own!"

"Repeal the barbaric law!" shouted another. "Are we savages? *Four hundred* for one?"

Finally the presiding consul waved his arms in desperation and recognized Senator Gaius Cassius, one of the most respected legal minds in the Empire. The Fathers waited expectantly, hoping he would inject some sanity into the terrible impasse.

Slowly the aging senator rose, faced the chamber, and said, "Your outcry, my colleagues, is a tribute to your humanity, and I sympathize with it. We must, however, face realities. A former governor, a senator, and city prefect has been murdered in his own home by the treachery of his slaves. Each of those slaves knew the penalty, but not one warned his master. You claim it's not fair that all should die? By all means, then, vote impunity! But henceforth don't think your rank or your purple-banded tunics will protect you from similar stabbings. Not when the prefect of Rome has fallen! Not when 399 were unable to protect one!

" 'Only one hand plunged the dagger,' you say. And true it is. But did the murderer decide to kill his master without dropping a threatening word or hint to anyone? Could he pass the night watch, open the doors of the bedroom, carry in a dagger, and then stab Pedanius without *anyone* knowing it? A crime has many advance symptoms. Unless our slaves tell us those symptoms, we're all dead men."

Senator Cassius paused for a moment, letting the Fathers digest his words. Then he concluded: "Will some innocent lives be lost? Of course they will! Yet when one of our cohorts shows cowardice on the field of battle, don't we decimate? Don't we seize every tenth man in the ranks and club him to death, including some innocent brave ones? Shall we then spare slaves if we don't spare freeborn Romans? In every great precedent, there is some injustice, which, though it injures the individual, works to public advantage. Therefore, my colleagues, you *must* decree the death penalty . . . to all!"

The chamber rattled with loud applause. Senators still calling for lenience appeared disorganized. Some, like Quintus, were too numbed by the implications of the case to find the proper eloquence for a firm rebuttal to Cassius. In the civic emergency, only the narrow mind of that legalist had prepared itself.

The consul called for a vote. "All those in favor of condemning to death the private and public slaves of Pedanius Secundus—in numbers about four hundred—pass to the right. Those opposed, to the left."

A dramatic reshuffling took place, and it was several minutes before senators stopped bumping into each other as they made their emphatic move to one side of the chamber or the other. The consul studied the line of demarkation and announced, "To me, it looks as if there is a majority for execution."

"Take the count! *Take the count!*" the lenient faction called out.

For the next half hour, the clerk of the Senate did a roll call of the Fathers. Then he added his columns and handed the results to the consul, who announced, "The vote is 188 in favor of execution, 158 against. The motion for the extreme penalty is upheld."

The cheers of the majority were suddenly drowned out by an angry chorus of shouts outside the Senate house. The walls of the chamber started clattering with what sounded like hail, and the consul hurried outside to investigate. A vast, threatening mob of Romans had surrounded the building, shrieking, "*Clementia! Misericordia!* Mercy!" They were pelting the walls of the Senate house with stones and shaking firebrands to underscore their threat: they would burn the place to the ground if all but the murderer were not released.

Inside, the Fathers quavered in fear, knowing that several times in the past century, the Senate house had indeed been burnt to ashes by such a mob and rebuilt at great expense.

"*Clementia!*" the shouting grew into a crescendo. "*Quadringenti pro uno?* Four hundred for one?"

Now there was an even greater tumult as thousands of praetorians wedged through the throng to permit Nero to enter the Senate. The senators stood and cheered when the emperor stepped inside the chamber. Clearly, he would not have been there unless enough praetorians were outside to protect him—and them.

Stalking over to the presiding consul, Nero asked him what the

Senate had decided about Pedanius' murder. He nodded, and then addressed the chamber.

"You have decided well, my colleagues. The ancient precedent is proper, and such a dastardly crime will never be repeated after the example we set today. I am ordering the entire Praetorian Guard to line both sides of the route along which the condemned will be taken to execution. The people will not prevent them."

The chamber applauded until a sycophant stood up and said, "I go farther, noble Caesar. I propose that all *freedmen* of the deceased Pedanius also be condemned, at least to exile."

"*Veto!*" said Nero. "This is excessive. Our law, which mercy has not tempered, must not now be aggravated by unnecessary cruelty."

The emperor was cheered for his clemency. The crowd was dispersed by force, and a majority of the senators went home to a comfortable dinner in good conscience.

But an enraged populace pommeled the praetorians lining the streets along which Pedanius' slaves were dragged. Yet they could not break through, and the terrified four hundred were finally herded inside the courtyard of the Castra Praetoria. Only the guards could now hear the pathetic pleading of aged men and women, the crying of boys and girls, or see the furious hatred in the eyes of the younger slaves. The sole culprit was crucified in a spot overlooking the chopping block. While he gazed down in horror, his fellow slaves were made to bend over the block, one by one. Arms tired quickly. Blades dulled. Ears deafened at all the screaming and shrieking and moaning. A growing stench filled the air, and tribunes had to bark at their men to get them to pile the bodies into carts, heads into separate tubs, and trundle them off.

Self-respecting Romans were horrified. Where in the Senate, some asked, was the voice of Thrasea Paetus? Or of Aulus Plautius? Of Flavius Sabinus? Many, patricians and plebes alike, were calling it Rome's darkest hour. They could not know that a blacker night was approaching.

Sabinus and Plautia were entertaining her parents at their new villa in Tibur. Most of their neighbors had returned to Rome in early fall, but they were so entranced by the natural beauty of the area that they planned to stay on for several more weeks, and they finally prevailed upon Aulus and Pomponia to pay them a visit. Aulus needed the change. He had been putting in long hours, advising Nero on how to put down the massive revolt in Britain under Queen Boudicca.

Then, on that morning they would not easily forget, a praetorian courier galloped up to their villa with an urgent note for Sabinus. It bore only four lines:

Afranius Burrus and Annaeus Seneca to Flavius Sabinus, greeting. Urgent that you return to Rome immediately and come to the palace. The messenger will inform you of the tragic news. Farewell.

The spoken tidings were a relentless succession of shocks. Sabinus had to hear that his successor had been murdered and four hundred lives sacrificed in retribution. Aulus collapsed onto a couch and held his head in his hands. Sabinus' knuckles whitened as he fired furious questions at the courier, his ire boiling over when he realized that some of his former trusted slaves at Rome's city headquarters had also been executed.

A fast horseback ride of about an hour brought Sabinus to the vestibule of the palace. Seneca and Burrus, who were waiting for him, whisked him into an anteroom and asked if he had learned everything.

"That Rome is drunk on the blood of innocent slaves? Yes," he seethed. "That some of my ablest men in the city prefecture were cut down? Yes . . . yes . . . that too!"

"A *horrible* business," said Seneca. "I've always taught that slaves are our equals. It's the Stoic creed. But we had nothing to do with it, Sabinus. You must be sure of that first of all."

"Of *course* you didn't, Seneca!" snapped Sabinus. "Any time anything goes wrong in the state, you and Burrus are *never* responsible!"

"Look, Sabinus," Burrus shot back with ire, "you can save your sarcasm. The *Senate* condemned the slaves, and without consulting the Palatine. Nero only confirmed their judgment. I'm sorry he did— he asked neither of us. As far as my men were concerned, it was a nauseating, disgusting mess."

"To come to the point, Sabinus," said Seneca. "Rome very desperately needs a city prefect. Immediately. The people are muttering. Rebellion's in the air. We need a firm hand at the helm as soon as possible. Nero asked us this morning whom we would recommend. Naturally we suggested you. He actually brightened and asked whether we thought you would accept after the way he dismissed you. We told him we'd ask you."

"You mean he *really* wants me back as city prefect?"

"Yes. Enthusiastically."

Sabinus thought for several moments. Then he replied, "My answer is no. Emphatically."

Seneca and Burrus stared at him blankly. To refuse high public office was almost unheard of, and, in the present case, at least unexpected.

"Now, Sabinus . . ."

Sabinus did not want to hear a discourse from Seneca. "Haven't I served the state? In the magistracies here at Rome? In Britain? In Moesia? In Gaul? In the Senate? As city prefect for five long years?"

"Yes. You have. Admirably."

"And will you believe me if I tell you that I've enjoyed the past months *immensely?*"

"Yes, I believe it," Seneca replied. "But what's the *real* reason, Sabinus? I know you better than to think you'd shun high office for any of those reasons. Politics is in your very blood."

Sabinus brushed a shock of black hair up from his forehead. Then he looked the philosopher in the eye and said, "You're right, of course. And the answer is I will *not* serve under an amateur esthete masquerading as emperor—a poor recitalist, but an excellent fratricide, matricide, tyrant, and, above all, voluptuary. And now a mass murderer too!"

"*Sshhh,* Sabinus!" Burrus cautioned. "Merciful Minerva . . . what if he should hear? On some days Nero rules well enough and makes the right decisions . . ."

"Don't tell me you're still trying to train a 'philosopher-king,' Seneca?"

Slowly Seneca shook his head, a little wistfully.

"Well, you aren't going to quarrel with my reasoning, then, are you?"

Seneca paced the chamber twice. "Yes, Sabinus," he finally said. "Yes, I will quarrel with it. If you love Rome, I think you should accept precisely *because* of what you say about Caesar. If we had an able emperor, our city prefect could be mediocre without much harm to the state. But quite the opposite is the case. Burrus and I are fighting a losing battle, Sabinus, and we need help. We need help desperately. I'll put it to you squarely: if you refuse the post, Nero will probably fall back on his untried, horsy friend Tigellinus, who knows nothing about administration. If he takes the office instead of you, Burrus and I will simply resign and go into retirement."

"No," said Sabinus. "You mustn't. You . . . you can't do that."

"We can. And we will," Burrus affirmed, a strange hoarseness in his voice that Sabinus had never heard before. "My health is failing. And why should you be permitted the luxury of avoiding high office and not we?"

They had won the argument, of course. It took Sabinus several more quiet moments and then he conceded. Seneca and Burrus grasped his hand and shook it. The trio then walked up to the imperial suite.

Nero seemed effusively friendly, though he avoided Sabinus' eye while he managed some unlikely excuse for having dismissed him a year earlier. Then he offered him his old office.

Sabinus' reply was curt and direct. "First I must register my indignation, my outrage at the execution of the four hundred slaves, Caesar. In view of this attitude, do you want to change your mind about offering me the prefecture?"

Nero shook his head, saying quietly, "I only endorsed what the Senate had already decided."

"You could also have vetoed it, Caesar."

Seneca and Burrus were alarmed by his bluntness, but the emperor merely replied, "Perhaps."

"If I accept," Sabinus resumed, "may I have a free hand in administering the city henceforth?"

Again the jaws of Seneca and Burrus dropped slightly, but Nero only nodded.

Sabinus formally accepted. Then he hurried down to his old offices across the Forum and assumed charge of Rome once again. His former staff was delighted to have him back in command. The next day, he addressed his four police cohorts in the Castra Urbana to the north of Rome. In words that would be repeated across the city, he bitterly denounced the Senate majority for condemning the four hundred, and promised to use the office of city prefect to assist relatives of the victims. He also freed all slaves still attached to the city prefecture so that if he himself were assassinated, they might not be punished.

One week with Flavius Sabinus at the helm, and Rome had regained her composure. The people even held a long torchlight pa-

rade to hail his return to power. Plautia stood by his side on the
Quirinal, watching people file by for a whole hour, shouting their
appreciation. She had never been prouder of her husband. And
never more concerned.

With the new year, A.D. 62, Sabinus' natural optimism was tempered by the severe illness of Afranius Burrus. The voice of the praetorian commander was little more than a raspy grunt, and an interior
swelling in his throat was slowly suffocating him. Palace doctors pronounced the cancer incurable. Still, Sabinus was shocked when a
courier from the palace told him the crusty old soldier was already *in
extremis*.

Hurrying across to the Palatine, Sabinus was met in the vestibule
by Seneca, who whispered, "Caesar is ready to appoint Tigellinus as
Burrus' successor."

"*Gods*, no!"

"Well, you could see it coming. The scoundrel's already commander of the night watch."

"We've got to block him."

When they reached Burrus' bedside, Nero was asking him solici-
tously, "How are you, dear friend?"

With great effort, Burrus managed a husky whisper, "*I*, at any
rate, am well." Then he turned his face to the wall. An exquisite insult, Sabinus thought, a declaration of independence on his very
deathbed. Nero merely lowered his head and walked over to a corner
of the room.

Sabinus bent over his friend and received a victorious smile.
Burrus was then seized with a fit of coughing. The tumor blocked
the return air flow and he started turning bluish-purple. Sabinus
yelled for the doctors, who tried to force a breathing tube down his
throat. But Afranius Burrus had ceased his struggle in death.

Sabinus, Seneca, and Nero paid solemn respects to the old commander and left the room. It was Nero who spoke first. "Well,
gentlemen, whom do you recommend as Burrus' successor? Sorry to
bring this up so soon after his death, but . . ."

They said nothing at first, too shaken by the passing of their
friend. But Sabinus seemed to hear Burrus' gravel voice upbraiding
them, "Open your mouths, you simple ninnies, and block that scheming swine Tigellinus."

"Faenius Rufus is your man, Caesar," Sabinus quietly advised.

"Hmmm. The prefect of the grain supply?"

"He'd be an excellent choice," Sabinus replied. "Rufus has kept Rome well fed, and he's run the office without profit to himself—"

"A rare enough accomplishment," Seneca added.

"You wouldn't want to command the praetorians yourself, would you, Sabinus?"

"I thank you for your confidence, Caesar. But no—I don't want to return to the military."

Nero pondered several moments more. "Well," he finally said, "Rufus it is, then." Flashing a curious grin at Sabinus, he added, "You see, Prefect . . . I'm not so uncooperative, am I?"

Sabinus returned him an uncomfortable smile and then left. At the door of the palace, he told Seneca, "Well, we won that round, friend. We should be able to build a new triumvirate with Rufus, not?"

"I . . . hope so," Seneca said, a little dejectedly.

Seneca wished he could share Sabinus' optimism, but he could not. On the way to his suburban villa that night, the philosopher sensed it for the first time. Then he pondered it, and finally spoke the word to himself: the *conversio*. Yes, he reflected, the *conversio* had probably come, that remarkable Latin word which meant "turning point," or "change of fortune."

Providence had favored him enormously: wealth, power, fame, wit—his beautiful wife Paulina—nothing more to be desired. How delightful to be a Stoic and accept all such pleasant "inevitabilities." But the Stoic creed cut both ways. Had he been a slave, dying in torment, he would have been obliged to bring the same affirmative response to whatever Providence had provided for him. Well, the *conversio* in his life had come. His very bones told him it had. He would now learn whether he were a genuine Stoic or a fraud.

Seneca's prescience was richly, if ominously, validated in the next weeks. He saw his influence over Nero eroding rapidly. The death of Burrus shook his position, and he watched in revulsion as the reptile from Sicily slithered snugly into Nero's favor. Tigellinus became Nero's companion in vice, the agent who arranged—and shared—his most intimate debauches. Gratefully, Nero soon promoted him to the very summit. Suspicious of Rufus as sole prefect, Nero now made a dual post of it, appointing Tigellinus as co-prefect of the Praetorian Guard.

Sniffing victory in his precipitous rise to power, Tigellinus and his coterie began a studied campaign to undermine Seneca's waning influence. At first there were merely slurring asides. If wealth were the topic of discussion at the palace, someone would observe, "Seneca's so rich he's a kingdom unto himself." If Nero were delighted with some new touch he had added to the palace gardens, the inevitable comment followed, "Almost as lavish as Seneca's parks."

Once, when Nero had finished a new composition on the lyre, Tigellinus responded, "Magnificent, Caesar!" Then, shaking his head mournfully, he added, "I can't understand why others . . . disparage your voice."

"Who does?" Nero finally responded.

"Seneca, for one. But only in private, of course." Tigellinus smirked. "I'll tell you this, Caesar: I'm sick and tired of that critic. *He alone* claims to be eloquent. He alone knows what diversions are right or wrong for his emperor. Nothing is thought brilliant except what *Seneca* has composed. That pedant is perverting our leaders into some kind of cult centering on himself."

Nero darkened and pursed his lips.

"Maybe I spoke out of turn, Caesar, but I'll merely add this. Do you know what the man on the street is saying about you? 'Surely Caesar's boyhood is over,' they're saying. 'Can't he get along without that old hypocrite tutor of his?' "

"They are?"

"Yes, and I agree with them. Why not look to your divine ancestors for any further instruction? Not the Spaniard."

What Tigellinus reported was true only of the smart young voluptuaries in Rome with whom Nero was intimate. Seneca still had enough close friends in the palace to report to him everything that was being said behind his back. He hoped Nero would consider the source of these comments in evaluating them.

Unfortunately, it seemed he did not, for Nero now sought him out less and less for advice and began limiting their social contacts, while he and Tigellinus became inseparable. It was the end, then, Seneca sadly realized, for it would now be impossible to salvage Nero's career. Besides, he was a ripe sixty-six years old. There was no other course . . . no other course at all. He would resign.

Arranging a private conference with Nero, he respectfully asked his permission to retire, pleading ill health and the desire to devote himself full-time to writing and philosophy. Nero was eminently of age now, he argued, and he himself would remain grateful for the rest of his life for the emperor's many favors.

Nero urged that his tutor stay on, but his plea sounded routine and hollow—something a student would *have* to say out of respect to an old teacher. The two exchanged a stiff embrace, and Seneca started vacating his office suite at the palace. Altering his way of life dramatically, he retired to his country villa and seldom appeared in Rome. The philosopher had only one regret at retiring from public life: since Rufus, the praetorian co-prefect, was being ruthlessly eclipsed by Tigellinus, there was now only *one* man of principle left in power. Flavius Sabinus now had to bear the burden alone.

The ominous change of climate on the Palatine blanketed Rome with clouds of foreboding. Over on the Quirinal, Plautia could feel it simply by watching new furrows deepen on her husband's brow each day when he returned from city headquarters, muttering something decidedly unpleasant about Tigellinus. Sabinus knew that a fateful turning point had come in the imperial government with Seneca's retirement, but he could not imagine that political murder would come into fashion again so quickly.

It was after one of the Friday councils of state that Nero called Tigellinus, Rufus, and himself into his office. "I want you to see what just arrived, my friends," he said, with a twinkle. "Until today, I feared only two human beings on this earth. But no longer, thanks to Tigellinus." Standing on a table adjacent to his desk were two large jugs of creamy Egyptian alabaster. Reaching into one of them, Nero pulled a human head out of preservative brine, holding it by the hair.

Sabinus shook at the knees and nearly fainted.

"Sulla here was mailed to us from Marseilles," said Nero. "He was descended from the great dictator of the same name, and might have raised Gaul against us. But I wonder. Look at his premature gray hair." He dropped the head back into the brine with a hollow splash.

Rufus had blanched. Sabinus noticed Tigellinus smirking at him, and for that reason alone he swore he would maintain his composure.

Nero reached into the other jug, extracting another head. "This is Rubellius Plautus, of course, fresh from Ephesus. A short while ago, there was as much Julian blood flowing inside his head as in mine.

He might have raised Asia against us. But why did I ever fear a man with such a nose?"

Nero dismissed the council and sent a letter to the Senate, claiming that both men had endangered the state. Fearing for their own heads, the Fathers decreed a thanksgiving, and, at least tardily, they also expelled Sulla and Rubellius from the Senate.

With all his imperial rivals dead, Nero found no reason to maintain his loveless marriage with Octavia. No longer was she his key to empire. Dear Poppaea had been so patient about their own postponed marriage. To be sure, she had hounded him about it from time to time, but she had not withheld her favors in the meantime. Now, finally, he could make his beloved empress of Rome.

On what basis could he divorce Octavia? Tigellinus tried to torture Octavia's slave girls into accusing her of adultery, but one of them actually spat in his face.

Rather than press the adultery charge, Nero divorced Octavia on the grounds of barrenness—though everyone in Rome knew why the empress had not conceived. Twelve days later, amid much official rejoicing, he formally and finally married Poppaea Sabina.

"You will go down in legend, my empress," Nero cooed as he embraced her in their first legitimate night together. "People will forget Helen of Troy . . . for Poppaea of Rome."

"How *long* . . . I've waited for this evening," she whispered.

"Yes, love," he soothed, fingering the strands of her shimmering golden hair. "But now, my goddess, I'll worship your happiness."

The deposed Octavia, however, remained extremely popular at Rome. Some underground rumor now surfaced that Nero regretted his latest marriage and planned to reinstate Octavia as empress. An excited throng, delirious with joy, toppled statues of Poppaea in the Forum and thanked the gods for restoring Claudius' daughter. Then they threaded their way up into the palace grounds to cheer the emperor's decision and thank him personally. "Come out, Caesar!" they shouted.

Nero came out—in a furious lather, and only long enough to order his praetorians to beat down all treasonable demonstrations in behalf of the divorced—yes, irrevocably divorced—Octavia.

Terrified by the demonstration and worried lest Nero be swayed by the people, Poppaea flung herself at his knees. "I'm not some

. . . some *rival*, fighting for your hand in marriage," she sobbed. "I thought we were already married, Nero."

"We are, my darling. We are," he consoled.

"No." She ignored him. "What I'm fighting for . . . is my life itself. Octavia and her followers—they want my head. *They're* the ones who stirred up the people." She broke into a flood of tears.

"I'll protect you, my goddess."

"Do you know what the people might do, Nero? They might find Octavia a new husband. And then he—not you—will be Caesar."

Her logic was studded with flaws, but the sure and proven way to bring out the worst in Nero was to alarm him, Poppaea knew. And alarmed he certainly was. She could tell it by the way he began tapping his left thumb while pondering a course of action—always a sure sign.

"This time we'll have to make the charge of adultery stick," he finally said. "And it will have to be *treasonable* adultery too. But with whom?"

He thought of various friends who owed him favors, but none could really serve the purpose. A tightening cramp of apprehension reminded him of another time when he had felt the same way. Yes. When he was trying to decide how to eliminate his mother. Anicetus!

Nero sent for the fleet commander, and detailed the reasons why he had to "confess" to adultery with Octavia. Anicetus was startled and reluctant. "But why me?" he wondered.

"That's the treason part of it: she involved you because you both planned to raise a rebellion against me with the fleet."

"Oh, *fine*," Anicetus muttered sarcastically. "And what will happen to *me* because of all these 'crimes'?"

"First, I'll present you with a considerable fortune, Anicetus. And, of course, I'll see to it that your 'punishment' is nothing more than sailing away to some delightful retreat. Though publicly, we'll call it exile, of course."

"And if I refuse?"

Nero was taken aback and glared at Anicetus.

"I mean, this *is* rather dangerous, you know."

"Well, I consider the Empire at stake," said Nero loftily. "If you refuse, I'll . . . well, put it this way: you'll have outlived your usefulness to me."

"Clear enough." Anicetus smirked grimly. "When do I testify?"

"Tomorrow. Today I've just 'discovered' this horrible plot. I'll summon a judicial council in the morning."

The tragic comedy was acted out in due course. Nero and his assessors were duly horrified by Anicetus' "confessions," which were even more lurid than Nero had suggested. The adulterous treason was then announced to the general public. The fleet commander was banished to Sardinia, where he lived out an opulent life, basking in the Mediterranean sun amid luxuries of every kind.

Octavia was exiled to Pandateria, a little island near the Bay of Naples. The modest girl was only twenty, yet she was now irrevocably doomed in her pathetic prison. For memories she could look back on her years with an adulterous mother who had been executed, a father and a brother who had been poisoned, and a husband who hated and maligned her.

And would now kill her too. The orders came a few days after her arrival on the island.

"No!" she screamed. "I'm no longer Caesar's wife! Just his sister! I'm no threat to anyone!"

After some preliminary atrocities, she was thrown into a hot bath and scalded to death.

The Romans who had once shouted in behalf of Octavia were now hushed with horror. The only sounds heard were those of a few parasites offering up public thanksgiving to the gods in the temples of Rome.

21

SABINUS decided that he could no longer work under a man who murdered wives and played with severed heads. He drafted a letter of resignation and then showed it to Aulus Plautius on the Esquiline.

"It's excellent," his aging father-in-law said, in the seclusion of his library. "But now you must crumple it up and throw it away."

"Why? Too dangerous to resign now?"

"Much too dangerous. Nero would take it personally. And more than that. With Seneca and Burrus gone, someone with conscience must stay in the administration."

Sabinus looked about to make sure no servant overheard. Then he leaned over to whisper, "Have you heard any of the . . . ah . . . talk about . . . assassination?"

Aulus nodded. "Quintus has dropped several hints, but I've tried to discourage his involvement. Too premature. Too disastrously dangerous."

"Who's mainly involved? In rumors you've heard?"

"Two groups, it seems. The Stoics—principally Thrasea, Seneca, and their friends—are now philosophically against Nero, though I don't know if they'd go as far as assassination. It's the other group that may: Quintus and a small circle of republican senators and equestrians, but I have no details."

Sabinus frowned. "It may have to come to that—if things get any worse."

Aulus' hands wrestled with each other. "Maybe our problems are deeper than Nero, Sabinus. I recall moments of despair under Claudius also, when he was too blind to see what his wives and freedmen were doing to him—and the Empire. *Ergo*, maybe our whole system of government is wrong. Maybe no individual should ever be given the powers of a Caesar."

"Are you saying that Quintus and his group are right, then? Save the body of the state by cutting away its putrid member?"

"Perhaps. But it may not be that simple. What would happen if Nero were assassinated, and the Republic were restored—and Rome *still* didn't return to her former health? I mean, her condition was hardly better in the late Republic. Maybe a rot exists at the very *core* of Rome—in our moral fiber. I don't think we have many real Romans left, Sabinus. There's you, there's Thrasea, Lateranus and his group, a few in the Senate with the courage to speak out when necessary. But otherwise our government is riddled with time-servers and sycophants, toadies and flatterers, parasites, leeches—all of them Nero's lickspittles, heaping slavish praise on him to his face while shaking their servile heads in dismay behind his back."

Sabinus stood up and walked over to a window that looked out across a stand of pines. Then he turned and said, "Much of what you say is true, Father, but—I don't mean this disrespectfully—but it seems I've heard some of this before. Didn't Scipio find his Rome demoralized too? Didn't Cato? And Augustus after him? Weren't they all trying to revive the 'old virtues' in their days? I wonder if each new generation inevitably suffers by comparison with the old."

Ignoring the last, Aulus observed, "Augustus thought our state religion could restore morality to Rome, but he was wrong. No intelligent Roman can actually believe in that menagerie of gods the Greeks freighted to us." Then he shifted his stance and smiled. "Now don't laugh, Sabinus, but there are times when I wish everyone in Rome had the ethical standards of my Pomponia's beliefs. Because those Christians give a person a *reason* for trying to live the good life. And they certainly avoid the excesses that are making Rome stink in the nostrils of the world. But here's my point: I wonder if we could *use* a few of their beliefs to try to . . . rebuild our civic morality. Anything, I think, would be better than that feast of hypocrisy we call our state religion."

"Well, it's clear that Rome does need *some* source of inspiration, Father, something to motivate it for the better—I'll grant you that. *True* leadership from the Palatine would help. If only Nero had filled one quarter of the hopes Seneca had for him—"

"We all had those hopes."

"By the way, *one* of Nero's crimes I think you'll forgive: old Pallas just died, and it's clear that Nero gave nature a hand."

"Poison?"

"Locusta's best. Nero wanted his enormous wealth."

With a faint smile, Aulus remarked, "I only hope the spirit of Narcissus has been duly informed." Then he resumed a frown of concern. "What does Nero think of *you*, Sabinus?"

"I don't know. At times he can be quite friendly."

"Well, he should be. You're taking good care of Rome. That leaves him free to tend the Empire . . . *or* practice his singing."

"In fact, I think he wants to conciliate us Flavii. I was going to let Vespasian tell you, but I'm sure he won't mind: my brother's been appointed governor of Africa."

"Wonderful!" Aulus beamed. "So, Vespasian's really going to do something with his life?"

"I hope so," Sabinus sighed. "He's just been treading water here, getting deeper into debt. But at times I feel sorry for him: his wife's sudden illness and death . . ."

Aulus nodded, then brightened. "By the way, how's that magnificent girl you spirited away from me?"

"Plautia? Any day now, Grandfather!"

Their second child was a masterpiece of timing. Just as the great end-of-the-year festival was getting under way, Plautia provided Sabinus with a tiny, warm Saturnalia present whom they named Flavius Clemens.

Sabinus looked down into the tortoise-shell cradle and beamed with joy at the wiggling infant, a pink ball of baby fat with chubby cheeks and light hair. Two *boys*? Could any Roman father be happier? He lavished kisses of adoration on Plautia, as if she and she alone had made it all possible.

Plautia had had a much easier delivery this time, and seemed to glow with happiness. "So much for the men in this family," she said. "Next time, a girl?"

"It can be arranged," he replied, with a confident grin.

The palace was looking forward to similar joy. Nothing was more important to Nero than an heir to the throne, and he carefully conveyed the pregnant Poppaea to his seashore villa at Antium. He had been born there, and so the future emperor of Rome must also be born there. Late in January of 63, Poppaea gave birth to—a girl. It was one of the only circumstances in the Empire that even Caesar could not control.

But his disappointment easily mellowed into joy—a gladness which was only fleeting, because in May the infant fell sick of a fever and died. Nero plunged into a grieving despondency that lasted for months. He would not be consoled, even when the Senate decreed the baby instant deification, a temple, and a priesthood.

It was not cares of state which finally snatched him from despair but his career as an artist. He was twenty-six, the last vestiges of puberty were safely past, and his now-reliable bass voice had sung through several test recitals in the theater at Naples. Should he give concerts also in Rome? Was the city finally ready to appreciate good music? Perhaps. But only if the people really wanted to hear him.

Tigellinus saw to that. A crowd gathered outside the palace, pleading that Caesar's "celestial voice" be heard at the Neronia festival.

Nero threw up his hands in sweet surrender, and on the great day of the festival, he cast his own lot into the urn with the rest of the contestants. It was Sabinus himself who now had to shake the lots and announce Nero's turn: "Number Four." To his disgust, Sabinus, as city prefect, had been drafted into serving on the committee of judges for the event, along with Gallio and Gaius Petronius, Nero's adviser in matters of taste.

During the first three performances in the jammed theater, Sabinus toyed with the thought of disqualifying Nero for all the noise he was making, tuning his instrument, clearing his throat, hawking, and even spitting resoundingly. When the emperor's turn came, something of a parade trooped out onto stage. Tigellinus and Rufus both carried his lyre, followed by a cohort of friends, apparently to keep Caesar from feeling lonesome on the vast stage.

When Nero had taken his place, a herald announced, "Our beloved Caesar will favor us with a rendition of . . . *Niobe.*"

"Great Hercules, not *Niobe!*" Petronius whispered to Sabinus, adding an exquisite curse, for this was an endlessly long opera about Apollo slaying twelve children, and Nero was singing the entire work.

Secretly, Petronius was also the emperor's shrewdest critic, and Sabinus' only amusement that afternoon was to read some of the comments he jotted down from time to time:

> Contracts his throat . . . squeezes his singing into a raucous buzzing . . . a hollow, grating sound . . . a few tones are gentler and therefore passable. . . . But his respiration is short, his breath never sufficient . . . hopeless.

It was late afternoon when Nero finally finished the last stanza of *Niobe.* While his claque was applauding, the three judges huddled in strategy. "It's too late for anyone else to perform," said Gallio. "So let's simply give Nero first prize and be done with it."

"*Never!*" huffed Sabinus. "What do you say, Petronius?"

"I'll give him first prize . . . for making a jackass of himself!"

"Well, what'll we do?" Gallio worried.

Sabinus stood up and announced, "Since there is hardly time for the other contestants to perform, no prize can possibly be awarded. Learn from the way Caesar accepts this verdict the measure of his obvious fairness! *Vale,* Citizens!"

Tigellinus glared at Sabinus, his mouth forming unheard epithets. Yet Nero seemed to be smiling. *Niobe,* in fact, had been part of his defensive strategy. Its very length was supposed to crowd out anyone else who might have snatched first place from him.

Later, on the Quirinal, Plautia called her husband's conduct "foolhardy."

"But honest, my love," Sabinus replied, a little smile on his lips.

Rome's nobility found Nero's theatrics beneath contempt, particularly since he was now also stagestruck to the point of donning masks and acting in operatic tragedies. His favorite role was *Canace in Childbirth,* where his grunting and groaning as if in difficult labor caused several women in the audience to faint.

Thrasea's circle of Stoics was beginning to doubt Nero's sanity, while others, like Aulus Plautius, wondered if it might not be a case of someone finding his true calling. "He can't govern," Aulus observed, "but he can play the mime."

"Or try to," Sabinus agreed, adding wryly, "no man is ever a complete failure. He can always serve as a horrible example!"

Was it the word failure that prompted Aulus to ask, "By the way, how's Vespasian doing lately?"

Sabinus had a long, sad answer to give, for his brother had returned penniless from his year governing the province of Africa. He had even been pelted with turnips while trying to put down a riot near Carthage. True, Vespasian had been honest in his administration there—his low level of finances was proof of that—but now his credit was gone, and the expense of setting up housekeeping again in Rome was too much for him.

"I need a . . . a very substantial loan," he told Sabinus, soon after his return.

"Again?"

Vespasian nodded his broad and balding head. "Something on the order of . . . a couple hundred thousand sesterces."

Sabinus' eyes widened.

"But this time I'm mortgaging my property to you as collateral."

"Not necessary, Vespasian."

"I *insist*, Sabinus!" he snapped. "Jupiter knows it's embarrassing enough to have to come to you again like this. Let me salvage *some* scrap of personal honor."

"All right. If you insist. But I'll never foreclose. Now tell me, what're you going to do to support yourself?"

Vespasian lowered his head and shook it. "I . . . I don't know, Sabinus. For now, I'm going to . . . deal in mules. It's the only thing open . . ."

"*Great gods!* My brother a *mule-trader?*" Sabinus was on the verge of saying, but he checked himself. Instead, he put his arm around Vespasian and said, "Carry on, old fellow. Let me know whenever I can be of any help."

Later, Sabinus thought about Vespasian's continuing run of vicious luck. His only real success in life had come in Britain, and even earlier when he served as street commissioner, Caligula had personally pelted him with mud from the gutter as reminder to keep the streets clean. *Why* did everything Vespasian touched crumble to ashes, Sabinus wondered. Would his fortunes *ever* turn?

High on the Esquiline, Pomponia was happily aloof from Roman politics. Whatever Nero did or did not do left her quite uninterested, unless it affected Sabinus and Plautia, since her life now centered in the growing Christian movement in Rome. A happy day for her was a visit from Aquila, especially when he brought along one of Paul's latest letters. The apostle had returned from Spain and was now on a round of pastoral visits in the eastern Mediterranean.

That spring, Pomponia was excited by news of Simon Peter's arrival in Rome. Jesus' prime disciple had just taken up lodging in the house of John Mark on the Viminal. Mark had joined Paul's circle in Rome, and stayed on in a dwelling near Paul's when the apostle and Luke left the city. Here he had begun writing the gospel that would one day bear his name. What Luke was to Paul, Mark now became for Peter—colleague, secretary, fellow missionary, and chronicler.

The first Sunday evening after Peter's arrival, Pomponia joined a throng of Roman Christians who crowded into Aquila's house on the Aventine to see and hear, even touch, the man who for more than three years had been Jesus' closest associate. Pomponia knew she would be easily impressed by this human link with the Christ. But the burly, hulking figure of Simon Peter would have been impressive in any case. After Aquila's glad introduction, Peter stood up to address the crowd, which had stilled to a hush broken only by the crackle of the pine torches illuminating the hall.

The tall, muscular frame of the man seemed almost necessary to support that full and strong head of his, covered with short, curly gray hair matched by a similar beard. His skin was leather-tough, browned by the sun of seventy summers. "The Fisherman," they called him, and his brawny arms and hands made him look the role. Pomponia thought it interesting that in the famous story of the huge draft of fish, it was the nets that finally gave out, not Peter's arms in hauling in the catch. So this was the man who pulled out his sword and thought to fight off, singlehandedly, the police arresting Jesus! Well, he looked the Samson type. And yet there was also a certain kindliness in his features that contrasted starkly with the man's build, a warm glint in his brown eyes and a gentle set to his mouth.

With deep, sonorous tones to match his appearance, Peter congratulated the Roman church on its growth and vitality. "Such numbers! Such fervent faith! And there are several thousands more like you in other congregations across Rome, I understand. We are especially proud of the church in Rome, because it was founded, not by us apostles, but by you lay men and women who returned from Jerusalem on that first Christian Pentecost. Some of your faces I recall seeing there thirty-one years ago, for you were among the first converts after my address.

"It was you, then, who were the seed of Christianity here in Rome, and now you've grown into a sturdy tree of faith. Some of you are Jews, some are Gentiles, but all are one in Christ. Some come from the nobility," he said, looking at Pomponia in her patrician stola, "while others are soldiers or servants or slaves. But all *are* one in Christ."

Peter then told of his days with Jesus, but it was clear that the people had not heard enough. They begged for more. And so the apostle continued every Sunday evening that spring, telling a new chapter about that luminous life which, he predicted, would one day change all of history.

June A.D. 64 was awash with social engagements for Sabinus and Plautia. Restraint had been thrown to the winds at a string of lavish parties given by the patricians of Rome. There were eighteen-course dinners with live birds flying out of the roast at a touch of the carving knife, and garish menu oddities like braised flamingo tongues, purée of pheasant brain, or sow's udder. Plautia quickly learned never to ask what she was eating, and usually picked through such delicacies like a sated sparrow.

Yet the feast and garden party given by Nero himself would easily outdo anything that Rome had ever seen. Plautia refused to attend until Sabinus pointed out that rejecting *this* particular invitation would be undiplomatic, if not dangerous.

The banquet, set for midafternoon, was held at a magnificent wooded park in western Rome called Agrippa's Pond. Guests were directed onto a huge pleasure barge, paneled in ivory with gold trim, on which long banquet tables stood ready. Tigellinus, who was directing the extravaganza, assigned places to each—the nearer to Nero and Poppaea, of course, the greater the honor. To Plautia's dismay, she and Sabinus were not only at the head table, but rather close to the emperor.

Tigellinus now clapped his hands three times. The barge cast off slowly, drawn by several smaller boats rowed by a corps of pretty young boys in gilded loincloths, their cheeks rouged to resemble

Cupids. Some were plucking at golden citharas fashioned in the shape of Cupid's bows, while others chirped greetings to the guests.

Sabinus squinted at them and scowled. "I think they're catamites," he whispered to Plautia.

"What's a catamite?" she asked.

Sabinus gave a low chuckle. "Better you don't know."

When they reached the center of the pond, the Cupids quit rowing and drew their craft alongside the imperial barge, where the rarest delicacies were now served along with exquisite vintages to wash them down. The gold-rimmed palace china was all but hidden by the small glassworks of Phoenician crystal surrounding each place setting. Plautia had to watch the empress out of the corner of her eye to see which glass was used for what purpose, and she was forever nudging her husband to identify the exotic white, amber, and red wines and spirits.

A cornet sounded and one of the groves at the edge of the pond quivered to life with strains of sensuous music and a troupe of dancing girls. The forest nymphs were wearing silver sandals but nothing else. Sabinus questioned Nero's taste—no emperor but Caligula had treated a mixed company to such a show.

The other guests, however, started applauding, but no one so loudly as Nero. "Nearer!" he yelled to the Cupids. "Row nearer!"

Poppaea nudged him under the table with a jeweled sandal, but it had no effect.

"Where did you ever find them, Tigellinus?" Nero exulted. "They're beautiful!"

"They're the finest pros— ah—'women of pleasure' in Rome." Then he added, with a tone of pride normally used for vastly different situations, "I chose them myself."

"Aha! What taste!" Nero beamed.

"What taste indeed," Plautia muttered, perhaps too loudly, for Tigellinus now stared at her with a growing smirk.

The dancing nymphs, incredibly libertine, gave even more of themselves as the imperial barge touched the shore of their grove. The girls swarmed onto the deck, fluttering among the guests with coy smiles and giggling each time a sated patrician finger tried to poke them. Then, just when it seemed several of the younger men might make nuisances of themselves so early in the party, Tigellinus gave the signal to cast off while the nymphs scampered back into their grove to continue the show.

"Oh, *must* we leave all this?" Nero wailed.

"Wait, Princeps. There's more to come," Tigellinus promised.

There was more food, of course, and much more to drink. In the darkening twilight Sabinus and Plautia were the only nearly sober ones left at what had all the marks of turning into an imperial bacchanal. For Tigellinus now stood up and announced, "Several of you are asking, 'Where are the *favors* at this banquet?'"

He glanced about and there was much good-natured nodding of heads.

"Well, I'll tell you. From Caesar you anticipate only the ultimate favors—not flowers or jewels or turbans, but this," he extended his arm in a vast circular sweep, "all around this lake—something to delight every taste. Look to the eastern shore, where you boarded the barge: do you see all those purple lanterns burning? Well, purple marks nobility, and those lanterns will show you where women of high rank are waiting impatiently to favor you in tents and arbors."

There was much oohing and aahing, but, incredibly, no one doubted Tigellinus. In the jaded aristocracy of Rome, he had had no trouble finding eager participants.

"There on the south shore," he pointed, "behind the flickering pink lanterns, you'll find groves for those whose taste runs to virgins —young virgins, that is." He flashed a wicked grin.

"Splendid, splendid, Tigellinus!" Nero cackled. "Better than I thought possible."

"Ah . . . will they . . . will they really permit us?" a leering old senator inquired. "What if they . . . resist?"

"No problem," Tigellinus chuckled. "The girls will comply, I assure you. My men are on guard in every grove."

"My prefect thinks of everything," Nero snorted. Then he sniffed the evening air and exclaimed, "Gods, that smells wonderful, Tigellinus! What is it? Incense?"

"Well, incense of a special kind, Caesar. It's an aphrodisiac. We have braziers burning it around the entire pond."

The guests roared with delight, though Plautia was becoming ill as the unbelievable proportions of Tigellinus' scheme unfolded.

"Now some of you seemed attracted to our dancing nymphs on the opposite shore," Tigellinus laughed, with studied understatement. "Well, they're through dancing now, and they're waiting for you with . . . specialties of every kind. Look for the green lanterns.—Now, this barge will continue circling the shore all night, so you can board and disembark at will. And don't forget, there's *much* more to eat and drink."

"*Well!*" Poppaea finally huffed. "You seem to have taken care of all the *men*, Tigellinus! But what are we *women* supposed to do in the meantime?"

"Anything, Empress!" he replied grandly. "Men are waiting on shore too. I've chosen only my handsomest guards to surround the pond. Or, if your taste runs to our Cupids here, help yourself."

Soon it was all happening exactly as Tigellinus had indicated. While lascivious music and ribald song filled the night—and enough drink to keep anyone from fully realizing what was happening—the barge began its series of slow sweeps around the pond. The banquet revelers, men and women, giggled and clucked as they scampered ashore, made their selections, and then disappeared with their tittering favors into some shadowy glade. From the eastern strand came some shouts of embarrassed recognition and delighted surprise. On the south shore, there were a few problems—screams from the unwilling and several curses—but Tigellinus' men soon had the situation well in hand. And from the professional far grove, there were sounds and scenes that beggared all description.

Reeking with wine, Nero stumbled onto shore hand in hand with Pythagoras, the most beautiful of the catamite Cupids. Poppaea, who was tipsy, raised her golden head when Nero left and scowled contemptuously. But then a·dark smile tugged at her crimson lips, and she rolled over to Sabinus, twining her arms about him and whispering, "With me, darling Sabinus! I think I've been in love with you for months."

Stunned, Sabinus tried to disentangle himself and snapped, "*No,* Empress!"

"But you *must,* my love," she murmured, while fondling him, "your empress *commands* it."

"Impossible!" Sabinus hissed. Then, using any excuse that came to mind, he said, "Never! Not with my wife here!"

"Ooohhh," she cooed, languidly, while covering his face and neck with kisses. "But isn't Tigellinus taking care of her?"

Sabinus flashed about. To his horror, Plautia was gone!

"*Where?*" Sabinus demanded. "Where did they go?"

Poppaea let a smug pout warp her lovely face and whined, "Why should I tell you . . . and spoil everything?"

Sabinus had in mind to strangle the truth out of her until he recalled that she was empress of Rome. Instead, he clutched the soft, imperial shoulders in his hands and started squeezing them until Poppaea winced and finally shouted in pain, "Stop it! Back over there!" she pointed westward.

It was a dark section of the lakeshore, between the pink and green lanterns. Sabinus' eyes combed the darkness. Squinting, he thought he saw a tall, stalking white tunic carrying something kicking. He sloshed his way onto shore and ran after them. It *was* Plautia, and she was screaming for help.

"Put her down!" Sabinus yelled.

"Who gives orders to the praetorian prefect?" Tigellinus turned his head and growled.

"The city prefect, you filthy fishmonger!" He made a lunge for Tigellinus' shoulders and pulled him over backward. Plautia's fall was cushioned by Tigellinus' chest, knocking the wind out of him. While he lay gasping for breath, she struggled free of him and rushed sobbing into Sabinus' arms.

"Are you all right, little darling?"

She nodded, her face wet with tears. "He . . . he put his hand over my mouth. Didn't you hear me scream?"

"No. Did he do anything else? I'll kill him if he did. Here and now."

She shook her head. "No, no."

"All right. Let's get out of here."

They started walking out of the grove, but just before they left the beach, Sabinus felt a sandy, wet hand clawing the nape of his neck. A voice grumbled, "As I indicated, you Sabine scum, it's your wife I want." Whirling about, he saw the leering face of Tigellinus.

He had no time to block Tigellinus' jab to his stomach, which doubled him over in pain. A swift uppercut followed, but Sabinus managed to dodge to one side so it only grazed him. Tigellinus had swung so hard that he threw himself off balance, easily tripping over Sabinus' hand clutching at his sandals. The two rolled over and over in the sand, pommeling one another while Plautia looked on in terror. She was going to scream for help but suddenly realized that any help would probably kill Sabinus, since only praetorians were guarding the park. Mercifully, there was enough music and noise to cover the grunts of the struggling men.

It was no contest. Sabinus was younger and had the advantage of being comparatively sober, too. When he saw he was losing, Tigellinus screamed a coward's call for help, and that instant Sabinus realized his mortal danger from the praetorians. Taking careful aim at Tigellinus' chin, he staggered him with an enormous, sweeping blow from his right fist, the knuckles tearing into his lower cheek. Tigellinus dropped over backward and lay very still on the wet sands. Sabinus flashed about to see if any praetorians had seen them, but apparently they were preoccupied with other pursuits.

"Did you . . . did you *kill* him?" Plautia whimpered.

"I hope so!"

"Sabinus!"

"No. He's breathing. Let's go."

It took Nero a day or two to get over the aftereffects of his garden party, but he certainly looked better for the ordeal than did Tigellinus. Puffy-faced and blotched with purple bruises, Tigellinus would tell no one what had happened to him. "If it's a woman you were with, she must have been *quite* the Amazon!" Nero taunted.

A few days later, as a kind of after-party, Nero summoned several of the principal merrymakers—not including Sabinus—to his "wedding with Pythagoras." He had been so taken with the pretty youth that he now played bride, donning a flaming red veil and reciting the marriage formulas. His friends formally witnessed the ceremony, a dowry was announced, wedding torches were lit, and Pythagoras led his imperial bride to the nuptial couch in the palace.

Seething with rage at the grotesque news, Poppaea called Nero names he had no idea she knew.

"It was only in fun," he lamely tried to fib. "I mean, we were only *acting*."

Poppaea was not convinced. Neither was Rome. After the city rocked with reports of the great orgy at Agrippa's Pond—one of the few events that could never be exaggerated—it was fully prepared to believe anything about Nero.

The following Sunday evening on the Aventine, Simon Peter altered his series of addresses to the Christians. That night he talked less about Palestine and more about Rome. Gone was the benign expression. His massive features had firmed into a look of prophetic fury while his eyes blazed with wrath.

"Has Rome become Babylon?" he thundered. "Has the capital of the world degenerated into a new Sodom on the Tiber? Certainly

Sodom's vices are being practiced here! And what happened to Sodom? What befell Gomorrah? The *fire of the Lord* swept down on those cities, and his anger consumed them in brimstone. And it may take flames to purify Rome!" Like an angry lion, his right hand was pawing the air as he scored the city's vices.

Finally, his face softened, and the kindly eyes of The Fisherman sparkled once again as he said, "But the Lord was ready to spare Sodom and Gomorrah if only a few righteous people lived there. May he spare Rome . . . because of you, my beloved."

22

THE WEATHER was very hot and very dry that July. No rain had fallen for weeks, and Rome seemed to shimmer in the parching heat. The colors of the city had dulled to drab and brown. The grasses in the parks and gardens had turned straw yellow. Only the pointing cypresses and the flat-topped umbrella pines offered any green, but even that seemed sick and wilted and thirsty.

Those with country villas had fled the city. The emperor, whose flab could no longer endure the stifling atmosphere, was off to his seaside villa at Antium. Sabinus planned to whisk his family off to Tibur in a short time. But Romans of the lower classes had to stay in town and suffer, waiting for breezes that never came, searching the deep blue skies for puffy rain clouds or even a heavy haze to filter the blistering tyrant sun. But there was nothing, just an impossible succession of clear, burning days that buckled paving stones in the streets and softened the tarry pitch that held them together into a gooey mess.

Finally, on July 18, the air began stirring. Breezes gathered and became a wind. But when the wind started blowing in force, all Rome groaned, for it was a hot blast from the southeast—a mid-summer sirocco that was born in the deserts of Libya and seemed to gather strength as it shot up the Italian peninsula to smother an already sizzling Rome with a suffocating blanket of thermal air.

The night brought no relief. An inflated, rust-colored moon was floating upward in the eastern sky—it was full that evening—but its brilliance only seemed to add warmth to the hot night.

Just east of the Circus Maximus, in a flat area between the Palatine and Caelian hills, stood a ramshackle collection of squalid huts and shops. It was one of the foreign quarters of the city, and a colony of Greek and Syrian traders lived here, selling their wares in the daytime, and retiring to living quarters in the back of their shops at night.

Hermes the contractor lived here too, although Sabinus had urged him often enough to move into better quarters. But it was a matter of convenience for Hermes. Living here, he could keep an eye on his lumber yard and his oil depot too, for recently the canny little city engineer had branched out into the oil business as well. Romans needed olive oil for everything from soap to lamp fuel, and Hermes was making a killing in the commodity.

On that broiling night, however, he wished he had taken Sabinus' advice and been living high on one of Rome's hills rather than sweating to death in that miserable valley. He stalked into the kitchen and found a source of additional heat—the charcoal stove on which his wife had cooked their supper of beans and boar's flesh. Uttering a choice curse in Aramaic, Hermes flung open the door of the stove, scraped the live coals onto a small shovel, and flung them out of his back window.

Under any other circumstances, the coals would have glowed down to ash and gone out. But these fell onto some woodchips, which curled, blackened, and began smoldering. A lazy spiral of smoke twisted upward, looking like a thread of silver in the moonlight. A blast of the sirocco struck, and the wood shavings burst into flame. Yet another quick gust blew them out again.

The chips continued smoldering away until a steady, building wind fanned them back into open flame. Now all the shavings were kindled, and flickering tongues of fire licked onto some boards stacked against the back of the house. Before the pile was half burned through, it had passed the blaze onto the wooden siding of the structure itself, and soon the back of the house was a quivering sheet of flame.

Hermes was preparing for bed when he saw the ugly orange glow and shouted his sleeping wife awake. Dashing outside, he tried desperately to beat out the flames. But several helpless swats with a cloak told him it was too late for that. He must now save what he could.

He and his wife emptied their closets of clothes and jewelry and threw them into the street on the north, screaming for help with each new trip to the window. Finally, when neighbors responded, he yelled, "The vats! Roll the oil vats outside!"

They crashed into his depot and feverishly began tugging at the great earthenware jugs filled with olive oil. Rolling them along their bottom edges, they trundled several of the vats to safety. Then two who found themselves tugging at the same jug from different directions cracked the huge vessel, and oil poured out of the cleft, cascading across the floor toward the living quarters, which were now belching flames through the partition wall into the shop itself.

The sirocco was the giant bellows that provided the final swell of air, and the oil suddenly ignited in a great flash. Flames soared into the night sky, using Hermes' entire premises as their wick. In a trice, houses on both sides caught fire, and their screaming and cursing residents watched their life's possessions blaze away. Playing with the fire like some bright new bauble it had discovered in the darkness, the sirocco sent the flames surging west, then northwest, then north, and back again. They leaped from house to house, and soon the whole block was ablaze on both sides of the street.

Seeing the spreading smudge of orange from their station on the Aventine, the *vigiles* (night watch–firemen) from Region XII trumpeted a fire call and then hurried over to the blaze, where they were soon joined by colleagues from neighboring Region II. In an instant the vigiles saw the mortal danger. They had no hope of saving the immediately surrounding blocks, but they would try to contain the inferno by creating firebreaks ahead of the flames in a line running north from the Circus Maximus, then due eastward to the Caelian.

Rousting sleeping families out of bed, they began demolishing their homes before their drowsy, then dumfounded eyes. Water from a nearby aqueduct was diverted into declivities between the Palatine and Caelian, and, with any luck, they would hold the holocaust to "Hut City"—no great loss, thought the firemen, since the place was a stinking slum anyway. The wind seemed to be abating, and they dared to hope for success.

But again the slumbering sirocco came to life. Shops with paint and other combustibles hissed and sputtered and sizzled. There were muffled explosions and sharp, cracking sounds, each catapulting some still-burning substance into the air, which was wafted upward in the fierce heat. Then the southeast wind took control of the flaming ash and pelted it northwestward in great arcs far beyond the firebreak. Some of the ash blew out. Some did not, and wherever it fell, tinder-dry structures gave it shelter and nourishment.

The Circus Maximus was next to go, not the lower tiers of stone seats surrounding the vast hippodrome, but the rickety super-structure of wooden boards that hovered around the stadium, in-creasing its seating capacity by 100,000. Several blobs of flaming cin-ders landed on the northern tier, and soon it was a crackling pyre of reddish-orange, its seats perfectly spaced to provide the flames all the air they required. Since the great hippodrome lay along the same axis as the wind, the hungry blaze leaped voraciously from row to row, gallery to gallery.

Along the entire northern edge of the Circus lay the Palatine and Nero's palace. With mounting, almost hypnotic horror, the palace staff watched the vigiles trying to contain the fire at the base of the Palatine. All seven cohorts of the night watch had now been alerted, and they were desperately ringing the imperial hill, trying to smother the flaming ash raining down on it. Palace slaves were scur-rying over the grounds with jugs, splashing water onto the orange blotches that lit up the hillside and steaming them back into dark-ness. They were coughing and choking in the smoky stench and per-spiring in a stifling night suddenly grown drastically warmer.

Nero had just put the finishing touches on what he called the Domus Transitoria, a great new wing of his palace that extended eastward, connecting the Palatine with the Esquiline. Now, almost as if the flames had been ordered to attack precisely this structure, they joined to converge on the Transitoria, for it was the last barrier between them and the valley leading into the Forum. All four stories of the new wing became a thundering, blazing inferno, consuming Nero's works of art, his library, wardrobe, museum, his dozen different lyres and costumes—in fine, everything that had made the man the artist. The palace staff now fled northward for their lives, since the hot breath of the sirocco bloomed the flames into an infer-nal tour of the Caelian and the Palatine, igniting the rest of Nero's palace as well.

Beyond the Palatine lay the Forum, but the conflagration paid scant respect to its antiquity. The Via Sacra—the world's central street—became a river of fire, hissing and spilling flame into Rome's most ancient monuments, scorching the marble and turning the white travertine into heaps of charred rock. The Vestal Virgins ran screaming from their quarters because the Temple of Vesta, where Rome's sacred fire was kept burning, was now its own gargantuan flame. As of that point, it was the worst disaster the city of Rome had suffered in five centuries, and it was far from over.

On the Quirinal, earlier that evening, Sabinus and Plautia had been preparing for bed when she noticed it first. Standing at their bedroom window for a wisp of fresh air before retiring she looked to the south and saw the Palatine encrusted in a halo of shimmering apricot.

"Come here and look, Sabinus!" she said. "Look at the palace. Isn't that the strangest light you ever saw? It couldn't be fire—there are no flames . . ."

"By all the gods!" Sabinus whispered. "There must be a flaming hell on the other side!"

Jumping into his tunic, he dispatched one of his aides northward. "Alert all Urban Cohorts to converge on city headquarters and meet me there." Then he rushed down to his offices, where the grim-faced commander of the night watch told him, "Started east of the Circus Maximus. Half of Regions III, X, and XI are gone. The Domus Transitoria is going now. You may be next here."

"How did it start?"

"Who knows?"

"Are all your vigiles on duty?"

"Yes. By now. They're trying to build another firebreak behind the Domus along this line." He traced his hand along the great city map hanging in Sabinus' office.

"Too close to the fire. You won't get everything torn down in time with the wind blowing the way it is. Let's let nature help us out: why not the valley between the Caelian and Esquiline farther north? Here."

The commander of the vigiles nodded. "You're probably right. But where are your men, Prefect?"

"They're on their way. Do you want them to help fight the fire or stay on security?"

"Why not have about a thousand help us clear your Esquiline valley line? But you'd better keep the other three thousand on police duty. We already have reports of looting."

"Has anyone alerted the emperor?"

"Ten minutes ago we sent a rider out to Antium."

"All right. Let's set the other firebreak immediately north of the Forum—here." Sabinus pointed. "We should be able to save the rest of central Rome."

"Right. But aren't your headquarters dangerously close to the Forum?"

"Yes, we may not be able to save all this. But I'm not hauling out our documents until we're in imminent danger."

By now the Urban Cohorts had arrived, and Sabinus went out to give them their orders. Then he hurried eastward with the company assigned to clear the firebreak at the base of the Esquiline. If the blaze broke through here, the house of Aulus and Pomponia would be in mortal danger.

Several hours later, about 4 A.M., he and his men had toppled most of the structures likely to transmit the flames when Nero and Tigellinus suddenly appeared, their mounts frothing after a frantic ride up from Antium. Nero, who had been giving a recital when he was alerted, had not even had time to change from his costume as a cithara player. Sabinus gave them a full briefing on the fire.

Tigellinus smirked as he spat out the words, "Can't you manage the city while we're away, Prefect? You've *really* let things get out of hand this time!"

"I expected that from you, Tigellinus." Sabinus glowered. "But instead of making asinine comments, why don't you order your praetorians out to help us?"

"Yes, yes, yes, Tigellinus—*do* get the praetorians!" Nero wailed. "But first, both of you, let's see it all from Maecenas' Gardens."

The gardens lay several hundred feet farther up the Esquiline, and a terrace there provided an ideal vantage point from which to survey Rome and lay strategy for containing the fire. Reining their horses to a halt after the steep uphill ride, the three dismounted to look at the smoldering city. The eastern skies were beginning to flush with the first delicate coral of dawn, but they stared only at the ghastly sight before them. Other Romans were also streaming to that spot, first in curiosity at reports about "some fire in south Rome," then in horror at what the panorama actually showed them. The great valley of the Circus Maximus lay in a million embers, while the Caelian and Palatine were belching up gigantic wriggling cones of flame from a vast, crackling sea of fire. Every time some structure collapsed, a huge column of flame shot upward for several moments, spattering the sky with clouds of luminous gold dust.

Nero broke down and wept. "Sweet goddess Roma!" he wailed. "My new palace? My old palace?" His face was contorted with shock and grief. "Will you look at the Palatine, gentlemen? Only *my* property is burning! Augustus' mansion still stands. So does Tiberius' palace. But my Transitoria is a cinder! All my apartments . . . gone! My treasures, my Greek statues . . . my trophies . . . library . . . wardrobe. Even my buskins!" Each item recalled seemed to strike new torture into Nero.

Sabinus tried to say something, but Nero held up his hand for silence. Now he walked to the balustrade of the terrace and peered at the spectacle before him. The flames, even though they were ruining him, had a terrible beauty of their own. The artist in him was touched deeply by the sight, and he started singing a mournful dirge of his own composition, *The Capture of Troy*. Only Priam's great city had suffered the disaster Rome was now enduring. Verse after verse poured out from Nero's quaking voice as he gestured across his city in tears.

Sabinus struggled to contain his impatience, though he realized Nero must have his moments now or his emotions might overcome him later. Some of the bystanders were moved by the emperor's performance. Others thought it undignified and unnecessary, and they would tell others what they had seen.

Sabinus would not see his wife again for five days. Getting what little sleep he could on a makeshift bed at city headquarters, he was on duty day and night in the crisis. Drawn with worry, Plautia kept watching the flames from the Quirinal but getting reports that her husband, as well as her parents, were safe. In the daytime, the view seemed the most ominous: great belching clouds of angry gray smoke polluting the air, rising from areas that had become scorched and ugly black. At night the scene was more disastrously beautiful as the flickering line of a thousand separate islands of fire seemed to advance northward in a vast arc. Little Flavius stared with childish fascination at the marvel, happily ignorant of the multiplied thousands of personal horrors being perpetrated by the holocaust.

But his father saw it all firsthand. Sabinus and his police were working with the vigiles, trying to copy their techniques. Like the firemen, Sabinus divided his cohorts into siphoners, who tapped the nearest aqueducts for water; blanketeers, who smothered flames with blankets soaked in water and vinegar; and netmen, who, with outstretched mattresses and nets, cushioned the fall of those jumping from windows. But in a catastrophe of this magnitude, even the disciplined firemen were having little success with such procedures.

If fire touched one house in a poor district, the whole block was lost, for homes on those narrow, crooked lanes were built onto one another to save the expense of building a fourth wall. Worse still was the fate of those caught in the upper stories of the many flimsy tenements in Rome.

Sabinus saw and smelled and heard it all: the screams of terrified men and women as the five or six stories of a tenement collapsed in a vast shower of golden sparks . . . the pleading cackle of those too old and decrepit to escape the flames . . . lost children shrieking for their parents . . . men carrying their household possessions awkwardly before them, jostling and shoving one another . . . others, in agony at failing to rescue their families, plunging into the flames to end it all . . . mothers hurrying their children from place to place in a mad flight from the crackling, whirling thunder of the blaze . . . hordes of the homeless occupying every foot of ground in whatever parks and open fields they could find, and then being beaten off by those who got there first.

As in all disasters, Sabinus saw the conflagration bringing out the worst—and the best—in people. Some became clawing animals, looting and thieving or seizing firebrands and adding insanely to the chaos. Bands of gladiators, drunk with wine plundered from burning taverns, roamed the city for new pillage. Slaves, freed by the catastrophe, were chattering in Greek, African, and Asiatic dialects, some vengefully ravaging the mansions that had held them captive. Other citizens heroically found strength to rescue the helpless while disregarding reports that their own homes were on fire. Mortally burned without knowing it, some kept battling the flames until they collapsed.

Strangely, it was not the searing heat that bothered Sabinus the most but the smells—the pungent, acrid odor of smoke, fumes, smoggy haze, and more smoke—that stinking pall hanging over the city, almost darkening the sun and turning day into night. Sometimes the smell was pleasant: if a tall, aged pine went up in flames and the wind blew right, his nostrils could relax. But moments later came the stench of scorching animal or human flesh and he would gag again. From time to time he tried to spit out the taste of soot and ash in his mouth, but in minutes it was back.

He met with Nero, Tigellinus, and the commander of the vigiles twice a day to discuss strategy, and the emperor surprised him by plunging boldly into relief efforts. He threw open to the homeless hordes the great public buildings, temples, and basilicas in the Campus Martius. He set up shelters and food stations in the parks of Rome and converted his gardens in the Trans-Tiber into a vast tent city. Ordering massive supplies of grain from government storage bins in Ostia and neighboring towns, he reduced the price of wheat to three sesterces a peck. No one, he swore, would go hungry.

The firebreak at the base of the Esquiline was holding. After demolition of all structures there, the eager flames met only bare ground and open sky. Sabinus dared to hope that the worst was over. On the morning of the sixth day, with the rest of Rome out of danger, the vigiles finally advanced into fire-gutted areas and extinguished the last remaining embers.

Sabinus staggered home and fell, exhausted, into the arms of Plautia. He slept straight through the next sixteen hours.

"Sabinus!"

He felt Plautia's hand tugging at his shoulder. Cracking his eyelids, he saw her bending over him, her eyes clouded with fear. "Someone from the vigiles is here," she was saying. "It's urgent. Something about fire breaking out again."

Sabinus was instantly awake. "Impossible! Send him in."

The courier marched into Sabinus' bedroom and gave a stiff salute. "Pardon the intrusion, Clarissimus," he said, "but fire's broken out again. It's raging out of control in the Campus Martius."

"What? When did it break out?" Icy disbelief clutched at Sabinus.

"About . . . two hours ago, we think. All the monuments there are in danger."

"How did this one start?" A feeling of nauseous dread was now suffusing him.

"We've no idea."

Fastening the last strap on his sandals, Sabinus caught Plautia about the waist for a hasty kiss. "This one's closer to us, carissima. It could be more dangerous. So if a strong west wind develops, you must leave the house. Take the children and servants over to your parents' place on the Esquiline. It'll be safe there."

"All right. But be *careful*, Sabinus!"

While he hurried off to the blaze, she stood in the doorway of their home, clenching a fist over her mouth.

Again the vigiles were sweating at their task when Sabinus and his police arrived, but this time he saw that he would have a problem with morale too. The firemen were losing heart: six days of fighting the ghastly inferno now seemed to be in vain, and the men were muttering darkly about a general curse hovering over the city— that Rome must inevitably go the way of Atlantis and Troy and Carthage.

"We can't fight the gods, Prefect," one of them moaned.

"Oh, to Hades with the gods!" Sabinus bellowed.

Several looked aghast at his impiety, but he pressed the point. "Did any of you see Vulcan hobbling about, putting Rome to the torch? He should have been involved, after all: he's the god of fire."

No one would admit to it.

Though it seemed a ridiculous time to deal in pleasantries, Sabinus could now build on the low chuckle of the vigiles. "No, men, don't blame this on the gods. So far, they're the biggest losers in this blaze: about forty of their temples are now in ashes! But we should have an easier time containing this fire. So man the siphons, vigiles! My police will use the Via Lata to set up a firebreak to the east!"

But the perverse sirocco, which had died down, suddenly came back to life and blew a sizable section of northwestern Rome into another raging furnace. This time, some valuable monuments, theaters, and aged temples were charred and ruined, while pleasure arcades in the gardens were seared into blackened wasteland.

Mercifully, however, there was less contagion in the new outbreak, and Sabinus found much less loss of life—none of the roiling scenes of human horror that would never erase themselves from his memory. Soon the sirocco exhaled the last of its baleful breath, and the second conflagration could be stamped out in three days.

Fully drained of all his energy reserves, Sabinus could barely see as he peered across Rome for the last time, searching for any lingering pockets of flame. But the holocaust was finally over. Only some random columns of smoke filtering up harmlessly from blackened acreage told the end of nine days of terror. Dizzy and bewildered from extreme fatigue, Sabinus could not later recall that it was his aides who finally had to carry him home to the Quirinal, where he collapsed and slept as one dead.

Plautia looked at the sooty, deep-breathing figure of her husband and—for some reason—thanked her mother's God for his safe return.

It was a note from the emperor that finally roused him two days later. Nero wanted a written estimate of the total damage Rome had sustained. It was to be delivered to him at his temporary quarters in the Servilian Gardens on the Aventine.

After an ugly week of trudging through the ashes and wreckage to interview survivors, Sabinus and his staff drew up a map of the city showing the fire-damaged areas [see back endpaper] and a table of losses, and presented them to Nero.

REGIONS HEAVILY OR COMPLETELY DESTROYED

III Isis et Serapis
X Palatium
XI Circus Maximus

REGIONS PARTIALLY DESTROYED

II Caelimontium
IV Templum Pacis
VII Via Lata
VIII Forum Romanum
IX Circus Flaminius
XII Piscina Publica
XIII Aventinus

REGIONS UNTOUCHED

I Porta Capena
V Esquiline
VI Alta Semita
XIV Trans Tiberim

PRIVATE MANSIONS DESTROYED

132

TENEMENTS DESTROYED

Over 4,000 units

Injured: Not available   *Dead:* Not available

"The last two figures will have to be determined in the next weeks," Sabinus explained to Nero.

"But what these figures *don't* show are the irreplaceables," Nero mused. "Romulus' temple, Numa's palace, Vesta's sanctuary . . ."

"Not to mention the archives."

"And my statues—Greek originals. Now we have only copies of those masterpieces." Then he stopped and smoothed his brow. "But we must look to the future, gentlemen. We must rebuild Rome. And we'll *not* rebuild her helter-skelter as our ancestors did after the Gauls burned the city. No, no! We'll have broader streets—"

"And straighter, I trust?" Sabinus smiled.

"Yes, straighter. We'll require open spaces between buildings and limit the number of stories in them."

"What about all the masses of rubbish from the fire?" Tigellinus inquired.

"I'll pay for clearing it away," Nero volunteered. "But where will we put it all?"

Sabinus pondered a moment, then suggested, "Why not have the grain barges return down the Tiber loaded with ashes and dump them in the marshes around Ostia? They're trying to raise that land anyway, aren't they?"

Nero smiled. "Inspired, Sabinus. Inspired."

"And I think your greatest problem now, Caesar, will be to lift the mood of the people in the devastated districts. They're crushed with this loss. They may not have the heart to rebuild."

"What do you advise, Prefect?" Tigellinus sniffed. "Shall Caesar buy them new homes while you massage their spirits?"

Coolly ignoring Tigellinus' inanity, Sabinus made a proposal. "Why not offer something like a bounty to owners of ruined property? If they rebuild within a specified time, they can claim the reward."

"Hmmm," Nero pondered. "Sounds reasonable, provided the bounty isn't too high."

"Proportion it to the loss sustained."

"All right, Sabinus. They're good suggestions. All of them. We'll incorporate them in our edict."

Nero did what he had promised. He also led Rome in publicly appeasing the gods so that the disaster would not be repeated, offering solemn prayers to Vulcan. At the same time, a somber parade of

Roman matrons trooped up to the Capitoline, which had been spared the flames, and humbly implored Juno to cool her anger, bathing her statue with water from the Mediterranean and holding all-night vigils in her honor.

As wife of the city prefect, Plautia was expected to join Poppaea in leading the women of Rome in these sacred duties, but she would not.

"It's all hypocrisy," she told her husband. "Not one of those women seriously thinks Juno is cocking an ear to their prayers. Or has the necessary existence to do so."

Sabinus, who let Plautia make her own decision in the matter, had to smile at her resolve. He recalled his own exclamation during the great blaze: to Hades with the gods indeed!

23

THE CEREMONIES OVER, Nero plunged into rebuilding a palace for himself. But where? The black wastes of the Palatine were haunted with bad memories, and the Fates seemed to frown on that hill. Severus and Celer, the emperor's master architects who were directing the rebuilding of Rome, pointed out the obvious spot: the great valley below the Esquiline, where everything had been demolished to serve as the massive firebreak.

Nero and Tigellinus hurried over to the site with Severus and Celer, and soon they were captivated by the prospects of a great new palace in that setting. Eyes blazing with faraway visions of future grandeur, Nero suggested its dimensions. The men caught their breath. Nero was stepping off an area of some 130 acres, larger than both Forums.

"Now listen carefully"—Nero beamed—"here's what I have in mind: the four of us are looking at the portals of the new palace . . . say about there." He pointed.* "Inside the vestibule, we ought to have something to symbolize the place. But what?"

Tigellinus picked up the cue. He knew Nero's dream had been to have a gigantic statue of himself erected, so he quickly responded,

* To a place where the Colosseum would later stand, itself named for Nero's colossus.

"Your colossus must stand there, Caesar. In truly heroic dimension."

"You really think so, Tigellinus?" Nero grinned. "Well, that might be appropriate. How . . . large should the statue be, do you suppose?"

"I said a *colossus*, Caesar, not a statue. Let it be at least, say, twenty times your size."

Severus was frowning. "But that would be well over one hundred feet high! And the vestibule housing it would have to be higher still."

"Aren't you and Celer capable of designing something like this?" Tigellinus sniffed.

"Of course, but if the palace stands that high it will also have to be extremely long to keep the proportions in balance."

"Oh, I intend it to be long," said Nero, in a matter-of-fact tone. "I had in mind a great hall of columns forming one axis of the building, running from here to . . . say, that great oak over there at the end of the valley."

Severus' eyes boggled. "But that's almost a mile away!"

"Of course it is!" Tigellinus growled. "We're planning a genuine palace here—not one of those hovels on the Palatine."

"But with this difference," Nero added. "Anyone can throw up *huge* structures. What I want is a *great* structure. Caesar is not merely emperor. Caesar is also an artist, and his residence must reflect that fact. Now, follow me. Here's what I have in mind . . ."

He took them on a tour of his future abode, his arms busy as he pointed out the prospective gardens, lakes, and even fields stocked with game that would surround the palace. Splashing fountains and groves with statuary were to set off separate pools for fresh water, seawater, and even sulfur baths piped in from the hot springs at Tibur.

The architects finally caught Nero's spirit. Several weeks later, they presented him preliminary sketches that were as breathtaking as they were lavish. They also had several surprises they knew would delight his fancy: a grand dining room in which a domed ceiling with sun and stars would revolve to symbolize the day and night skies. The halls would be covered with so much gold and jeweled inlays that they suggested a name for their project: the Domus Aurea.

"The 'golden house'?" Nero mused. "Yes. Yes, I like that very much. Build it, gentlemen."

Severus and Celer laid their plans on Sabinus' desk at city head-quarters. He studied them for several minutes as every muscle in his body seemed to tauten. Walking over to the great wall map of Rome, he moved his left hand over a massive arc of Rome to the west and north. "Here, gentlemen," he said, his voice exuding sarcasm, "here are several sections of the city that you *haven't* reserved for your new palace. Otherwise, you'll have most of Rome!"

"We know, we know," Severus huffed. "But we didn't come here to listen to caustic comments, Prefect—we're just following orders, after all. We *are* here to ask for work crews for the new palace."

"Every last city crew and all private contractors are at work rebuilding Rome."

"Yes, but Nero has to have a place to live too," Celer observed. "We're authorized to take over your crews if you won't cooperate."

Sabinus struggled to contain his fury. He searched for theoretical options and alternatives, but found none in fact. "I want you both to know," he finally said, "that the people of Rome will know *exactly* why the work crews are being diverted."

"Fine," said Severus, shrugging his shoulders. "Now, here's what we'll require . . ."

As many thousands of laborers who had been toiling to rebuild the city were suddenly shifted to the vast project along the Esquiline, Romans frowned and began grumbling. The rumblings grew louder as they saw the incredible dimensions of Nero's new palace and its financing through forced contributions from all over the Empire "for rebuilding Rome." Was it an accident that six great landowners in Africa were suddenly executed on trumped-up charges and their vast estates—virtually half the province—confiscated by the emperor?

The Golden House only served as capstone to an ugly arch of rumor that had been building across Rome ever since the great fire. People were whispering it to their neighbors. Graffiti were shouting it from the walls. Homeless thousands were shaking their fists and screaming it. And Nero's enemies were trying to prove it: as a climax to all his other crimes, *Nero himself* had set fire to Rome!

But why? Finally it was obvious, they thought: to clear out the slums at minimal expense; to be given glory for founding a new city, probably to be renamed Neropolis; and, above all, to seize vast acreage in the very heart of Rome for his Golden House. These were the main motives. And there were others: Priam and Troy were immortalized by their fiery, disastrous end. Nero too wanted to go down in legend, and so created his own catastrophe.

And the proof? Look where buildings were demolished for the firebreak. And the scene of Nero surveying his burning city from the Esquiline terrace had been embellished from mouth to mouth in the retelling. In place of tears, he now wore a dark smile. Instead of merely singing his dirge, he now plucked rapturously at his lyre, nearly salivating over the flames.

"Nero *played* while Rome *burned!*" The obvious, angry slogan had arisen shortly after the flames were extinguished. Sabinus, who wanted to be fair, tried to scotch the rumor. "Nonsense!" he countered publicly. "People *always* blame the person in power at times of catastrophe."

But then the colored reports, the misinterpretations, the rumors started saturating the city at a time when Romans were prone to look for culprits and incendiaries. A plebe who had lost his wife and baby on the Caelian stood up in the tent city and shouted, "My cousin works in the palace. She told me that at one of Nero's dinner parties, someone quoted a line from Euripides: 'When I am dead, may fire consume the earth.' But Nero replied, 'No! Rather *while I live!*'"

But the greatest fuel for the rumors flowed from the efforts of the firefighters themselves. People saw them demolishing buildings or setting counter fires, and the police were even helping them. Hence it must all have been done at Caesar's orders!

Nero had heard the first rumors while the smoke was still curling up from the blanket of ashes that was south-central Rome, yet he had passed them off as idle gossip. But with the Golden House project, the angry mutters became open shouts. Now the city was rumbling with furious demonstrations as a hundred thousand accusing fingers seemed to rise from the rubble and point toward him.

The graffiti of Rome used to be simple and obvious, merely taunting Nero for matricide. But now there were fresh themes:

A House of Gold is swallowing Rome!
Let's flee to Veii and make it our home!
But the palace—it grows so much faster than hell,
That soon it'll gobble up Veii as well.

and:

> Who set Rome on fire?
> The man we must admire
> For killing his wife, and taking the life
> Of mother and brother and so many others
> While plucking his damnable lyre.

Nero made no effort to find the authors of such graffiti—a hopeless quest in any case—but he grew alarmed when people no longer spoke of Caesar, but of "The Incendiary" or "The Arsonist-Matricide." Verging on panic, he called a conference at his temporary residence of all heads of government, including his council of state.

Sabinus had forebodings about the imperial conclave. Nero was always at his worst when threatened. All his crimes had been committed when he felt threatened. But now there was a new complication—the voice of the people—for Nero was extremely sensitive about his popularity. With the people against him too, Nero would doubtless be cowardly, suspicious, volatile, and ready to clutch at any convenient solution.

Sabinus was not disappointed. Nero was all this and more. His ruddy face had blanched with a clammy pallor, and it seemed to have fattened over the past months, for the outlines of a double chin were unmistakable and his bull neck was never more ponderous. The sensuous lips now seemed thick enough to touch his nose, Sabinus thought, or were his nostrils stretching down to guard his mouth from overeating?

Nero quickly sounded the keynote of the conference. "I've gathered you all, my colleagues—and even my beloved Poppaea here—to help me decide what to do about the terrible slanders circulating in the city. The people are holding meetings in the streets. They're demanding that I be burnt in the 'troublesome tunic'! Great Vulcan, the incredible injustice! I—who suffered most from the fire—am accused of setting it! Everything I valued is now ashes, and they want to say I made Rome a blazing hell!"

His pudgy hands, sprouting coarse amber hairs, were busy smoothing his tiers of curls at the back of his head or tugging at the purple silk handkerchief about his throat—Terpnus ordered such protection for the "celestial voice." Nero then recounted his losses once again, a list Sabinus had heard so many times before he could recite it from memory.

"Has anyone discovered the *true* cause of the conflagration?" Petronius inquired.

Nero looked to Sabinus and said, "Perhaps our city prefect can enlighten us."

In fact, Sabinus knew exactly what had caused the outbreak. Long before the embers had glowed down, a guilt-ridden Hermes had confessed his accident to Sabinus. Realizing Hermes' life was at stake, Sabinus had sworn him to silence. So now he replied, "As far as we can determine, it was merely an accidental house fire in an oil dealer's shop east of the Circus that set it all off. The sirocco took over, and that was that."

"But *I* get the blame," Nero moaned. "I who was thirty-five miles away at the time. *I* sent incendiaries into the city . . . at the time of a full moon, no less! Fiery Vulcan! In that case, why didn't I get placards painted to advertise the scheme: 'These Flames Courtesy of Nero Caesar'."

"And how you bungled it, Caesar," Tigellinus continued in the same irony. "You were after the Esquiline property, but you destroyed a third of the city before getting the flames that far!"

"Including everything I owned. So I repeat, my friends, what shall we do?"

Silence filled the chamber until Tigellinus asked, "Why don't we find the *real* culprits?"

"The real culprits?" Nero stared at him blankly. "But there aren't any. The fire was accidental."

"I know, I know. But, you see, the people *want* culprits . . . they *want* to believe it was caused by arsonists. So let's supply them."

"You mean, pin the blame on some innocent people?" Petronius asked.

"Yes, innocent of this, but . . . guilty of something else. We could find some criminals—perhaps even some foreign elements we don't like—and indict them to clear Caesar."

"Hmmmm," Nero reflected. "The plan has possibilities . . ."

"Utterly and morally wrong, Caesar," Sabinus countered. "The criminals would confess they'd been put up to this, and you'd be worse off than ever. The only solution is to tell the truth about how the fire started."

"But we've *tried* to do that, Sabinus," grumbled Tigellinus, "and the people just won't believe it."

"Hear me out. Let's circulate a full explanation of the causes of the fire—sworn testimony from survivors on the street where it started—and then add a list of Caesar's own great losses and many relief efforts afterward, and people *must* believe his innocence."

"I'd support that," said Petronius. Several other heads nodded, but Nero seemed less than impressed.

"Disgusting!" he pouted. "It's disgusting that I have to prove my innocence—as though somehow *I* were on trial. If we publish such a statement, Sabinus, it will look as if I'm on the defensive in this matter."

"With all respect, Caesar, you *are*," said Sabinus. "However unjustifiably, the people of Rome have put you on the defensive and you must answer them, clear yourself, and tell the true story. Publish the facts. They'll believe them."

Again there were some moments of silence. Finally Tigellinus said, "You don't understand the people of Rome, Prefect. The common man is a sensation-seeker. That's why feeding him is not enough: we must dazzle his eyes as well as fill his belly. Circuses must follow bread. Now, what does the public *prefer* to believe? That the great fire started by accident—as fires most often do—or by design? The people have already opted for the latter. They always prefer the sensational to the actual. If we try to prove it was an accident, they'll never believe it now. They'll say we're only covering up the truth, and the murmuring will continue as long as Nero rules. Conspiracies will multiply. Assassinations will be attempted."

Nero tightened his eyes and looked visibly alarmed as Tigellinus, who knew his emperor's weaknesses so well, continued. "That's why we *must* protect Caesar by clearing him completely. And the only way to do that is to give the people the victims they want. So I suggest we decide on some gang of 'incendiaries,' indict them, 'prove' their guilt, and then give them a very dramatic execution before the people in one of the great hippodromes. We'll burn . . . we'll torture . . . we'll crucify them while our citizens watch it all. Those who lost their loved ones will finally drink the sweet nectar of revenge as they watch the agonies of the 'arsonists,' and they'll quit blaming their innocent emperor."

"But . . . it's . . . *wrong*, Tigellinus!" Sabinus objected. "Unjust! Immoral! A show, a farce. It could cause complications of the worst kind. Rome's never—"

"Who says what's right or wrong? Are you putting the lives of some wretched criminals ahead of Caesar's own?"

Unhappily, Tigellinus' plan seemed to gain support among some of the advisers, and soon Nero was openly praising it. "The people *do* have to have a show after all this misery," he said. "Imagine how happy it would make them! And that point about getting their vengeance while watching the guilty suffer—it's true, you know. People *are* like that. Yes. Yes indeed! That's the solution, my colleagues. Let's do it."

Sabinus entered an even stronger protest, this time calling on the memory of Nero's ancestors who had governed in justice and equity. But Nero grumbled, "Oh, shut up, Sabinus. You're not much help here. If you can't sing a new song, why don't you leave?"

His ire rising, Sabinus got up to leave the room.

"No, wait!" Nero ordered. "Stay. As city prefect, you'll have to be in on these plans, of course.—Now, Tigellinus, who will the victims be?"

"I don't know." The praetorian prefect shrugged. "The idea just occurred to me. We'll have to think about it."

"Well, how many should there be?"

"Not just a few, Caesar. This must be a spectacle. We'll have to fill the arena of one of the hippodromes with a whole crowd of arsonists."

"Yes, yes. Perhaps several dozen, at least."

"More like several hundred, I should think." Tigellinus smirked. "The greater the number of victims, the greater the feeling of revenge among the people."

"Gods, what sage advice, Tigellinus!" Nero smiled. "Do you see, my friends, why I chose this man as praetorian prefect? Now, where can we round up a gang of criminals this size?"

"Or foreigners . . . cultists . . . any group in society that we despise."

"The followers of Isis and Osiris?" Gallio ventured. "After all, fires raged through their Region III."

"Which means they're innocent," Tigellinus objected. "They'd hardly destroy their own area of the city. Let's look at sections *not* touched by the fire."

Nero called for the city map that Sabinus had shaded in to show the burned-out districts. Spreading it out on their conference table, they studied it for some moments. Suddenly Nero exclaimed, "Do you see what I see, gentlemen? There are only four regions absolutely untouched by fire. Of these, we can eliminate Regions V and

VI, since only the wealthy live on the Esquiline and the Quirinal, not cultists and foreigners. That leaves only Regions I and XIV."

"What are you getting at?" asked Petronius.

"Simply this: what foreign group has settled heavily in both Region I, the Porta Capena, and XIV, the Trans-Tiber?"

"Why . . . the Jews, of course." Tigellinus brightened.

"The Jews. Exactly." Nero smiled. "We have to clean them out of Rome from time to time, but they always manage to come back. *The Jews* set fire to Rome!"

Sabinus was shaking his head in despair, and Poppaea too was frowning. "But there are too many Jews for your purposes." She spoke for the first time. "There must be 30,000 in Rome alone."

"We'd merely ask them for several hundred," Nero replied. "Most of our citizens don't like them anyway. They'd be perfect scapegoats."

"No," Poppaea said, quietly but firmly. "If you'd kill a hundred, the people would go after all the others too and kill many thousands. It would be a horrible blood bath. The Jews are innocent . . . they're loyal. They intercede for you in their synagogues, Nero. You can't do this to them."

"Not even to save your husband, Empress?"

"Don't you *dare* to put it that way, Tigellinus!" she hissed. "Whatever you decide, gentlemen, it will *not* be the Jews."

Silence again dominated the room. Suddenly Sabinus' heart began pulsing in a wild cadence, and he fought to keep his face from reddening and betraying what had just occurred to him. In the horror of the moment, he prayed the great Father of the Gods that Tigellinus was not thinking of the same possibility. He stole a quick glance at him, then looked away again, but his horror was richly confirmed: Tigellinus had been staring at him with a slowly broadening smile. He waited several moments longer to let Sabinus suffer before saying, "Well, Caesar. Search no further. We've found our arsonists."

"Who?"

"Who?" Tigellinus grinned as the full implications became clearer to him. "Simply that special brand of Jews who are not Jews at all, as Sabinus helped me prove in the trial of one, Paul of Tarsus, three years ago. I lost that case, you'll recall. But I think I'll win this one."

"Oh . . . you mean the Christians," Nero replied.

Tigellinus nodded slowly and said, "Exactly. The Christians."

For several moments they all paused to ponder the possibility.

"By the immortal gods, that's *good*, Tigellinus," Nero finally commented. "Excellent . . . in fact, a *superb* suggestion. Our people hate the Christians as much as the Jews, and there are far fewer Christians. They'll suspect them more. They're a weird group anyway. They could so easily have done it."

"Their main congregation is on the Aventine," Tigellinus added. "And the Aventine was almost untouched by the fire."

Sabinus was queasy at the horrendous turn the conference had taken. Hundreds of innocent lives were now hanging on his ability to turn the dreadful decision the conclave seemed to be pondering. By now, of course, he had become *persona non grata* in that discussion, but he would never be able to live with himself unless he made the supreme effort.

"My colleagues," Sabinus began slowly. "I'd like to expand on the very eloquent objection raised by the Empress Poppaea. She was absolutely right in suggesting that our people will not be content with the punishment of a few. They will indeed go after the many. Now, there are more than a few hundred Christians in Rome. By now there are thousands—"

"Oh, he's thinking of his dear mother-in-law, of course." Tigellinus smirked. "Don't worry, Sabinus. We won't touch Pomponia."

"Entirely apart from Pomponia," Sabinus continued, "people of every rank in Rome are now Christians. It's an innocent religion, Tigellinus. Some of your own praetorians are Christians—and the better for it. Some of your own household slaves are Christians, Caesar."

"They *are?*" Nero darkened.

Instantly, Sabinus knew it had been poor timing for that particular argument, since it could feed Nero's suspicions. He resumed as best he could. "They pray for you, Caesar. They're good citizens. And they would never admit to the falsehood that they set fire to Rome."

"They would under torture," Tigellinus huffed.

Ignoring the comment, Sabinus argued, "If you blame the Christians, the hundred innocents you gather in the arena won't be the only victims. The people will seek out the rest and cause a general slaughter. I plead with you, my friends, by all the gods and goddesses we honor, that you choose another group, if choose you must—convicted criminals, perhaps."

"No. Criminals can't be trusted," Tigellinus sneered. "They might expose us—wasn't that your original argument, Sabinus?—and besides, I don't trust the Christians anyway. If they *are* growing here in Rome as you say, then they're a dangerous and subversive element—a state within a state. And maybe they *do* commit those atrocities mentioned at Paul's trial: they meet at night, like a pack of sorcerers and magicians—"

"And the point is that people *think* they do all these things." Nero smiled. "If they murder babies and despise our gods, they might easily have hated Rome enough to burn it too."

"By the gods!" Tigellinus suddenly exclaimed. "I hadn't thought of it until this moment! I've had two of my praetorians attending their meetings on the Aventine to spy out their teachings. Now, their *other* major leader recently arrived in Rome—a Galilean fisherman named Simon, I think it was. Yes, Simon Peter. And what, do you suppose, he told his people just after our . . . magnificent party at Agrippa's Pond?"

"What?"

"I don't recall the exact words, but it went something like this. He told about some cities in Palestine being destroyed by fire, and then he said, 'It may take fire to purify Rome also'—or something like that."

Nero's eyes widened. Then he smiled. "It's settled, then. The Christians set fire to Rome."

"No!" Sabinus interjected. "That was only a figure of speech—a simple coincidence. It means nothing. Certainly Peter never advised arson. Christians are law-abiding—they don't set fires—they rather—"

"Oh, shut up!" Nero bellowed. "At this point I don't care in the least if they do or don't set fires. Again you're missing the point: it's now a question of this government *surviving* or not. Are you too dense to see that?"

"I only know this," Sabinus shot back, a volatile mixture of fury and also anxiety welling up inside him. "Arson is a capital offense. And such crimes in Rome are tried before the *city prefect*. I promise you that in trying the Christians, I'll judge them individually—not as a group—and I'll convict *none* of them because the fire was an *accident*. We know where it broke out."

Sabinus knew it was a desperate statement—no one talked to Caesar like that—but it might cause Nero and the conclave to rethink their decision.

Nero merely turned to Sabinus and gave him an elaborate frown. Then he opened his thick lips and muttered contemptuously, "Do you *really* think we'd wait while you processed your Christians one by one, Sabinus? Releasing all? Convicting none? Embarrassing us— turning us into liars as well as arsonists? *Forget that!* Do you take us for *fools*, Sabinus? *Eh?* You're treading on *very* dangerous ground, Prefect!" He fixed his menacing stare several moments longer, and then commented, "No, we can't use someone as spineless as you in this operation.—What alternatives do we have, Tigellinus?"

"Simple enough, Caesar." He smiled, touching the tips of his fingers together. "My praetorians will take care of it. We're the government police anyway, and we'll use our channels to find out who the Christians are and arrest them. I'll judge them myself of course."

"Excellent! Round them up and bring them into the Circus. No, we can't use the Circus Maximus! Let's use the stadium where I race my horses . . . over in the Vatican Gardens across the Tiber. Great Jupiter! *You* again, Sabinus? What do you want?"

"I . . . I feel it only proper to submit my resignation as city prefect, Caesar. I find this one of the worst and most degrading solutions imaginable. Under these circumstances, obviously, you can't want me to continue in your administration."

Nero's lips quivered, as the veins on his neck were distending. "Let Caesar do his own deciding, will you?" His filmy blue eyes, narrowing in rage, glared into him for several moments. Then he muttered. "Yes, I *should* let you resign. I should *fire* you for that matter! Or *worse!* But I haven't time to look around for a new city perfect just now. You will therefore *not* resign, Flavius Sabinus! You will continue in office for as long as I wish it. Do you hear me?"

24

BARELY COMPREHENDING THE HORROR about to unfold, Sabinus hurried over to the Esquiline to alert Aulus and Pomponia. He had failed to avert disaster. Now he could merely warn of its approach.

Aulus recoiled at Sabinus' dreadful report, while Pomponia broke down and wept. "What . . . whatever should we do?" she asked, between sobs.

"Make a list of all the Christians you want notified. No time for them all. Dispatch your most trusted servants at once to warn them. Aquila, Priscilla, and certainly Peter and the other leaders should go into hiding at once."

"But where?"

"Anywhere. Not here, though. Tigellinus will probably search this house first. Oh yes, he promised not to touch you, Pomponia, but I'd never rest on his word. Your Christians, though, should get out of the city—*at once*—before it's too late. Better yet, I'll hurry over to the Aventine myself and warn Aquila. Meanwhile, go to Peter— *now*—since he's staying near the Castra Praetoria. If necessary, hide him at our villa in Tibur."

With that he rushed out across Rome, much of which was still littered and scorched from the great fire, and hurried up the slopes of the Aventine. Huffing for breath, Sabinus rapped furiously on the door of Aquila's chapel. There was no answer.

Finally the door opened. Priscilla beamed and said, "What an honor, Prefect! Peace be with you."

"Where's Aquila? Get him if he's here, Priscilla! *Hurry!*"

She called her husband. The moment he appeared, Sabinus announced the mortal danger. "I feared, I feared," Aquila said. "I had the feeling someday it would happen. Jesus said, 'If they persecuted me, they will also persecute you.' What should we do, Prefect? Is there any hope?"

"Not if the praetorians catch you. Warn your nearest Christians to flee Rome if they can. Hide if they can't. Each must relay the message."

"When will they come to arrest us?"

"*Imminently.* You must leave here at once!"

"But . . . but we can't just—"

"I almost forgot. You don't have any list of believers here, do you, Aquila? Any records of who your Christians are?"

"Yes, certainly . . ."

"Gods, man! *Burn* them. Now! At once! Show me where they are."

As they stepped into Aquila's office, there was an ominous clack, *Clack*, CLACK, *CLACK* of approaching troops. "*Cohort . . . halt!*" a tribune shouted. "*Surround this house!*" There was a banging on the door.

Priscilla gasped. The door came crashing open and troops marched inside. Alongside the tribune was Tigellinus himself, who rasped, "Where's your husband?"

Priscilla, horrified, said nothing. They combed the house and easily found the office, but it was empty. Tigellinus looked out its open window, then crawled through it into the back garden.

"So, Sabinus," he laughed. "What are you two doing back here?"

"Just warning a few innocents that a slaughterer is coming."

"I'd say the city prefect is consorting with the enemies of Caesar. That's treason, you know."

"Only by your warped definitions, Tigellinus."

"So bold, Sabinus? At a time when I have a few scores to settle with you? At a time when this house is filled with my men? Why don't I simply arrest you here and now for high treason?"

"I'll tell you why: because Nero doesn't want to take on the whole senatorial class at the moment, does he? The plebes already accuse him for the fire. If the patricians join them too because of your bungling . . ."

He let Tigellinus draw the conclusion. He had to play for time, and in any case he could be of more use to the victimized Christians as prefect than as fellow victim.

Tigellinus gave him a long, supercilious stare. Then his eyes shifted. "Your name's Aquila?"

"It is."

"You are a Christianus, Aquila?"

"Yes. I am."

"You and your wife are under arrest."

"For what reason?"

"Don't you know?" Tigellinus smirked. "For burning Rome, of course. You're an arsonist, Aquila. Learn the term well, for you'll have to confess it."

"I will not confess to something I did not do."

"Oh yes you will. Let's go."

They returned inside. Sabinus tried to say something comforting to Aquila and Priscilla, and then left. He had not gone far when Tigellinus yelled down to him from the chapel: "That's *very* interesting reading material you buried next to the roses, Sabinus!"

Sabinus winced as if he had been skewered with a spear. They had not had time to burn the membership list, hastily burying it instead! Now hundreds would die. His second, horrendous failure that day plunged Sabinus into black despondency. Knowing Tigellinus' methods, however, he would probably have ferreted out the information anyway. At least Aquila and his wife would now be spared torture . . . a small consolation. A pathetic people, the Christians— believing in a god who obviously was unable to save them. Was he so much better, Sabinus wondered, believing in a state that was unable to save innocent citizens?

He groped for alternatives. Should he try to counter Nero at the summit of power? He could ask the consuls to convene an emergency meeting of the Senate, where he could present Hermes, expose the plot against the Christians, and paint Nero and Tigellinus for the cowardly liars they were. Nero's reputation with the Fathers would reach a new low and he might even be deposed, while the innocents would be spared.

Dreaming. That's all it was, he knew. Even if the senators

believed him, would they be courageous enough to stand against Nero? And even if they were transformed into 500 Thraseas and finally rose from their marble benches to depose the emperor, Tigellinus would merely order the 10,000 men of the Praetorian Guard to advance on the Senate. Against this force, Sabinus could field only the 4,000 in his Urban Cohorts, and it was doubtful that they would fight a civil war against these odds. The 7,000 vigiles would doubtless side with Nero—they had been accused of doing a miserable job in containing the flames and were also looking for scapegoats. If only the legions were prepared to revolt. But they could never be reached in time.

So there was no hope. Tigellinus' terrible scheme would become reality: Nero would rescue himself with the blood of others.

Tigellinus' praetorians functioned with ruthless efficiency. They began by purging any in their own cohorts who were Christians, and they were shocked to find twenty-six who admitted to being converts. These were tortured until one of them finally broke and identified the other congregations in Rome besides Aquila's. Praetorian squads were immediately dispatched to these locations and the premises impounded. Where membership lists were not found, members were. And they were tortured until they divulged the names of others. Many revealed nothing at all, even though the flames of a candle were played along the bare soles of their feet. Then there were the terrified marginal members who, to save themselves, exposed others.

In a short time, several hundred Christians were imprisoned at the Castra Praetoria—the camp had not seen such a throng since the 400 slaves of Pedanius were executed—and they were still arriving by the dozens. Nor was Nero's own palace staff exempt. Nothing shocked him more than to learn that some slave whom he trusted implicitly turned out to be a Christian. Rome was harboring what evidently was a larger conspiracy than he or Tigellinus had imagined, for he was beginning to believe his own story. But Simon Peter, the ringleader, was still at large.

With Nero's permission, Tigellinus now published the following edict:

NERO CAESAR to the SENATE AND THE ROMAN PEOPLE, Greeting! By the favor of the gods, the arsonists who burned our beloved city have finally been identified and are now being arrested. They are a criminal cult of foreign misanthropes known as Nazarenes or Christiani. (Their name comes from Christus, a felon who was crucified in Judea by one of our governors.)

If you know of any such Christians, report them at once to any member of the vigiles or the Praetorian Guard. They are now being tried at the Castra Praetoria, and will be publicly executed at special games in the Vatican Circus beginning Monday next. You are all invited to witness their punishment. Thanks be to the gods!

The notice was posted throughout the city, and Tigellinus was overwhelmed with the success of his scheme. The Roman people, always fickle, easily transferred their hatreds from Nero to that cult of little-known fanatics who had tried to infiltrate the city with their silly belief about a dead criminal being some kind of god.

The trials at the Castra Praetoria were abnormal exercises in justice. Brought in groups before his tribunal, the Christians were judged by Tigellinus through his power of *coercitio,* a magistrate's authority to enforce public order at his own discretion. Everyone denied the charge of arson, but "witnesses" were found who testified that they had seen the second and the fourth person in each front row with a firebrand in his hand on the night of the outbreak. Tigellinus then asked if they were Christians, and this, in fact, soon became the fundamental charge. For as Christians they were guilty of what he called *odium humani generis*—hatred of the human race —for they sought its violent destruction by means of fire, conspiracy, vice, and treason. The *odium* charge was also the standard indictment against the poisoners and magicians of Rome—a happy association, Tigellinus thought.

Such a high proportion of those arrested actually confessed to being Christians that Tigellinus released all who denied such belief. He would have more than enough victims for the Circus. He wondered why many more did not try to save themselves by feigning unbelief. Did it have something to do with their fanatic faith? Or maybe they had no idea what sort of punishment awaited them. In any case, he was careful to condemn each group without specifying punishment. He wanted obedient, docile sheep marched out to the slaughter.

"We were able to reach most of our church leaders before the praetorians arrived," Pomponia told Sabinus over on the Esquiline.

"Did they flee? Or are they in hiding?"

"At first they didn't want to hide at all. Mark and Luke insisted that they ought to suffer with the other Roman Christians. But Peter ordered them to go into hiding. 'Apart from God himself,' he said, 'the future of the Faith lies in your hands, my brothers. You must survive to finish writing your gospels.'"

"Where are they hiding, then?"

Pomponia looked down and said, "At your villa in Tibur, Sabinus. I'm sorry. I just didn't know where else to send them."

So, then, he reflected, he was now harboring fugitives wanted by the state. And even though not a Christian, he could easily share their fate if discovered. "It's all right," he finally told Pomponia. "I'll go out to see if I can help them."

Sabinus reached Tibur after a short, hard ride. Peter and about twenty others were huddled in the atrium of his villa, looking anxiously at the doorway. Their tense, frightened faces melted in smiles when they saw him.

For the next hour, Sabinus reported on conditions in Rome and debated their best course of action. The question to which Peter returned again and again was whether the persecution would be limited to Rome, or extend throughout the Empire. Sabinus thought it would remain local, though with Nero, anything was possible.

"In any case, we must alert Christians everywhere, especially in the East. Silvanus"—Peter turned to a recently arrived friend who had also accompanied Paul on some of his journeys—"I'll dictate a letter for you, and you must carry it to Greece and Asia."

The silver-haired amanuensis, who looked like someone's benevolent uncle, went for his pen and some sheets of papyrus.

"But what if Silvanus is arrested?" asked Sabinus. "All roads out of Rome are being searched."

"I hadn't thought of that."

"I'll write out a safe-conduct pass for him," Sabinus decided. "Who else will be leaving? Give me the names, and I'll prepare passes. Luckily, I thought to bring my seal along."

Peter and the elders made a quick decision as to who should flee and who stay. Then he handed Sabinus a list of names.

"I don't see your name here, Peter. They want you more than anyone else."

"I must stay . . . to help our Roman brothers and sisters in this terrible hour."

Instantly the elders were clustering about the big fisherman, pleading with him to flee "for the sake of the church at large."

"No, no. I *must* stay," he repeated.

"You must—and you will—go," insisted Linus, one of the elders.

Finally, Peter gave in, asking, "Will you take care of the flock while I'm gone?"

Linus nodded, solemnly.

"Very well, then," said Peter. "Kindly prepare a pass for me also, good Prefect. But Silvanus must leave ahead of us—as soon as possible, in fact."

"I can take him over the back roads around Rome to a point on the Appian Way well below the city," Sabinus volunteered.

"That is gracious of you, Prefect."

While Sabinus sat down and wrote out the documents, impressing each with his city prefect's seal, Peter started dictating to Silvanus and quickly came to the point of his letter. "Rejoice in your salvation," he said, "though now for a little while you may have to suffer various trials. . . ."

From time to time, Sabinus listened to snatches of the dictation:

. . . Be subject for the Lord's sake to every human institution, whether it be to the emperor as supreme, or to governors as sent by him. . . . Honor all men. Love the brotherhood. Fear God. Honor the emperor.

"*Why?*" Sabinus interrupted. "Excuse me, Peter, but how can you say something like that—after what Nero is doing to your Christians?"

"Because it's what Jesus would say. He told us, 'Love your enemies . . . pray for those who despitefully use you and *persecute* you.' And isn't it important that Christians be known for these qualities? Aren't we charged with hating humanity and dishonoring Caesar?"

"I suppose you're right." Sabinus shrugged, returning to his documents. When he had finished the list, he shuddered a bit thinking of what would happen if any of the leaders were arrested and his pass seized, impressed as it was with the city prefect's seal. Now Peter was concluding:

. . . After you have suffered a little while, the God of all grace will himself restore, establish, and strengthen you. To him be dominion for ever and ever. Amen. . . . The church that is at Babylon sends you greetings, and so does my son Mark.

"Babylon?" Sabinus inquired.

"Yes." Peter smiled. "It's our name for Rome."

"Good name!" Then Sabinus bade them all good-bye and led Silvanus safely to the Appian Way, where they parted. "Better avoid Naples," he advised. "Go on to Brundisium and take a ship from there."

BOOK FOUR

THE HOLOCAUST

25

THE HIPPODROME in Nero's Vatican Gardens with its lofty central obelisk was first built by the emperor Caligula. It was he who had barged the huge granite spire from Egypt and set it upright on the *spina* of the stadium, a spinelike platform in the center of the racecourse. But it was Nero who embellished the place, for here he had raced horse and chariot for the first time, to the plaudits of an adoring claque. It was here that suspicions of his putting Rome to the torch would finally be purged. The Senate and all heads of state were invited—the language had more the flavor of "commanded"—to attend, while the people of Rome were promised a spectacle they would never forget.

The last Monday in October dawned bright and clear. An autumn rain had washed the air the night before, and the day gave promise of being warm, perhaps even hot. Bridges across the Tiber were swarming with plebes and patricians alike heading for the Vatican hippodrome. In a short time, all 60,000 seats in the stadium were filled, but Tigellinus had erected extra galleries to accommodate the crowd. By midmorning, however, it was obvious that all places, even for standing room, had been taken, with thousands outside still shouting for admission and pounding on closed gates.

Tigellinus had his praetorians shower them with tokens and announce, "Tomorrow we will have exactly the same games as today! Only half the Christians will be executed today. Present these tokens tomorrow and you will be seated first."

Nero, meanwhile, stepped out of his litter, clad in a rich new amethystine toga, generously accented with gold trim. He took his place in the imperial box, which was situated in the middle base of the south tier so that he would not have to face the sun. Poppaea joined him, resplendent in a chlamys of spun silver that flashed with a brilliance approaching that of the diamond strands about her delicate pink neck. Tigellinus, Rufus, and other emperor's friends also filed into the imperial box, while senators were taking their seats in a large reserved area just behind them.

Directly opposite Nero, in the center of the north tier, was the box of the city prefect, the second most distinguished area here and in the other stadiums of Rome. Nero squinted across the hippodrome to Sabinus' box and frowned. It was empty.

"He'll come, won't he, Tigellinus?"

"After your note 'requiring the presence of the city prefect in view of the large crowd'? Of course he'll come."

"Are your . . . prisoners under control?"

"They're in the stables at the west end. A strange group . . . they're actually singing—hymns of some sort."

"Have you caught their leader yet? That fisherman?"

"Simon Peter? No. Not yet. We will."

"Well now," Nero toyed, "a fishmonger should be able to find a fisherman, don't you think, Tigellinus? Aha! Ahahaha!"

Tigellinus ignored the comment. Then he said, "Sabinus is just arriving" and pointed.

Nero squinted across the stadium through a large concave emerald that he used to correct his myopic vision. "Yes, there's his pretty wife, too. *And* her parents. But the rank effrontery," he wailed. "Her mother's dressed in *mourning* clothes!"

"Nothing new. She often wears them, I understand. Are you ready, Princeps?"

Nero stood up, held out a white napkin for some moments to build the dramatic effect and then dropped it, as if starting a horse race.

A cohort of praetorian trumpeters marched onto the central spina and blasted out a brassy fanfare, repeating the flourish at each corner of the obelisk. Then a tribune, known for his booming bass voice, cupped his hands around his mouth and announced: *"Welcome, O Senate! . . . Welcome, O People . . . of Rome!"* The hesitation between phrases was necessary to give echoes time to spend themselves in the vast hippodrome. *"We have . . . taken the omens . . . and they . . . are favorable!"*

A lusty cheer arose from the stands, sending all birds in the area fluttering off in fright. Then cries of *"Pompa! Pompa!"* welled up from the massed thousands.

"Very well!" the herald boomed. *"You shall have . . . your pompa!"* He flung his arms to the west. *"The procession . . . of those . . . who set fire . . . to Rome!"*

Waves of deafening applause cascaded down into the arena, as the praetorian trumpet corps blasted out the flourish of victory. Doors sprang open at the western end of the stadium and the Christian victims were marched out between files of praetorians. Even though they were distant, Sabinus had little trouble identifying the couple leading the column of Christians. Unmistakably, it was Aquila and Priscilla. They were followed by a motley cavalcade of people of every sort—aging matrons, young men in their prime, terrified children, slaves, an occasional praetorian marching along in what was left of his uniform, derided by his former comrades.

The galleries were howling with hatred. A thousand fingers were raised in obscene gestures, ten thousand fists shook at the procession, as if dripping off the finally-to-be-avenged fury at the fiery loss of a wife, a baby, a friend, a house with all its possessions. *"Arsonists!"* many hissed.

"Anarchists!" *"Madmen!"* others cried.

"Fools!" *"Atheists!"*

"Incendiaries!" *"Dregs!"*

"These shouts are even sweeter music than what I hear from my lyre." Nero smiled, as he leaned back contentedly on his couch. "They'd been calling *me* those names, Tigellinus. You've done *well*, my friend. Very well indeed!"

"Thank you, Caesar. Your happiness . . . your security are my only concerns."

Directly opposite them, Aquila and Priscilla were now marching past Sabinus' box. Just behind them were their friends Hermes and his wife. Incredibly, the man accidentally responsible for burning Rome was arrested as a Christian, not an arsonist. Sabinus looked at the four, and his eyes misted. Pomponia began sobbing and made the sign of the cross over her friends. But the red thatch and russet beard of Aquila stood tall and determined as he returned the sign of the cross, and Priscilla even managed a farewell smile. Poor Hermes, though, seemed in a trance.

Finally the procession of the condemned had wound its way around the racecourse and returned to the stables. Again there was a blistering trumpet fanfare. When the final notes had reverberated and died, the herald bellowed out, "And now . . . the venatio!"

For the great "wild beast hunt," ten of the sturdiest Christians— men in their burly prime—were thrust into the arena. At the opposite end, iron gates were drawn up, rasping and creaking, as six Libyan lions padded suspiciously out of their cages. They sniffed the air and grunted several times, their slitted yellow eyes squinting at the unaccustomed brightness of the arena. They seemed unconcerned by all the people, for the masses were sitting dead still and holding their breath as the lions started prowling suspiciously about the arena.

The ten victims, who had just finished praying, stood in a circle, naked but for loincloths. Several looked about for anything that would serve as a club, but they found nothing. They were supposed to "hunt" the beasts barehanded.

The lions, which had been cruelly starved, approached the circle stealthily, stopped and sniffed, but then padded by it again on their slow lope around the racecourse. Now they were below Nero's box. He leaned over to the beasts, pointed to the victims, and cried, "There! Over there, my friends! Food!"

One of the lions stopped, walked over majestically toward the imperial party, opened its massive mouth, and emitted a great, guttural roar in Nero's face. There was snickering from the senatorial section behind the emperor, and Petronius whispered to Quintus Lateranus, "Bravo, lion! Only you can address Caesar so frankly."

Nero leaned over to Tigellinus and said, "Get those cursed beasts to attack, will you?"

Tigellinus stood up and brought his flattened right hand down in a perpendicular arc onto his left open palm—the signal to cut. A band of praetorians rushed out at the circle of Christians and crisscrossed their skins with knife cuts so that the lions could see and smell blood. Some hissing actually boiled up from the galleries, since this was an unusual gesture and quite unsportsmanlike.

Now the lead lion raised his head and again sniffed the air, this time heading back toward the Christians with a low, graceful lope. The others followed and soon they halted in a pack to stalk the ten. Several began growling with anticipation, scratching the ground with great, tawny paws. The other lions answered with menacing snorts, panting as their manes rose.

One of the Christian men, who had a strong, baritone voice, now cupped his hands around his mouth and yelled to the crowd, "We're *innocent!* We did *not* set fire to Rome! *Falsely convicted!*"

The massed thousands answered with a vast booing. The matter was settled. They were certainly guilty, and it was normal for criminals to shout their innocence. Besides, if they were innocent after all, there would be no show.

The booing startled the lions, and it was nothing more than one of the Christians turning about suddenly that set off the pack. Rumbling a fearful roar, they attacked the circle with great leaps, their open jaws salivating with anticipation and their huge jagged teeth tearing into human flesh. The agonized screams of the victims set the spectators on the edge of their seats, the women whimpering with horror, feigned or real, and clutching at their husbands who were sitting rod-straight as they stared at the ghastly sight, trying to affect an air of cool detachment.

Since the lions had singled out two of the bloodiest victims for their first attack, the other men pommeled their tawny hides and beat them off. The largest of the ten actually charged one of the beasts and knocked him off his feet. Another smashed the snout of a lioness so forcefully that the dumfounded animal backed off dizzily and was out of the fight for some moments.

But whenever the pack retreated, it returned to attack again and again. The lacerations and bites were draining blood from the men, and soon six of them were sprawled on the ground, dying or dead, while the remaining four still fought on hopelessly. A smaller lioness planted her teeth into the ribs of one of the fallen victims and dragged him off to the other side of the arena so that she could dine in peace. The largest of the men, the last to fall, seized an interim to make the sign of the cross over his fallen comrades, and he knelt down in prayer before he, too, was struck down.

Sitting on their haunches in pools of gore, the six beasts voraciously tore away at their prey until the area lay strewn with bones. The wind was from the west, and it carried the sickly odor of blood across the lower tiers of seats in the arena. Women made faces and lunged for their vials of perfume, dabbing several drops under each nostril.

Nero reached for his emerald looking glass and peered across the stadium at Sabinus' box. He saw the two men sitting motionless in their seats, but Plautia seemed to be cradling her mother's head in the folds of her stola.

Again the trumpets sounded and the herald announced, *"And now . . . a typical meeting . . . of the Christians!"*

Men, women, and even children—about forty in all—were brought to the center of the hippodrome and made to sit down on the spina in rows resembling a congregation. Before them stood one of the prominent preachers in the Christian community, the upper half of his body fitted into the costume of an ass. At a signal from Tigellinus, a praetorian squad tore the clothes off the congregation and tied the members together in indecent postures to dramatize the familiar slander against the Christians. The galleries quaked with peals of laughter. But the victims were crying *"Pro Christo!"* to one another. "For Christ." Then the praetorians dashed back to the sidelines, because someone had given the signal for the dogs prematurely.

From the eastern end of the stadium a frenzied chorus of yelping and snarling was heard as more than a hundred wild dogs came dashing down the hippodrome and vaulting atop the spina. Like all the animals used that day, they had been starved to build a voracious hunger. But unlike the lions, the hounds attacked immediately, for they had been goaded and prodded to fury in their cages, and made to smell great hocks of raw meat. The crazed canines ran riot through the "congregation," lacerating, tearing, devouring until at last they had their fill and almost meekly waddled out of the stadium with bloated stomachs.

The four who were sitting in the box of the city prefect huddled in horror. Aulus was muttering to himself, defining Nero in terms he had not used since his military days, while Pomponia, who had been pleading to her God, was now moaning in despair. Mercifully, her sight was heavily blurred by her own tears. Plautia was bearing up, but she was pale and frozen in disbelief. Sabinus didn't know why he had let her come. This was a sight only for those who enjoyed wallowing in brutality. But the women had insisted on coming out of some very dubious sense of loyalty to the persecuted victims.

Sabinus was not really that surprised by the inhumanity of it all:

a regime that took four hundred lives for one could quite easily prepare the pitiless panorama of pain unfolding in the arena. But he was utterly nauseated at the reactions of his fellow Romans: presumably civilized men and women, gloating over the grisly horror below. If they were moved by pure vengeance against people they believed truly guilty of arson he could understand it, and doubtless it did explain the delight of some in the vast hippodrome. But what about gladiatorial games, where Romans cheered themselves equally hoarse over the deaths of people who had not wronged them? Was brutality part of the Roman personality, he wondered, and if so, could one justifiably speak of Roman "civilization" in any genuine sense?

Now a figure costumed as Mercury glided out into the arena, waving a wand of red-hot iron. Gracefully, he danced among the bodies of the slain Christians, touching each corpse with his poker to see if it moved. Several did. With a circular swing of his wand, Mercury signaled a band of colleagues, dressed like Pluto, who sallied forth with little mallets and clubbed to death all who were still breathing. Next a squad of arena slaves, costumed like demons of the underworld, swarmed onto the spina, dragging the dead off by their feet and raking over the pools of blood. Meanwhile, a chorus of boys clad like Cupids ran about, scattering rose petals and flowers and spraying perfumes.

A fresh round of trumpets. A new announcement: *"Another meeting . . . of the Christians . . . a more accurate scene!"*

A new congregation was paraded out, and the crowd howled with laughter at what they saw: the victims were all sewed up inside animal skins. The men were standing African leopards. The women, covered with hogshide, were trying to peer through the eye sockets of hollowed-out pig heads, while their children were dressed in dog skins. This time a pack of yapping Iberian hounds came bounding down the stadium, halting to sniff at the strange beings on the spina. A child shrieked, and the hounds then attacked with hungry rage, as if angry at the sham perpetrated on them. The shrill screams of children made many of the women spectators cower on their benches, while men with some shred of conscience were starting to question Tigellinus' taste.

Inside the stables at the western end of the hippodrome, meanwhile, hundreds of Christians were living out their last minutes in prayers and hymns. But leaning against a manger at the far end, one man was moaning uncontrollably.

"My fault! My *wretched* fault!" Hermes groaned again and again, kneading his hands into one another. "My own idiotic, hellish, foolish fault!"

"Nonsense, Hermes. It was an accident," Aquila consoled. "How could you ever know—"

"*My coals did it!*" the little Syrian suddenly stood up and shouted. "My simpering stove was *made in hell! It set fire to Rome!*" He yelled for the guards and bellowed out in a manic rage, "*I'm* the arsonist! *I'm* the killer! *I'm* killing all these people!"

He started raving, and Aquila reached out and slapped his cheeks several times. "Sit down, Hermes!" he commanded. "Compose yourself! Play the man!"

Hermes collapsed and started sobbing uncontrollably. Some minutes later, he looked up and remarked, coolly, "All right. I'm . . . back in control of myself, Aquila. Sorry about the scene." Then he added, with quiet determination, "But I'm going to do it."

"Do what?"

"I'll speak to the chief centurion and tell him I have life-and-death information for the emperor. Then, when he brings me to Nero, I'll tell him that I, alone, set fire to Rome. And I'll tell him how. Then he must release everyone else."

Aquila smiled at Hermes' naïveté. "That would be useless, dear friend. Nero must have his show. In fact, he'd either laugh in your face, or justify himself with a great announcement to the crowd. Can't you hear it now? 'Lest some of you doubt that Christians *did* set fire to Rome, here's the chief arsonist himself, confessing it all!' No, Hermes, don't give him that satisfaction."

"I don't know, Aquila. I think I must."

Out in the hippodrome, a detail of praetorians began dropping tall posts into holes that had been dug earlier along the circumference of the arena. Then they laid a *patibulum* or crossbeam at the foot of each to prepare for crucifixion.

"*The founder . . . of the Christians . . . died this way,*" the herald shouted. "*So should . . . all their leaders!*"

The captured clergy and elders of the Roman congregations were now paraded out into the arena. To the astonishment of the multitude, they were all singing a triumphant hymn, "*Christus regnat.*"

Then each was led away to a separate cross. Tigellinus leaned over to Nero and said, "See that one with the red hair just below us, getting his wrists nailed onto the crossbeam?"

"Yes . . ."

"His name's Aquila, one of their chief leaders. You may recall him from the trial of that Paul of Tarsus."

With a stinging jerk, two men hoisted up the crossbeam with its victim attached, stepped onto little wooden platforms on each side of the post, and lifted the crossbeam over and onto it, resting it snugly in its mortise. They took another spike, drove it first through a broad wooden washer, and then pinned both feet to the cross. Moving on to the next of the condemned, they repeated the process. With grim efficiency, the praetorians managed to crucify the forty leaders in just fifteen minutes.

"I'd say it was a record, Caesar," Tigellinus admitted proudly.

"And now they have the proper vantage point from which to watch the rest of the games. A touch of genius, Tigellinus! There's art in your planning." Nero lolled backward on his couch, staring with fascination at the bloody panorama before him while clutching a silk handkerchief to his mouth and neck to protect his voice from drafts. Glancing over at Poppaea, he wondered why she was so quiet.

On the opposite side of the stadium, a perspiring and trembling Plautia could no longer look at the appalling spectacle. She heard a quiet sigh and turned to see her mother blanch and faint across Aulus' lap, a lifeless heap of mourning garments.

"Enough, Father. Enough," Sabinus said. "You take the women home. They've seen too much already. *Far* too much. I'll stay on until the end."

Plautia made a feeble objection, but the aging senator, almost as sick as the women, nodded in resignation. Several of Sabinus' aides helped them out of the hippodrome and back to the Esquiline.

Now alone in his box and numb with revulsion, Sabinus felt one consistent emotion: a mounting, throbbing hatred for Nero and Tigellinus. Yes, Lateranus and his circle had the only real solution after all: assassination—the excision of two putrid members from the race of Roman man. But if only it had happened *before* all these useless deaths! He also felt stabs of self-recrimination: why hadn't he been able to divert all this that day in the imperial conclave? He, the chief officer of the city of Rome . . . as helpless before the tyrant as the lowest beggar.

His thoughts were punctuated by another flourish from the trumpets. "*Now let's teach . . . these Christians . . . our true national religion!*" the herald cried.

A burst of applause and cheering broke into the announcement, as strange-looking contrivances were wheeled out into the arena. Everyone knew the time had come for scenes from Greco-Roman mythology, always a popular feature.

"*Ixion!*" the herald shouted. "*Ixion, father of the Centaurs . . . tried to seduce Juno . . . whereupon Jupiter . . . bound him to a wheel . . . which turns forever down in Hades!*"

Now young men, by twos, were selected from the remaining victims and fastened onto opposite sides of iron wheels. While slaves worked gears that slowly turned the disks, the praetorians set fire to combustibles beneath each wheel. When these blazed up, there was just enough reprieve on the upper portions of each revolution to keep the victims from fainting so that they could experience the sensation of roasting to death above the flames.

"*Daedalus and Icarus!*" the herald cried. "*Their wings of wax . . . melted in the sun!*" Much whistling arose, for this act promised to be spectacular. This time the victims, always a man and a boy with flimsy cardboard wings pinned to their tunics, were attached by hooks to a rope pulley running to the top of Caligula's obelisk. Each time they would be hauled up almost to the top of the spire, where the hooks would open, dashing them to the ground. Several victims grabbed hold of the ropes when the hooks opened, but this only made more fun for the crowd, since the praetorians would wait until the victim was doing a mad hand-over-hand in trying to lower himself and then tug the rope back up again until he finally dropped from exhaustion.

Nero now nudged Tigellinus. "It looks as if your friend may be dying there."

Tigellinus peered at the cross directly in front of them. Then he shouted, "Don't die yet, Aquila! We have a final surprise for you!" Then he signaled the herald.

"*A special treat!*" he announced. "*Priscilla . . . wife of the leader of the Christians . . . as Dirce!*" Spectators drew in their breath. They knew that Dirce, Queen of Thebes, had been strapped to the horns of a wild bull for persecuting the mother of Castor and Pollux. As a further refinement of cruelty, the herald added that Priscilla's husband Aquila was watching from his cross in front of the imperial box.

Sabinus grasped the railing before him. He felt nauseous. He had not known that Aquila, on the opposite side of the stadium, had already been crucified.

Several minutes later, a great white bull charged into the arena, desperately shaking its head to try to get rid of the naked woman tied tightly across its neck and horns. The bull charged wildly down the hippodrome until it came to Nero's box, where praetorians waved some brightly colored blankets to distract the beast and bring it to a halt. Wife and husband exchanged a final, meaningful glance. Then, completely maddened at the heavy load across its horns, the bull lowered its massive head and charged directly into the wall below Nero, killing its victim instantly. The figure on the nearest cross groaned deeply, shook, and then hung lifeless.

Aides told Sabinus what had happened—his view had been blocked by the spina—and he could only lower his head in rage, grief, and utter helplessness.

By now it was late in the afternoon and the shadows were lengthening. Tigellinus conferred with Nero, then dispatched new instructions to the herald.

"By now," he shouted, "you must all . . . be rather hungry!"

There was much head-nodding but also laughter, since many had quite understandably lost their appetites.

"Caesar has provided . . . dinner for all of you . . . in the gardens outside . . . The food and drink . . . will cost you nothing . . . if"—he paused—"if you return . . . after supper . . . for the climax . . . of these games!"

An enthusiastic roar thundered up from the massed thousands. Cries of "HAIL CAESAR!" and "GRATIAS, IMPERATOR!" ricocheted throughout the vast stadium.

Tigellinus turned to Nero and said, "I do believe your old popularity has returned, Princeps."

"Thanks to you, dearest friend," Nero fawned, then winked, "and the Christians! Come, precious Poppaea. A real feast is waiting for us, I understand."

Sabinus walked about in the Vatican Gardens, watching the plebes gulp down great quantities of food and wine, wondering how

people who had just witnessed the gruesome, torturous deaths of almost 250 people could manage to find such an appetite. He carefully
avoided the imperial table in the gardens, unsure if he could resist
the burning impulse to haul out his prefect's dagger and plunge it
into Nero—and Tigellinus, too, if he could possibly manage. He was
starting to lose all hope for that species known as *homo Romanus*
until, in the clusters of senators who had finished eating, he started
overhearing some surprising comments, even from Nero's friends
and leeches.

"He's overdoing it," said one.

"Any more and he'll make heroes of these Christians . . ."

"That woman tied on the horns of the bull . . . too cruel."

At an outer edge of the garden, Sabinus came upon a small group
of republican senators clustered around Quintus Lateranus. When
Sabinus appeared, they suddenly quit talking and looked up a little
apprehensively. "It's all right," said Sabinus. "I'm one of you now."

Quintus smiled. "I knew you'd be, Sabinus. But for the moment,
you should be one with us in spirit only, not in plans."

"Why?"

"Because you're too important as city prefect. We may need someone who is absolutely untainted by association with the likes of us."
He smiled.

"All right, then. But you must let me know when the time is
ripe."

"We will. And Sabinus, much as you may feel like it, don't even
think of resigning as city prefect. Under *any* circumstances. Do you
understand me?"

"Yes. I think I do." Then Sabinus added with a wry smile, "Besides, Nero won't let me resign."

While walking off, Sabinus took stock of the faces he saw huddled about Quintus. Senator Piso he recognized, as well as Senator
Scaevinus and the poet Lucan, Seneca's nephew. And yes, it had to
be—at the far end—the olive-tan face and balding scalp of Faenius
Rufus, the *other* prefect of the Praetorian Guard! This would be no
minor conspiracy.

A blistering trumpet on the upper rim of the stadium summoned
everyone back inside. There was grumbling and jostling as people
tried to find their places again. Many tripped in the darkness. Some

were angry that others had taken their lower seats and they now had to climb higher.

Again they were trumpeted to silence, and the familiar voice of the herald boomed out: *"You are asking . . . why you returned . . . when you can see nothing?"*

A rumble of affirmatives showed that the people did indeed have the problem in mind.

"People of Rome! . . . Is there . . . a more appropriate . . . punishment for arson . . . than being burned alive?"

There was a shivering blast of cornets as pinpoints of flame began fanning out across the blackened hippodrome. They were praetorians clutching torches, over a hundred of them, racing into the arena until they formed a huge, oblong horseshoe of fire. Then, when Nero himself called out a *"Now!"* the praetorians touched their torches to the posts before them, and a hundred pillars of flame flickered into life and soon bathed the entire stadium in a bright orange glow. The people rose in a standing ovation for the spectacle.

But the posts came alive, and began crying out in piercing human screams of agony. They were Christians, each chained to the top of a post and wearing the *tunica molesta,* the notorious "troublesome tunic"—a shirt that had been heavily saturated in nitrates, sulfur, and pitch. The posts had also been steeped in a resin and oil mixture, and now served as gigantic wicks to illuminate the darkness. Most victims quickly crisped in the scorching, unbearable heat, choked on the smoke, and mercifully lapsed into unconsciousness and death. A few struggled with their chains before they succumbed, uttering prayers until the flames reached them. Their blackened bodies would continue carbonizing down to ash, for the posts would flame on for some three hours.

Nero was so impressed that tears of joy gathered in the corners of his eyes and trickled along the sides of that ruddy, bulbous ridge that was his nose. "Such art, Tigellinus!" he sighed. "Such beautiful, beautiful candles!"

Another trumpet. Another silence. Another announcement. *"Thanks, Christians . . . for enlightening us!"* The laughter was not as much as the herald had hoped. *"And now . . . Hercules in Flames! . . . But this time . . . we'll have the Danaides . . . put out his pyre!"*

The galleries laughed uproariously, for the fifty daughters of the Argive King Danaus were condemned to pouring water into a container down in Hades that was full of holes. Fifty men were now chained down onto separate pyres before the eyes of their terrified wives, and the pyres were ignited.

"Quick!" the praetorians urged the women. "Save your husbands! Take these buckets and bring water from the fountain over there." The women grabbed the buckets and filled them. But each pail had been riddled with holes, draining all but a worthless splash.

High above the blazing scene, lofty and detached, stood the statues of the gods of Rome, each resting on a column that plunged down to the spina on both sides of the obelisk. From time to time Sabinus pulled his eyes away from the horror and looked up at this pillared pantheon. He almost thought he saw the great head of Jupiter smiling and winking at Vulcan in the glimmering scarlet of the flames, while the statues of the nymphs clustered about them were wearing gleeful grins.

The blazing panorama was too much for Nero. The flickering beauty of the flames and the sensational scenes he had witnessed that day made him, in a monstrously perverted fashion, almost jealous of the Christians. They, not he, had trodden the boards that day. They had put on the outstanding, if painful, spectacles. The actor in him was offended. He craved the eyes and plaudits of the people too.

Leaning over, he whispered something to Tigellinus. In a moment, the prefect had vaulted over the balustrade and was running down to the stables. Meanwhile, Nero, under cover of darkness but before the gaping eyes of Poppaea, crawled out of his purple toga and exposed the tunic he had been wearing that day. It was the garb of a charioteer in the colors of the green faction!

Tigellinus and several aides soon returned along the racecourse, leading a team of four horses hitched to Nero's golden chariot. Almost ecstatically happy, the emperor descended from his box, climbed aboard his quadriga, and took the reins.

The herald now announced: "*As the final . . . presentation tonight . . . Caesar himself . . . will display his prowess . . . as charioteer! . . . Hail Caesar!*" he saluted.

"HAIL CAESAR!" the crowd replied, their arms similarly extended.

Giving his snorting steeds a whack, Nero drove them in a furious run around the hippodrome, sweeping into turns he knew so well at dangerous speeds and cutting corners with abandon. Certainly he was showing off, he chuckled. But, then, he had so much to show off . . . such versatile talent. He whipped his horses to a frenzied lather, while careening about the course in a mad race with his own shadow. He arched backward as he stood in the lurching chariot, reins bunched in one hand, for that was the most graceful stance of the charioteer. The wind was in his face, the adoring people of Rome around him, and the flickering human lamps showed him the track. Some turns he took on one wheel. Several times he skidded and almost fell out of the cab. But each time, he always managed to regain his balance. For he led a charmed life.

Slowly, the people threaded their way out of the stadium. Some were debating when they had begun to sicken of the spectacle. Was it the poor woman tied to the horns of the bull? Was it when the wind changed and the nauseating stench of the human torches blanketed the galleries, those sickly-sweet whiffs of grilled flesh? Or was it the idiotically parading emperor himself, displaying his wheeled toy like some overindulged child and providing an incongruous close to what had been, after all, a monstrously grim spectacle?

Others started wondering about the Christian victims. They had only Nero's word that they were the arsonists. Had they really been destroyed for the public good? Or was it to glut one man's cruelty? Or to cover his cowardice? Or to hide his guilt?

That night, Sabinus returned to the stadium with one of his Urban Cohorts. They searched the smelly heap of bodies outside the western end of the hippodrome for any survivors, but they found none. Mercury, Pluto, and the demons had done their work with ruthless Roman efficiency. Sabinus and his men gave the victims a mass burial. And he was armed with a proper excuse if Nero protested that gesture: the city prefect was responsible for the public health of Rome.

26

IN THE DEAD OF NIGHT came an urgent rapping at Sabinus'
door. An hour earlier, he had returned, exhausted, from the Vatican
hippodrome and his eyes only half opened when his steward said,
"I'm sorry to bother you, Clarissimus, but a man and a woman are
waiting in the atrium to see you on an urgent matter."

Sabinus threw a robe about his night tunic and sleepily padded
out into the hall. Then he stopped in his tracks and bristled with
utter shock. There stood Aquila and Priscilla!

"Forgive us, Prefect," Aquila apologized, "but—"

"*Gods!*" Sabinus exclaimed. "But you . . . you headed the procession . . . the cross . . . the horns of the bull!"

"Let me explain . . ."

"Wait a moment." He ran out of the atrium and returned, dragging in Plautia who was only half awake. But one glance at the
pair and her eyes and mouth shot open simultaneously. "You . . .
both of you . . . how . . . a resurrection?" she stammered.

"No, Lady Plautia." Aquila smiled. "But I must hasten to explain."

"By all means!" Sabinus could scarcely believe his eyes.

"After I had conducted a final worship for our people in the stables at the hippodrome, a centurion called for Priscilla and me, and

we knew our hour had come. The officer was a secret member of our congregation who thought he could do more for us by *not* revealing his Christianity. Imagine our shock when we came to the main gates of the stables and the guard on duty merely saluted and let all three of us pass outside!

"Our centurion explained that the guard owed him a personal favor, and that a couple in prison who look very much like Priscilla and me would assume our names in case Tigellinus issued special orders regarding us. Priscilla and I thanked him, but we were on the point of returning to die with our people when he said, 'Your elders knew you'd never save yourselves, but they decided that you *must* escape to tell the story of the great Roman martyrdom.' He said the Christians were thrilled with the prospects of delivering us—it would make their last hours happier—and finally we agreed . . . We've been in hiding since then. But now we must know: what happened in the stadium after we left?"

While Plautia prepared refreshments, Sabinus reported the brutal events of the afternoon and evening. It was a corrosive experience for him, watching the horror burrowing into their lives, but when he finally had to tell about the cross and the horns of the bull, Priscilla broke into convulsive sobbing, while Aquila seemed on the verge of black despair.

As Plautia brought in food and wine, tears were glistening in Aquila's eyes. "We're . . . we're going back," he said. "We can't go free . . . not after what they've been through."

"Yes, we must bring comfort to our brothers and sisters still in prison," Priscilla added. "And then gladly share their martyrdom."

Sabinus disagreed. "Nothing would demoralize your friends more than to see you captured again after all their planning. *Don't* disappoint them."

Aquila slowly shook his head.

"Peter himself said the leaders must survive," Sabinus argued, "and there's no time for further delay. I hope you understand, Aquila, I will physically prevent your returning."

The couple looked startled, but saw only determination in Sabinus' eyes as he continued, "Now, you'll sleep here till morning. Then I'll give you money and whatever else you'll need, and my men will see you out of Rome. I'll write out a pass that will carry you to the East. Where will you go?"

For several moments they said nothing. Finally Aquila nodded and said, "Corinth. Yes, we'll go to Corinth again, and then try to rejoin Paul."

"Give him our fond greetings when you see him next," said Plautia.

"Prefect," said Aquila. "Thank you for trying so hard to avert this disaster, and thank you for your help now. Give our special farewell to beloved Pomponia and her husband."

About the time that Aquila and Priscilla were traveling safely down the Appian Way, Nero's games were beginning once again. Another capacity crowd had jammed into the stadium. While thousands of previous spectators were surfeited and had no stomach to return, their reports merely inflamed the dregs of Rome to besiege the entrances to the stadium from early morning.

The senatorial section behind Nero, however, was pockmarked with empty places, and he was on the point of suggesting that Tigellinus take a roll call of the Conscript Fathers. But he became too intrigued by the opening events, in which a pack of German bears was let loose on the procession of the condemned even before they had returned to the stables. There was a screaming stampede for the exit.

"Ah!" Nero smiled. "That was a new twist, Tigellinus!" Then, his emerald looking glass raised to his better eye, Nero noticed that the box of the city prefect was occupied once again.

Over the protests of all in the family, Pomponia had insisted on returning that day. "When my fellow Christians are dying," she insisted, "I should be at their side—at least to witness their triumph over death." Aulus and Sabinus found her last phrase incomprehensible, but they knew Pomponia would probably be worse off if she stayed at home.

Early in the again grisly afternoon, one of his aides came running over to Sabinus' box. "Quick, Prefect. Come with me. It's urgent."

Sabinus followed him out one of the exits and down to the sprawling stables where the remaining prisoners were being guarded. There he was met by a smirking Tigellinus. "Aha, Sabinus! I wanted you to be the first to know." He grinned. "Guess whom we have here? . . . Well, we finally found your fisherman after all. I trust you know Simon Peter?"

"Yes, I know him," Sabinus replied, as calmly as he could, though his heart was pounding. Depending on how Peter had been arrested, he himself might never leave the stadium alive. Yet he had to gamble that Tigellinus knew nothing of the pass he had supplied Peter, so he said, "Why don't you return to your butchery out there, Tigellinus, like the vulture you are?"

"Certainly, certainly." Tigellinus smiled. "Good friends are always allowed a parting visit." Then he left them.

"Where did they find you, Peter?"

"They didn't find me. I returned to Rome of my own accord."

Sabinus' jaw dropped. "Are you mad?"

"Jesus didn't escape when he saw the police coming into Gethsemane Garden. A servant is not above his master. Should I have tried to escape what awaited me in Nero's gardens?"

"Yes. You should have. For the future of your cause."

"The Faith is well seeded across the Mediterranean now, good Prefect. And I *know* the Master wants me to stay here in Rome."

"How do you know that?"

"Once, after his resurrection, He told me, 'When you are old, Peter, you will stretch out your arms and be bound fast, and be borne where you don't wish to go.' I'm old now. My mission is accomplished."

"The cross? Did he mean crucifixion?"

Peter nodded. "And in case I doubted that this was the time, let me tell you this: I was indeed taking the route you suggested—the one avoiding Rome—when I seemed to see Jesus in my mind's eye. He looked as he did on the way to his own cross, so I asked him, '*Maran, la'an att azel?*'"

"What does that mean?"

"'*Quo vadis, Domine?* Where are you going, Lord?'—It's Aramaic, the language we always used in Palestine.—And then he seemed to reply, 'I am going to Rome, to be crucified again.'"

"And such a *vision* brought you back to this inferno?"

"No, far more than that, Sabinus." Peter smiled. "I *must* share these sufferings of my people, also as a witness for the future. Though he doesn't know it, Caesar is accomplishing much today for the church."

More of that Christian logical nonsense, Sabinus thought. That faith loved to deal in paradoxes: enemies are loved, the first is last— the last is first, death brings life, defeat is triumph.

"I do have a bit of happy news for you, Peter," he suddenly

recalled. "Aquila and Priscilla were able to escape. They'll be joining Paul in Greece."

"The Lord God be praised." The apostle beamed.

"But is there . . . anything I can do for you, Peter?"

"Yes. I've left documents and instructions for the church inside
that large blue vase on your desk at Tibur. Please see that the surviving elders get them. And bid good-bye for me to your wonderful
family, especially dear Pomponia, and accept the thanks of all Christians for what you've done for us, Prefect."

"So little." Sabinus shook his head. "So pathetically, painfully little." He looked a last time into the leonine but kindly face of the
apostle and said, "Good-bye, Simon Peter."

"God bless you, Sabinus. Tell everyone *not* to weep for me, because my death is only the portal to a triumphant eternity with
Christ."

With that, several praetorians stepped over to take Peter down the
hall and thrust him into prison. Sabinus could hear the glad shouts
of joyful recognition mingled with moans that the apostle had been
arrested. But in several moments, all was quiet as Peter addressed
comforting and yet, Sabinus thought, victorious and bracing words
to his fellow prisoners.

By the time he returned to his seat, the grand announcement was
being made: *"The Galilean fisherman . . . the leader of these criminals . . . is now in chains . . . in this very stadium!"*

A great oohing and aahing welled up from the multitude.

"His name . . . is Simon Peter," the herald continued. *"He
stands . . . before the emperor."*

Amid thunderous waves of applause, Nero propped himself up
from his couch, grabbed his emerald, and studied Peter. "A big
enough fellow," he commented. "Otherwise unimpressive. How do
you plan to kill him, Tigellinus?"

"Crucifixion, of course." The commander smiled. "It seems so . . .
fitting."

"Did you torture him for additional information about the Christians?"

"Yes. A little. But he said nothing more than prayers to his god.
Besides, we really don't need any more victims, do we, Princeps?"

Nero smirked and then broke out laughing. "No, I suppose not.
How many will have died by the end of the day?"

"Total? Over the last two days? Between six and seven hundred."

"Well, that should just about rid us of the pestilence."

"Yes. We'll never hear of 'Christians' again!"

In the arena sands below the imperial box, Peter, clad only in a loincloth, was told to lie down so that his hands could be fastened to a crossbeam. "Would you do me a favor, Tribune?" he asked the officer in charge of the execution detail. "Crucify me head downward instead of the regular way."

"Why?"

"I'm not worthy to suffer in the same way Jesus the Christ did."

The tribune looked at him and smiled. "Sorry, old man. It just isn't possible to do it that way. Oh, it's *possible,* I suppose, but it's not very practical. You see, the crossbeam is mortised onto the *top* of the post there."

Peter nodded in resignation. They spiked his wrists to the ends of the crossbeam and hoisted him up to face the south, the sun, and the imperial box. Nero's courtiers vied with each other in shouting crude mockeries at Peter, but he ignored them. Apparently, even hanging on the cross, he seemed in an attitude of prayer.

The grotesque events continued throughout the afternoon. Ixion's wheel turned again, dogs tore into new groups of Christians gathered at the foot of Peter's cross, and victims dropped around him from the top of the obelisk. Each new group of condemned first looked to the apostle before undergoing their torture, and he made the sign of the cross over them with his head, as if imparting a final blessing.

Again it was too much for Pomponia. But this time, instead of fainting, she stood up in the city prefect's box, turned about, and held up her hands for silence.

"What kind of Romans are you?" she screamed. "Cheering while innocent people are dying? While children are strangled and women roasted? What kind of . . . *monsters* have you become?"

Aulus was startled and embarrassed over the scene his wife was creating. He rose to whisk her out of the stadium and take her home, until the force of what she was saying suddenly registered with him and he sat back down.

"Can you *really* believe that these innocent victims set fire to Rome?" she continued. "Look at me! Do *I* look like an arsonist? Because I'm a Christian too! Go on, then. Kill *me too!* And cheer like the bloodthirsty *beasts* you've all become!"

A swath of humanity in the north tier of the stadium within earshot had stilled to a hush, an almost guilty silence. Pomponia sat down, buried her face in her hands, and shook with sobbing. Sabinus summoned guards from an Urban Cohort and gave Aulus and Pomponia protected escort out of the stadium.

"I've never been prouder of your mother," Sabinus told Plautia.

"Nor I," she replied. Then she broke down and wept. "But why, Sabinus? Why? *Why?*"

Hermes had just been crucified opposite them. Sabinus feared that he might still try to confess his role in the great fire, but the little contractor was clearly a changed man. Peter had had some words with Hermes just before his own crucifixion, and now, far from losing control over himself, the Syrian, for all his pain, was actually regaling the multitudes with a long recitation of Nero's outrages, including details on the collapsible ceiling he had ordered for his mother's bedroom.

The sensational disclosures easily won him the sympathy of the crowd, and some discernible mood of pity was building also among people in the south tier. Nero and Tigellinus had overdone it again that day, and even the hardened, brutal mind can endure only so much horror. People began leaving the hippodrome in droves, and some of the more outrageous spectacles were starting to draw hissing and boos.

Meanwhile, the serenity of Peter's last hours was also affecting spectators. Late in the day, with his strength ebbing and his arms in agony, Peter looked at Nero, the senators, and magistrates during a lull in the executions and called out in a surprisingly loud voice for one presumed to be almost dead, "*We forgive you, Caesar!* We are all *innocent* victims. But still we pray for you. And forgive you."

Much of the tier quieted abruptly to hear the extraordinary statement.

Nero blanched and his lips twitched with ire. "I don't *need* your forgiveness, fisherman," he sneered.

"Oh, but you *do*, Caesar! The one sovereign God, who is above all, will judge you for all your crimes if you don't repent."

"What crimes, wretch?" Nero's naturally ruddy countenance now flushed to a deep crimson.

"Too many to list, Caesar. You know them. The whole Empire knows them. There is no form of murder you have not committed, no depravity or vice in which you have not . . . wallowed. You have stolen from Romans of every class. Your Senate sits there behind you now, cringing in terror before your tyranny. You are a *stench* in the nostrils of the world, Caesar!"

A muscle in Nero's left jowl twitched involuntarily and he nearly lost control of his bowels. Seething as he snorted for breath, Nero finally stammered, "Shall I have your tongue cut out, you prattling cultist criminal?"

"The truth will triumph no matter what you do, Caesar! Your rule is temporary . . . passing . . . a shadow. But the kingdom of God is eternal."

Petronius, who was sitting just behind Nero, was deeply impressed with Peter but shook his head in embarrassment at Nero's attempts to match wits with him. Tigellinus, meanwhile, whispered that it was beneath the emperor's dignity to continue any conversation with a condemned criminal, while Poppaea was tugging at her husband.

But Nero ignored them and cried, "Oho! *You* can make such lofty claims, fanatic fisherman? What have *you* accomplished in that miserable life of yours besides deluding a superstitious rabble into arson and treason? And now death too?"

"As for these innocent victims, you've only sent them to be with our Lord in paradise. For that . . . we even thank you."

"Oh, *shut up*, you . . . you maddened misanthrope!"

"A misanthrope hates mankind, Caesar. We Christians *love* humanity. Even you."

"Gods!" Nero whined petulantly. "The trumpets, Tigellinus. Have them blow some flourishes so we don't have to listen to this babble."

But the last hour of the afternoon made Nero increasingly uncomfortable. From time to time his eyes darted back to the cross on which Peter was hanging, and each time the apostle's eyes seemed to be riveted on him. Peter, however, was thinking back to the days in Galilee when someone had come up to him while he was casting fishing nets and said, "Follow me," and how he had done just that—down to the present moment.

But soon the superstitious Nero was so uncomfortable that he told Tigellinus, "Kill him."

When Peter saw a tribune approaching with a thrusting spear, he closed his eyes and said, "Blessed Lord, to be like you, even in this!

Receive my spirit." The tribune thrust his javelin deep into Peter's side. The apostle quivered once and then died. His head fell, but his eyes opened in death, and they were again focused directly on the emperor, for the pupils had snapped up toward the eyelids. But Nero was looking elsewhere.

Some minutes later, however, he glanced back at Peter's body and saw the unblinking eyes staring at him. "By the Furies!" Nero shrieked. "Get him off that cross, Tigellinus. Get him off!"

"What's the matter, Nero?" Poppaea inquired.

"I don't know," he said, cold beads of perspiration erupting on his forehead. "Haven't you . . . had enough of this, my dear?"

"Yes. Hours and hours ago."

"So have I. How many more prisoners are left for this evening, Tigellinus?"

"About a hundred or so."

"Well, you can burn them without me. We're going."

"Certainly, Caesar."

Just as he was climbing into the imperial litter, Nero leaned out and asked, "What sort of victims are left for tonight?"

"Men, mainly."

"Are they sturdy? Full grown?"

"Most of them."

"Then why don't you stop it all now? We can use them as slaves in building my Golden House."

"An excellent plan, Princeps." Tigellinus bowed, a perfect weathercock to Nero's wishes.

That evening, under the red-amber glow of their torches, Sabinus and his Urban Cohorts buried the second pile of bodies in a mass grave within a nearby cemetery, which lay along the Via Cornelia on the sides of the Vatican hill. He personally searched for the tall, burly frame of Simon Peter and found it rather easily. Did he imagine it, or was the horror playing tricks with his mind? But it seemed that the rugged features of the apostle had softened into a serene and slumbering face of peace. Sabinus washed Peter's body and reverently buried it in a separate tomb in the cemetery.

"May you enjoy that 'triumphant eternity' with your Christ, Simon Peter," said Sabinus, trying to mirror the apostle's words as a kind of oral epitaph. He himself could not really fathom the faith of the Christians. Jesus told his followers to turn the other cheek to enemies. And Peter had made his suicidal return into Rome to do just that. But he himself swore, on Peter's grave, that he would instead turn Nero's cheeks for him—round and round until that bloated bull neck of his was twisted and throttled in death.

27

IT WAS A CHILL, RAINY NIGHT in March of 65 that Quintus
Lateranus and Faenius Rufus climbed the Quirinal for a secret conference with Sabinus. Plautia was whisked out of the library and
told to keep all servants out of earshot.

"The time's come to tell you the names and the plans, Sabinus,"
Quintus confided. "Since Rufus here is one of us, we have *great*
hopes for success."

"I should think so." Sabinus smiled.

"Tigellinus, of course, also commands the praetorians, but he's
spent so much time on the Palatine he's lost touch with the troops.
Rufus, here, sees them every day. Besides, two of the leaders in our
plot come from the ranks of his officers . . ."

Sabinus' eyes widened. "Who?"

"Subrius Flavus and Sulpicius Asper."

"Aha! A praetorian tribune and centurion, no less."

"Poor Flavus is really champing at the bit," Rufus chuckled,
while scratching his balding scalp. "Twice now he almost did Nero
in. Once during the fire he came up behind him with a hand on his
sword, and the other time he was going to garrotte him with a lyre
string while he was performing."

"Why didn't he?"

"For the same reason that Nero continues to breathe today," Quintus replied. "Everyone wants Nero dead. But everyone wants to live on after the great deed!"

Sabinus smiled. "That's the 'sticking point' in any conspiracy. But proceed."

"Well, among the senators, the leaders are Piso, Scaevinus, and Quintianus."

"Yes, I saw them with you in the Vatican gardens."

"Now, we're all agreed that Nero must go. Beyond that, there's some division among us as to whether to replace him with another emperor or restore the Republic. Some want Piso as emperor *pro tempore*. Some are talking of Seneca. But for now, Piso will hold it all together and the takeover will be announced in his name."

"Why Piso?" Sabinus wondered. "Oh, he's a tall and handsome sort—"

"He's eloquent . . . comes from high nobility. Why do you ask?"

"Oh, nothing," Sabinus hesitated. "It's just that . . . do you really think he has the *character* to see it through? Piso seems to me more the pleasure-loving, passive sort. Lacking in firmness . . ."

"Right. My feelings too." Rufus was nodding. "But those very qualities may be a blessing when we want to replace Piso with the man we all finally decide on. Maybe Seneca. Maybe you, for that matter, Sabinus."

"Oh, please!" Sabinus held up his hands.

"Not unlikely," said Quintus, looking at him seriously. "Your name has been mentioned several times. But to continue: Seneca knows what we're doing and approves . . . tacitly, of course. He's a close friend of Piso, as you know, but he wants no part in the actual assassination."

"Can't blame him," said Sabinus. "Nero suspects him anyway."

"But his nephew Lucan, the poet, is heavily involved with us. Nero's jealous of his poetry and won't let him publish." Rufus smirked.

"Well, Lucan's also very republican in his themes," Sabinus commented.

"Anyway, those are the leading names," Lateranus explained, "and there are more." He went on to mention a dozen prominent equestrians, while Rufus identified six more of his officers who were party to the plot.

Sabinus was appalled. "But you have *more* than enough now. Each new member only adds to the risk of exposure."

"I don't think so," Quintus objected. "*Sixty* were in on the conspiracy against Julius Caesar."

"But they hadn't been plotting as long as you have. In fact, it's almost miraculous that your conspiracy hasn't been exposed already."

"Well, we're getting ready to strike," said Rufus. "That's why we're here."

"Oh, let's tell him the whole truth, Rufus. The fact is, we *have* to strike now, Sabinus, because the plot *was* almost exposed a week ago."

"Yes, that accursed woman just couldn't wait!" Rufus snapped. "Always hounding us for action."

"A *woman* is in on the conspiracy?" asked Sabinus.

"Her name's Epicharis," Lateranus admitted. "She's . . . quite a charming freedwoman—the mistress of Seneca's brother Mela. She tried to get the navy behind our plot by going down to Baiae and calling on Proculus to—"

"Our fleet captain?"

"Yes, he had some grudge against Nero. So she played on his wounded feelings and on his vanity—he'd go down in history, and so forth—if only he and his sailors would kill Nero during one of his vacations down there."

"Anyhow, Proculus turned the tables on the simple fool," Rufus sneered. "He went and told Nero the whole story."

"*Sweet Jupiter!*" Sabinus cried. "It's all over then!"

"Wait." Rufus continued. "The idiot captain forgot to ask Epicharis for the names of the other conspirators."

"So, when Nero summoned her, she put on quite a performance," Quintus interposed, "laughing away any thought of a conspiracy. It was only a lovers' spat, she explained. She had decided to end her affair with Proculus, and this was his way of repaying her."

"What did Proculus say?"

"Well, he's not entirely bright, you know. He just stood there with his arms hanging down, lamely insisting it was all the truth, but the dolt didn't have a scrap of evidence to support him, and there were no witnesses to their conversation."

"So Nero *believed* her?"

"We think so. At least he discharged her into loose custody. What's the latest from Baiae, Rufus?"

"My agents say he's making a few inquiries, but he's learned nothing at all. He doesn't have one name."

"Well, you'll obviously have to strike at once, then," Sabinus sighed. He put his fingers together in thought, then parted them. "Piso often entertains Nero at his villa in Baiae, doesn't he? Why not simply invite Nero to dinner there and do the job?"

"Exactly our thoughts, Sabinus. But we just had a meeting of all the conspirators at Piso's place, and he vetoed the scheme. For a host to murder a guest within his own home would be a sacrilege against the household deities, Piso claims. So we plan to do it here in Rome . . . at the Festival of Ceres on April 12. Nero always attends the opening games at the Circus, and so he'll finally be outside his villa and we can get at him. Now, I'm to make the first move. You know the passageway that leads to the imperial box in the north tier of the Circus Maximus?"

"Yes . . ."

"Well, at the end of the passage, I'll fall down at Nero's feet, as if begging him for some special favor. Now, I'm a fairly husky fellow, and I plan to reach out, grab Nero's knees and tackle him, pinning him to the ground while the others stab him to death. Scaevinus has reserved the privilege of striking the first blow. Then Rufus and the others will finish him off."

"You see, there'll be an interesting coincidence." Rufus smiled. "Most of my men in on the plot will happen to be Nero's guard that day."

Sabinus cupped his chin and paced about the library. Finally he smiled. "The plan has a simplicity about it that's excellent. It should work. Very well indeed. The key, of course, is Rufus and the bodyguard nearest the emperor. Scaevinus and the others will have to place their blows well lest some guards not in the plot try to save Nero."

"We'll control the others," said Rufus.

"So then." Sabinus grinned. "You're really going through with it, are you? And you a consul-designate, Quintus. My, my!" he trifled. Then he grew serious again. "All right, then. Where do I fit into the scheme?"

"At first we wanted you to send one of your Urban Cohorts into the area to support us," Quintus replied, "but that might get Nero suspicious. Besides, we won't need them. Your job comes *after* the assassination, Sabinus. Have only a small component of your police patrolling the city that day. Keep most of them in the Castra Urbana. The moment Nero's dead, we'll signal you from the Palatine by torches—the roof of the Tiberian palace. You'll immediately have your men stand for assembly. Make a careful speech, listing Nero's crimes, then announce his death, have your men swear allegiance to Piso's provisional government, and then send *all* your cohorts into the city—"

"To keep order at a very critical time." Sabinus nodded. "Yes. Good. Easily done. And I'm glad you've thought about what should happen *after* the assassination. Most conspiracies fondly imagine everything will solve itself once the tyrant's dead."

"It never happens." Quintus smiled grimly. "You can ask Brutus and Cassius about that!"

"In fact, I have only one worry about your plans, my dear plotting friends: I wish *tomorrow* were the beginning of the Festival of Ceres, not two weeks from now. All conspiracies have one great enemy . . ."

"What's that?"

"Time."

On the evening of April 11, Senator Flavius Scaevinus was returning to his mansion on the Esquiline. He had spent the afternoon with an equestrian friend named Natalis, and the two had rehearsed final details of the assassination. They had even practiced stabbing daggers through various thicknesses of cloth into a chunk of beef, seeing how much force was required to make a lethal penetration. Scaevinus looked anxiously at the sky overhead but then smiled at its limpid deepening purple. Hardly a cloud cluttered the horizon. Soon the stars would appear. Surely it would not rain in the morning, and the games for Ceres would take place as scheduled. And, if any just gods controlled the destiny of Rome, this would be Nero's last night.

His flabby frame had a certain vigor that evening, Scaevinus thought. Let his wife and friends tease him about his corpulence and various excesses. After tomorrow they would laugh no longer. They would learn that his was the mind that had first conceived the great strike for freedom—he had kindled the original flames under Piso and welcomed Lateranus into the plot—and soon all Rome would know that his blade had been the first to taste Nero's blood. Yet for now he must control himself. Though fidgety and nervous to the gut, he must register serenity and composure. But if only his heart would stop its reckless throbbing!

No sooner had he arrived home than his wife asked why he had ordered so elaborate a dinner for the household that evening.

"All will become clear later," he replied, with a twinkle. "Now, come to our suite, my dear. I've something to show you."

He opened a drawer and took out several documents. "It's my will. I leave everything to you, my darling." Then he called, "Milichus!"

His freedman aide appeared moments later.

"Here . . . witness my signing this." Scaevinus sat down and wrote his name with a flourish. Milichus then added his, and the senator sealed the documents.

"Why are you doing this?" his wife asked, with rising concern.

"I just want you to know you're always first in my thoughts." Scaevinus expected to survive the violence on the morrow, but this gesture would add to the heroism and drama of it all, he thought. Now he stood up, walked over to a trunk, and took out a sheathed dagger. Fondling the weapon, he slowly withdrew the blade from its scabbard and examined it.

"Family heirloom, Milichus." He smiled. "I consecrated it in the Temple of Safety up in Ferentinum. But it's old . . . and very blunt. Take it downstairs and sharpen it on the whetstone till its edge glitters."

The dinner that night was more of a banquet, with all its ostentatious food and drink. But through it all Scaevinus seemed moody. One moment he was obviously deep in thought, the next he was affecting a cheerfulness that was all too contrived. His comments were random and disconnected, and he drank more wine than usual. At the close of the dinner, he startled the household by awarding freedom to his favorite slaves.

Milichus thought this conduct all rather strange, but not as weird as the final orders he received from Scaevinus that night: "Prepare a pile of bandages for me, Milichus. And ligatures. And styptics for stanching blood." The senator was about to add, "And please don't ask me why," but found it unnecessary. He had given Milichus his freedom. For that he must never question his former master.

But questions were indeed churning through the freedman's mind as he assembled the first-aid supplies. Scaevinus' behavior pointed clearly to some mortal crisis the next day, and he had overheard enough comments from the senator in the last months to guess who might be the intended victim of a plot. He placed the sharpened dagger and the pile of bandages in front of Scaevinus' bedroom door and retired for the night.

But Milichus could not sleep. Turning toward his wife, who also was awake now, he voiced his thoughts about Scaevinus' mysterious conduct that day. "What does it all add up to?" he asked finally.

It took her only an instant to reply, "He'll try to assassinate Caesar some time tomorrow."

"That's it, of course. Now, help me solve this second riddle . . . I must *not* betray Scaevinus: he gave me my freedom and I must protect my patron out of gratitude. Yet I *must* betray Scaevinus: for if the plot miscarries—and from all those bandages, he doesn't seem too optimistic!—then I'm a dead man. It was I who sharpened the blade that will have been used in an attempt to murder Caesar. It was I who will have failed to warn him. Now, solve the riddle for me, dearest."

She thought for some moments, and then replied, "You forgot to add that Caesar would reward you handsomely for alerting him. He might even take you into the government for saving his life."

"Oh . . . I doubt that last."

"You must preserve yourself in any case. If Scaevinus was fool enough to perform as he did this evening, how do you know the other servants here aren't thinking exactly the same things we are? And if any one of them gets to Nero first, you *are* a dead man, Milichus: you prepared the bandages and yet you didn't warn him."

Milichus turned over in bed and said nothing for some moments. Then he whispered, "We'll steal out and go at daybreak."

Suddenly he vaulted out of bed and tiptoed down to the doorway of the master bedroom. Thank the Fates! The dagger was still there. Carefully he picked it up and stole back to his quarters. "We'll need this as evidence," he said.

28

BECAUSE the Golden House was not yet completed, Nero was still residing at his temporary quarters in the Servilian Gardens at the south of Rome. It was here that the lanky Milichus and his tiny wife arrived with the first roseate glimmer of dawn. The gates to the palatial villa were locked, and they pounded on the grating. Finally a sleepy gatekeeper stumbled out of his shack, stared at the improbable couple, and demanded, "What—by the Forge of Vulcan—do *you* want?"

"Let us in. We have *urgent* information for the emperor!"

"Don't we all? Go back home. You must be daft."

"But it concerns his personal safety!" Milichus persisted.

"You'll be concerned about your *own* safety if you don't clear out. You must be a pair of imbeciles, coming here at this hour!"

"Let . . . us . . . in, I say!" Milichus hissed. "Caesar's in danger! He must be warned! If anything happens to him, we'll accuse *you* of preventing us."

The gatekeeper cocked his head and smiled. "You have any idea how often we get warnings like this? And what are you doing with that dagger? Maybe *you're* the ones who are endangering Caesar."

"Do you want us to scream for the guards?" Milichus' wife chimed in. "We will, you know." Milichus gave her a swift pinch in the back, for it suddenly occurred to him that maybe they had already said too much. What if the guards were in on the plot too?

"Take 'em to Epaphroditus," a voice called from inside the gatehouse.

Presently another porter stepped out, the gate creaked open, and the pair was escorted into a vestibule of the rambling villa where they awaited Nero's freedman secretary.

Epaphroditus took his time about coming out to see them. First he ate a leisurely breakfast. Then the stocky, swarthy little Greek poked a pomaded head into the anteroom off the vestibule where they were waiting and inquired, "Are you two the bearers of the 'urgent information'?"

"We are . . . yes," said Milichus.

"Let's have it," Epaphroditus yawned.

When Milichus started listing the symptoms of conspiracy that he knew and the rumors he had heard in recent weeks, the sneer on Epaphroditus' face gave way to a look of alarm. "That's enough," he said. "Follow me. But I'll take that dagger, if you don't mind."

They were led up to Nero's suite. Several guards searched them at the doorway, and then they were admitted. Nero was lounging in his night clothes, eating a hearty breakfast.

"Sorry to disturb you, Caesar," said Epaphroditus, "but this sounds rather serious. Quite serious indeed . . . a plot against your life."

Nero scowled, threw down the piece of honeyed bread that he was munching, and wiped his mouth. "Who are they?" he demanded. "And who's involved?"

"My name is Milichus, Caesar. I'm a freedman of Senator Flavius Scaevinus. And this is my wife."

"Scaevinus' freedman, you say? Who wants to kill me? Tell me everything you know."

Milichus was detailing every strange gesture of Scaevinus the previous evening when Nero interrupted him. "If what you say is true, it certainly looks as though he was up to no good. But how do you know I was to be the victim? Did he say I was?"

"Certainly not. And he mentioned nothing of any assassination, of course. But my master has been critical of you, Caesar, *very* critical. He also belongs to a circle of senators who bitterly oppose you. And he has no other enemies. What would you have concluded? And why did he ask me to sharpen the dagger there which he en-

dowed with religious significance if he had merely planned to use it
for common purposes?"

"Let me see it," Nero said to Epaphroditus. Then he fingered the
keen edge of the blade and winced.

"And lest you think this any idle accusation," Milichus resumed,
"I suggest that you summon the senator himself. I'll be happy to
repeat my charges in his presence." Such a confrontation was inevitable, of course, but Milichus' suggesting it served to strengthen his
case, he thought.

"*Guards!*" Nero called. Several praetorians marched into the
chamber and saluted. "How many of you are on duty at the moment?"

"The usual cohort, Caesar."

"Double the number. And take fifty men and go immediately to
arrest Senator Flavius Scaevinus and bring him to me. Hurry! And
send Tigellinus in here."

The guards saluted and left the chamber. In the interval, Nero sat
lost in thought, staring at the yellowing morning outside while tapping the side of the dagger blade against his open left palm.

When Tigellinus arrived, Nero pointed the dagger at Milichus
and said, "Repeat your story for the praetorian commander here."

Tigellinus listened to the tale with a dark, constricting frown
until a sparkling glint took command of his eyes. He knew that
soon, again, he would be playing his favorite role of high inquisitor.

Milichus had just finished retelling his story when Scaevinus himself arrived, flanked by columns of guards. As the senator saw Milichus, his eyes narrowed momentarily with horror and rage.

"Come in, Senator, come in," said Nero, still flipping the dagger
blade across his hand. Then he stopped and held it up. "Have you
ever seen this before?"

Scaevinus hesitated some moments while flushing fiercely. Then
he regained his composure and said simply, "Why yes, Caesar. It
looks like my dagger."

"Why did you ask Milichus to sharpen it?"

"The blade was getting blunt and rusty. It's an old heirloom from
my ancestors and I keep it in my bedroom. My *ex-slave* here must
have stolen it." He shot Milichus a glance of deadly hatred. "Why
do you ask, Caesar? Why was I brought here?"

"Suppose we let your freedman tell us. Milichus?"

For the fourth time that morning, Milichus began his story, this

time giving the fullest version he had yet offered, his wife adding
details from time to time. All the while, Nero kept his dull blue eyes
riveted on Scaevinus to see how he was taking the disclosure. When
it was finished, Nero asked him, "What's the matter, Senator? You
don't look very well. Not at all."

"For obvious reasons." Scaevinus now scowled fiercely. "Wouldn't
you be ill, Caesar, if suddenly you heard Tigellinus here tell a pack
of lies about you? This is an idiot's attempt at the great game of
playing informer, but what a stupid and threadbare case you've
presented, Milichus! You steal my dagger, sharpen it, and call it 'evidence.' You make a great affair of my preparing a will. *Great gods!*
Must the implications be ominous when a person merely plays the
role of paterfamilias? I adjust my will from time to time, Caesar. It
means nothing more than that we live in uncertain times. Just last
year, my place was almost destroyed in the great fire."

"All right." Nero nodded. "But what about your . . . strange timing in awarding freedom to your slaves?"

"Strange timing? May I respectfully remind all of you what today
is? The beginning of the great Festival of Ceres! What more appropriate time than to honor the goddess of grain who sustains us all?—
Well, I will admit another motive also, Caesar: my fortune isn't
what it was. My creditors are pressing. I don't know if my will will
hold. Better to give my favorites the liberty they deserve than have
my creditors foreclose and take them over as slaves. Yes," he
laughed, "maybe it was a bit of sharp dealing. But really, Caesar,
you do understand, don't you?"

Nero smiled. "I'd have done the same thing, Scaevinus. But the
lavish dinner?"

"That's the stupidest charge of all," the obese senator chuckled.
"To this jealous ingrate I suppose it looked lavish enough. He still
prefers his slave's beans and garlic. But I *always* dine that way"—he
patted his paunch—"as you do yourself, Caesar. We're epicures. We
love good food. Our tongues find it succulent even while our ears
hear the hungry carpings of our critics."

"True enough," Nero tittered, looking down at his own swelling
girth. "But what about all those bandages and ligatures, Senator?"

"You'll remember that was where my face was turning various
colors during Milichus' servile slanders. The bandages, you see, are a
bald and stark and total *lie!* I gave Milichus no such orders. His
slave's mind tells him, 'Now if I cut up pieces of cloth, I'll claim

they're bandages and use them as evidence.' He's taking us all for
fools, Caesar. What would it prove if he delivered a whole cartload
of medical supplies to you? Nothing more than my dagger there."

"That's true, of course. All right, the final charge is that Milichus
overheard you and other senators making critical remarks of me."

"What sort of remarks?"

" 'The actor will soon go off his stage' . . . 'This lyrist must also
give recitals for Father Hades' . . . that sort of thing."

"Lies. And in bad taste, too. You can tell a slave invented something so obvious as that. Oh, I'll admit to occasional criticisms, Princeps. I once called your verses . . . well . . . inferior. And in a
group of senators, too."

"You *did?*" Nero frowned.

"Yes." Scaevinus nodded. "I said they were worthy of a Virgil
. . . or a Horace . . . or even Homer, for that matter, but not of
you, Caesar. You could exceed them all."

"Oh." Nero smiled, relaxing once again. "Then you didn't say my
singing could 'harmonize only with the howling of Cerberus' three
heads'?"

"Is *that* what he told you?" Scaevinus grinned, knowing, of
course, that he had indeed said that very thing. "What a twisted
mind in that knave! No, Caesar, if you take the lies of a villainous
freedman over the word of a senator, things have come to a sorry
pass. Milichus is a wildly ambitious wretch. He thought I should
have given him a minor fortune along with his manumission. I did
give him his freedom, and this is how he repays me: with a cock-
and-bull story he thinks will earn him great rewards from you."

Nero slowly turned to the freedman. "Everything Senator Scaevinus has said suits the facts, Milichus. Do you have any other evidence, any *proof* for your charges? Anyone who can bear out what
you say? Or infer?"

"The other servants saw what I saw yesterday."

"That's not proof, Milichus." Nero shook his head. "We get
many rumors here. If we believed them all, we'd go insane. We have
to have proof."

Milichus was agitated and now perspiring. He looked down and
slowly shook his head. "I have nothing else. I . . . I was only trying
to do the right thing and protect you, Caesar."

"You mean you were only trying to reap a fast fortune, Milichus,"
said Scaevinus. "I trust you'll punish him, Caesar. Otherwise, once

this story gets out, every slave will be accusing every master in Rome. They've tried such tactics before."

"Have you any idea what the penalties for false accusation are, Milichus?" Nero was frowning.

But Milichus was not listening. His wife was whispering something into his ear. Suddenly he brightened and said, "Yes . . . yes indeed, Caesar. We *do* have what may be additional evidence. Before returning home yesterday, the senator had a long conference with Antonius Natalis. Now both Natalis and my master are on very close terms with Senator Piso, and Piso is the name we keep hearing in whispers. Why not question them too?"

Nero turned to Scaevinus and asked, "*Did* you see Natalis yesterday, Senator?"

"Well . . . yes . . . but it was only to discuss—"

"*Guards!* Take fifty men to the house of Antonius Natalis and bring him here immediately!"

Tigellinus leaned over and whispered to Nero, "This may be the chink in the affair. You have a golden opportunity to question them separately."

"I know, I know," Nero sniffed. "Now, Scaevinus, please continue. Tell me *exactly* what you and Natalis discussed yesterday afternoon."

"Ah . . . it was nothing of any secret or extraordinary nature"— Scaevinus chuckled—"the Festival of Ceres . . . the games . . . that sort of thing."

"How long was he gone, Milichus?"

"Most of the afternoon."

"Come, come, Senator. You'll have to do better than that." He was staring at him with crinkle-eyed suspicion.

"No, that was it, Caesar. We were planning a . . . a party for some of our friends in connection with the festival. That . . . and travel plans for the summer. Really, it was as simple as that."

"On what day is the party to be?" Tigellinus interjected.

"Ah . . . the last day of the festival."

"Who is giving it?"

"Well . . . it's at my place."

"I see," Tigellinus continued. "And where do you plan to travel for the summer?"

"Well, I was thinking of . . . ah . . . Greece."

"And Natalis?"

"He was speaking of Egypt."

"Very well. We'll see."

Natalis arrived a half hour later. When he saw his friend Scaevinus standing there also, his eyes tightened with apprehension.

"Natalis," said Nero, again beginning in a kindly tone, "what did you and Senator Scaevinus discuss yesterday afternoon?"

"I . . . I don't understand."

"I believe I was speaking plainly, Natalis." Nero scowled.

"Go ahead and tell him," said Scaevinus jovially. "Tell him about the party we were planning for the festival, Natalis."

"*Shut up*, Scaevinus!" Nero glowered furiously. "One more word or sign from you and I'll hail you up for high treason! Is that clear?"

Scaevinus nodded his perspiring head.

"Go ahead, Natalis. And look only at me."

"Ah . . ." he hesitated, "just as the senator said. We discussed a party. A party . . . yes . . . for the Festival of Ceres."

"When had you planned to give the party?" Tigellinus inquired.

Natalis hesitated. "Oh . . . soon. On the Ides. In the middle of the festival."

"I see," said Nero, without registering emotion. "And who is giving it? Where will it be?"

"At my place," said Natalis.

"And what else did you and the senator discuss?"

"Ah . . . we talked over . . . ah . . . property . . . investments . . . that sort of thing."

"A final question, Natalis. Were you and the senator planning any trips away from Rome this summer?"

"Uhh . . . no. We both plan to stay in town."

"*Guards!*" Nero shouted. Several praetorians advanced.

"Chain these men immediately! You're both under arrest for high treason and criminal conspiracy!"

Tigellinus barked several other commands at his tribunes: "Tell Rufus to march five praetorian cohorts over here at once and surround the entire villa! And bring torture equipment. All guards' liberties are revoked as of this moment. Do a security check throughout the villa!" Then he whispered something to one of the guards and finally added au bly, "Have the executioner erect his platform in the rear of the garden."

"And go out to the games, someone, and tell them I won't be attending today," Nero added, with a trace of regret in his voice.

"What shall we do with these men?" a tribune asked.

"Nothing. We're not through with them yet," said Tigellinus. "May I take over the inquiry, Caesar?"

"Certainly, Tigellinus."

"Now, gentlemen. You're lying about your conversation yesterday. We've proved that. Are either of you prepared—now, immediately— to reveal this entire conspiracy?"

Natalis looked down, but Scaevinus made the final effort. He raised a shackled hand and said, "What conspiracy, Prefect? It was only—"

"*No more lies!*" Tigellinus shouted. "We're finished with lies, Scaevinus. Only the truth. Only the truth from now on. We'll reward honesty with lenience."

Neither made any response.

"All right, then, the alternative is this: Caesar's life is at stake, so we'll stop at nothing to ferret out the facts." He paused, letting his face assume a vicious grin. "Do you recall how the Christians were tortured to death, gentlemen? I can assure you that their punishment will seem a merry romp around the gardens compared to what's in store for you if you don't tell us—immediately—all the plans, and all the names."

Neither said anything. Both were looking down at the floor. A guard signaled Tigellinus. He nodded. "Throw them on the floor and remove their sandals," he ordered. Suddenly Natalis and Scaevinus found themselves pinioned, while a guard brought Tigellinus a sword that had been heated over coals until it glowed.

"This," said Tigellinus, holding up the red-orange blade, "is only a little appetizer in the feast that awaits you, gentlemen. The main courses are on their way over here from the Castra Praetoria . . . a very delicious menu indeed," he said, with relish, "the scourge, pincers to claw your flesh, red-hot plates applied to your—well, you'll see. Honor of rank, Senator. We'll try the equestrian first."

Slowly Tigellinus approached Natalis' bare feet with the glowing blade. Natalis tried to take the searing pain stoically, until the tender arch of his foot began baking and he screamed at agonies he could not believe that painful. "*O immortal gods!*" he shrieked. "Stop it! I'll tell you."

"Everything?" Tigellinus inquired, not moving the blade.

"Yes. *Everything!*"

"All right." He pulled the sword away. "Take Scaevinus into the next room. We'll want it all corroborated separately."

As the senator was dragged off, Natalis actually assumed the offensive. "What you want is quick, solid information so that you can save Caesar, correct?"

"Precisely."

"And if I'd stall or tell you half-truths and not expose the whole conspiracy, you might not be able to save Caesar even now. So here's my bargain: I'll tell you everything I know—quickly and honestly— and you will grant me impunity."

"I can't promise that," said Tigellinus.

"I can," said Nero, now desperate for his own safety. "I pledge it, Natalis. Now tell us what you know."

Natalis was playing a reckless game, selfishly saving himself certainly, but also trying to limit the extent of the punishments. He would claim to reveal all the conspirators but would not do so in fact. He told of the plot at the entrance to the Circus, but did not mention Rufus or the praetorians. Yes, Piso was to be the new emperor. Quintus Lateranus was part of the plot too. And Seneca.

Nero's mouth dropped but then slowly twisted into a smile. At last he had the evidence he needed to put away his tutorial gadfly.

After the disclosures, Natalis was taken out of the chamber and Scaevinus brought in. Now, of course, it was simple to loosen the senator's tongue. Tigellinus simply led off with what Natalis had told him, suggesting that he merely wanted Scaevinus' corroboration. With everything in the open, Scaevinus saw no reason to remain silent, and he admitted other names in the conspiracy.

Within several hours, these, in turn, were summoned to the Servilian Gardens, confronted with the evidence, and falsely promised impunity for further information. With astonishing speed, Tigellinus had most of the names by nightfall, though no one had yet named Rufus, Sabinus, or the praetorian officers.

"That woman!" Nero suddenly remembered. "Get her out of custody and bring her here, Tigellinus."

"Epicharis! Of course! She's part of it, then. And a woman will never be able to take torture."

The guards brought the girl before Tigellinus, but she would admit nothing. He showed her the rack in the basement of the villa, where the torture equipment had been set up. She scorned it.

A leer on his face, Tigellinus ordered her stripped and then strapped to the instrument. He had her lashed with a scourge while he paraded the known names before the prostrate form now swelling with contusions. "We know they're all involved in your plot. But who else? Talk, woman!"

Epicharis said only, "It's all untrue. They're innocent."

"You half-witted incompetents," Tigellinus taunted the torturers, "you're letting a *woman* get the best of you!"

Now they wound the gears of the rack. Her limbs slowly stretched until her left arm popped out of joint. Epicharis shrieked and lost consciousness. When she came to, Tigellinus said, "That was only one joint. Three more to go. Who are the other plotters?"

"No one," she mumbled, after which she was stretched again until both her legs were dislocated. Then they threw the mercifully unconscious form into prison for the night. The next morning, while being carried back to the torture chamber in a chair, she managed to slip off her breast-band, hook it over the back of the chair as a noose, and strangle herself.

Epicharis would quickly find her way into Roman legend, the woman and ex-slave who did not betray others under the most intense agonies, while freeborn men, untouched by torture, were hastening to betray friends and relatives in a mad effort to save themselves. Seneca's nephew Lucan, the poet, had even named his own mother as a conspirator, though no one took him seriously.

Nero, meanwhile, was horrified at the lengthening list of conspirators. What he had imagined as merely a private grudge of several in the nobility was blooming into a broad and devastatingly dangerous plot against his life. Tigellinus surrounded him with a triple guard of only his trusted minions, while he garrisoned the walls of Rome with praetorian cohorts, occupying even the coastlands and river banks. Until the plot was fully exposed, they had no idea if attack from the outside were imminent. Nero placed special confidence in his German cavalry, foreigners who were paid by—and trusted—him alone.

Earlier on the day set for Nero's assassination, while Sabinus waited for the signal from the Palatine and could not know the plot was miscarrying, Quintus Lateranus hurried down to the Forum to bring Piso news of Scaevinus' arrest.

"We now have only one option left," Quintus told Piso. "We must dash to the Castra Praetoria and have Rufus and his men declare for you. Then we march back here with the entire Guard. You'll mount the rostrum and win over the people. Sabinus will fall in with his Urban Cohorts. Then it'll be Rome versus the praetorians on duty protecting Nero. We'll win!"

"I . . . I don't like it, Quintus. Too risky."

"*Risky?!* With Scaevinus and Natalis probably revealing the whole plot, naming you as Nero's successor? What other course is there?"

"I . . . don't know. How do you know they'll talk?"

"Torture. Neither of them is man enough to take it."

Still Piso said nothing.

"Look, we're all destroyed if we don't act, Senator. It's our one and only hope," Quintus pleaded. "You'll see: Nero *has* to collapse. By all the gods, if competing lyre-players terrify him, how about rebellious praetorians!"

But Lateranus could see from the perspiration on Piso's pallid face that he was losing all nerve. Hesitantly, Piso stopped a passing plebe and asked him, "You . . . what would you say if Piso became your next emperor?"

The commoner looked up at him and wrinkled his brow. "Piso? Who's Piso?"

A defeated look on his face, Piso said, "See, Quintus . . ."

"That proves *nothing!* We must act!"

"I . . . I'm going home now, Quintus. I'm . . . sorry. Very sorry. You'd better do the same."

While Lateranus stood gaping, Piso walked back to his town house and wrote out his will. It was riddled with loathsome but necessary flattery for Nero, necessary because he wished his wife spared. Then he heard the sounds of troops surrounding his house. Looking out, he saw that they were all young praetorian recruits. So! Nero didn't trust his veterans—as well he might not!

Piso hurried inside his bedroom, propped up his legs and trunk on the bed with pillows, and let his head and arms dangle over the side. Then he nodded to a servant, who carefully slashed the arteries in both arms from the wrists upward.

Quintus had just stepped inside his mansion on the Caelian and kissed his wife when the place was suddenly surrounded by praetorians. The tribune Statius entered and announced, solemnly, "Quintus Plautius Lateranus, I have here the order for your immediate execution, signed by the emperor."

It all seemed miserably unreal to Quintus, that the sweet adventure called life should end because Fate seemed blind to the proper course of Roman statecraft.

"May I choose my own death?" he asked the tribune. "It *is* traditional, you know."

"Sorry, Senator. My orders are immediate execution by the sword. I'm also ordered to take possession of this house in the name of Caesar."

"I understand. But my wife and children are to be spared, certainly. They have no idea what this is all about."

"I have no orders concerning them. I assume they'll be untouched."

"Very well, then. May I . . . bid my children good-bye?"

Statius, shaken by emotion and almost breaking into tears, said, "I . . . I'm sorry, Senator. Caesar said, 'Drag him off to the Sessorium the moment you set foot in his house!' It's too long already. My men could report it . . ."

Quintus gave his sobbing, almost hysterical wife a tender kiss and said, "Tell the children how much I loved them—and you, carissima. Some day, too, tell them . . . what I tried to do for the state."

In all her agony, she still managed to nod her quivering head.

"And tell that twin brother of mine to look after you. *And* the cause!—He'll understand." Then he let Statius and his guards drag him off to the Sessorium, a place just outside the Esquiline Gate reserved for the execution of slaves. The tribune himself, trembling and threatening again to give way to tears, whispered to Quintus as he bent over the block, "Thanks, noble friend. I'll imagine it's Nero under me when I swing."

Saying not a word, Quintus stretched his neck across the block.

That night, Statius wept the bitter tears he was holding back. He himself had been a prime conspirator, but Lateranus had maintained a resolute silence about it. The noblest of the plotters was dead.

Sabinus, meanwhile, had been keeping his cohorts on alert inside the Castra Urbana, while waiting anxiously for the fire signal from the roof of Tiberius' palace. A flaming torch was to be waved back and forth three times if Nero were killed, but ten times if he were only wounded or the plot miscarried—the signal to be repeated twice for accuracy.

Sabinus' eyes strained as he watched the Palatine minute after minute, but he saw only the clear cerulean of an April sky atop the palace. Nero had been expected to enter the Circus Maximus at mid-morning, but it was now an hour later than that and still there was no signal.

Another hour passed. His nerves tingled. His armpits dampened. How much better to have been at the Circus waiting for Nero than linger, safely but helplessly, in an agony of anticipation. Again his eyes flashed toward the palace, but, other than one fleecy cloud blooming up on the southern horizon, there was nothing.

Suddenly, the jangling rhythmic thud of marching men filled the eastern end of the Forum. He looked and saw praetorian cohorts marching south around the Palatine. This was *not* part of the plan! One . . . two . . . three cohorts. Going where? The Circus Maximus? Now there were *four* cohorts.

Still no signal. Something must have gone desperately wrong if they forgot even to signal the plot's failure. Sabinus climbed down from his pinnacle, canceled the alert at the Castra Urbana, and committed the normal number of police cohorts to the streets of Rome.

When he returned to city headquarters, Rufus' closest aide, the tribune Flavus, was waiting for him, ashen-faced and trembling, his great mound of blond hair disheveled from haste. He reported the whole story of the plot's exposure to that moment, culminating in the latest word: Piso's suicide, Lateranus' execution.

Rippling with horror, Sabinus staggered backward and slumped into a chair. His face was pebbled with perspiration and blotching with anger, dread, and despair. He felt nauseous as his heart galloped recklessly.

"That histrionic idiot!" he finally muttered.

"Who?" Flavus inquired.

"Scaevinus." He spat the name out as if it were a piece of wormy apple. He wanted to pommel the flabby body of the ostentatious and theatrical Scaevinus until it was a battered heap, for it was his showy stupidity that would now rain more deaths on Rome. But the maelstrom of moods ripping through him seemed to change by the moment. Now grief eclipsed vengeance: cousin Quintus Lateranus was no more. That lovable rascal with the blazing sense of humor who had also made him rich was *dead!* The Twin Brothers had been cut apart. There would be no more financial triumphs for the Gemini. Castor . . . or Pollux—they never did decide which was which —had gone to the gods. How would he ever tell Plautia?

"Tell me, Tribune," he asked Flavus, "is your commander . . . planning anything further . . . so far as Nero's health is concerned?"

Flavus caught the meaning perfectly. "No, Prefect, quite on the contrary. Rufus never even *heard* of the plot now. By philandering Jupiter, if *only I'd* had sense enough to stab that swine when I had the chance! But I've got to leave now, Prefect. They want me over at the Servilian Gardens."

"*Vale,* Flavus." Then Sabinus added, "If you ever find yourself in such a position again, thrust, my man, thrust!"

"I will, Prefect. I'll try hard to find that black heart of his beneath all the lard! *Vale.*"

Sabinus left shortly after him for the Quirinal. His roiling thoughts had difficulty finding any mooring. Now he was even beginning to hate the gods of Rome. He had never believed in them since childhood, of course, but now he resurrected them only long enough to hate them cordially. Jupiter and his crew had let Rome burn herself to ashes, and later they had not intervened while hundreds of innocents were slaughtered. And now they had spared a murderous tyrant with disastrous consequences. No, the gods didn't exist. Gods like that didn't deserve to exist. For that matter, the god of the Christians—milder and more logical as he seemed—was also, evidently, powerless before some higher, impersonal force. Perhaps Fate?

No sooner had Sabinus stepped inside their house than Plautia rushed up to him, sobbing, as she twined her arms around him, burying her face in the folds of his toga. She had learned the tragic news about her favorite cousin in a cruel fashion: Quintus' widow and children, beside themselves with grief, had arrived on the Quirinal earlier to beg shelter.

Aides were arriving hourly with reports that other conspirators were being rounded up. His own prospects heavily shrouded in black, Sabinus quickly wrote out his last will and testament and prepared himself for the end as best he could. He went over all the alternatives with a weeping Plautia. Flight from Italy? It was too late for that. Turn state's evidence to save himself? Unthinkable. Revolution? Earlier, perhaps, but now it was no longer possible.

Actually, the only very slender hope of emerging from the disaster intact was to pursue "business as usual." When his affairs were arranged, Sabinus gave Plautia a long, tender, and meaningful kiss. Then he hurried back to city headquarters.

Columns of manacled prisoners were arriving at the gates of Nero's villa and the trials had begun—brief, emergency affairs which assumed all defendants guilty until proven innocent. Nero sat behind a judiciary table, flanked by his assessors: Tigellinus, a senator named Nerva, and Rufus, who was flooded with conflicting emotional currents. He tried desperately to mask his own role as a leader of the plot by fiercely browbeating his fellow conspirators, praying all the while that they would be gentlemen enough not to expose him.

Finally the flaxen-haired Flavus, who was standing at Rufus' side, could stand it no longer. "Thrust, my man, thrust!" Sabinus had advised. Nudging Rufus, he gave him a wide-eyed look while his hand went to the hilt of his sword. Rufus caught the message: "Shall I kill the tyrant here and now? Can you control the praetorians in this place?"

Rufus thought for an instant, almost breaking under the strain of history waiting for his decision. Rome's destiny would be altered by a movement of his head one way or the other. His heart pounded and his body bathed itself in sweat. In a crisis, take the safest course —the old rule. He shook his head at Flavus. The tribune's hand dropped away from his sword. Nero would live on.

Retirement had been kind to Annaeus Seneca. He had been traveling in southern Italy with his beloved Paulina and penning his finest Stoic treatises, the *Moral Letters*. But on the very day set for Nero's assassination, he had returned to his villa just four miles south of Rome.

Now he was reclining with his wife and two friends at dinner, trying to take in stride news that the conspiracy had failed. He himself should have provided leadership in the plot, Seneca sadly realized. Then it might not have come to grief.

Halfway through their simple dinner, they heard the clatter of troops surrounding the villa. A tribune burst inside and announced the charges against the aging philosopher. One last play in the game of life, Seneca thought. He rose serenely and responded to all the charges against himself with a witty defense.

Leaving his cordon of guards, the tribune returned to Nero with the message. The emperor asked him, "Did it seem as if Seneca was . . . preparing to take his own life?"

"Not really. At least I saw no . . . sadness in his words or looks."

"Then go back and announce the sentence of death to him, Tribune. Only him. No one else."

When the tribune returned with his fatal message, Seneca's wife Paulina broke into tears, and their two friends joined her.

"Why should this surprise you, dearest friends?" the philosopher frowned. "Everyone knows about Nero's cruelty. After murdering a brother, a mother, and a wife, what's left but the destruction of a guardian and a tutor? But enough of tears," he huffed. "Where are the maxims of our philosophy? If Stoicism teaches anything, it tells us how to meet misfortune."

Then he turned to his wife and embraced her tenderly. "Don't mourn, lovely Paulina. Well . . . only a little while for appearance's sake. Console yourself with virtue."

"I . . . I've decided to die with you, dearest."

"I won't have it, Paulina." He stroked her hair.

"I must."

"Noble, but unnecessary."

"I have *resolved* it, Annaeus. We will not be separated in death."

Seneca looked into her eyes. They were cool and firm with determination. "So?" he whispered. "Do you really prefer the glory of dying too?"

The tiny mouth of the handsome woman smiled serenely and she nodded.

"I won't begrudge your setting so noble an example, precious Paulina. May your courage in death outshine mine"—he smiled—"and win eternal praise."

Together they drew a knife across their wrists. Then he kissed Paulina good-bye, and bade her retire to the bedroom lest they weaken at seeing each other suffer. Unbeknown to Seneca, the praetorians would check her bleeding—against her will—and bandage her arms. She would live on.

As his life drained away, Seneca called in a secretary and dictated his final thoughts for posterity. "See that the city prefect, Flavius

Sabinus, gets this and all my other manuscripts," he told him. Then he added, wistfully, "Nero and Sabinus were my two greatest hopes in life. *One* succeeded, the Fates be thanked!"

Now he asked his physician for poison hemlock—Socrates' last drink—but even that had little effect, for his spare and aging body failed to absorb the drug. Finally, he ordered himself carried into an overheated bath.

"My offering to Jove the Deliverer!" were his last words. Suffocating in the steam, the sixty-nine-year-old Seneca collapsed and died.

Nero's tribunal ground on relentlessly. It was during a second, intensive questioning of Scaevinus that Rufus overplayed his role as inquisitor, browbeating Scaevinus mercilessly. Finally the perspiring senator had enough of Rufus' dual role as accomplice and yet judge. "Oh, that's enough play-acting, Rufus!" he sneered. "No one knows more about the plot than *you* do! Show your gratitude to so 'good' a prince! Go ahead and tell him, Rufus. Tell him *everything!*"

Blanching with terror, Rufus tried to stammer out a denial, but he was a military man, not an actor.

Nero's heart almost stopped in horror. Vaulting up from his chair, he ran over to Tigellinus and clutched him like a frightened child. "Sweet goddess Roma!" he bawled. "Not the man who's been sitting next to me at the tribunal! My own bodyguard! *Gods!*" He cringed.

"*Guards!*" yelled Tigellinus. "Seize the Prefect Rufus and bind him fast. Triple sets of fetters!" Then, turning to Nero, he said, "Maybe now, Caesar, you'll realize that my suspicions of this . . . reptile were not ill-founded."

"Here I thought you were only jealous of someone sharing your rank, Tigellinus," Nero whimpered. "Who *else* among the praetorians is involved?"

In a short time they had discovered them. Flavus and Asper gave a much better performance than the cowering Rufus. When they were hauled up before Nero, the tawny-haired Flavus objected, "Me? Do you really think a rough army type like myself would associate with this . . . ladylike Scaevinus and his fairy friends?"

But when pressed, the tribune made a glorious confession of his whole role in the plot. "Yes, Caesar, three different times I planned to kill you: once, when you were holding a long and very sour note on stage . . . the second, during the great fire . . . and then here at your tribunal."

"Why, Flavus?" asked Nero, his mouth quivering.

"Because you preferred playing butcher, or buffoon, or pervert to emperor."

Nero clutched at the arms of his chair and clenched his teeth. "And you, Asper?" he finally managed. "Why did *you* try to murder me?"

The centurion replied coolly, "It was the only way I could really *help* you, Caesar."

A great vein swelled up across Nero's forehead, and his face darkened to a turgid purple. He opened his mouth several times to say something, but brought up only frothy grunts. Finally he signaled the guards by swinging a flat, trembling hand across his own neck in the "cut" gesture. Both men were dragged off into the garden and decapitated.

Then it was Rufus' turn, later Lucan's, then Scaevinus'. The final total stood at nineteen deaths, twelve senators exiled, and four praetorians degraded in rank.

So much for punishments. As for rewards, the freedman Milichus was lavished with gifts and the term Soter ("Savior") was added to his name. Nero awarded triumphal honors to Tigellinus and other officers who had helped expose the plot. Honors should also have been due the city prefect for keeping Rome secure at a critical time, but Nero did not single Sabinus out for any special award. Tigellinus, in fact, had fondly hoped that someone would raise Sabinus' name in connection with the plot. But Sabinus' only bridges to the conspiracy had been Lateranus, Rufus, and Flavus. They had not exposed him, and all three were dead. Amid the fountains of blood that had splashed across Rome's governing circles, he had survived.

But Sabinus was not particularly grateful to Destiny for that survival. The inner logic of existence was fading in Rome, he thought. The man who should have died did not. Instead, hundreds of slaves and hundreds of Christian victims had been tortured and killed. And now, too, patriots like Quintus, philosophers like Seneca, and a circle of Roman statesmen had been cut down. *Madness!*

Time, high time, to do something about that madness. Sabinus stalked out of city headquarters and crossed into the Forum. It was twilight, and the place was largely deserted. Wandering among the monuments and columns that were the very heart of the city and the Empire, Sabinus felt almost tangibly the judgment of Rome's glorious past against her murky present. Each pillar seemed to issue its separate challenge to him. He and his bystanding friends had wrung their hands while gazing with alarm for too many months, no, years, now, and even those who had just acted should have done so earlier —and successfully. A true tyrant can never be cut down too soon. But past was past.

Now he was standing before the great marble columns of the Temple of Castor and Pollux, wedged into the southern base of the Palatine. Inevitably he thought of Quintus and his last message through his wife: "Tell that twin brother of mine . . . to look after the cause. He'll understand." Yes, he understood well enough.

Climbing up the steps of the deserted temple, he paused before the magnificent bronze statues of the Gemini, and his eyes filled with tears as he recalled several of his escapades with Quintus. Then it suddenly occurred to him: for centuries, Rome had regarded Castor and Pollux as guardians of her liberty. Vengeance now buried grief.

"All right," he finally resolved out loud, "enough of Flavius Sabinus the passive protagonist. Everyone else has failed, but I shall succeed. I *will* overthrow Nero. I will do it legally or illegally . . . peacefully or violently. But the tyrant must be toppled. And if he resists in the slightest"—he paused and almost reverently drew out his prefect's dagger—"then this must assist me. I swear by my ancestors and for my children, I must then kill him. For the Senate, for the people, for Rome, I *must kill Nero*."

29

IT WAS A LATE AFTERNOON in May when Pomponia jumped down from her litter and rapped on the door of her daughter's house on the Quirinal.

"Paul is back in Rome," she told Sabinus, "Paul of Tarsus."

"What? He couldn't have come back at a worse time. Where's he now?"

"At the Castra Praetoria. He was arrested."

"I . . . I'm sorry, Mother." Sabinus shook his head. "I doubt if we can save him this time. You know why."

"I know, Sabinus. Just . . . do what you can."

Sabinus went over to the Castra and peered into the darkness of the dungeon, trying to locate the apostle, when he heard the rattle of chains.

"Prefect," a familiar voice from the shadows called out. "How *very* kind of you to come." Paul was walking toward him from a corner of the prison, carrying part of his chain so it would not make so much noise. Sabinus saw that unmistakable wiry face looming out of the darkness, and the pointed, prying gray beard.

"Hello, Paul. Despite all this you look well. Are they giving you enough to eat?"

"Not always so tasty, but always enough." Paul smiled.

"What happened? Why were you arrested again?"

"It was in Ephesus. At one time I thought I'd never return there—and the way matters developed, perhaps I shouldn't have! But the church in Ephesus is so important for all of Asia that we couldn't tolerate what was happening."

"Persecution?"

"No, the Christians there were being perverted by a false teacher named Alexander. Alexander the Coppersmith. He used to be a Christian, but he got caught up in Gnostic philosophy. Then he tried to subvert other Christians there, so Timothy, Luke, and I had to step in. The Ephesian church finally excluded him from membership. It's an unhappy story, Prefect. Alexander grew so resentful that he formally indicted me before the Roman governor of Asia."

"And again you invoked your Roman citizenship to appeal to Caesar?"

"I'm not sure that would have been so wise." Paul smiled. "No. The governor himself sent us both to Rome, Alexander to repeat his charges here. You see, he knew Caesar had persecuted the Christians, and he wasn't clear on their present legal status in the Empire. So he wanted to make no decision one way or the other."

"When does your hearing take place?"

"It already has."

"What! When?"

"Shortly after my arrival six weeks ago."

"Why didn't you let us know about it, Paul? I'm not sure we could have done much . . . but we could have tried."

"At the time, I was allowed no contacts outside the prison. But even so I wouldn't have bothered you."

"Why not?"

"Because my time has come, Sabinus. And you were all . . . concerned about the recent crisis here in Rome."

"Well, what happened at your hearing? Who served as judge?"

"Nymphidius Sabinus."

"The new praetorian co-prefect? Rufus' successor?"

"Yes. Caesar and Tigellinus didn't want to be bothered with my case again, so they turned it over to Nymphidius and several assessors. They wanted to 'give him judicial experience,' so I'm told." Paul smiled.

"What happened? How did they decide?"

"Well, Alexander the Coppersmith did his worst, painting me as a seditionist, a rabble-rouser, but above all, as an arsonist. He thought he was being shrewd with that charge, since Nero himself tormented us for that. So he said, 'This man is guilty of complicity with those who burnt your city.'"

"Who defended you?"

"No one. Several witnesses I'd hoped to summon all deserted me. May it not be held against them.—But the Lord stood by me, and I showed the judges how ludicrous it was to believe that I, in faraway Ephesus, had touched off the flames that consumed Rome. A fuse almost 900 miles long?"

Sabinus chuckled. "He didn't absolve you, then?"

"No," Paul said wistfully. "Not enough A tablets this time! The vote was NL . . . 'not proven.' So my trial is postponed for further evidence."

"Any idea when the next hearing will be?"

"No."

Sabinus nodded. "They'll probably get Alexander to drop the arson charge and focus instead on your being the leader of an illegal sect. And ever since the persecution, this has been impossible to refute, Paul. I'll tell you candidly: your fate is beyond any of the courts. It's all in Nero's hands, now. Oh—'and God's', I'm sure you'd add."

"You're learning, friend." Paul smiled.

"I doubt that." He shook his head. "I'm far from a Christian, Paul." Then, leaning close to the grating so no one else could hear, he asked, "How can anyone believe in a supreme god who lets Nero live on while Peter and hundreds of your Christians died—horrible deaths?"

Paul looked about cautiously, then whispered, "You can't imagine how many of our members were *not* seized! We're also finding a new attitude toward Christians in Rome—'pity' or 'sympathy' would be too strong a word—but we feel it, Sabinus. Romans are embarrassed at what Nero did to us. It was all *too* violent, *too* horrible. Luke is back in Rome again, and he reports inquiries about the Faith *because* of the persecution—good pagan Romans wondering how people could die with that sort of courage and conviction."

"Still, I'd advise you all to be very careful, Paul. By the way, how are our friends Aquila and Priscilla?"

"Fine. They're guiding the church in Ephesus now. We'll need their strength when Alexander returns. They want to be remembered to you, of course. They owe their very lives to you."

"I admire your conviction, Paul. You don't think of yourself, only of your 'future church.' Well, I'll make whatever discreet inquiries I can about your case, but I'm afraid there will be . . . so little to promise. Send Luke over from time to time. He can be our contact."

Paul clasped Sabinus' shoulder through the bars and smiled his gratitude.

The Neronia festival was approaching once again. The thought of Caesar returning to the stage, always a disgrace to the state, particularly irked the Fathers in view of the political funerals that year. But Thrasea Paetus found a deft solution. He stood up in the Senate and said, "I propose that we award Caesar the victory in advance of the games—he will surely win anyway—and now he need not even compete."

"Euge! Euge!" the senators agreed, and then voted it into law.

Nero was less than pleased with the news. "I *don't need* any special favors—least of all from the Senate," he pouted. "I'll win my honors by merit alone."

Eagerly he returned to the stage, this time shod with high-soled buskins to improve his stature. In bowing to the opening applause, Nero was delighted to note that Sabinus was not only sitting in the city prefect's box adjacent to that of Poppaea but had brought along his brother Vespasian. Now, costumed in rags and fetters, Nero launched into a spirited rendition of *The Frenzy of Hercules.*

Sabinus rippled with repugnance at Nero's theatrics but coolly masked it, for he was attending, not as spectator, but as hunter, stalking his prey. He now wanted to observe every last trait, each mannerism of his quarry so he could learn where Nero was vulnerable and attack successfully where others had failed.

Nero was now pleading so plaintively for help in *Frenzy* that a young praetorian, standing on guard in the wings, actually rushed on stage to assist him. "No, no, you fool!" Nero snapped. "It's just an act."

Sabinus was trying to smother his laughter when he heard a woman's voice near him wondering out loud, "By all the gods, when will he *ever* shut up and sit down?" The voice belonged to Poppaea, who was trying to cover her yawn with a hand. The empress, who seemed to have put on weight, looked dreadfully bored.

During the rest of the warm afternoon, Nero returned to his lyre and launched into another of his interminable epics. Praetorians were guarding all exits so that no one could leave, although several plebes jumped down from the stands rather than listen any longer. Vespasian, who could never sit longer than a quarter hour without nodding, was having a terrible time staying awake. An occasional jab from Sabinus' elbow was enough to return him to the land of the conscious, but later Sabinus also got sleepy and had all he could do to keep himself awake. But Vespasian's eyes snapped shut and his head dropped. It was one of Nero's aides who now hovered over the dozing Vespasian and gave him ringing slaps across the cheeks.

"Vespasian here was *sleeping!*" he huffed to Sabinus. "A grievous insult to Caesar!"

"Nothing of the sort," Sabinus quickly covered. "My brother always concentrates better with his eyes shut. Don't *you* think Caesar's singing should get the most dedicated hearing?"

The aide scowled and ambled off. Vespasian leaned over and whispered, "Thanks, brother. You're always getting me out of trouble, aren't you?"

After his concert, Nero also watched several races and finally made a tardy return to the palace-villa at night. He received an expected scolding from Poppaea that hardly seemed to faze him, for he had assumed his most imperial pout and was indulging the role of a wronged princeling.

Finally Poppaea ventured the obvious query. "All right, Nero. Out with it. What's the matter? *I'm* the one who should be furious with you . . . coming home as late as this."

After several more moments of studied sulking, he replied, "Each time I've returned from one of my concerts, you've told me how *well* I did. This time you said nothing. You even left before I finished. You even acted . . . well, *bored* during my singing. I saw you! I always watch you from the corner of my eye."

"I wasn't feeling very well. Have you forgotten I'm pregnant again?" she sighed. "And . . . I'll admit it: I *was* bored, Nero."

"You were . . . *what?*" He looked as if his soul had been lacerated.

"Bored, Nero. Yes, bored to death . . . and more than a little offended."

"Why, Poppaea?" he asked in a high, gulping voice.

"Because it was *too long,* for one thing. You acted *all morning.* You sang *all afternoon . . .*"

"But . . . but the epics *are* that long."

"Then maybe they shouldn't be sung at all. Especially by you."

"Why you . . . you uncultured little sow."

"Listen, you pompous, bloated bag of wind, I'm only doing this for your own good! *Somebody* has to tell you, Nero! Some of your performances are barely acceptable. A few are even acceptable. Others, like today's, are *terrible!*"

Nero was cut to the quick. He groped for words and finally found them. "Why, you ungrateful little trollop: you went from man to man until I found you and made something of you. But your ears and your mind—they're clearly beyond any help!"

"You can talk to me like that? At a time when I'm carrying your child?"

"Whose child is it really, Poppaea? Tell me true?"

"*Monster!*" she shrieked, giving him a stinging slap across the cheek. "Worthless, would-be artist who *kills* rather than creates! You're a *disgrace,* Nero! A disgrace to the whole Empire!"

Quivering with rage, Nero drew back his right foot and gave Poppaea a hard, painful kick in the abdomen. Shoved off balance, she fell to the floor, striking her head on the marble pavement. Her eyes snapped shut. She lay motionless, huddled under a green silk house robe.

Nero quickly hovered over her. "Oh, my precious Poppaea!" he cried. "Talk to me! Are you hurt, carissima? I'm sorry . . . sorry . . . sorry, darling! Speak to me! Poppaea?"

She made no stir. In a frenzy, Nero summoned the palace doctors. They examined the prostrate empress and then carried her up to bed. Nero sat at her bedside in anguish.

In the early morning hours, she regained partial consciousness, but then she suffered a miscarriage. Attending physicians tried desperately to halt the hemorrhaging that followed. They were not successful.

By noon, Nero's beloved Poppaea Sabina, empress of Rome, was dead.

Sabinus had never particularly admired Poppaea, but he now regretted her death because it threw Rome into turmoil and severely complicated the plot he was formulating against Nero. The emperor canceled their weekly conferences and spent weeks moaning about the palace, calling for Poppaea to return from the dead and forgive him. He would sit for hours in her bedroom, staring blankly at the walls, playing with items that used to delight her. Fearing for the emperor's sanity, Tigellinus tried hard to shake him out of his grief. He eventually resorted to a trusty device that had worked so well before: scaring Caesar.

It worked again. Nero's extravagant grief turned into a paranoid vengeance against the "conspiracies" swirling about him, most of them merely products of Tigellinus' depraved imagination. Sabinus felt a second wave of terror strike across Rome, which, in many ways, was more terrifying than the first. In the ruddy wake of the Pisonian conspiracy, the blood list had been drawn up quickly and the executions carried out with ruthless efficiency. But this time it was different: no one could tell whom Nero and Tigellinus would strike—or when—or how—or really why. People like himself were targets of the current purge, Sabinus quickly saw, and if he understood Tigellinus correctly, the man would not rest until he had sipped the nectar of revenge over his own prostrate body. A good hater, Tigellinus was nothing if not relentless, and it was astonishing that he had not yet been able to link him with the original plot against Nero.

Suspected republicans, rivals, critics—types who might plot against Nero in the future—were rounded up and mercilessly dispatched. The two brothers of the dead Seneca were indicted. Mela was accused of sharing his son Lucan's role in the plot. In fact he was innocent, but he saw no alternative to suicide. The same "guilt by relation" felled the eloquent Gallio, tidings that stunned and saddened Paul in prison, who would outlive his judge in Corinth.

Thrasea Paetus was giving a garden party for a few of his friends and had invited the aging Aulus and Pomponia to attend. They were listening to the discourses of a visiting philosopher when a messenger hurried into the grove with ugly tidings: under enormous pressure from Nero, the Senate had just condemned to death its one courageous voice, the most incorruptible of the Fathers, Thrasea Paetus.

Aulus stood up from the table. In a quaking voice, he cried, "May all the spirits of *hell* fatten on Nero's bloated body . . . first his voice, to halt its ghastly grunting. May the Furies—"

"Aulus, my friend," Thrasea cheerfully interrupted, "everyone knew the trail of death would finally wind to this door. After all, I have the honor of having been Nero's earliest and most implacable enemy. And for years on end. The wonder is that I've survived this long."

Then, a smile of serenity on his face, Thrasea hustled his guests out of the grove lest they be incriminated by contact with him. But Aulus refused to leave him, sending Pomponia back to the Esquiline. When the praetorian officer arrived to announce sentence of death, Thrasea took out a knife and neatly slit both of his wrists. "A libation to Jove the Deliverer!" he cried, turning to the soldier. "Mark this well, young man: you've been born into times when it's advisable to steel the spirit with examples of courage."

Aulus and the praetorian helped Thrasea onto his deathbed. Tears rolling down his leathery cheeks, Aulus told the officer to wait outside. Then he whispered into the ear of his dying friend, "Sabinus *will* destroy Nero, Thrasea. He will. Believe it. I know his plan."

"Then I can die a happy man," Thrasea replied, still smiling. "Nero can kill me . . . but he can't harm me."

Had he been a bachelor with no attachments, Sabinus would long ago have plunged his prefect's dagger deep into Nero during any of their conferences. He and Tigellinus were the only armed men allowed in Nero's presence, and he would gladly have sacrificed himself for the state. But he could not demand that his wife and children and their aging parents make the same sacrifice, for Tigellinus' vengeance would surely seek them out. And so he was trying to work out a plan that would spare his family.

It was hard enough sustaining Plautia's spirits through the agony of uncertainty. She was crushed by news of her "Uncle" Thrasea's suicide, and worried incessantly about her husband as the circle of deaths seemed to constrict around him. Her one comfort was the tenderness he showed in their habit of standing together on the roof terrace each day after supper, watching the evening sun drop over the Vatican Gardens across the Tiber. He would stand behind her, his arms locked deliciously about her waist, and whisper in her ear, simply, "One more day, my love."

They had been given another twenty-four hours together. She would nod her dark curls appreciatively and try to pull his arms even tighter about her lissome body. She had never before thought of time as a gift. But with a maturing love—was it actually being intensified by all the danger?—each extra day or week was its own consolation.

Petronius, the imperial arbiter in matters of taste, had invited them to a banquet at his country villa, promising that neither Nero nor Tigellinus nor any of their minions would be present. He wanted only to help break the somber mood hovering over Rome, the invitation insisted.

Sabinus and Plautia both needed the change and were enjoying themselves immensely at the lavish feast, the first time they had laughed or smiled in weeks. As the dessert wines were being served, Petronius leaned over and said, "I almost succeeded in bringing Caesar a little culture, Sabinus. He actually read—and even half understood—my *Satyricon*."

"Why do you say 'almost succeeded'? Nero calls nothing witty or elegant unless you first tell him it is."

Petronius frowned abruptly. "It's that brutish clod Tigellinus. He was afraid I was winning Nero away from him—and I was!—so he bribed a slave to swear I was a ringleader in Piso's conspiracy." Then he shrugged his shoulders and smiled. "Well, I'm leaving tonight, Sabinus. This all is just a friendly farewell."

Before Sabinus could even respond, Petronius had gotten to his feet and raised his hands for silence. "You all know, my friends, how much Caesar has envied my collection of murrhine vases," he said. "I might modestly add that they *are* the finest grouping in the Empire, and worth an entire wing of Caesar's . . . ostentatious new palace."

He clapped his hands twice. Servants filed out of the kitchen, each lifting one of the priceless urns out of Petronius' museum case. A slight nod from the host, and all vases were hurled onto the tessellated floor of the dining hall, shattering into a thousand fragments. To the astonished, indrawn breath of his guests, Petronius continued, "Now the sweaty hands of Caesar will never caress their cold porcelain. Let this symbolize the larger purpose of our *final* dinner together, my dearest friends."

In just moments, Petronius conveyed the grotesque news that the rest of the banquet would be not a grisly deathwatch but the happiest of wakes. "And *please* no remonstrances or sympathies or tears. Seneca left the stage philosophizing"—he grinned—"but for me no serious discussions on the immortality of the soul, if you please. And certainly no philosophy."

There was silence in the hall until Sabinus ventured, "What then, Petronius?"

"Why, bawdy tales, of course," he chuckled. "Light poetry." He lifted a silver razor and made small incisions in his wrists "for a deliciously gradual departure." Then he reclined again to hold his crimsoning arms out of view below the table.

"And now some frivolous verses," he challenged.

Guests told some, he others. From time to time he bound up his wrists to stop the bleeding and win time for several more stories. However unlikely the scheme would have seemed, Petronius was actually bringing it off with verve and style, Sabinus thought, sadly.

Now the host called in two secretaries to record his will. "One copy goes to the Vestal Virgins," he directed. "The other is for Nero." Then he read aloud the codicil he had just added to the will:

I know, Caesar, that many of your victims hope to save a little property for their families by leaving bequests for you and your tasteless leech, Tigellinus. But in this document you shall find only what you deserve, to wit:

I. *A Critique of Your Artistry*

You have sought this for many months, and I am now happy to supply it. Let history judge your other crimes, Caesar, your endless slaughter of relatives and friends and statesmen. I shall not even mention your novelty in devising a new and unprecedented outrage: *double* uxoricide. No, as a parting favor, I shall reveal only your master atrocity, which is this: that you have the brazen effrontery to imagine that your throaty warble should be called singing, and that your caterwauling on the lyre and your sins on the cithara pass, in any sense, for art. An offense to the ears? Certainly! An abrasive test for the nerves? That too. But art? Never! In the name of the Muses, we crave your silence, as we also ask that hopeless laughingstock of the actor in you to take his *final* bow.

II. *A Private Inventory*

Since your recollection of friendships is so very short, you may forget some of your depravities as well, and what would

Nero be without his vices? The following table, however, should refresh your memory. You may be shocked that I should have known about these novel gymnastics of yours, but this makes me all the happier . . .

What followed was a long listing of three columns, each headed, respectively: *"Names . . . Dates . . . Specialties, Preferences, Novelties."*

Against gales of laughter, Petronius signed the documents and sealed each with his signet ring, which he then crushed to forestall any future forgery. Now he reopened his bandages, bidding farewell to Sabinus, a very pale Plautia, and his other guests.

Nero read Petronius' will the next afternoon. Mortified that his private revels were such public knowledge, he fell into such a rage that he lost control of his bodily functions. Vainly, Terpnus pleaded with him to "spare the celestial voice."

By evening, however, Nero had calmed down. "Well, Tigellinus," he sighed, "with the deaths of Thrasea and Petronius, I feel truly *free* for the first time. All my enemies are now dead or banished. I can breathe again. I no longer have to worry—thanks to you, dear fellow."

For Tigellinus this was unhappy ebullience, since his power rested on manipulating Nero through fear. "I . . . I hope you're right, Princeps," he said.

"What do you mean 'hope'?"

"Oh . . . nothing, really."

"Tell me, Tigellinus. Is there anyone *else?*"

There was. Someone Tigellinus hated more than he could believe. Someone he would indict when a full case could be built against him. But for now he merely replied, "Several people bear careful watching, Caesar. Your city prefect, for one."

"Sabinus? He *seems* all right. I see he's finally attending all the public functions. My concerts, too."

"If you call 'attending' sitting there drowsy and put upon. At your last performance, his brother even fell asleep."

"Ohhhh," Nero winced. "Do you suppose we should indict them?"

"Not yet. Vespasian's innocent, at any rate. He's just an unartistic ox who may yet be useful to us in the army. Sabinus is the one to watch—I *still* think he plotted with the Piso group. He recommended Rufus to us, don't forget, and he was so very friendly with the Christians. *And"*—he smirked—"I just learned that he and his wife attended that treasonable banquet at Petronius' place."

Nero's eyebrows arched. "So? Shall we arrest him then, Tigellinus?"

"Soon, I would think. Let me get a little more evidence first.— Now, Caesar, before I leave, here's a list of cases awaiting your pleasure."

Nero scanned the schedule of trials pending. His eyes narrowed when he came to "Alexander the Coppersmith *versus* Paul of Tarsus."

"Paul of Tarsus . . . Paul of Tarsus? Oh, is that the little Christian fellow—all eyes, hook nose? Aha ha! The case you lost to Sabinus?"

"The same," Tigellinus sneered. Then he reminded Nero about the first hearing of Paul's second trial.

"Why is he still alive?"

"He was stupidly prosecuted on a charge of arson, and Nymphidius got a *non liquet* result."

"Well, I won't see *him* again. I warned him not to come back, didn't I? And we can't let him off—not when all his followers died. Simply reconvene your special tribunal at the Castra, Tigellinus, and condemn him for being one of those treasonable haters-of-mankind. Yes, crucify him, just like that . . . ah . . . what was his name? That fisherman?"

"Peter? Simon Peter?"

"Yes, Peter."

"That's not possible in this case, Princeps."

"And why not?"

"Paul's a Roman citizen. Peter was not."

"Very well, then, the sword."

Luke was able to alert Paul's close friends only after his death sentence, so quickly and without warning had Tigellinus struck. They had all they could do to arrive at the Castra Praetoria in time to accompany the apostle on his final journey. Pomponia was there—red-eyed and mournful—and so were Sabinus and Plautia, though Aulus was confined to the Esquiline with a respiratory illness.

Tigellinus had offered Paul his choice of sites for the execution, "just so long as it's outside the city walls."

Paul chose to die and be buried near the concentration of Christians on the Aventine, so he replied, "Beyond the Ostian Gate."

"All the way across Rome?" Tigellinus scowled. "Which would give you extra time with your friends, wouldn't it, Paul? Very well, then, the Ostian Gate.—Tribune," he called, "you're in charge of the execution. Take only a small detail. I don't think these sheep will give you any trouble." With a haughty smirk, Tigellinus bade them good-bye and left the Castra. Sabinus was merely grateful that Paul's final hour was not besmirched by the presence of Ofonius Tigellinus.

Young Timothy, Mark, Luke, and other elders were waiting outside the Castra and now joined the small, grieving company that wound its way southwestward across Rome. As Tigellinus had surmised, Paul used the time to good effect in giving final directives to the elders of the Roman church. Now they passed under the red brick arches of the Ostian Gate and continued a mile down the Via Ostiensis in order to avoid curiosity-seekers who might be alarmed at the execution of a Roman citizen. Finally they reached a green and level spot, surrounded by low, rolling hills, called Aquae Salviae, "Waters of Sage."

While the tribune and his men carefully set up a chopping block beneath a pine tree, Paul took leave of his friends. He commended the church to God, promising, "This is only the beginning of a cause that will one day be far greater than the Empire. We are *not* ashes, we are embers. Glowing in the Spirit, we shall rekindle the Faith so that Christ *will* triumph!"

Then he gave Pomponia and Plautia parting kisses. Plautia whispered something to him and a great smile bloomed across his face. Finally, he extended a firm hand of gratitude to Sabinus.

For the last time, Sabinus looked into the cool serenity of the apostle's eyes, and then glanced down in remorse. Once again, the chief magistrate of Rome could not prevent the execution of an innocent.

The tribune indicated that all was now ready.

"The time of my departure has come, beloved friends." Paul's face was wreathed in a peaceful smile. "As I once wrote you, Timothy, I have fought the good fight. I have finished the race. I have kept the Faith. And now the prize is waiting for me . . . the crown of righteousness which the Lord, that perfect judge, will award to me on that great day. And not to me only, but to you as well . . . and all who await his coming. Peace be with you all."

Then, bending over the block, he prayed, "Into your hands, O Lord, I commend my spirit."

The tribune raised his sharpened sword with both hands and brought it down in one clean sweep.

Pomponia, Plautia, and several others burst into tears. But Luke consoled them all with the assurance of the resurrection in which Christians confidently believed.

Sabinus had the execution detail help them bury Paul under an oak in a small parcel of wooded property nearby that The Twin Brothers owned. The much-traveled Paul of Tarsus had come to rest at last, buried, appropriately, near the side of a highway.

On the quiet trip back to Rome, Sabinus asked Plautia, "What did you whisper to him? What made him so happy?"

"I told him that I believed. That I was going to become a Christian too."

BOOK FIVE

THE EMBERS

30

PLAUTIA'S CONVERSION should not have surprised him, Sabinus told himself, but it did all the same. She had inherited her mother's sensitivity, and Roman women had always been more religious than their men. And yet in a happy marriage, such as theirs, everything was to be shared. But could he ever really share Plautia's Christianity? He doubted it.

For one thing, it was all so . . . un-Roman—something imported from the East, like Judaism. That there should be one god, not many, was easy to believe, he thought. In fact, it was intellectually satisfying to pin one's worship to a supreme deity, a better-than-Jupiter sort who was in final control of the universe. Yes, the Jews did well to be monotheistic, and it was not surprising that some members of the Roman nobility had become proselytes to Judaism. Even the learned Varro confessed his belief in the one great Soul of the Universe who could also be identified as the god of the Jews, he wrote. And Seneca seemed to share the belief. And Vergil. And Cicero.

But to go beyond this and claim that the one god extended himself into human form in the person of Jesus was difficult to accept. True, it was more rational that the deity should appear as a *man* rather than the various disguises Jupiter assumed when he chose to visit the world—like a snow-white bull or a lusty, rutting eagle. But suppose for a moment that the deity did exist and was sophisticated enough to embrace humanity intimately in the form of a man. Wouldn't he really have brought it off differently?

The Jesus figure, in that case, would not have been born in obscure circumstances at a tiny corner of the Empire far across the Mediterranean, but in the center of the world—in Athens or Rome. And he surely wouldn't have selected twelve uncultured, uneducated types as his disciples. A Paul of Tarsus, perhaps, and a Peter, but the others would have been ranking intellects of the day like Aristotle or leaders like Alexander—*if* the message were to take root in the Greek East. Inevitably, then, like all things Greek, the movement would filter westward into Rome. Here, in the hub of the Empire, the Jesus phenomenon and his disciples would set up their school and convince the Senate, the philosophers, and the masses. From Rome, in turn, the message would reach out to all the world. And if the deity were still suicidally minded—if he insisted on sacrificing the Jesus figure in a crucifixion—then Rome could serve as platform for that too. And wouldn't the cross show up far more prominently on the summit of the Capitoline ("The Place of the Head") than on that small ridge outside of Jerusalem called Golgotha ("The Place of the Skull")?

It was a quarrel between his two boys that pulled Sabinus out of his reverie. But before it all broke into separate shreds and dissolved, he was struck by one thought: even though it had not happened in the artless and obvious manner he had projected, the *result was the same*. The message had indeed reached Rome from the Greek East, and it was beginning to spread out from the capital.

Plautia was happy with the way Sabinus had accepted her new convictions. If he had uttered one critical word on the way home from Paul's burial, she would have collapsed, she felt. But he had maintained a wise, mature silence. And in the days following, while he had not applauded her resolve—that, she knew, would have been hypocrisy—he seemed to have understood it. Mother Pomponia, of course, was radiant at the news. For her it was the perfect antidote to grief in the days following Paul's execution.

She had no choice but to decide as she did, Plautia thought. The gods of Rome were sleeping, or dead, or had never existed—to let the city endure what it had. There was also the problem of focus: *whom* to worship. The pious Roman was supposed to juggle his loyalties between several dozen gods, goddesses, spirits, shades, demigods, and heroes. And dead emperors too! Against such a confusing mélange, the story of a one true God had come almost as an exuberant relief, and the reports that Paul and Peter told about the Christ carried their own indescribable authority and conviction.

But would her faith make any difference to their marriage, she wondered. That she could never have endured, for her joy with Sabinus was something sacred in itself—a kind of religion of its own. But her husband seemed to be adapting rather well to the circumstances. In fact, once when she asked him about it, he laughed and said, "Don't worry, darling. I think it's much more dignified to see you bowing your head in prayer from time to time than poking around a sheep's liver for clues to tomorrow."

His wan smile was broadening as he announced, quite pompously, "You know, I've just discovered the key to the moral problem of the Roman Empire . . ."

"What is it?"

"Romans have been getting their omens from animals for so long that they're starting to behave like them too. Have I told you the latest from the palace?"

Nero still sorely missed his beloved Poppaea. Remorsefully, he remembered that she had remained faithful to him, despite his numerous extramarital affairs. One afternoon at twilight, Tigellinus unveiled a surprise for him. A figure entered his suite dressed in one of Poppaea's favorite costumes—her gossamer turquoise tunic—and redolent with her favorite perfume. Nero stared as the girl came closer, and he clutched a handkerchief to his throat. There, beneath that transparent veil she frequently wore, was—*impossibly*—his beloved herself!

"Poppaea?" Nero asked hoarsely. "Goddess? Poppaea?" His knees shook and he nearly fainted. "My . . . my darling Poppaea?"

Tigellinus reached over and removed the veil. Nero staggered to his knees and clutched at his heart. *"Great Olympian gods!"* he shouted. "It *is* Poppaea! S-s-*say* something, dearest! H-have you forgiven me for what I did?"

"Relax, Caesar. No, it's not Poppaea." Tigellinus reached over and removed the blond wig the figure was wearing. "It's little Sporus. Growing up, isn't he?"

"You . . . you mean . . ."

"Remember that beautiful freedman's boy you once said looked so much like Poppaea? Well, he certainly does . . . more like her every day, in fact."

"By the gods, Sporus! You . . . you *are* so much like her."

The youth blushed prettily and gave Nero a coy smile.

Though no one outside Rome could really believe it, Nero actually started courting Sporus and soon fell in love with him. Several weeks later, he asked the boy to marry him.

Sporus did have an objection, though not the obvious one: "You're already *wife* to Pythagoras, Caesar," he pouted.

"But I'll be your *husband*, Sporus," Nero crooned, caressing his cheek.

Happily, Nero assigned Sporus a regular dowry, wrote up a nuptial contract, and later he publicly celebrated his wedding to the catamite, Tigellinus giving the veiled bride away. Guests even prayed that children would be born from such a union.

When Sabinus learned of it, he told Plautia, "Well, our palace pervert has finally exhibited *all* his talents. No other combinations are possible, I think."

Plautia, who barely understood such things, replied, "If only Nero's father had had a *wife* like Sporus!"

"Excellent, my dear!" Sabinus laughed.

One morning, as he walked into city headquarters, Sabinus found a huge graffito painted in ugly red lettering on the wall near the entrance:

THE FOES OF CAESAR *ALL* LIE DEAD?
AND HAS SABINUS NOTHING TO DREAD
FOR PLOTTING WITH PISO? CUT OFF HIS HEAD!

The shock bristled even the smallest hairs on his neck. But he heard his own voice calmly telling a custodian, "Whitewash this garbage off the wall."

He tried to forget about the incident. But later in the day he was summoned to the palace, his first conference with Nero in some time. Sabinus found the emperor strangely agitated, more like a suspicious, frightened canine ready to leap at him. Gingerly, Sabinus avoided touching on anything Nero might construe as a bone, while

avoiding a defensive posture lest he seize on it as some proof of guilt.
Once again, the frozen mask of normality.

After some banal platitudes, Nero brought him up short. "What
if it *were* true, Sabinus?" he asked.

"What, Caesar?"

"That you *were* one of Piso's men? That . . . that you actually
would have taken my life? You were friends with all the conspirators—Petronius, Seneca, Gallio. Quintus Lateranus *was* your relative
and business partner. You recommended the traitor Rufus to us.
And on the day set for the assassination, just *why* were your Urban
Cohorts on alert? No, don't look away, Sabinus, look me in the eye!"
And the imperial eyes were glistening with a new ferocity.

Sabinus fought to contain the icy flux within him so the climate
at the surface would remain unchanged. "The cohorts?" he replied.
"They were on alert for one very obvious reason, Caesar: to control
any disorders at the Feast of Ceres. And I recommended Rufus
purely because of his record in the grain supply." Then he tried a
desperate gamble by seizing the offensive. "If you're trying to be hu-
morous, Princeps, I consider it in *very* bad taste. You raised me to
highest office in Rome twice, so my loyalty should be obvious. Can
you find any fault with my record? Any at all?"

"I . . . I always thought you were reliable, Sabinus. But no one
else seems to think so."

"By that you mean . . . Tigellinus, I suppose?"

Nero turned away. "Tigellinus and I will be leaving for Greece in
early September—the games, the concert tour are finally confirmed.
Now, my freedman Helius will be in charge here while we're gone.
You'll be minding Rome while he minds the Empire." Then, facing
Sabinus directly again, he lowered his voice. "Helius will be watching you, Sabinus, *watching* you. Closely. He wonders, for example—
and so do I—why you daubed a coat of whitewash on your prefecture with . . . such embarrassing haste."

Sabinus' throat went dry, but he did not stammer his reply beyond a quick, inaudible gulp. "Perhaps Helius should be more concerned at finding the liars who defaced city property than in the
maintenance of those properties."

"That's all, Sabinus." Nero frowned, waving him off.

He was already out of the imperial offices when he heard Nero
call after him, "Oh, Prefect, I thought you'd like to know: your

brother Vespasian will be accompanying us to Greece as military aide. His son Titus, too."

"I'm delighted to hear that, Caesar."

While returning to city headquarters, Sabinus pondered both the news and its timing. Put baldly, if not unfairly, *why* had Nero chosen a mule-trader as military aide? Coincidence? More than that, it suddenly seemed clear. Nero and Tigellinus were serving him plain notice: "Don't try anything while we're gone, Sabinus. We have your brother and nephew as hostages."

Curse the Fates who were presiding over the insane course of Roman destiny! He had indeed planned to make his move against Nero while he was in Greece. It would have been the perfect time for it. But now his blundering brother was along as hostage. Unless—. He must have a talk with Vespasian immediately.

Ever since he convinced himself that he was an artist, Nero had been planning his concert tour of Greece, for only the aesthetic Hellenes could truly appreciate genius in a commoner or an emperor —to them it made no difference. Now, in the fall of 66, he set sail with a great chorus of Augustiani and a virtual army of entertainment laden with lyres, citharas, masks, costumes, and buskins.

Curious Greeks craned their necks to see the lord of the world as he disembarked in the land he so admired. By now his paunch had grown, his pustules had never really cleared, and his slender legs seemed more spindling than ever. But, as a kind of compensation, he had let his darkening blond locks grow long, and they now hung down his back in cascades of curls.

Nero had ordered that all the Greek festivals be held during his visit—something sacrilegious and unprecedented—and he carefully enrolled himself in each of the contests, performing from his repertory as tragic actor, reciter of his own poems, lyrist, and charioteer. The judges were very discerning, he thought: in every contest, they declared him the victor! He won everything there was to win at Olympia, Corinth, Delphi, and elsewhere—a grand total of 1,808 trophies and prizes.

Once, though, he nearly made a false step, as Vespasian wrote Sabinus. During a chariot race at Olympia, Nero tried to handle a ten-horse team, but careened out of his cab and was nearly killed. For several moments, everyone had the unparalleled spectacle of seeing the Roman emperor rolling over the sands of the hippodrome. Judges halted the race until Nero, skinned and bruised, could be loaded back onto his chariot. When he had completed the laps he had missed and several more for good measure, the judges ordered the race resumed, but Nero was unable to hold out and gave up before the end. The victor? Nero, of course! Whereupon he lavished Roman citizenship and a million sesterces on the judges.

The Greeks were no fools. If the emperor wanted to play, they would play too—and win immense concessions in the process. Early the next year, Nero proclaimed at least local self-government for the Greeks.

In Rome, meanwhile, a courier delivered another letter from Greece to the Quirinal. "It's from Vespasian!" Sabinus called to Plautia. Then he slit the heavy wax seals and began reading aloud to her:

T. Flavius Vespasian to T. Flavius Sabinus, greeting.—You will not believe the incredible changes in my life, dear brother! At first my prospects were typically terrible. I began by offending Caesar at Eleusis. He was about to participate in the Mysteries there when the herald, as usual, warned "all the wicked and godless" to flee before ceremonies began. Nero got so frightened he refused to participate! And that's when he saw me shaking with laughter.—Then, during another of Caesar's concerts here, I—you will surely be disgusted with me—I fell asleep again. This time Nero went into a rage. "I never want to see your ugly face again!" he cried, and expelled me from the imperial party.

"But where shall I go?" I asked Phoebus, his freedman. "Go to Hades!" he shouted. So I went—not really to Hades—but into exile at a little cottage near Corinth. I'd be there today but for the Jewish revolt in Palestine.

The rebellion there is getting much worse: our forces have been driven out of Jerusalem and most of Judea. Since there's no other general around, Nero was forced to use me, and I've now been appointed supreme commander in charge of 60,000 troops to put down the revolt. You wouldn't believe the praise and flattery Nero is heaping on me, now that he has need of me!—I am just leaving Corinth, and my Titus will join me with

a legion from Egypt. Farewell from "the liberated hostages."
Good hunting!—Given the Ides of February, A.U.C. 820.

Sabinus put the letter down and broke out laughing for joy. "The
vicissitudes of Fortune!" He beamed. "From commander to mule-
trader and back to commander again. *Good* for Vespasian!"

"He should be able to carry his own weight from now on." Plautia smiled. "Did he ever repay the money you loaned him?"

"Part of it. But he's a good risk now." Sabinus grinned. "Though
I can't say the same for Nero." His jaw was clenching with determination and his eyes stared off over the top of her head for several
moments. "Good hunting *indeed!* At last," he whispered, then
louder, "Yes, *at last!* It's not just that Vespasian's no longer a hostage
—he's now one of the strongest men in the Empire! *At last,* carissima! Our great hour has *finally* come."

Minutes later, Sabinus paced about his office in a cadence that
sounded to him like the drumroll of destiny. One last time he
searched out and dissected the alternatives he had been mulling
every day over the past months. Actually, there were only three—just
three ways to topple a Roman emperor. *One:* assassination. But ever
since the Pisonian conspiracy, Nero was more closely guarded than
ever. *Two:* revolt of the Praetorian Guard. But with Tigellinus and
Nymphidius as co-commanders, that was clearly impossible. *Three:*
revolution by the provincial legions. If enough commanders could be
persuaded, it was also the most formidable way to dethrone a Caesar.

It *had* to be the legions, Sabinus reflected. Commanders across the
Empire were furious at the fate of General Corbulo, who had gen-
erated miracles for Rome on the eastern front. Suspecting a conspiracy, Nero had summoned Corbulo and two commanders from Germany to a conference in Greece, where he had all three commit
suicide. That, in fact, was why only Vespasian was available to put
down the Jewish revolt, Sabinus now realized. The commanders
were murmuring indeed. They were also tired of the Praetorian
Guard deciding when to make and unmake emperors. They were
tired, too, of trying to maintain discipline in the troops at a time
when their commander-in-chief was an actor, recitalist, multimur-
derer, and pederast. *The legions!* His brother now suddenly controlled the East. He must therefore win over the commanders of the
West.

"Vindex," he whispered to himself. What had his protégé in Gaul at the time of the census said in his last letter: "If ever I can serve you, Sabinus, command me: I owe my entire career to you!" And Vindex, one of Nero's most caustic secret critics, was now Governor General of Gaul! Time to contact Vindex!

Sabinus paced his office several minutes more to formulate all the arguments. Then he sat down at his desk to write out the most important letter of his life, a solemn call to revolution in the name of saving Rome. He also suggested that Governor Galba of Spain and Otho of Lusitania—Poppaea's former husband—would doubtless make common cause with Vindex, tearing the whole West from Nero's grasp.

Imprisoning the message in a cocoon of canvas and sealing wax, he called in his most trusted aide, hung the message around his neck, and gave him a secret briefing. At the end of it, he said, "Leave at once. And remember, no one but *Vindex himself* sees this. If he agrees, you then visit Galba and Otho to coordinate it all."

Nero staged his triumphant return to Rome in January of 68. A portion of the city wall was breached so that he could ride through it in his chariot, a traditional gesture permitted Olympic victors. Rome was decked with garlands, blazing with lights, reeking with incense and perfume. Nero himself was clad in purple and gold, and crowned with the Olympic victor's wreath of wild olive. All the trophies he had won were paraded through the city, along with signs identifying them, and then put on permanent display in his rambling—and now cluttered—private quarters.

"I understand I have Helius to thank for this fine reception, not you, Sabinus," said Nero, in their first encounter after his return. They were wandering through the nearly completed Golden House, a lavish labyrinth of gilded, pearled corridors with ceilings of fretted ivory. Sabinus took his cue from their surroundings and lied, "It was more a division of labor, Princeps. Helius took care of your reception. I thought it best to keep our city crews busy with this." He spread his arms.

Nero seemed satisfied for the moment. He walked to a corner of the dining room and pulled a lever. Ceiling panels opened to let flower petals flutter down on them while hidden jets sprayed perfume. Then he peered out of a window. The new palace was surrounded by a countryside of lakes, woods, and vineyards—all in the very heart of Rome.

"Good," Nero finally commented. "Now I can begin to live like a human being."

The guttural voice of Ofonius Tigellinus intruded. "Caesar and I have been discussing your record, Prefect. And your sympathies. We quite agree that . . . you are not to leave the city of Rome until further notice."

"I take my orders only from Caesar, Tigellinus. Not you." Sabinus struggled to remain calm. "Am I under some indictment, Princeps?"

Nero looked away nervously. "No, Sabinus," he said quietly. "But . . . do stay in Rome."

For the next weeks, Sabinus lived in a clutch of suspense. His courier had returned from Gaul and Iberia with a strong but secret positive response from the governors there, and Vindex had been particularly enthusiastic. But no further word had arrived from the West. All the while, his own Quirinal mansion was being put on continual surveillance by a series of poorly disguised praetorian agents skulking near the place, who were doubtless reporting everything they saw directly to Tigellinus. After bumping into them several times, Sabinus ordered an equally continuous guard at his place from the Urban Cohorts to show Tigellinus that he would not, under any circumstances, be intimidated.

Well and good at the surface. But how disguise the gnawing dread that was devouring the happiness of each day and converting the life experience into a lingering nightmare for himself, Plautia, and her parents on the Esquiline?

Early in March, she did brighten his life by presenting him their first daughter, a tiny infant with remarkably long raven hair, whom they named Plautilla, "Little Plautia," a glad interim in all the stress. But even while dandling the very apple of his eye, Sabinus could not help but wonder what kind of world it was into which they had brought another human life.

Just a week after Plautilla's naming day, her grandfather Aulus hurried into city headquarters with tears in his eyes. "Get them out of here!" he commanded, as Sabinus dismissed several urban secretaries. Only then did he notice that they were tears of excitement and joy.

"It's *happening*, Sabinus!" he exulted. "We *just* got word in the Senate! Vindex has issued a formal proclamation, calling on imperial armies everywhere to rise in revolt against Nero! He has one hundred thousand troops massed in Gaul for revolution!"

Sabinus let out a whoop of joy. "What about Galba and Otho? Any word?"

"That's just the point." Aulus caught his breath. "They're *joining* the revolution! Galba's Spain, Otho's Lusitania, and Vindex's Gaul— the *whole west* is demanding that Nero abdicate!"

Sabinus' open palm went crashing down onto his desk. "At last!" he exclaimed. "*At last!* How is the Senate reacting?"

"I've never seen such . . . private joy in the Fathers' faces. Because of the praetorians, of course, they can't do anything at the moment."

"I'll write Vespasian at once," Sabinus decided, "even though he could hardly break off the Jewish War to advance on Rome!"

At that moment, Nero was down in Naples watching wrestling contests. It was shortly after lunch when Tigellinus ran almost frantically into the arena with the ominous news from Gaul. Nero merely leaped down from his seat to join in tussling with the wrestlers. Eight more days he idled in Naples, and it was only when Vindex issued another taunt against "Bronzebeard the Bad Lyre-Player" that he was finally stung and wrote the Senate "to take care of the Gallic matter."

More ominous messages finally sent him in a huff to Rome. He set a price of ten million sesterces on the head of Vindex, but Vindex offered even more for Nero's: "Anyone bringing me that buffoon's head can have mine in return," he vowed. Sabinus, now moving in a delirium of joy, knew he meant it. Vindex was a patriot.

Several days later, when Galba's revolt was also confirmed, Nero kicked over his breakfast table. Then he tore his robe, beat his brow, and carefully fainted onto a bed, where he lay prostrate for an hour. Then he roused himself and officially declared Galba a public enemy, confiscating all his property in Rome. In turn, Galba declared Nero a public enemy and seized all his property in Spain. Auctions were held in both places, and Galba came off far the richer from the proceeds.

Still Nero refused to appear in the Senate. One night, instead, he summoned the leading senators, Sabinus, and all his prefects to a conference at his villa. Carefully masking his elation at the revolt, Sabinus was planning to give Nero all the wrong advice. He was amazed at how badly Nero was degenerating physically. A red face and blondish hair still marked the man, but now his sly, suspicious eyes peered out at him between bulges of oily flesh that had puffed up his face. He was a heap of bloated fat, poorly concealed under the costliest garments. Old at thirty, Nero conducted the conference as if he were oblivious of events outside Rome.

Then, with a wave of his handkerchief, he suddenly broke off the conclave. "Come with me, gentlemen." He smiled. "I've something to show you." He led them into a hall where some lofty and strange-looking contrivances were standing—pipes, vertical and horizontal, and keyboards of some kind. "They've just arrived from Alexandria," he effused.

"What . . . are they, Princeps?" Sabinus wondered.

"Hydraulic water organs, silly! The wind pressure for the pipes is kept constant by these columns of water," he pointed. "Here, I'll show you how they sound." He clapped his hands. "That's so the slaves will start pumping."

Like a child with a tantalizing new toy, Nero began tooting away at the largest organ, covering his ears at the chirping, high notes and bringing the most out of the instrument's booming bass. "How's *that*, my friends?" he exulted.

"Superb, Caesar," said Tigellinus, in a rising flush of embarrassment. "Now about Vindex and the—"

"I've discovered how to get even lower notes from it." He beamed and went on to lecture on the theory of water organs, demonstrating various note combinations on the instruments. "I plan to have these set up in the theater and give a concert soon—all, of course, with the kind permission of Vindex." He winked.

Sabinus left the impromptu recital with a lighter heart than he had known in months. Apparently, it would all go easier than he had feared, and he was angry with himself for not having launched the revolution earlier. Nero had clearly lost touch with reality. He was tottering and must soon fall. If only Rome could be spared further bloodshed in that collapse.

He must now keep Nero off balance, Sabinus resolved, also because of what this did to Tigellinus. He could still see the perplexed and wounded look in Tigellinus' eyes during Nero's organ recital. Hurrying over to his agent on the Caelian, who was now supervising Twin Brothers Enterprises, he asked him, "Do we still supply Nero's wine?"

"That we do, Prefect." He smiled. "Caesar drinks as much Gemini brand in various vintages as all others combined."

"Excellent! Now tell me this: is there any way you can double the alcoholic content in bottles you supply him? Or increase it in some way?"

"We've been trying to distill stronger wines, but our only success is with the grapes from Mount Etna. Wine from them is almost twice as powerful. But why would—"

"Don't ask. Make another delivery to Nero's villa and replace Gemini bottles already in his wine-cellar with the stronger stuff. Soon as you can, all right?"

"Certainly, Prefect."

Sabinus hurried off with a low smile. Nero's lethargy after meals would be even longer now, his wits more addled than ever. His wine consumption had been on the steady increase as it was.

Only military force could now put down the rebellions, Nero finally realized, and he prepared a legion to invade Gaul. Crush Vindex, and Galba and Otho would have to sue for peace. Tigellinus was working out the strategy with his praetorian officers' staff when one of the tribunes complained that massive funds from the war chest were being diverted at Nero's orders.

Storming over to the imperial villa, Tigellinus found Nero in his cups, still reclining languidly at lunch although it was late afternoon. He was, however, able to account for the missing funds. They were for a train of wagons that would carry his concubines and theatrical instruments to Gaul. "It needn't actually come to bloodshed," he told Tigellinus. "No, not at all. I'll simply stand in front of Vindex's forces and . . . and do nothing more than weep. The troops will be so touched at the sight of their emperor in tears that they'll stop their rebellion. And then I'll give a concert in honor of the glorious victory." Nero was smiling. And he was serious.

Tigellinus stared uncomprehendingly.

Sabinus, meanwhile, was trying to coordinate the revolution through a mass of secret correspondence with Vindex and the other legionary commanders. He urged a general invasion of Italy by the western legions, his brother to join from the East once the Jewish rebellion had been quelled. Everything now depended on the attitude

of Rome's seven legions along the Rhine River, which had not yet
joined the revolt, even though Sabinus had pleaded with them to do
so.

Early in May, his personal aide arrived with the latest message
from Gaul. "I have . . . *extremely* bad news, Clarissimus. You . . .
you'd best sit down for this."

"What happened?" Sabinus tensed.

"Verginius Rufus, commander of our Rhine legions, finally made
his decision. He . . . stayed loyal to Nero and attacked Vindex's
forces in eastern Gaul. Defeated them. Badly. He killed about
20,000."

"What about Vindex himself?"

"Committed suicide just after the battle."

Sabinus sank slowly into his chair, clutching a roll of cheek flesh
in his fingers until the skin was tawny white. "Vindex . . . Vindex,"
he muttered, in a daze. "Oh, *brave* and *faithful* Verginius! Such a
loyal soldier!" Tears welled up in his eyes. "Stupid, stinking *dullard,*
Verginius! Blasted *dolt!* Helping that murderous voluptuary out of the
grave in which he belongs."

For some moments his hands covered his face. Finally, he asked,
"And Galba . . . Otho . . . what'll they ever do now?"

"They're in a fiercely bad position, of course. But what *can* they
do, Prefect? Retract the nasty things they've said about Nero? Apologize for treason?"

"They *might,* believe it or not. Because Nero's under pressure,
he's in a *very* forgiving mood lately. I've *got* to steel them up. It's our
only chance."

He sat down at his desk, lost in thought for some minutes, and
then carefully wrote this note:

Sabinus to Galba, *Salve!* Forget the code. This message gets
through or the cause collapses. Despite poor Vindex, *you and
Otho must continue the revolution!* Nero remains very much
off balance. At the moment, he's more worried about rival actors
catching the public fancy—"taking advantage of Caesar's busy
days," he puts it—than in saving the Empire. Exactly four
weeks from today, I am mobilizing the Urban Cohorts and the
Praetorian Guard in your behalf. My aide will supply all the
details. *Start marching,* Galba! Given the Nones of May,
A.U.C. 821.

The aide was awestruck. "The Praetorians? But . . . but with Tigellinus, they'd never—"

"Leave that to me. Now, here's my plan . . ."

In the days following, Sabinus kept his ears to the ground. A true revolution could never succeed without the people, he knew, and he wondered how the plebes were taking the current crisis. The common people were always more amused than terrified by Nero. He had purged none of their ranks but treated them instead to a series of sensational shows. Yet even the plebes were starting to murmur, Sabinus found, and in not very muted tones. They were hungry. Nero had mishandled the wheat supply. One day, though, news reached Rome that a grain fleet was sailing into the harbor at Ostia, and thousands of plebes hurried over to the port to help unload the cargo. All of it turned out to be *sand* for the Vatican hippodrome! Already surly, the people's mood now curdled.

Good, Sabinus concluded. Now was the time. Months ago he had abandoned the comparative luxury of merely treading water in the vicious whirlpool of Roman politics for direct involvement against Nero. But others, not he, had taken the prime risks. No longer. The time had come at last for direct exposure, whatever the hazards. Nero had to be overthrown—immediately. The Western legions were taking far too much time. If the Rhine legions marched south, or if Nero recovered his wits in the interim, he might yet survive.

Sabinus made his move. On the night of June 1, long after Plautia and the household had gone to bed, he held a clandestine encounter at his place with only one man, who had arrived without escort. A broad-shouldered hulk with hair no lighter than ebony, the man was Nymphidius Sabinus, co-commander of the Praetorian Guard, the judge who had presided at the first hearing of Paul's second trial.

"So," said Sabinus, as he escorted him into his library and carefully shut the door. "The civil and the military heads of Rome finally meet in private."

"And we're both named Sabinus." Nymphidius smiled, showing a row of milk-colored teeth. But this was the extent of any pleasantries, for his muddy visage tautened again and his eyes narrowed suspiciously.

"First of all, Prefect," Sabinus began, "where is your colleague Tigellinus these days?"

"Why do you ask?" Nymphidius inquired, with a frown.

Sabinus bit his lip. Nymphidius was not giving an inch, at least not at the start. It might all be more difficult than he had imagined. How did two conspirators—or one conspirator and one candidate— ever get into serious dialogue without tipping their hands? What were Cassius' opening words to Brutus?

"Very well, I'll be more direct: who *really* controls the Praetorian Guard now, Nymphidius? You or Tigellinus?"

"We're both in charge. What do you mean?"

"A simple question. Why are you being so evasive?"

"I'm just wondering what you're driving at . . . why you called me here . . . why you insisted on all this secrecy."

"If you knew me better, my friend, you wouldn't have to ask such questions. And if you've gained your impressions of me through Tigellinus, you must know I'm a scheming traitor who ought to be eliminated." He paused briefly, then resumed. "But I'm only a Roman, Nymphidius, a Roman who would still like to pride himself on that designation years from now. And so I'll be candid, whatever the risks." He paused, pondered the syllables that would forever change his life, and then spoke them: "The time has come . . . to depose Nero."

Sabinus carefully studied the praetorian commander for a reaction. A sudden look of shock or horror on the man's face could seal his own doom. But Nymphidius merely crinkled his eyes.

"Go on," he said.

"I'll tell you how I'd *much* prefer to see Nero deposed: an edict of the Senate, pure and simple, with your praetorians following their lead. But I'm not sure the Fathers would make such a decision without cocking their ears in the direction of the Castra Praetoria. The Guard made both Claudius and Nero."

"Aren't some of the legions marching against Nero?" Nymphidius asked, with a smirk.

"And it's taking them a blessed long time to get here. But they *will* get to Rome—eventually. And then what will your praetorians do? Fight for that murdering actor and parricide, poisoner and pervert? Will you really drench Rome with more blood? Or do the sane thing and abandon him for Galba?"

For several moments, Nymphidius studied his sandals. Then he said, "Galba's no prize."

"Of course he isn't! But next to Nero, he'll look like Romulus himself. And he also has the advantage of being seventy-three years old: he can't make that many mistakes before he dies. But Nero must go in any case. And *now*. Otherwise the state's lost."

Nymphidius scratched his scruffy cheek for some moments. Finally he said, "So—you want me to get the Guard to declare for Galba?"

"The moment you do"—Sabinus nodded—"I'll introduce a motion in the Senate to depose Nero. It will pass, I can assure you, because my Urban Cohorts will also be declaring for Galba. Your praetorians will make it unanimous."

Suddenly Nymphidius gave him a vicious scowl and dripped the words out of his mouth like sour wine: "You're committing treason, Prefect . . . outright, treacherous *treason!* Tigellinus has been looking for an excuse to sever your head, and it's obvious why." He walked over and held his face just inches from Sabinus. "I could expose you in twenty minutes and you'd never see dawn. In fact, why don't I do just that?"

"I could physically prevent your leaving this house, Nymphidius," Sabinus answered coolly, staring back at the commander without blinking.

"Your servants? You think I'm afraid of them?"

"I was referring to *myself*, Prefect! I once gave Tigellinus a battered face. I seem to do well against praetorian prefects." He glared at him for several moments, and if one board in the floor had creaked it might have come to blows. Then Sabinus said, "But I won't try anything so obvious this time, because I'd have to kill you to keep you quiet. And I'm no murderer."

"You wouldn't get that far, Sabinus," he sneered. "So, then, what happens when I tell Nero?"

Sabinus hesitated, but then the words poured out. "Civil War, Nymphidius. I'll order my Urban Cohorts to join the legions against you and the praetorians."

"Ha! We'll win. We'll smash your police."

"I'd never give you the chance to shed more blood here in Rome, Prefect. My cohorts are on alert to march out of the city the moment I give the order. We'll establish contact with Galba's forces in north Italy."

"Oh, I'm impressed," said Nymphidius sardonically. "But the Rhine legions are loyal. With them we can beat your friends Galba and Otho."

Sabinus shook his head. "Discontent is brewing also in the Rhine legions, I understand. But if not, think, dear Nymphidius, *think:* where else does Rome have legions?"

A gathering frown suddenly shaded the face of the praetorian commander. "The East," he muttered. "Your brother, Vespasian . . . would he really march on Rome?"

"I believe he could provide the . . . necessary honor guard," Sabinus admitted, with a wan smile. "Of course, that would delay things a bit. But meanwhile, there would be no police to keep order in the city, and your praetorians would have their hands full trying to keep the lid on a rebellious lot of citizens who hate Nero almost as much as I do."

"You . . . you'd actually do that, wouldn't you, Sabinus?"

"My troops are armed and ready."

Instantly Nymphidius' face bloomed into a great smile as he reached over to clasp Sabinus' shoulder. "I'm with you, Prefect! I'm *with you!* For the last couple of weeks I've been looking for an excuse to drop my allegiance to that . . . blundering buffoon of a Caesar. But I *had to be sure* of your politics. *And* your determination. Nero's agents are *everywhere* lately."

Slowly Sabinus sank onto a couch and wiped his brow. "*You* should be on the stage, Nymphidius, not Nero. What a front! Excuse me a moment . . ."

Presently, Sabinus reappeared with a wine flask and poured out two generous goblets for them.

"Now, as I was asking," Sabinus continued, smiling with profound relief, "who commands the Guard? You, or the elusive Tigellinus?"

"We don't even know where Tigellinus *is* for sure," Nymphidius chuckled. "He simply abandoned Nero: couldn't stand the way he was facing the crises . . ."

"When?" Sabinus could hardly believe the good news.

"Two days ago was the last anyone saw him. And Tigellinus *is* a master coward, you know. Just like the proverbial rat scampering off a foundering galley, he's left Rome."

"What's the mood of the praetorians? *Will* they sack Nero and declare for Galba?"

"Yes—*if* I promise them enough of a gift from Galba. But it's Nero's German bodyguard I'm worried about. They have a deadly loyalty . . ."

"The Germans?" Sabinus paced the room in thought. Then he stopped and smiled. "Let's simply get rid of them."

"How?"

"Wasn't Nero planning a trip to Egypt?"

"Yes—he wanted to give concerts there, but now he's sailing there for his own safety."

"All right. Why not have him send the Germans on ahead? To 'check security in Alexandria and welcome him on arrival.'"

Nymphidius nodded emphatically. "Yes. Yes indeed. He'll do it too, if I suggest it."

"When does he plan to sail?"

"June 9 or 10."

"All right, then. Here's the schedule: the German bodyguard goes off at once. Then, on June 8, I'll enter the Senate and ask it to depose Nero. Aulus Plautius, my father-in-law, will support my motion with news that your praetorians are deciding the same way. Meanwhile, my Urban Cohorts will have declared for Galba, and we'll all march over to the Castra Praetoria and help you convince the Guard, if necessary." Sabinus' eyes were blazing. "Well, what do you think of it, Nymphidius?"

He smiled and reached out to clasp Sabinus' hand. "It has to succeed—*if* we stay in close touch."

"Twice a day from now on. Let me know when the Germans have sailed."

"Right."

Now Sabinus grasped his cup and held it high. "*Roma resurgens!*" he toasted.

Nymphidius nodded. "To Rome—rising again!"

31

AT LAST Nero grasped that he was in serious circumstances, and he cast about for help. But Tigellinus had deserted him—the scoundrel was rumored to be somewhere in southern Italy—and only his palace staff was left. But if he kept his wits, his charmed destiny would see him through once again, Nero reasoned, toying with a string of amber worry-beads. His aides were already in Ostia preparing escape ships, for if he could but reach Egypt, he would support himself there as a lyre-player, if necessary. "This little talent of ours will afford us daily bread," he claimed. He did, however, procure a vial of greenish poison from the witch Locusta in case his escape plan miscarried, hiding it inside a golden box in the bedroom of the villa where he was still residing.

Maybe, though, escape wasn't necessary after all. Hurrying into his office, he rehearsed a plan with his private secretary. "I'll dress in black, Epaphroditus, walk into the Forum, and mount the rostrum. There I'll beg the people to forgive me for any past offenses. I'll even fall on my knees if necessary . . ."

The rotund little secretary looked up at him and replied, "Do you *really* think you could soften their hearts in such a way, Caesar?"

"I think so. Why not? But if they won't have me back, I'll ask for something less . . . say . . . the prefecture of Egypt. Or maybe the kingship of Jerusalem?"

Epaphroditus shook his pudgy cheeks in dismay. "The people are hungry, Caesar. They're angry. They might even tear you to pieces before you reached the rostrum."

"Gods!" Nero whimpered. "What . . . what can I do, Epaphroditus?"

"I don't know, Caesar. It was foolish of you to send your German bodyguard on to Egypt, I think."

"But Nymphidius advised me to . . ."

"Yes, and I wonder why. Any word from Ostia yet on the escape ships?"

"No." Nero's pout now faded into a smile. "But I know I'll get through all this: when I was in Greece, the Oracle at Delphi told me, 'Watch out for the seventy-third year!' Bah! I'm only thirty. I still have a long life ahead of me."

The freedman looked up at him. "Princeps, did it ever occur to you that Galba . . . is seventy-three years old?"

Horror gripped Nero as he stalked out into the Servilian Gardens and paced their wooded lanes, plotting desperately. Returning to his villa about midnight, he summoned the palace guard. No one replied. All the remaining praetorians had left. He yelled for anybody who was there to show himself. Epaphroditus and several freedmen appeared. "But where are my friends?" Nero wailed pathetically, and then went from door to door in the palatial villa to find them. The rooms were empty.

In a panic, Nero fled to his bedroom, which he found in shocking disorder. While he was out roaming the gardens, even his valets had deserted him, taking all his valuables, including the golden box with the poison. Nero collapsed onto his bed, pressing his head between his hands. "They could have *had* the box," he cried, tears streaming down his face, "but I needed the poison."

Now he darted up from his bed and ran out of the villa.

"Where are you going?" Epaphroditus called.

"To fling myself into the Tiber!" he replied, "–iber," "–iber," re-echoing through the cavernous halls.

In a short time, though, he was back. "I need some place to hide while I plan my escape," said Nero, with a new determination. "Where can I go?"

Phaon, another of his freedmen, replied, "I have a villa in the northeastern suburbs. It's between the Via Nomentana and the Via Salaria . . . near the fourth milestone."

"Good, Phaon, brilliant. We'll go there . . ."

Barefoot and dressed only in a tunic, Nero put on a faded cloak, covering the lower part of his face with a handkerchief, then mounted a horse and rode out into the night. Epaphroditus, Phaon, and the catamite Sporus accompanied him on other mounts. Their route led them dangerously close to the Castra Praetoria, near enough for Nero to hear shouts of "Victory to Galba!" and "Nero has warbled his last!" Everything was happening exactly as Sabinus had scheduled.

The dark early hours of June 9 were awesome to the horsemen. Flashes of lightning in the distance and rumbles were heralding an approaching storm, but nothing terrified Nero so much as comments of late-drinking roisterers who were making their way home: "Who're they?" one asked. "Prob'ly after Nero."

At the outskirts of Rome, they rode through some low hills until they came to a bypath leading to Phaon's villa. Here they turned their horses loose and made their way on foot through bushes, brambles, and reeds. Just behind the villa was a sand pit, where Phaon whispered to Nero, "Hide here until I can dismiss my household staff tomorrow morning."

"Oh no," Nero objected. "I'm not going underground while I'm still alive."

"Sshhh, Caesar!" Phaon warned. "All right, then. We'll dig a secret entrance into the basement. Help me, brothers."

All helped except Nero, who walked over to a water hole nearby where he scooped up the water and drank it from his hands. "So this is Nero's snow-cooled, distilled water," he remarked grimly. Then he sat down and pulled the briars out of his cloak.

When the passage tunnel was ready, Nero crawled on all fours into the villa and lay down on an old couch in a small, empty slave's room. His companions brought him coarse bread and water. In whispers, they now plotted Nero's escape.

"Well and good to declare him a public enemy," Sabinus told a predawn meeting of his officers, "but where is the man himself? He's escaped so many times before."

Quickly mustering two companies of mounted police, he rode to the villa in the Servilian Gardens where Nero was last reported. Bursting through the main entrance, they clattered inside.

"In the name of the Senate and the Roman People," Sabinus called out, "I have orders to arrest Lucius Domitius Ahenobarbus, formerly Nero Caesar!"

Only echoes replied.

"Search the place," Sabinus commanded. "Bring me anyone you find."

The police fanned out into the villa. Minutes later they came back with a gardener and two kitchen servants.

"Is this *all* you could find? Out of a staff of hundreds?" Turning to the three, Sabinus asked, "Where's Nero?"

The women shrugged their shoulders.

"Do you know?" he asked the gardener.

The man slowly shook his head, avoiding Sabinus' eyes.

Sabinus grabbed him by the shoulders and held him tight. "Where is Caesar?"

The gardener cleared his throat and said, "He was always kind to me . . ."

"But he was a monster to hundreds of others. Your last chance, or I'm arresting you for high treason."

Sadly, the man nodded. "Late last night . . . on horseback. Epaphroditus, Phaon . . . I couldn't see the fourth."

"Did they say where they were going?"

"No. Well . . . one of them did mention the Via Salaria . . ."

Sabinus studied the floor for several moments. "Phaon's villa." He suddenly brightened.

"One contingency we must admit, Caesar," Phaon whispered in the basement of his villa. "May the gods forbid, but you *may* be found here . . ."

"In which case I must . . . die first. Yes, let's . . . get all that ready. Why not here . . . in the floor?"

"What, Caesar?"

"My grave," Nero said, trembling. "Dig it to the proportions of my body. And Phaon, do you have any pieces of marble around? Find something. The earth alone . . . seems so common. And Sporus dear, do fetch some water and some wood."

"Why? Oh . . . to . . ." Then he broke into tears.

"Yes, water to anoint the body," Nero said in a hollow tone, warped by dread. "And fire to consume it after you've put it . . . down there. But remember, there's to be *no* mutilation of the body. The"—he broke down and wept—"the head must not be severed from the body." He could not bring himself to say "my head."

He tried to get some sleep during the early morning hours, but he started at every sound—a dog barking, a twig breaking in the wind, the rustle of a bush. With the first light of dawn, a courier delivered a message to Phaon.

Nero snatched the dispatch out of Phaon's hands and read it. It was a public notice from the Senate:

WANTED FOR ARREST

Lucius Domitius Ahenobarbus

formerly *Nero Caesar*, whom the Senate has declared a public enemy. He shall be punished in the ancient fashion. Anyone knowing his whereabouts must report them immediately to the nearest magistrate.

"What's that? Punishment 'in the ancient fashion'?" Nero groaned.

No one seemed ready to tell him, and Nero grew angry.

"All right," said Epaphroditus. "The criminal—or rather, the victim," he corrected himself, "is stripped naked, his neck is chained inside a V-shaped yoke, and he is marched through the city . . ."

"And? And then?"

"Then he is beaten to death with rods, and his body is thrown down into the Tiber."

"*Great Jupiter,* no!" Nero cried, and now began shedding tears in earnest. He reached down to his belt for two daggers he had carried with him from the villa, trying the point and the edge of each. "This one," he said. "But only if necessary."

Then he gingerly tested the size of his basement grave by crawling into it. Whimpering a bit, he then climbed back out and pleaded, "Why won't anyone say anything? Sporus? Little Sporus, sing a lament for me, my dear. Or cry a little, will you?"

Sporus lowered his pretty head and tried.

"I have it." Nero smiled. "Maybe one of you could set me an example by . . . taking your own life ahead of me." He held out his hand and eagerly offered one of his daggers. But no one seemed ready to accept his suggestion.

"For shame, Nero," he frowned, chastising himself. "This doesn't become you . . . doesn't become you at all. *Courage*, man!"

He walked to a corner of the basement and stared at the stone and mortar for several moments. Then he whipped about and said, "I wonder if we aren't giving up too easily, my friends." He had a glint in his eyes, which started twitching with excitement. Fresh energy seemed to suffuse him as he paced the basement in thought, his dark blond curls swinging with every step as he cocked his head low and tightened the muscles in his bull neck for an attempted charge out of the constricting corral of Fate.

"Yes." He smiled. "Yes, there *is* a way. We'll stay under cover during the daylight hours. Then tonight, we steal out, head eastward across the Apennines, and go down the coast to Brundisium. There we'll get a ship and—*what's that?*" he suddenly cried, blanching with terror.

Horses' hoofs were thundering to a crescendo outside. Phaon darted upstairs to investigate. Nero quavered, whispering a line from the *Iliad*: "Hark! The hoofs of galloping horses strike my ear!"

Phaon returned, crying, "Urban Cohorts, Caesar! They've come to arrest you."

His face white, his forehead wet with sweat, Nero turned to his secretary and pleaded, "H-help me, Epaphroditus . . . if it's necessary." Clutching a dagger, he brought it up to his throat and said, "*Qualis artifex pereo!* What an artist dies in me!"

Then he plunged the point into his throat, avoiding his voice box. But the blade had entered only an inch. Nero's wild, agonized eyes told Epaphroditus what he had to do. He gave the dagger a penetrating thrust several inches deeper into Nero's thick neck and then moved it from side to side, widening the wound. Soon Nero collapsed at his feet, and the floor of the basement was washed in a warm tide of imperial blood.

There was a loud pounding at the door upstairs. Brushing aside the domestic who answered it, Sabinus and his centurions stormed inside, calling out the arrest notice. A groan from the basement broke the silence, and they rushed downstairs—to a pathetic sight. Nero, his eyes pink with tears and burning with pain, was clutching the end of a dagger buried in a flowing belt of red girdling his neck.

Sabinus was staggered. He had come to the villa, saturated with vengeance—the spirits of dead friends and hundreds of victims driving him on. His one great dream over the past months—no, years—

had been to load Nero with chains and present him triumphantly to the Senate, or happily slash a sword through his squat, ugly neck if he resisted in the slightest.

But the gasping, kicking victim below him wrenched out a measure of pity. Hurrying to Nero's side, he ordered a centurion to try to stanch the bleeding by putting a cloak next to the wound. Nero looked up at him. "Too late, Sabinus," he gurgled. "This . . . *is* loyalty."

A final gasp and kick and he stopped breathing, his eyes gaping open in their sockets. Sabinus and the others shuddered at the sight. The thirty-year-old ruler of the world—the last of the Julio-Claudian Caesars—was truly dead.

Shaking his head in persistent disbelief, Sabinus gave Epaphroditus and his friends custody of the remains. Then he left.

Nero's body was taken back to Rome, laid out in white robes embroidered with gold, and quickly cremated lest it be mutilated by the people. His two nurses from childhood carried an urn full of his ashes to the family mausoleum of the Domitii on the summit of the Pincian hill at the north of Rome and deposited them in a sarcophagus of porphyry. There was only one other mourner at the simple interment: the woman who had remained faithful to Nero despite his multiple marriages and tangled perversions—his first great love, the beautiful Greek freedwoman Acte.

32

SABINUS returned to Rome at a furious gallop and called the Senate into extraordinary session within the hour. He also sent special word to Plautia and her parents to come to the chamber at once and witness the great scene.

By midmorning, nearly all Conscript Fathers were in their places, filling the chamber with a buzzing drone of anxious dialogue. The presiding consul stood up and announced, "Our distinguished city prefect, Titus Flavius Sabinus, has urgent news for us. I will only add that for years now, Clarissimus, you have been the one rock of stability in the . . . earthquake around us. The Senate and the Roman People are . . . profoundly grateful."

The Fathers started applauding enthusiastically and even rose in unanimous support of the consul's opinion.

Moved by the sight, Sabinus hurried to the dais with a great smile and motioned the senators to be seated. "Thank you, my colleagues!" he responded, to an instant hush. "My gratitude is that brief because the extraordinary news cannot be denied you any longer. You are, of course, wondering about the former emperor. Last night, he fled from Rome with three aides. At dawn today, we found them hiding at the house of his freedman Phaon northeast of the city.

Honorably judging himself, Nero took a dagger to his throat, and died—not quite three hours ago."

A deathly hush hung in the chamber for several moments. Then it was shattered by a general uproar—a shouting, applauding near-hysteria of jubilation—the final release to years of searing frustration for the Fathers, of enforced hypocrisy and clutching anxiety. Up in the gallery, Pomponia clasped Plautia to herself in exhilaration, staring through her tears at Aulus, who was beaming up at them from below.

It was fully ten minutes before Sabinus could continue. Even then there were still pockets of applause and shouts of "Sabinus for emperor!" "Sabinus Caesar!" "Our new princeps!" Holding up his hands for silence, Sabinus unleashed a broad smile but shook his head. He went on to supply details of Nero's last hours and then answered as many of their questions as he could before dismissing them. "The people of Rome have a right to hear the happy news also. Let each of you be a herald of joy."

In minutes, the city of Rome was erupting in a symphony of rejoicing, each class providing a glad orchestration of its own. The oppressive pall of fear that had smothered the people was dissolved at last. The rich were talking to the poor, commoners were embracing slaves, and even the crime rate dropped. A sense of civic joy was everywhere.

Sabinus and Plautia finally celebrated spring that second week in June, calling their friends up to the Quirinal for a lavish festivity in honor of freedom. The aging Aulus happily brought Pomponia over in the brightest costume she had worn in years. One of the first things he did was to lead a toast in memory of his friend Thrasea Paetus, his nephew Quintus Lateranus, "and all the many victims." The entire company arose in solemn remembrance.

Sabinus, who had aged markedly in the last months, bowed his gray-streaked head, relieved that it was still attached. He thought of how the irrepressible Quintus would have relished the present moment, and his eyes misted at memories of the twin brother. He also wondered if any other age had witnessed so extraordinary a clash of good and evil, so grotesque a collision of violence and depravity with idealism and love.

Plautia played the role of serene and happy hostess at the party, still lovely and suffused with the bloom of youth. When his friends were bantering Sabinus for keeping a child bride on the premises, Plautia loyally proved her age by calling in their eldest and showing him off to the guests. Young Flavius was now almost eight years old, and, with his tousled brown locks, he seemed the very image of his father—in younger days.

Not to be outdone, little Clemens scampered into the atrium as well. His hair was still a childish flaxen yellow, bleached by the hot spring sunshine of Rome. He was aping all the movements of his older brother and showing off to his heart's content until Plautia whisked them both out of the room. Off near the center fountain sat Aulus, his eyes burning with all the grandfatherly delight the old soldier-senator could muster. If only Plautia had brought out baby Plautilla too, his bliss would have been complete.

Pomponia looked at Aulus and breathed a prayer of gratitude to her God. Never had she been happier about her husband. After almost twenty years of scoffing at her beliefs, Aulus was now becoming intrigued by the extraordinary hopes which animated her faith. It had occurred to him one day earlier that spring as he was sitting in his garden study: no other philosophy, no other religious system had such definite plans for people after they died. The concept of a higher existence was appealing enough for one, like himself, who would soon find out if anything lay behind—and beyond—this life. Now he was sure that the Christians could not, as he had earlier supposed, merely be *used* as moral props for Rome, because what they believed had to have a validity of its own, or it was nothing.

Soon the men had withdrawn into the peristyle, where the conversation turned to the new emperor, Servius Galba. Several younger senators in the group voiced qualms about Galba. "Yes, he comes from an old senatorial family," said one of them, "but power has corrupted more than one good citizen in that position. I say let's have done with it all."

"Yes, end the Empire!" a colleague responded. "Restore the Republic!"

"One thing at a time, gentlemen." Sabinus smiled. "Nero's gone, and that's most of the battle."

"Seriously now, Sabinus," one of the older senators remarked, "quite a number of us think that *you* are easily the most qualified man in all Rome to wear the purple."

"Yes indeed," another agreed. "Augustus would—"

"No, no, no, good friends," Sabinus laughed. "Haven't I put in my time? Besides, my brother Vespasian is the one who now controls almost half the Roman legions."

The tall figure with Greek dark hair was late in arriving, and he excused himself for that. Pomponia and Plautia ran to the vestibule and welcomed him with outstretched arms. Sabinus, too, gripped the hand of Luke enthusiastically.

"The Beast is dead, thanks be to God!" said Luke, with a warm smile. "And to your efforts, Prefect! Nero tried to exterminate us . . . but failed. And now the embers of the Faith that Paul spoke about are indeed rekindling into flame. Someday all nations will be brightened with their glow!" Luke's eyes blazed with a distant look, as if peering over their heads centuries into the future.

"What are you carrying under your arm, Luke?" inquired Sabinus.

"Aha!" Luke chuckled. "Well, it's finally safe to give you these." He handed Sabinus two large brown leather cylinders with scrolls inside. "One is what I call my *Evangelium,* my 'Glad Tidings.' The other is my *Acta,* the record of our faith. I"—he paused and looked at the women with a broad smile—"I've dedicated both treatises to *you,* Prefect, because of how you helped us all."

"*Me?*" Sabinus' eyes widened.

"But in order to spare you any embarrassment or even danger, I've not used your personal name—Titus Flavius Sabinus—but rather a code name—Theophilus—a combination of the beginning sounds of your three names. And since Theophilus means 'friend of God,' I thought it quite appropriate."

Sabinus could not know that someday the entire world would know him, not as Flavius Sabinus, but as Theophilus, because the first scroll would soon be called the Gospel According to St. Luke, and the second, the Acts of the Apostles, both biblical books addressed to a certain "Theophilus." Nor could he know that the scrolls would one day so impress his children and even himself that they would share the Faith also.

EPILOGUE

SABINUS AND PLAUTIA might well have wondered if the future would be dull in comparison with the harrowing past. But the strangest twists lay in store both for Rome and their own family.

The emperor Galba—aged and inept—ruled only seven months before the praetorians killed him in favor of Otho. Otho, in turn, was forced to take his own life after only twelve weeks as Caesar. The Rhine legions replaced him with Aulus Vitellius, the son of Claudius' toady adviser, who proved to be a worthless glutton.

The eastern legions finally lost all patience with the praetorians and the western legions, who had enthroned three worthless successors to an unbearable tyrant. In the summer of A.D. 69, they declared for the commander who was putting down the revolt in Palestine, whose son Titus would conquer Jerusalem while he himself assumed emperorship. Incredibly, it was the former bankrupt mule-trader who got pelted with mud in Rome or turnips in Africa, a man who literally could not stay awake in some circumstances to save his own life—Sabinus' debtor brother, T. Flavius Vespasian. With the proper challenge, he "did something with his life" after all, as one of Rome's ablest emperors. Vespasian gave Rome a decade of peace, prosperity, and freedom, erected the great Colosseum over the ruins of Nero's Golden House, and founded the Flavian dynasty of emperors.

And Sabinus? He gave his life for the Flavian cause, fighting heroically on the Capitoline hill to deliver Rome to his brother. The Senate decreed Sabinus the highest funeral the Empire could bestow and erected his statue in the Forum.

Tigellinus was found—surrounded by mistresses at the sulfur baths down in Sinuessa, where he took a razor and slit his own throat. Locusta, the witch, and Helius, the puppet, were led across Rome in chains and executed. Sporus committed suicide.

Two structures, finally, have a fascinating epilogue of their own. Quintus Lateranus' mansion, confiscated by Nero and retained by succeeding emperors, was given at last by Constantine to the Christian bishop of Rome. Eventually, it became the headquarters of the Western church, the Lateran Palace of the popes and site of the famous Lateran councils—a clear perpetuation of Quintus' name. Today, its base is incorporated in the Basilica of St. John in the Lateran, the mother church of Rome.

And the Egyptian obelisk that witnessed Nero's persecution of the Christians stands today at the center of the great circular colonnade in front of St. Peter's Basilica at the Vatican. St. Peter's itself marks the presumed site of Peter's grave, while the Basilica of St. Paul ("Outside the Walls"), that of the other great apostle.

HISTORICAL NOTE

ALL CHARACTERS and all major and many minor episodes in this book are historical and have been documented in the Notes below. The portrayal of imperial politics under Claudius and Nero is fully authentic. However, the connective material and much of the dialogue was contrived, but done so on the basis of probabilities with no violation of historical fact. Because of missing evidence, some relationships were necessarily presumed. The true name of Sabinus' wife, who bore Flavius and Clemens, is unknown, but she may indeed have been Plautia, an otherwise unrecorded daughter of Aulus Plautius and named for her father, a supposition based on facts explained in the Notes. Plautia's is the only proper name in this book not attested by an original primary source.

Demands of the novel required the trimming away of several minor historical characters to keep the cast from becoming unwieldy, such as Hosidius Geta, who also received honors at Aulus' ovation on the Capitoline, and Antonia, daughter of Claudius by Paetina.

The role of Aquila and Priscilla in this story is partially presumed, but they were leaders of the earliest Christian church in Rome and were closely associated with Paul in both East and West. Since the persons and circumstances involved in Paul's Roman trial(s) and death are almost unknown, they were reconstructed from all shreds of available evidence. Because of the source problem, the role of Peter in Rome was even more difficult to restore, but avoiding, as in the case of Paul, the rich encrustation of legends, the portrayal in these pages has tried to flesh out what faint clues we have.

Finally, Sabinus' efforts in behalf of the Christians are only presumed, but they are, again, in accord with the sources, which show him a noble-minded peacemaker and father of the probably Christian Clemens. His exact role in the overthrow of Nero is unknown. Other items are clarified in the Notes.

NOTES

THE PEOPLE, places, and events portrayed in this book can be documented in the following ancient sources: Tacitus, *Annals*, xi–xvi; *Histories*, i–iii; Suetonius, *Lives of the Caesars*, v–xii; Dio Cassius, *Roman History* (hereafter "Dio Cassius"), lxi–lxiv. Additional evidence for the era A.D. 47 to 69—the time frame in these pages—was derived from the works of Arrian, Aurelius Victor, Eutropius, Josephus, Juvenal, Lucan, Lucian, Martial, Pliny, Plutarch, Seneca, Strabo, and, among Christian authors, Clement of Rome, Luke, Paul, Peter, Tertullian, and others. Archaeology and epigraphy are listed below.

While it would have been possible to document in much greater detail than the references below, only the very significant or disputed items are noted here, particularly where reconstructions have been necessary as a result of missing evidence.

CHAPTER I (Pages 3–19)

T. FLAVIUS SABINUS: Tacitus, *Histories*, i–iv *passim*; Suetonius, *Vitellius*, xv; *Divus Vespasianus*, i; *Domitianus*, i; Dio Cassius, lx, 20; lxv, 17; Plutarch, *Otho*, v; Josephus, *Wars of the Jews*, iv, 11, 4; Sextus Aurelius Victor, *De Caesaribus*, viii; and a mutilated dedicatory inscription in *Corpus Inscriptionum Latinarum* (hereafter *CIL*), VI, 31293. For an inscription recording two letters of Sabinus to the people of Histria (in Rumania), confirming their rights at a time when he was governor of Moesia, see *Supplementum Epigraphicum Graecum*, I, 329.

FLAVIUS VESPASIAN: Above references, and Tacitus, *Annals*, iii, 55; xvi, 5.

THE PLAUTII: For a catalogue of the prominent members of this Roman gens, see the article "Plautius" in Georg Wissowa, ed., *Paulys Real-Encyclopädie der classischen Altertumswissenschaft* (Stuttgart: Metzlersche and Druckenmüller Verlag, 1953 ff.), hereafter Pauly-Wissowa. For the authenticity of Plautia, daughter of Aulus Plautius, see Historical Note above, and the entry "Plautilla" under Chapter 30 below. Plautius Lateranus' first name is unrecorded, but since he was doubtless the son of Quintus Plautius, the consul in A.D. 36, it would most probably have been Quintus.

CHAPTER 2 (Pages 20–27)

MESSALINA'S STRATAGEM: Incredible as it may seem, Messalina's method of winning her lovers with apparent imperial approval is historical. As Dio Cassius states: "Claudius told Mnester to do whatever he should be ordered to do by Messalina. . . . Messalina also adopted this same method with various other men and committed adultery, pretending that Claudius knew what was going on and approved her unchastity" (lx, 22). Since Lateranus was seduced after Mnester, it is likely that he was subjected to the same ruse.

CHAPTER 3 (Pages 28–35)

THE GAIUS SILIUS AFFAIR: For the entire extraordinary episode, see Tacitus, *Annals*, xi, 12, 26–38; Suetonius, *Divus Claudius*, xxvi; Dio Cassius, lx, 31; and Juvenal, *Satires*, x, 328 ff.

CHAPTER 4 (Pages 36–49)

THE BACCHANAL AT SILIUS': Tacitus, *Annals*, xi, 31–32.

CHAPTER 5 (Pages 50–63)

MESSALINA'S REMARRIAGE A SHAM? Suetonius, *Divus Claudius*, xxix, suggests, contrary to Tacitus, that Claudius knowingly signed the contract for the dowry in the supposedly sham marriage to Silius, but I am inclined to agree with Suetonius' own words in introducing this version: "It is beyond all belief. . . ." THE PUNISHMENTS: Tacitus, *Annals*, xi, 35–38.

CHAPTER 6 (Pages 64–71)

AQUILA AND PRISCILLA: Acts 18:1 ff.; I Corinthians 16:19; Romans 16:3–4. Their contact with the Plautii is only presumed, but tentmaking was their occupation, and they were in Rome at this time.

CHAPTER 7 (Pages 72–83)

THE "CHRESTUS" RIOT: This was undoubtedly the first public notice of Christianity taken by the Roman state, and the earliest chronological reference to Christ by a secular author. In *Divus Claudius*, xxv, Suetonius writes: "Since the Jews constantly made disturbances at the instigation of Chrestus [*impulsore Chresto*], he [Claudius] expelled them from Rome." Some scholars have argued that Chrestus was the name of a Roman Jew who caused the riot, not Christ, and yet Suetonius would probably have used the term *quodam* in that case, "a certain Chrestus." That Chrestus was another form of Christus among Romans of the time is indicated by Tertullian, *Apologeticus*, iii, and Lactantius, *Institutiones Divinae*, iv, 17. The French word for Christian, *chrétien*, reflects this mode of spelling to this day.

EXPULSION OF JEWS FROM ROME: Suetonius, *loc. cit.*, and Acts 18:2, which refers also to the specific expulsion of Aquila and Priscilla and their arrival in Corinth. On the other hand, Dio Cassius, lx, 6, writes: "As for the Jews, who had again increased so greatly that because of their numbers it would have been hard to bar them from the city without raising a tumult, he [Claudius] did not drive them out, but ordered them, while continuing their traditional mode of life, not to hold meetings." Dio cites this in connection with events from A.D. 41, whereas Suetonius seems to suggest a later date, and the reference in Acts coordinates with Paul's visit to Corinth in A.D. 51, where he met Aquila who "recently" came from Rome. Hence A.D. 49, the date cited by Orosius for the expulsion (*Historiarum adversus paganos libri vii*, vii, 6) would seem preferable, since Dio appears to be summarizing some of Claudius' future acts in his lengthy discussion of the first year of the emperor's reign. He is correct, however, in suggesting that

Claudius could not possibly have banished *all* Jews from Rome.

PILATE's *Acta*: This wording is only presumed, but there is no question that Pilate would have made some reference to Jesus in his official *acta*. For his role in Jesus' trial and the A.D. 33 dating for the Crucifixion, see my book *Pontius Pilate* (Doubleday, 1968) and my article, "Sejanus, Pilate, and the Date of the Crucifixion," *Church History*, XXXVII (March, 1968), 3-13.

THE GRAVE-ROBBERY ORDINANCE: This inscription, discovered at Nazareth in 1878, remained unnoticed until F. Cumont published it in 1930. The Caesar mentioned in the ordinance is not identified, and some scholars claim that it may date back to Augustus, while others have suggested as late as the time of Hadrian. On the one hand, it is unlikely that any emperor would have set up so harsh an edict in any area not under direct imperial control, and Galilee (where the inscription was found) did not return to the Empire until the death of King Herod Agrippa in A.D. 44, ruling out emperors before Claudius. On the other hand, since the epigraphy indicates Greek writing of the first half of the first century A.D., Claudius would, in fact, seem to be the author of the inscription. For further discussion, see F. Cumont, "Un Rescrit Impérial sur la Violation de Sépulture," *Revue historique*, clxiii (1930), 241-66; F. de Zulueta, "Violation of Sepulture in Palestine at the Beginning of the Christian Era," *Journal of Roman Studies*, xxii (1932), 184-97; M. P. Charlesworth, ed., *Documents Illustrating the Reigns of Claudius and Nero* (Cambridge, 1939), p. 17; and Arnaldo Momigliano, *Claudius* (Cambridge, 1961), pp. 35 ff.; 100 f., though the author later changed his mind, see p. ix.

CHAPTER 8 (Pages 84-91)

AGRIPPINA's AMBITIONS: Tacitus, *Annals*, xii, 8-42. Pallas' successes are reported in xii, 53-54.

CHAPTER 9 (Pages 92-104)

CLAUDIUS ON FLATULENCE AT THE TABLE: Suetonius, *Divus Claudius*, xxxii.

THE DEATH OF CLAUDIUS: Tacitus, *Annals*, xii, 66-69. In addition to the standard account of Claudius' death, Suetonius, *Divus Claudius*, xliv-xlvi, also cites an alternate version that the eunuch Halotus supplied him the poison while he was banqueting with the priests on the Capitoline, but Dio Cassius, lxi, 34, confirms the Tacitean account. See also Pliny, *Natural History*, xxii, 92, who cites Agrippina as serving Claudius a poison mushroom. A few scholars have questioned whether or not Claudius was actually poisoned, but this would seem unduly revisionist. Later, Nero would jest that mushrooms were "the food of the gods," since his father became one by eating them (Dio Cassius, lx, 35), and Seneca's *Apocolocyntosis* is a play on the colocynth or poisonous wild gourd. Cp. also Juvenal, *Satires*, v, 147 ff.; vi, 620 ff.

CHAPTER 10 (Pages 107–23)

SABINUS IN GAUL: His appointment as *curator census Gallici* after his term as governor of Moesia is attested by the inscription in *CIL*, VI, 31293, but Agrippina's interest in him, while possible, is contrived.

CHAPTER 11 (Pages 124–31)

SENECA: Whether or not the philosopher was involved in the death of Claudius has never been proven. Nor have the circumstances causing his exile to Corsica been clarified, other than Messalina's charge of his adultery with Julia. Sources for Seneca are *passim* in Tacitus, Suetonius, and Dio, as well as the philosopher's own writings.

PLATO ON IDEAL GOVERNMENT: Plato, *Republic*, v, 473.

RETURN OF AQUILA AND PRISCILLA: Presumed from Acts 18:18 ff. and Romans 16:3—probably written in A.D. 56/7—in which Paul salutes them in his letter to Rome.

GALLIO: His "hook" remark is attested by Dio Cassius, lx, 35. See also Pliny, *Natural History*, xxxi, 62; Seneca, *Epistulae Morales*, civ, 1; Tacitus, *Annals*, xv, 73. Paul's appearance before Gallio in Corinth is described in Acts 18:12–17. An important inscription found at Delphi records a rescript of Claudius in which "Junius Gallio, my friend and proconsul of Achaea" is mentioned (Dittenberger, ed., *Sylloge Inscriptionum Graecorum*, Ed., 3, 801 D). The inscription is important not only in confirming the account in Acts, but in dating the life of St. Paul, for it styles Claudius as acclaimed emperor "for the 26th time," indicating A.D. 51–52. For further discussion, see F. J. Foakes-Jackson and Kirsopp Lake, *The Beginnings of Christianity* (London: Macmillan, 1920–33), V, pp. 460–64.

CHAPTER 12 (Pages 132–48)

THE DEATH OF BRITANNICUS: Tacitus, *Annals*, xiii, 14–17; Suetonius, *Nero, xxxiii*; Dio Cassius, lxi, 7. Tacitus cites his sources as
stating that Nero violated Britannicus some time before he poisoned him, but since this is not confirmed elsewhere, the lurid ad-
dendum is relegated to the Notes. Suetonius, *Divus Titus*, ii, has
Titus reclining at the side of Britannicus, but Tacitus' version of
a separate table for the youth at which they sat upright is preferable.

CHAPTER 13 (Pages 149–57)

SABINUS APPOINTED URBAN PREFECT: Pliny, *Natural History*, vii,
62, suggests that he succeeded Saturninus in A.D. 56. See also
CIL, VI, 31293.

CHAPTER 14 (Pages 158–68)

PRAEFECTUS URBI: The most complete discussion of the prerogatives
of this office is the article so entitled in Pauly-Wissowa.

NERO'S NIGHT GANGS AND JULIUS MONTANUS: Tacitus, *Annals*,
xiii, 25; Suetonius, *Nero*, xxvi; Dio Cassius, lxi, 8–9.

CHAPTER 15 (Pages 169–84)

THE TRIAL OF POMPONIA GRAECINA: The text of Tacitus, our sole
source, reads as follows: "Pomponia Graecina, a woman of high
family, married to Aulus Plautius—whose ovation after the British
campaign I recorded earlier—and now arraigned for alien superstition, was left to the jurisdiction of her husband. Following the
ancient custom, he held the inquiry, which was to determine the
fate and fame of his wife, before a family council, and announced
her innocent." (*Annals*, xiii, 32; John Jackson's translation in
Loeb Classical Library.)

The identity of the alien superstition (*superstitionis externae
rea*) is a matter of some dispute. Lipsius, the great classical scholar
of the sixteenth century, first suggested Christianity, and this conclusion has been adopted by the Loeb text and many scholars since
that time. However, Judaism, Isis and Osiris, and even Druidism
have also been suggested, though without any compelling basis.
Some have tried to see in Pomponia's retiring life an early form of
Christian asceticism, and there is archaeological evidence that

later Pomponii were indeed Christian, for the Christian catacombs of Callistus provide inscriptions of a Pomponius Graecinus and of the Pomponii Bassi, dating from the second century. See G.-B. De Rossi, *Roma Sotterranea Cristiana*, ii, 364. The objection raised by some commentators against Pomponia's Christianity, i.e., that she escaped any penalties in both A.D. 57 and 64, is easily answered: at the former date, Christianity was not yet illegalized, and at the latter, Nero's persecution by no means eliminated all the Christians in Rome.

The nature of the prosecution and the defense at Pomponia's trial is not given by Tacitus, but I have incorporated in the charges the standard calumnies which Romans raised against Christianity at this time and subsequently, as cited by Justin, Tertullian, Minucius Felix, and other Christian apologists. Cossutianus Capito as prosecutor is only assumed in the absence of other evidence, since he was the most notorious informer of that time (see Tacitus, *Annals*, xi, 6; xiii, 33). In the defense—again, Lateranus' role is only assumed—the verses cited from Paul's letter are Romans 13:1, 7–9, 13.

CHAPTER 16 (Pages 185–204)

OTHO AND POPPAEA: The sources vary widely on how Nero's romance with Poppaea began. The most reasonable version, offered in the text, follows Tacitus, *Annals*, xiii, 45 f. Tacitus does refer to an alternate suggestion that Otho *intended* his wife to attract Nero in order to build his own power over the emperor, but this seems unlikely and certainly proved to be a foolish plan, if true.

AGRIPPINA INCESTUOUS: There are more scandalous reports regarding Nero and his mother. Tacitus cites his own sources: Cluvius, for the version which he prefers and I have incorporated; and Fabius Rusticus, who said that it was Nero who took the initiative vis-à-vis his mother. Suetonius, *Nero*, xxviii, records that Nero had incestuous relations with Agrippina as they rode in a litter, the stains on his clothes betraying it. Cp. also Dio Cassius, lxi, 11.

THE PLOT AT BAIAE: Suetonius, *loc. cit.*; Tacitus, *Annals*, xiv, 3–5; Dio Cassius, lxi, 12–13. Strabo, *Geographica*, v, 245, provides the detail that it was an oyster boat which picked up Agrippina.

PAUL'S ARRIVAL AT PUTEOLI: Acts 28:11–13. That St. Paul approached Puteoli on the very night of the collapsible-boat episode cannot, of course, be documented, but the coincidence has considerable historical basis *if* the apostle reached Italy in A.D. 59, a date favored by many scholars. Paul and his associates wintered "three months" in Malta (Acts 28:11). Since the Mediterranean was technically closed to shipping until March 10, it is at least reasonable to assume that the voyage resumed on or about March 11, since maritime insurance could have been vitiated by an earlier voyage during *mare clausum*. Once resumed, the run from Malta to Puteoli, with stops at the various ports of call mentioned in Acts 28:12–13, took at least nine days, making the estimated date for arrival March 20. Since the Festival of Minerva was celebrated March 19–23, the banquet at Baiae could well have taken place on the second night of the festival, March 20, the same night as Paul's arrival in the above scenario. While hardly provable, then, the coincidence is not as remote as one might assume.

CHAPTER 17 (Pages 205–17)

THE MURDER OF AGRIPPINA: Tacitus, *Annals,* xiv, 6–12; Suetonius, *Nero,* xxxiv; Dio Cassius, lxi, 13–16. Whether or not Seneca and Burrus knew beforehand of the plot against Agrippina is not definite. Dio suggests that Seneca was indeed involved, but his bias against the philosopher is notorious. Tacitus, typically more careful, suggests that he and Burrus only "possibly" were in on the plot. The lurid mention in some sources that Nero carefully examined his mother's corpse, praising its beauty, need not detain us.

PAUL'S ARRIVAL IN ROME: Acts 28:14–16. The Western version of the Greek text at Acts 28:16 has this interesting variation: "When we came to Rome, the centurion handed the prisoners over to the commandant of the camp [*to stratopedarcho*], and Paul was ordered to remain by himself with the soldiers who were guarding him." In commenting on this variant, Theodor Mommsen defined the *stratopedarchos* as the princeps *peregrinorum* ("Zu Apostelgesch. 28, 16," *Sitzungsberichte der Königlich Preussischen Akademie der Wissenschaften zu Berlin* [1895], 491–503). But A. N. Sherwin-White more aptly suggests princeps *castrorum* as the best identification of this officer, for he was the "commandant of the camp" of the praetorians where Paul would most likely have been brought. See A. N. Sherwin-White, *Roman Society and Roman Law in the New Testament* (Oxford: Clarendon, 1963), pp. 108–10.

PAUL AND THE JEWS OF ROME: Acts 28:17–28. Where Paul lived in Rome for two years is unknown, but it must have been in the vicinity of the Castra Praetoria, in a house large enough to accommodate the crowd indicated in Acts 28:23.

CHAPTER 18 (Pages 218–29)

GROWTH OF CHRISTIANITY AT ROME: Paul's reference to praetorian converts is supported by Philippians 1:12–14. He also closed that letter with this salutation: "All the saints greet you, especially those of Caesar's household" (4:22, both RSV). There is some debate over whether the "prison epistles" were written in Ephesus, Caesarea, or Rome, but the scholarly consensus leans strongly to the last, particularly because of the verses here cited. Earlier, Paul had written the Roman church, greeting brethren "who belong to the family of Narcissus" (Romans 16:11), though whether Claudius' secretary is meant here is not known. Paul's claims to Christianity's growth are not inflated, because in just four years, an "immense number" of Christians would die in Nero's persecution, according to Tacitus, *Annals*, xv, 44. Jesus' statement about appearing before kings is Matthew 10:18.

L. PEDANIUS SECUNDUS, not Flavius Sabinus, was *praefectus urbi* in A.D. 61 (Tacitus, *Annals*, xiv, 42). Sabinus certainly succeeded him in office, and because Sabinus served Rome for twelve years as city prefect (Tacitus, *Histories*, iii, 75), most scholars conclude that Sabinus served *two* terms as prefect: A.D. 56–60, and A.D. 61/2–69. See the discussion in Pauly-Wissowa under "166) Flavius Sabinus, der Bruder Vespasians."

SABINUS' BABY: T. Flavius Sabinus was the eldest of Sabinus' children. Though the precise year of his birth is unknown, it is closely estimated to be c. A.D. 60. See Suetonius, *Domitianus*, x; Dio Cassius, lxv, 17. Cp. Tacitus, *Histories*, iii, 69 and CIL, VI, 20, 3828.

CHAPTER 19 (Pages 230–49)

ABSENCE OF PAUL'S PROSECUTION: Another reason may lie in the Temple Wall controversy. Angered that Agrippa II had erected a dining room atop his palace from which he could look into the Temple, the Jerusalem authorities raised the west wall of the Temple so that it obstructed Agrippa's view. Agrippa and Festus ordered them to pull it down, but the priests sent ten of their leaders to Rome to appeal to Nero. Through Poppaea's intervention, Nero permitted the wall to stand. (See Josephus, *Antiquities*, xx, 8, 11.) Accordingly, the Jewish authorities may have decided not to "press their luck" for what must have seemed the comparatively insignificant case of Paul.

PALLAS PROTECTS FELIX: Josephus, *Antiquities*, xx, 8, 9. Why Pallas should still have been in a position to intercede in behalf of his brother after his own fall from power is puzzling. In dismissing him from office, however, Nero did give Pallas extraordinary concessions.

TIGELLINUS: His role in Paul's trial is only assumed. It is known that he came to prominence at this time, and the actual prosecution at Paul's trial, if any, is unknown. But allowing another party to renew an accusation in the absence of the original accusers was permitted under Roman law (*Digestae*, xlviii, 16; x, 2).

PAUL'S ROMAN TRIAL is extremely difficult to reconstruct, since the primary source stops at Acts 28 with only a few hints in the epistles. Some scholars doubt that Paul ever appeared before Nero; others claim he did indeed. The only certainty is that he waited "two whole years" in Rome before any hearing took place (Acts 28:30).

On the basis of all scraps of evidence in the prison epistles (the above passages in which Paul looks forward to a positive resolution of his case), the political situation in both Palestine and Rome, and the known court procedure in appeals to the emperor, I have endeavored to reconstruct the trial as set forth in the text. The general outline would indeed be accurate, in that the basis of accusation would be the same three indictments cited by Tertullus in Paul's first hearing before Felix (Acts 24:1–9). On any appeal, the original character of the case was always preserved.

That Nero heard both accusation and defense on each specific charge before moving to the next was his judicial custom, according to Suetonius, *Nero*, xv. Whether Paul defended himself or had an advocate is not known. Sabinus' role here is only assumed, but Paul would not have disdained such help, for during his second trial he would complain, "At my first defense [in the second trial], no one took my part; all deserted me" (II Timothy 4:16).

Paul's record in Asia Minor, Greece, and Palestine is described in Acts 13–23. The incident regarding Trophimus and the four Jews is Acts 21:17 ff. The Temple notice prohibiting Gentiles (cited by

Josephus, *Antiquities*, xv, 11, 5; *Wars*, vi, 2, 4) has also been discovered by archaeologists. Agrippa's statement absolving Paul (Acts 26:31 f.) would have been powerful evidence for the defense, but whether it was included in any deposition from Festus is unknown.

The most complete discussion on Paul's trial in Rome is Henry J. Cadbury, "Roman Law and the Trial of St. Paul," in Jackson and Lake, *Beginnings, op. cit.*, V, pp. 297–338. Cadbury makes the interesting observation that any Judean prosecution, faced by heavy transportation and legal expenses, might have enlisted the help of Roman Jews for this purpose rather than making the trip themselves, and that the object of Acts 28:21 is to indicate that not even that recourse had been taken. Compare also Sherwin-White, *op. cit.*, pp. 108–119.

NERO DESPISING CULTS: Suetonius, *Nero*, lvi. The goddess in question was Atargatis.

PAUL ACQUITTED? There is strong, though not conclusive, evidence that Paul was indeed acquitted after his first trial at Rome. The pastoral epistles to Timothy and Titus cannot be fitted satisfactorily into the three missionary journeys, and they bespeak Paul's subsequent activities, although the authenticity of the pastorals is much debated.

There is no tradition that Paul was martyred before A.D. 64, and no dating of the apostle's life could reasonably have his two-year imprisonment end in 64. In the meantime, he may well have been released. Clement of Rome, in his epistle to the Corinthians of A.D. 96, states that Paul "reached the limit of the West" [*to terma tes duseos*] before he died (I Clement v, 1–7), which, for a Roman author, would imply Spain or Portugal. (Cp. Strabo, *Geographica*, ii, 1.) Romans 15:24, 28 show that Paul had certainly planned a trip to Spain via Rome, and a second-century document, the Muratorian fragment, states: "Then the 'Acts of the Apostles' were written in one book. Luke says . . . that the various incidents took place in his presence, and indeed he makes this quite clear by omitting the passion of Peter, as well as Paul's journey when he set out from Rome for Spain" (*Canon Muratorii*, xxxviii). This document, however, is somewhat late. Evidence against a trip to Spain is the absence of any local Christian tradition there recalling the apostle's visit. But this would have been brief in any case, and the long Moorish occupation may have expunged it.

While certainty in the matter is impossible, the evidence points to the *probability* of Paul's release after his first trial, and his rearrest, trial, and execution later on (see below). For further discussion of Paul's fate in Rome, see L. P. Pherigo, "Paul's Life after the Close of Acts," *Journal of Biblical Literature*, LXX (1951), 277 ff.; Sherwin-White, *op. cit.*, pp. 108 ff.; and F. F. Bruce, "St. Paul in Rome—Concluding Observations," *Bulletin of the John Rylands Library* (Manchester), L (1967–68), 266–79.

SENECA AND PAUL: While there is no evidence that the two ever met each other, some contact between Paul and Seneca would easily have been possible at this time. Seneca did, in fact, serve frequently as assessor, and it was his brother Gallio who judged Paul in Corinth. The "golden rule" statement by Seneca is from his *Epistulae Morales*, xlvii, but the famed correspondence between Paul and Seneca is a fourth-century Christian forgery that has no basis in fact.

LUKE'S RECORD: The cited passage is Acts 28:30–31, the last verse of Acts and perhaps the most unsatisfactory ending of any book in the Bible. While such an "unresolved fade-out" is very congenial to modern literary taste, it is rather extraordinary for an ancient author, especially one who has pointed his account toward the very matter to be resolved. Why the Acts end so abruptly has been vigorously debated by scholars, see especially Jackson and Lake, *Beginnings, op. cit.*, IV, pp. 349 f. I have suggested an alternative reason in the text.

CHAPTER 20 (Pages 253–66)

THE MURDER OF PEDANIUS SECUNDUS: Tacitus, *Annals*, xiv, 42–45.

THE DEATH OF BURRUS: Suetonius states that Nero "sent poison to Burrus . . . in place of a throat medicine which he had promised him" (*Nero*, xxxv), and Dio offers a similar version (lxii, 13). Tacitus, however, leaves open the question as to whether he died from illness or poisoning (*Annals*, xiv, 51). In view of this restraint by a hostile source and the fact that Burrus' symptoms did resemble cancer, Nero may be spared the responsibility for this particular death.

CHAPTER 21 (Pages 267–80)

FLAVIUS CLEMENS: Sabinus' second son probably had "Titus" as his first name, though it is unknown. Suetonius, *Domitianus*, xv; Dio Cassius, lxvii, 14. See discussion on Flavius Clemens in the lengthy note on Chapter 32 below.

NERO'S DEBUT IN NAPLES AND ROME: Tacitus, *Annals*, xv, 33–34; Suetonius, *Nero*, xx–xxi. Petronius' critique of Nero's performance reflects an opinion in the dialogue *Nero*, attributed to Lucian of Samosata, though probably written by the elder Philostratus.

THE ARRIVAL OF PETER: Whether or not Simon Peter ever visited Rome has been debated for centuries. Roman Catholic scholars have been virtually unanimous in insisting that, as first bishop of Rome, Peter must indeed have reached the capital. Protestants have been somewhat divided on the question, although the current consensus agrees that Peter came to Rome.

The evidence *against* Peter's presence in Rome is the silence of the New Testament, particularly Acts, as well as of the second-century Christian apologist who lived in Rome, Justin Martyr.

The evidence *supporting* Peter's presence in Rome is larger. If, as seems probable, "Babylon" were a cryptic name for Rome, then I Peter was addressed from Rome (I Peter 5:13), though there is some debate over its authorship. The crucial, early (A.D. 96) letter of Clement of Rome to the Corinthians strongly links the martyrdoms of Peter and Paul with those of the Roman Christians enduring the Neronian persecution (I Clement, v, vi). A short time later (c. A.D. 107), Ignatius of Antioch's *Epistle to the Romans* contains the revealing phrase: "Not like Peter and Paul do I give you [Roman Christians] commands" (iv, 3). Another early, indirect witness is the first-century apocryphon, the *Ascension of Isaiah*, which implies that one of the disciples—doubtless Peter— was delivered into the hands of the matricidal Nero (iv, 2 f.).

In the second century A.D., there are numerous references in Christian authors to the martyrdoms of Peter and Paul in Rome, and one of these is especially interesting. Eusebius refers to a second-century presbyter, Gaius, who stated: "I can point out the monuments [or trophies] of the apostles: for if you will go to the Vatican hill or to the Ostian Way, you will find the monuments of those who founded this church [Peter and Paul]" (*Ecclesiastical History*, ii, 25). The monuments marked the traditional sites of their martyrdoms and probably their places of burial as well, since Gaius was countering a claim from Asia of apostolic *tombs* in that province. At any rate, the emperor Constantine later erected the basilicas of St. Peter and St. Paul, respectively, at these locations.

Balancing the evidence, the historian is justified in concluding that Peter did, in fact, reach Rome. There is too much in its favor. On the other hand, suggestions that Peter conducted a lengthy, twenty-five-year ministry in the capital and opposed Simon Magus there already at the beginning of Claudius' reign is extremely unlikely, despite Eusebius' discussion of this tradition, *op. cit.*, ii, 13. Such a stay conflicts too grossly with the absence of any reference to Peter's presence or work at Rome in Paul's epistle to the Romans, or in the Acts narrative. The date of Peter's arrival in Rome cannot be determined, although it seems to have been shortly before his martyrdom. For further discussion, see Oscar Cullmann, *Peter—Disciple, Apostle, Martyr* (Westminster, 1962); and Daniel W. O'Connor, *Peter in Rome* (Columbia, 1969).

THE LAKESIDE BACCHANAL: This incredible episode is recounted in Tacitus, *Annals*, xv, 37; and Dio Cassius, lxii, 15. Cp. also Suetonius, *Nero*, xxvii. Dio's version is considerably more sensational —and less believable—than the restrained rendering in the text.

NERO "WEDS" PYTHAGORAS: Tacitus implies that it was a formal marriage (*Annals*, xv, 37), though Dio, lxii, suggests, quite obviously, that it was abnormal in any case. While one is tempted to ignore such reports of degeneracy as concoctions of hostile sources, this pattern is consistent with Nero's later affair with the boy Sporus (see below), and also explains Paul's comments in Romans 1:26 ff.

CHAPTER 22 (Pages 281–93)

THE GREAT FIRE OF ROME: Various versions are provided by Tacitus, *Annals*, xv, 38 ff.; Suetonius, *Nero*, xxxviii; Dio Cassius, lxii, 16–18; Pliny, *Natural History*, xvii, 5; and Seneca, *Octavia*, 831 ff.

The Cause: All ancient sources claim Nero himself as the arsonist, except for the careful scholarship of Tacitus, who begins his famous account with the words: "A disaster followed, whether due to accident or to the treachery of the emperor is uncertain. . . ." Scholars fall into five camps on this issue, concluding 1) that

Nero did indeed send his agents to set fire to Rome; 2) that the first fire arose by accident, but the second was kindled, under Nero's orders, by Tigellinus and his men; 3) that both fires were wholly accidental; 4) that the Christians, or several Christian fanatics, fired the city; and 5) that the Pisonian conspirators (see below) set fire to Rome to incriminate Nero.

Most recent scholarship leans to the third alternative. While some lines in ancient sources can be marshaled in support of all of the above alternatives except 4) and 5), the weight of circumstantial evidence would tend to absolve Nero of any responsibility for the blaze. Accidental fires were all too frequent in Rome, and Nero was miles away at the time—not, of course, a perfect alibi—but a true arsonist would have wished to witness his handiwork soon after its inception. It was the night of the full moon, as C. Hülsen first noted in *American Journal of Archaeology,* xiii (1909), 45. Nor could it have been Nero's violent "slum clearance project," since the worst slums in the Subura were untouched. His noble relief efforts would hardly seem appropriate for an incendiary. And, above all, Nero would hardly have had the fire kindled near the southeastern tip of his Palatine palace to burn down all his own priceless works of art and treasures. Again, this statement must stand: in terms of property destroyed, Nero was far and away the greatest loser in the fire. That it all began from a blaze at an oil merchant's shop is merely assumed, but the general location of its inception is accurate.

The Extent: Most sources exaggerate the devastation of the great fire. According to Dio, "the whole Palatine hill . . . and nearly two-thirds of the remainder of the city were burned" (lxii, 18), while Tacitus says that of the fourteen regions, only four remained intact, "three were leveled to the ground, while in the other seven only a few shattered, half-burned relics of houses were left" (*Annals,* xv, 40). But literary and archaeological evidence shows that the latter is particularly exaggerated, and the fire generally ravaged the areas indicated on the endpaper map. For further discussion, see Gerard Walter, *Nero* (London: Allen & Unwin, 1955); and Jean Beaujeu, "L'incendie de Rome en 64 et les Chrétiens," *Collection Latomus,* XLIX (1960), 5 ff.

DID NERO PLAY WHILE ROME BURNED? Probably the most popular misinterpretation in history is that "Nero fiddled while Rome burned." The violin, of course, was not invented until fourteen centuries after the fire. Tacitus has Nero appearing on a private stage to rhapsodize on the destruction of Troy; Suetonius has him singing, in costume, from the terrace of Maecenas, while Dio has him holding forth on the roof of the palace—an impossibility, since the palace was in flames. An unsensational version of Suetonius' account was used in the text, since Maecenas' terrace was indeed untouched by fire and would have afforded a good vantage point.

THE LOSS STATISTICS are based on a restrained interpretation of Tacitus, *Annals*, xv, 40, while the specific numbers of mansions and houses lost derives from the apocryphal correspondence between Seneca and Paul, Letter xii (Barlow ed.). While no suggestion is made that this correspondence is authentic—it is not—this estimate from a fourth-century author is the *only* surviving statistic we have on the great fire, and it was incorporated because the figures are quite probable in themselves, and the author may well have used an ancient source lost to us.

CHAPTER 23 (Pages 294–305)

THE GOLDEN HOUSE: Tacitus, *Annals*, xv, 42; Suetonius, *Nero*, xxi. Partial remains of the great Domus Aurea are visible today in Rome just northeast of the Colosseum on the sides of the Esquiline. The graffito referring to the expanding Golden House is authentic; see Suetonius, *Nero*, xxix.

CHRISTIANS BLAMED FOR THE GREAT FIRE: Tacitus, *Annals*, xv, 44. This passage, perhaps the most famous in the *Annals*, begins:

Therefore, to scotch the rumor [that he had set fire to Rome], Nero substituted as culprits, and punished with the utmost refinements of cruelty, a class of men, loathed for their vices, whom the crowd styled Christians. Christus, the founder of the name, had undergone the death penalty in the reign of Tiberius, by sentence of the procurator Pontius Pilatus, and the pernicious superstition was checked for a moment, only to break out once more, not merely in Judaea, the home of the disease, but in the capital itself, where all things horrible or shameful in the world collect and find a vogue. (John Jackson's translation in Loeb Classical Library)

That Peter ever made a statement involving the term "fire" which had anything to do with clinching Tigellinus' argument to persecute the Christians is only contrived, but for early Christians to castigate Rome's vices in such language was not untypical. Tigellinus may well have suggested to Nero that he punish the Christians, for this is at least implied in Melito of Sardis, *Apologia,* as excerpted in Eusebius, *op. cit.,* iv, 26: "Of all the emperors, the only ones ever persuaded by malicious advisers to misrepresent our doctrine were Nero and Domitian." At this time, Tigellinus was certainly Nero's principal adviser, and Juvenal, *Satires,* i, 155 ff., seems to link Tigellinus and human torch deaths.

CHAPTER 24 (Pages 306–13)

THE TRIALS OF THE CHRISTIANS: Whether Nero indicted them as a mere police action on the basis of the magisterial *coercitio* (punishing authority) or via a special imperial or senatorial edict against Christianity has long been debated. French and Belgian scholars have tended to follow the latter interpretation, while others, following Mommsen, conclude that the Christians were prosecuted as a police action under existing laws concerning public order. See Theodor Mommsen, "Die Religionsfrevel nach römischen Recht," *Historische Zeitschrift,* LXIV (1890), 389 ff.; and A. N. Sherwin-White, "The Early Persecutions and Roman Law Again," *Journal of Theological Studies,* III (1952), 199–213.

PETER'S LETTER: The phrases are taken directly from I Peter 1–5. There is, of course, some debate over the date and provenance of the epistle.

CHAPTER 25 (Pages 317–31)

NERO'S PERSECUTION OF THE CHRISTIANS: Suetonius, *Nero,* xvi; and the famed source passage in Tacitus, a continuation of *Annals,* xv, 44 (Jackson's translation):

. . . First, then, the confessed members of the sect were arrested; next, on their disclosures, vast numbers were convicted, not so much on the count of arson as for hatred of the human race. And derision accompanied their end: they were covered with wild beasts' skins and torn to death by dogs; or they were fastened on crosses, and, when daylight failed, were burned to serve as lamps by night. Nero had offered his Gardens for the spectacle, and gave an exhibition in his Circus, mixing with the crowd in the habit of a charioteer, or mounted on his car. . . .

There has been a vast literature on this passage. A few scholars in the last century tried to deny that such a persecution ever existed, on the basis of the following arguments: expressions in the passage unusual for Tacitus, silence of other sources at the time, and silence of the Christian tradition. But the great majority of scholars today accept the authenticity of this passage and of the persecution, since nothing in *Annals*, xv, 44 could not have been written by Tacitus, and recent studies have reaffirmed the validity of this passage, such as H. Fuchs, "Tacitus über die Christen," *Vigiliae Christianae*, IV (1950), 65 ff. Moreover, the secular and Christian sources are *not* silent. Suetonius writes that "Punishments were also inflicted on the Christians, a class of men given to a new and mischievous superstition" (*Nero*, xvi). Cp. also Sulpicius Severus, *Chronica*, ii, 29, and the earlier Christian tradition on this persecution is vocal enough in I Clement vi, and in other documents associated with the apostles cited above and below.

THE SPECIFIC PUNISHMENTS: Besides those indicated in *Annals*, xv, 44, that Christians and condemned criminals suffered in these and other ways may be documented as follows: Ixion (Tertullian, *De pudicitia*, xxii); Daedalus and Icarus (Martial, *op. cit.*, viii; Suetonius, *loc. cit.*). The punishments of Dirce and the Danaides are cited in I Clement vi, 1 ff.: "Besides these men of holy life [Peter and Paul], there was a great multitude of the elect, who through their endurance amid many indignities and tortures . . . presented us a noble example. . . . Women were paraded as Danaides and Dircae and put to death after they had suffered horrible and cruel indignities."

Victims fixed on poles in garments impregnated with inflammables and then set afire is cited not only in *Annals*, xv, 44, but in Juvenal, *Satires*, i, 155–57 and viii, 235; Seneca, *De Ira*, iii, 3; and Martial, *Epigrams*, iv, lxxxvii. The *tunica molesta* and being thrown to the beasts were standard penalties for arson, according to *Digestae*, xlvii, 9, 9, and 12. Several scholars have blunderingly attacked *Annals*, xv, 44 by claiming that the luminous combustion of the human body is physically impossible, but such human torch deaths did in fact take place: the wood of the posts and the *tunica molesta* clothing the bodies would indeed be luminous while the bodies themselves carbonized.

Finally, Hercules in Flames is cited by Tertullian, *Apologeticus*, xv. Other probable tortures, not cited in the text, included Pasiphaë and the Bull (Martial, *De Spectaculis*, v; Suetonius, *Nero*, xii), and Attis (Tertullian, *loc. cit.*)

THE TIME OF THE PERSECUTION: Paul Allard, *Histoire des Persécutions* (Paris, 1903) suggested August, 64 (I, pp. 48 ff.), but since the great fire was not extinguished until July 27, and it would have taken some weeks for planning the Golden House which finally pinned suspicions on Nero, August would seem much too early for the persecution, with October more probable. On the other hand, suggestions that would delay punishments until spring of A.D. 65 founder on Nero's diverting *fresh* public hatreds for suspected arson on the Christians and the fact that in the spring of 65, Nero's full attention was claimed by the Pisonian conspiracy (see below).

CHAPTER 26 (Pages 332–41)

PETER'S MARTYRDOM: Jesus' prediction of his death is given in John 21:18 f. The famous *Quo Vadis* legend first appears in a second-century manuscript, the *Acta Petri* (cp. later, Ambrose, *Epist.*, xxi). A much reduced version of the legend is included in the text because it is both ancient and moving. But it seems certain that if Peter did, indeed, communicate with the spirit of Jesus, he would doubtless have spoken to him in Aramaic, their common tongue, rather than the Latin *"Quo vadis, Domine?"* which would have been foreign to both of them.

The legend that Peter was crucified head downward has been common since Origen, as quoted by Eusebius, *op. cit.*, iii, 1. But this would seem an unnecessary, slightly ostentatious, and—in view of the way crosses were constructed—an unlikely embellishment, even if such crucifixions were not unknown (see Seneca, *Ad Marciam*, xx). But there was no early Roman tradition that Peter was crucified in this way, and the claim has an apocryphal ring.

For the historical sources on Peter's death, see references to Chapter 21 above. Most scholars now agree that Peter was likely martyred in some connection with the Neronian persecution, but the precise date of his death is impossible to determine. Similarly, there is no reliable evidence as to where the apostle was imprisoned, and the tradition pointing to the Mamertine prison is unlikely because it is very late, and the Mamertine was usually used only for high prisoners of state.

As to the location of his burial, Roman Catholic scholars generally concur that his grave lies under the great altar of the current Basilica of St. Peter in the Vatican; see Margherita Guarducci, *La tomba di Pietro* (Rome, 1959). Some Protestant scholars agree, while others conclude that it can only be proven historically that the Christian church of the second century A.D. *thought* that this is where Peter was buried, as Cullmann, *op. cit.*, and O'Connor, *op. cit.*

THE NUMBER OF VICTIMS in this persecution is set at 977 in the *Martyrologium Hieronymianum* (ed. Duchesne-De Rossi in *Acta Sanctorum* [Brussels, 1894], II, p. 84). But this figure need not be considered accurate and might well be reduced in view of the exaggeration of such documents. Tacitus' "an immense multitude" [*multitudo ingens*] in *Annals*, xv, 44 is certainly vague, and the two other places where he uses this expression in the *Annals* (ii, 40; xiv, 8) cannot be reduced to numbers. Clement uses a similar expression in I Clement vi, 1: "a very great number."

CHAPTER 27 (Pages 342–48)

THE PISONIAN CONSPIRACY: Tacitus, *Annals*, xv, 48 ff.; Dio Cassius, lxii, 24 ff. There is some debate as to whether Seneca was part of the conspiracy, but all circumstantial evidence points to his involvement, and most commentators conclude with Momigliano in *CAH*, X, p. 728: "There can be no doubt that Seneca shared in the conspiracy."

CHAPTER 28 (Pages 349–67)

SABINUS' INVOLVEMENT IN THE CONSPIRACY is only presumed, but the fact that so high a magistrate was *not* rewarded for loyalty at a time when his colleagues were would suggest that he was not above suspicion in Nero's eyes. Similarly, Walter, *op. cit.*, p. 196. The fact that Sabinus continued to be popular with both the Senate and the public *after* the fall of Nero, when death for Nero's minions was being demanded, more than demonstrates Sabinus' true loyalties.

CHAPTER 29 (Pages 368–81)

PAUL'S SECOND ARREST: If Philippians offers source material for Paul's first imprisonment, II Timothy provides it for the second. Although some are wary of using II Timothy and the other pastoral epistles as evidence, even critical scholars admit that the letter probably contains authentic Pauline reminiscences in verses such as 1:8 ff., 1:15 ff., 2:9, and 4:6 ff.—which are precisely the references to a second imprisonment in Rome. Evidently Paul did succeed in blunting the charges against him at a *prima actio* or first hearing (II Timothy 4:16–17), though he knew the outcome of the second would result in his death (4:6). Recent attempts to date the pastorals to an earlier, non-Roman imprisonment founder on II Timothy 1:17, as genuine a Pauline fragment as any.

ALEXANDER THE COPPERSMITH: While it is not certain if Alexander came to Rome to prosecute Paul, this may be implied from II Timothy 4:14 ff. Alexander the false teacher (I Timothy 1:19) rather than the Jew of Ephesus (Acts 19:33) seems intended here, and for a former Christian to turn against Paul is very well attested in I Clement v, 2, where the church father says that it was specifically "through jealousy" that Paul was delivered up to death.

THE REIGN OF TERROR: More prominent Romans fell than was possible to mention in the text. A list of other victims is supplied by Tacitus, *Annals*, xvi, 7 ff. and Dio Cassius, lxii, 25 ff. A young Aulus Plautius is a victim cited in Suetonius, *Nero*, xxxi, but he was likely a member of the younger line of the Plautii, and not Aulus' son.

THE DEATH OF PAUL: Nothing is known of the final trial and death of Paul other than that he was most probably executed in Rome under Nero (I Clement v, 5 ff.) Later, Eusebius states that Origen recorded the same fact in his commentary on Genesis (*Ecclesiastical History*, iii, 1). As an early church tradition has it, the execution probably took place outside the Ostian Gate of Rome at or near the present Basilica of St. Paul "Outside the Walls" (see the presbyter Gaius' statement on the "monuments of the apostles" under Chapter 21 above). His grave may be indicated under the high altar of the basilica by the fourth-century inscription, "PAVLO APOSTOLO MART." As F. F. Bruce points out, *op. cit.*, 274, the location may be "accepted provisionally" in default of any rival tradition, and in view of the corporate memory of an ongoing Christian community at Rome ever since the event. The fact that Paul's monument, like Peter's, lay in a pagan necropolis—not the area later Christian piety would have selected—adds a further touch of authenticity.

As to the date of Paul's death, some have suggested that the reference in I Clement v, 7 that Paul gave testimony "before the rulers" [epi ton hegoumenon] before he died implies that he was judged by Nero's vicegerents Helius and Nymphidius while Nero himself was away in Greece in A.D. 66–67. While ingenious, this suggestion makes too much of a phrase which is so common in early Christian testimony, that the apostles would have to testify "before governors and kings" (Matt. 10:18; Mark 13:9; cp. Acts 9:15). Paul certainly had already done this before Sergius Paulus, Gallio, Felix, Festus, Publius, Nero, and others. The tradition that Peter and Paul died on the same day, June 29, A.D. 67, on the basis of apocryphal "Acts" of the two apostles, is without historical value.

The names of those attending Paul in his last imprisonment are indicated in II Timothy 4, but whether any of them witnessed the apostle's death is unknown. The presence of Sabinus, Plautia, and Pomponia is only presumed.

CHAPTER 30 (Pages 385–403)

NERO's "MARRIAGE" TO SPORUS: Suetonius, Nero, xxviii, xxxv; Dio Cassius, lxii, 12–13. Even more depravities of Nero are portrayed in the sources, such as his attacking, like an animal, the genitals of nude men and women bound to stakes (Suetonius, Nero, xxix; Dio Cassius, lxiii, 13) though regard must be paid the hostility of the sources on Nero. About this time, the emperor also married Statilia, one of his mistresses.

CORBULO: His fate was linked to the Vinician conspiracy against Nero, named for Annius Vinicianus, son-in-law of Corbulo, which broke out at Beneventum in A.D. 66. Details on the nature and extent of this conspiracy are very sketchy, since Tacitus is missing here. See Suetonius, Nero, xxxvi; Dio Cassius, lxiii, 26.

PLAUTILLA: While young Flavius and Clemens are the only two children of Sabinus specifically mentioned in the sources because of their later political careers—Clemens as consul in A.D. 95—this does not rule out the possibility that the Plautilla who is mentioned as the "sister of Clement the consul" in the *Acts of Nereus and Achilles* was in fact the third child and daughter of Sabinus. Nereus and Achilles were early Christian martyrs who were originally servants of Plautilla, and ever since De Rossi's discovery of their memorials in the cemetery of Domitilla (*op. cit.*, i, 130 ff.) there is no doubt that they were real persons, an authenticity which should carry over also to their mistress, Plautilla. Since the diminutive "-illa" suffix in a daughter's name usually reflects a mother's "ia" ending, the mother of Plautilla would doubtless be "Plautia," as De Rossi first suggested, and the unnamed wife of Sabinus can provisionally be named after all. For further discussion, see R. Lanciani, *Pagan and Christian Rome* (New York, 1967, reprint), pp. 336 ff.; A. S. Barnes, *Christianity at Rome in the Apostolic Age* (London, 1938), pp. 138 ff.; and G. Edmundson, *The Church in Rome in the First Century* (London: Longmans, 1913), who suggests a slightly different family structure.

CHAPTER 31 (Pages 404–10)

Nero's Last Day, Death, and Burial: Suetonius, *Nero*, xlvii f.; Dio Cassius, lxiii, 27–29. Regrettably, the *Annals* of Tacitus break off with the forced suicide of Thrasea Paetus in A.D. 66.

CHAPTER 32 (Pages 411–14)

Theophilus: That Sabinus was so intended by the author of Luke and Acts is only conjecture. But since the man named in Luke 1:3 and Acts 1:1 is cited as "most excellent [*kratiste*] Theophilus," a form of address used elsewhere by the same author only for a Roman official (Acts 23:26; 24:2) and a title accorded Romans of the senatorial class, it may be assumed that the works were dedicated to some Roman of high position. Notes appended to some early manuscripts of the Gospels say that Theophilus was a man of senatorial rank. For the dating of Luke–Acts, see P. Carrington, *The Early Christian Church* (Cambridge, 1957), I, 182 ff., 278 ff.

The Religion of Sabinus' Children has long been a subject of scholarly debate. Both Christianity and Judaism have been suggested, on the basis of the epitome of Dio Cassius (lxvii, 14), which states:

. . . And the same year [A.D. 95], Domitian slew, along with

many others, Flavius Clemens the consul, although he was a
cousin and had to wife Flavia Domitilla, who was also a relative
of the emperor [his sister's daughter]. The charge brought
against them both was that of atheism, a charge on which many
others who drifted into Jewish ways were condemned. Some of
these were put to death, and the rest were at least deprived of
their property. Domitilla was merely banished to Pandateria.
(E. Cary's translation in Loeb Classical Library.)

That Sabinus' children, or at least Clemens and his wife, had converted to Judaism is one obvious interpretation of the source, a
view held by some commentators, including E. Mary Smallwood,
"Domitian's Attitude Toward the Jews and Judaism," *Classical
Philology*, LI (January, 1956), 7 ff., who suggests that they were
not full converts to Judaism but only "God-fearers" on the fringe.
   Other scholars, however, think Christianity is intended in the
reference, for Dio otherwise never refers to it by name—an apparently intentional slight—and "atheism" was a term hardly used
for Judaism, a legal religion in Rome, but frequently for Christians (who were also accused of practicing "Jewish ways") in that
they abjured the national religion of Rome. Eusebius, *op. cit.*, iii,
17 f., records Domitian's persecution of the Christians, the second
in history, and claims that the pagan historians recorded Domitilla's banishment for her Christianity, though he considers her
the niece, not wife, of Clemens, a much-debated problem. Since
classical sources do not record such a niece, Eusebius' tradition
would seem to be faulty at this point, and Flavia Domitilla is in-
terpreted as Clemens' wife by most investigators. Synkellos adds
that Flavius Clemens was executed because of his Christian faith
(*Chronographia*, ed. Dindorf, I, 650, 17 f.). Suetonius' description
of Clemens as a man of "most contemptible laziness" seems to
hint at his Christianity (*Domitianus*, xv), since pagan authors regularly faulted Christians for indolence and indifference to public
affairs. M. Goguel, *The Birth of Christianity* (New York, 1954),
p. 532, suggests: "Flavius Clemens may have secretly shared his
wife's convictions but, anxious to preserve his reputation and his
career and not to stand in the way of the future of his sons whom
the emperor [Domitian] had adopted . . . he decided not to enter
the church officially. This explains why he was not remembered
as a martyr."

But his wife Domitilla, not under the same obligations, may well have converted. In 1852, De Rossi uncovered an ancient Christian catacomb which proved to be the "Cemetery of Domitilla," with an inscription, *"ex indulgentia Flaviae Domitill[ae]"* and she is named as "granddaughter of Vespasian" (*CIL*, VI, 948, 8942, 16246). The cemetery had been dug on land that had belonged to Domitilla, which she gave to her dependents as a burial ground.

Finally, that Domitian did indeed persecute the Christians seems strongly supported in a contemporary document of highest authenticity. At the opening of I Clement (i, 1), the author speaks of the "sudden misfortunes and calamities which have fallen upon us one after another," and the date of writing is most probably A.D. 95–96, the tyrannical close of Domitian's reign. See also *CAH*, XI, pp. 254 f.

EPILOGUE (Pages 415–16)

GALBA, OTHO, VITELLIUS, VESPASIAN: Suetonius' *Lives* by those names, and Tacitus, *Histories*, i–v; Dio Cassius, lxiv–lxv.

SABINUS' MONUMENT: *CIL*, VI, 31293.

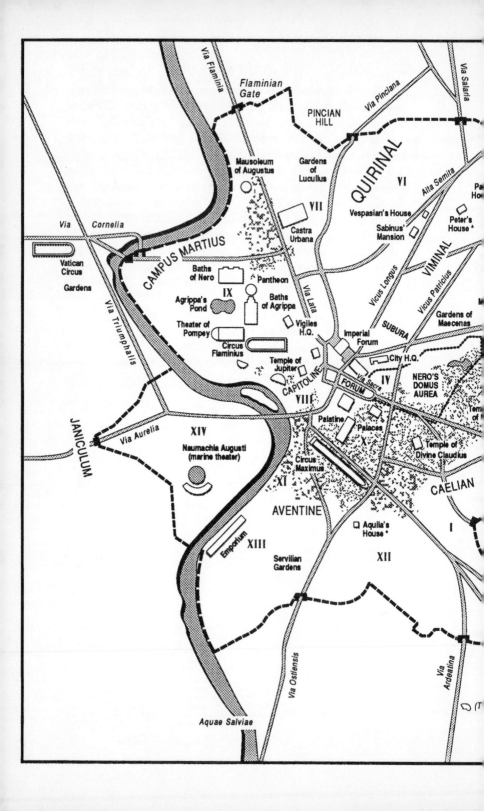

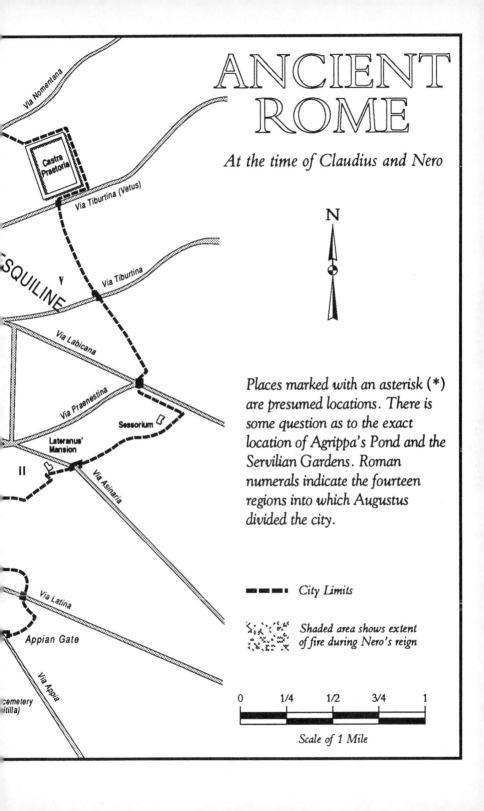

ANCIENT ROME

At the time of Claudius and Nero

N

Places marked with an asterisk (*) are presumed locations. There is some question as to the exact location of Agrippa's Pond and the Servilian Gardens. Roman numerals indicate the fourteen regions into which Augustus divided the city.

Via Nomentana

Castra Praetoria

Via Tiburtina (Vetus)

ESQUILINE

V

Via Tiburtina

Via Labicana

Via Praenestina

Sessorium

Lateranus' Mansion

II

Via Asinaria

Via Latina

Appian Gate

Via Appia

cemetery itilla)

▬ ▬ ▬ ▬   City Limits

Shaded area shows extent of fire during Nero's reign

| 0 | 1/4 | 1/2 | 3/4 | 1 |

Scale of 1 Mile